After a career in the Civil Service, Brenda Clarke began writing when her two children left school. Since then she has written over twenty novels, many of which were published under her maiden name of Brenda Honeyman. She now lives with her husband in Keynsham, Bristol.

Also by Brenda Clarke

THREE WOMEN
WINTER LANDSCAPE
UNDER HEAVEN
AN EQUAL CHANCE
SISTERS AND LOVERS

and published by Corgi Books

BEYOND THE WORLD

Brenda Clarke

CORGI BOOKS

BEYOND THE WORLD
A CORGI BOOK 0 552 13690 5

Originally published in Great Britain by Bantam Press,
a division of Transworld Publishers

PRINTING HISTORY
Bantam Press edition published 1991
Corgi edition published 1992

This book is set in 10/11pt Century Schoolbook by
Photoprint, Torquay, Devon

Corgi Books are published by Transworld Publishers Ltd.,
61–63 Uxbridge Road, Ealing, London W5 5SA, in
Australia by Transworld Publishers (Australia) Pty. Ltd.,
15–23 Helles Avenue, Moorebank, NSW 2170, and in
New Zealand by Transworld Publishers (N.Z.) Ltd., Cnr.
Moselle and Waipareira Avenues, Henderson, Auckland.

Made and printed in Great Britain by
BPCC Hazell Books
Aylesbury, Bucks, England
Member of BPCC

They that love beyond the world cannot be separated by it. Death is but crossing the world, as friends do the seas; they live in one another still.

WILLIAM PENN (1644–1718)

PART ONE
1985

CHAPTER ONE

THE EARLY MORNINGS were the worst: that first moment of waking in the cold bed, the summer light filtering through the half-drawn curtains; the knowledge that another day stretched emptily ahead. Never again would she see his face or hear his voice. Rowland was dead, and somehow or other she must force herself to accept that fact.

Christine Saxelby rolled on to her back and stared at the ceiling with its intricate plasterwork and delicate cornice of alternating Tudor roses and fleur-de-lis. The profusely carved oak bedstead, its headboard bearing the coat of arms of James I, dominated the room in which she lay and had been at Mallerby since 1812, when the house itself was already well over fifty years old. A late-seventeeth-century oak cabinet, inlaid with mother-of-pearl, stood against one wall. But, apart from these two items, the rest of the furniture was mainly made up of heavy Victorian mahogany pieces. Twenty years before, after her marriage to Rowland, Christine had introduced a touch of femininity into what was essentially a masculine room, by insisting on a pale pink carpet and damask curtains of a deeper rose. Make-up and scent-bottles, together with a pair of silver-backed hairbrushes, which Rowland had given her as a 'conscience' present after one of his many affairs, littered the dressing-table, and her satin dressing-gown was flung carelessly across the back of one of the chairs. Matching slippers stood ready at the side of the bed. Yet this was still Rowland's room, as it had been ever since he was a boy.

Even after all these years, there were times when Christine felt herself to be an intruder. The cuckoo in the nest.

She must have dozed for a while because, the next thing she knew, there was a knock at the door and a maid came in with her early-morning tea. The female domestic staff no longer wore the uniform of print dress, cap and apron, changing to black silk in the afternoons, which Christine had seen in old family photographs. Nowadays, very few of the girls lived in, most of them arriving from the village around eight o'clock in a varied assortment of clothing, mainly T-shirts and jeans. When Christine had first come to Mallerby, in the 1960s, some sort of uniform had still prevailed. Colette Saxelby, using all her Gallic charm, had managed to persuade the live-in servants to wear pale-green nylon overalls, and a plain, darker green dress later in the day. The only men on the staff, then as now, worked out of doors, in the greenhouses and gardens, unlike the halcyon days of Rowland's father and grandfather before the First and Second World Wars, when a butler, two footmen and four under-footmen swelled an already substantial payroll. In the mid-1980s, Mrs James, the cook-housekeeper, commanded a staff of three village girls and a cleaning woman, all of whom came in daily, and a couple of resident au pairs. The latter changed every two years or so, but were always the same nationality: French. Colette Saxelby, even after forty-eight years in England, still liked to have people around her with whom she could chatter in her native tongue.

'The English!' she would exclaim scornfully. 'They cannot even speak their own barbarous language properly, let alone a civilized language such as French!'

Christine half-smiled to herself as she sat up in bed, sipping her tea. At school, French had never been one of her strongest subjects, and twenty years of marriage to Rowland, who had been as fluent in it as his mother

10

and younger brother, had done little to overcome her native prejudice against speaking foreign languages. Like the vast majority of English-speaking peoples, she felt acutely embarrassed at being asked to perform the necessary contortions with her lips.

But at the thought of Rowland the agony of her loss came flooding back. It was a little over two months since his death, and the wound was still raw. It had been so totally unexpected. There had been nothing on that April morning, at breakfast, to warn her that she was seeing him alive for the very last time. It was true that his father had died of a heart-attack when in his early forties, but there had been no indication, at forty-seven, that Rowland could go the same way. He had complained of no pains in his chest, no shortage of breath. He had been for a medical check-up four weeks previously and been given a clean bill of health.

Thinking back, Christine remembered that he had looked tired, but his position as head of Saxelby's Merchant Bank, his hectic lifestyle were the obvious explanations for any symptoms of fatigue. It had never occurred to her that he might be feeling ill. His secretary, Marcia Corby told her later that he had asked for aspirin shortly after arriving at the bank, but she had thought nothing of it. A slight headache, he had said, with his usual courteous charming smile. A bit of a hangover, and he wanted to get rid of it before the board meeting at ten. He had gone into his office, the big ground-floor room overlooking Gresham Street, and shut the door. She was just getting a glass of water from the private bathroom adjoining her own office, when she heard him fall ... By the time she had summoned an ambulance and alerted Mr Julian Saxelby, he was dead.

At this point, Marcia broke down and cried. Christine guessed that she had been in love with Rowland. Had she ever been his mistress? Who could tell? There had

11

been so many women in his life. He had never been able to resist them, nor they him.

'I can't help it. It's in my blood,' he would excuse himself, with that lop-sided shamefaced grin which, to the last, had had the power to make her go weak at the knees.

She had always known, of course, to what he was referring. The Bérengers, his mother's family, claimed descent from a bastard daughter of Henri IV of France, Henri de Navarre, one of that country's greatest and most promiscuous kings. It had been a private joke between them to blame Rowland's womanizing on his illustrious ancestor; but it had been a joke without much humour and one which, over the years, had worn thin . . .

With a snap, Christine put her half-empty cup down on the bedside table and got out of bed, padding across to the big bay window which overlooked the gardens of Mallerby and the parkland beyond. She opened one of the casements and leaned out, breathing in the clean country air. It was so quiet, she could just make out the faint rush of tyres as early-morning commuters took the short-cut between the busy A30 and A303, on their way to work in Yeovil, Shaftesbury or Salisbury, or headed in the opposite direction towards Ilminster. They went too fast considering the narrowness of the roads which served the village of Hinton Malsherbes.

'The "Malsherbes" bit is pronounced "Mallerby",' Rowland had told her, all those long years ago, down in Devon.

'Yes, I know,' she had answered. 'I'm from Somerset myself.' She added with an ironic inflection: 'Weston-super-Mare.' And they had both laughed and exchanged hoary old jokes about the tide never being in.

But he hadn't told her then – in fact he hadn't told her at all: it had been Russell Jennings who had passed on the information – that he lived at

12

Mallerby House, one of the county's showplaces. Nor had he mentioned that his family were merchant bankers and had another home, Inglebatch House, near Hampstead Heath, nor that his mother's family owned a château in Poitou. There, again, she had been indebted to Russell. And how could she possibly have guessed, on first acquaintance, that the tall youth in scruffy old jeans and sweatshirt, with his gypsyish appearance – swarthy skin, greasy black hair and smiling brown eyes – was in reality a very wealthy young man? Besides, it hadn't really concerned her then.

Oh, she had fallen for him, of course, as nearly all women did; fallen for his charm and ease of manner, which sprang from his deep-rooted liking for, and genuine appreciation of, women. In that respect, he was like no other man she had ever met; certainly not like Russell, to whom she had been on the very brink of becoming engaged during that 1960s camping holiday near Slapton. Poor Russell, with his possessiveness and his unshakeable belief that women belonged almost exclusively in the kitchen and the bedroom. Even her father, who had prided himself on being a man's man, had never been quite such a male chauvinist as Russell Jennings. What on earth had she seen in him? No wonder someone like Rowe had been such a revelation.

Christine sat down on the broad window-seat and stared out over the park, where the sun was beginning to disperse the mist, leaving it swirling in tatters around the trunks of the distant trees. Once, many years ago, long before the war, there had been cattle grazing in the park, but Colette, coming as a bride to Mallerby, had insisted on her husband getting rid of them.

'What, I ask you,' she would demand of Christine in the oft-repeated story, spreading hands of Gallic dismay, 'was the point of a *dairy* herd in a place called

13

Hinton *Malsherbes*?' She always gave the village's second word its French pronunciation. 'The mind fairly boggles!'

Christine laughed, however many times she had heard the anecdote before, but also considered it an example of her mother-in-law's ruthless determination to get her own way. No one, however, could deny that Colette was an extremely practical woman; a practicality which had stood her in good stead when, at the age of thirty-two, after only twelve years of marriage, she had been left a widow with two small boys of eleven and eight to bring up. She had managed to get herself appointed to the board of Saxelby's in order to protect Rowland's interests until he came of age and assumed his rightful place as head of the bank. Her down-to-earth approach had also helped her to adjust, in due course, to the improvident marriages of both her sons.

Christine sighed and got up, going into the adjoining bathroom to run her morning bath. While the water gushed out, hot and steaming, thanks to Colette's insistence on up-to-date plumbing, she looked critically at herself in the mirror. She saw the face of a reasonably good-looking woman of forty-five, its frame of thick straight brown hair, beautifully cut and styled at one of London's top salons, beginning to show a little grey at the temples. Blue eyes, a straight nose and a wide generous mouth contributed to features which had always been pleasant, but not memorable.

'You'll never set the Thames on fire, my girl,' her mother used to say, 'but you're not bad-looking.'

It was true that from the age of thirteen onwards she had never been short of boyfriends, but she had put this down to her early physical development. She had needed to wear a brassière long before any of her friends. She was no beauty; never had been and never would be, unlike so many of the women Rowland had known. But, then, he had been able to have any woman

14

he wanted. She wondered who, of all of them, he would have decided to marry if he hadn't done the right thing, the gentlemanly thing — how outmoded an expression nowadays! — by her as soon as he knew about the baby.

She turned sharply away from the mirror and turned off the taps. She didn't want to think about the baby: that son who would have been twenty-three years old this month; whose death and her own subsequent inability to have more children had made her marriage to Rowland such a farce. And yet Rowland had steadfastly refused to let her divorce him, although she had offered him his freedom more than once. He had withstood all pressure from his mother to marry again and produce an heir.

'I have a son,' he would tell her with a smile. 'Why should I want another?'

'A bastard,' Colette would retort viciously, 'who can never inherit the business.' And then her face would soften. She was fond of her grandson.

Christine stripped off her nightdress and stepped into the bath. The scented water slid across her skin, and she let herself sink into its warm comforting depths. She, too, was fond of Patrick in her own way.

Patrick Brennan. Lucy Brennan's son. Nomadic, rebellious, uninhibited Lucy, wandering from country to country, from man to man. A true gypsy, who had believed in nothing and no one but herself. A vivid picture sprang into Christine's mind of the girl she had first seen at the camp-site in Devon: a pointed face beneath the straggling, waist-length, unkempt hair; the huge, thickly lashed Irish blue eyes; the soft, slightly trembling lips which made her seem, so misleadingly, vulnerable.

Patrick had the same appearance of vulnerability, the same mobile mouth and lazily smiling eyes as his mother. And Christine had the same sense of disquiet about him as she had had for Lucy Brennan. She

15

always felt that there was something a little devious, a little untrustworthy about Patrick, yet there was nothing she could put her finger on. She had known him for fourteen years, ever since, at the age of ten, his mother had abandoned him in a Paris hotel and Rowland had taken on the responsibility for his hitherto unknown son. And in all that time there was no specific incident to which she could point and prove that he had been underhand. Nevertheless, the feeling persisted, and she knew that Colette shared it, too.

'He has such charm,' her mother-in-law had once confided to her, referring to Patrick. 'It makes me very uneasy.'

Christine had smiled. The two women's initial antagonism had gradually faded over the years as they had been drawn together by their mutual love for Rowland. All the same, Christine had been unable to resist saying: 'But I thought you had a penchant for charming men, like your brother Lucien and that very handsome son of his, young Giles.'

Stepping out of the bath and starting to towel herself dry, it occurred to Christine that 'young' Giles was now thirty-three and had just assumed command of the Bérenger bank in Paris, following his father's retirement. He was only twelve years younger than she was.

'I'm beginning to think like a middle-aged woman,' she scolded herself, once again glancing in the mirror. 'I'm thinking like my mother, who thought she was old at fifty. For God's sake, forty-five is young these days! I still have so much of my life before me.'

But it would be a life without Rowland, and at the realization she froze. She had met him first twenty-five years ago, and there had rarely been a day since when he had been out of her thoughts. And always, *always* she had hoped against hope that his affection for her might ripen into love. Sometimes, in her more optimistic moments, she had believed that he did love her without being aware of the fact. They had had so many things in common: a sense of the ridiculous, the ability to laugh at themselves, a passion for seventeenth-century music and a deep abiding love for the countryside of England and France.

She was deluding herself! Christine snatched up her nightdress, suddenly angry, and returned to the bedroom to dress. Why had she put up with Rowe's infidelities? Why hadn't she made scenes, insisted on a divorce? But she knew why. She would have been the loser, not him. Her spurt of anger evaporated. He had never pretended he was in love with her. He had married her because of the child and because he was fond of her. That was all.

But was that really all? Fondness and affection for those twenty-odd shared years – could that truly be all that she had? She flung herself down on the bed, pushing her face into the tangle of sheets and blankets to stop herself from screaming. She pummelled the bedclothes with her fists. Rowe was dead, had died without a sign. Now she would never know . . . never know . . . never know . . . The words went round and round inside her head.

She sat up abruptly, recognizing the signs of hysteria, and made a determined effort to pull herself together. She was a grown woman. She must stop behaving like this.

She slid off the bed and began to dress, glancing towards the windows, bathed now in brilliant sunshine. It was going to be hot, which would make a pleasant change: so far, the summer had been extremely wet. She went over to the big double-fronted wardrobe and opened one of the doors, only to be brought up short. What subconscious impulse had made her go to Rowland's wardrobe instead of her own? It was a mistake she would never normally have made. What was the matter with her? She simply wasn't thinking straight. All the clothes he kept at Mallerby were still

17

hanging there. She caught the faint musky scent of his aftershave. The next moment, she found herself clutching the sleeve of one of his shirts and crying as though her heart would break.

Two arms came round her. It was Colette who, having knocked and received no answer, had entered the room unbidden.

'Hush, hush, *ma chérie*,' she whispered, rocking Christine to and fro. 'Rowe would never have wanted you to grieve so. He would have wanted you to be happy and go on with your life. Do you remember him quoting those lines of Christinã Rossetti to us once? "Better by far you should forget and smile/Than that you should remember and be sad." And this grief will pass, I promise you. I know. I have been through it all with Rowland's father. Now, finish getting dressed. You will feel better when you have had some breakfast.'

CHAPTER TWO

THE BREAKFAST-PARLOUR was at the back of the house, in one of the two wings which flanked the terrace and steps leading to the park and gardens. There were windows on three sides, including one of the bay windows which were so much a part of Mallerby. The original fireplace, wainscoting and frieze were still features of a room which had always been one of Colette's favourites, and was furnished very much in accordance with her tastes. Over the years, she had done away with the big handsome Victorian pieces she had found there, replacing them with some delicate ladderback chairs and a Regency gateleg table. A pale blue wallpaper, a settee covered in eighteenth-century needlework, whose tiny reddish-brown flowers echoed the colour of the velvet curtains, plus the fact that it caught any morning sun, made it one of the prettiest rooms in the entire house.

This morning it was awash with light. Christine, taking her place at the table, felt her spirits lift. She smiled at Colette, who was already seated, eating croissants and black cherry jam whilst reading the *Financial Times*. She had already dealt with her post, and letters, bills and empty envelopes were strewn across the white linen tablecloth.

Christine turned to her own mail, which had been neatly stacked beside her plate. Colette poured her a cup of coffee.

'Anything interesting?' she enquired.

Christine shook her head. 'Mostly circulars by the look of it. I wonder the world has any trees left, the amount of paper that's being used to print junk.' She took the proffered cup and saucer from her mother-in-law and added: 'Wait a minute. Here's a letter from Vivien. Give me a moment or two, and I'll tell you what she says.' Christine tore open the envelope and extracted several sheets of thick white notepaper, closely covered in a small, neat hand. She glanced through them quickly, then went back and read them again. 'She sends you her love. Giles is working all hours at the bank, and she doesn't see nearly so much of him now that he's chief director. Lucien and your sister-in-law are enjoying their retirement, and they all went down to Lussac-les-Châteaux last week for Madame's eighty-fifth birthday.'

'How is my mother?' Colette sighed. 'I ought to have gone over, I know, but somehow I just couldn't. I hope they all understood.'

'I'm sure they did.' Christine smiled reassuringly. 'Yes, look! Vivien says here: "We were thinking of you all, and wished you could have been with us, but realized that none of you was in the mood for any kind of celebration, however muted. It was much too soon after Uncle Rowe's death."'

Vivien was Julian Saxelby's daughter and, three years ago, had married her father's cousin, Giles de Bérenger. The marriage had not been altogether approved of at the time; but, remembering the events of 1980, everyone agreed that it might have been very much worse. Vivien had always been headstrong and unmanageable, but since her marriage she seemed to have settled down, taking her responsibilities as wife, and now mother-to-be, far more seriously than anyone could have foreseen. This had a lot to do with the influence of her great-grandmother de Bérenger, who, from her château above the River Vienne, still ruled her family with a rod of iron.

Christine took a croissant and nibbled at it, aware of her mother-in-law's bright eyes watching her, but she wasn't hungry.

'Eat it!' Colette commanded. 'Do you want to fade away to nothing? Do you think that's what Rowe would have wished?'

Christine made a valiant effort, but after a moment or two she slid the croissant to one side of her plate and picked up her cup. Coffee was all she really needed these mornings.

'Was there anything interesting in your post?' she asked, to divert Colette's attention.

Colette glanced shrewdly at her daughter-in-law. She knew perfectly well how matters had stood between her son and Christine, and wished with all her heart, for both their sakes, that things had been otherwise. She hadn't always felt that way: there had been a time when she had regarded Christine as a scheming minx; a little nobody who had trapped her precious elder son into marriage. But that was so long ago now that it was like looking back at a different woman. If she had any regret at all about her past, it was that she had not been kinder, in those early days, to Rowland's wife.

But she hadn't been wrong about her other daughter-in-law, Sophie. Drunk half the time, she must have slept with most of the men of her acquaintance. It was no wonder, with a mother like that, that Vivien had been so wild. Julian had done his best, but he was busy all day at the bank. Besides, it wasn't the place of a man to bring up a child. It said much for the underlying strength of Vivien's character that she had turned out as well as she had. Colette's eyes softened. She was fond of her only grand-daughter. A pity Rowe and Christine couldn't have had more children.

Colette was conscious of her daughter-in-law's raised eyebrows and remembered that she had been asked a question.

'No . . . No,' she said, smiling. 'Nothing of any interest in my post, either. Like yours, mostly circulars. A brief note from Julian, scribbled on the bank's notepaper, to say he's sorry he hasn't phoned. But he's desperately busy, as we might suppose.'

'How is everything going?' Christine took another sip of coffee and looked a little apprehensively at her mother-in-law.

Colette smoothed back a strand of hair which had strayed into her eyes. At sixty-eight, she was still a very pretty woman; as dainty and vivacious as on the day she had married Noel Saxelby in 1937. The huge brown eyes in the delicate small-boned face retained their sparkle, and the husky voice its attractive accent, in spite of the fact that she now spoke English as easily and fluently as she did her native French. ('When you begin to *think* in a foreign language, that's when you know you have finally mastered it,' she had once said to Christine.) Her bird-like movements had lost none of their quickness. Only the gleaming black hair had dulled to a uniform grey, with here and there just the odd glint of sable to remind herself and others of its past glory.

'I'm not certain, *ma chère*,' she said in answer to Christine's question. She tapped the *Financial Times* with a carefully manicured fingernail. 'There has been some loss of confidence in the bank since Julian took over, but one would like to think that that was only natural. A period of transition following the unexpected death of a man who was well liked and highly esteemed in the City is bound to create some little fluctuation in the price of shares.'

Christine put down her cup and broke a piece off her almost untouched croissant, without making any attempt to eat it. 'But you don't think that's the only reason?'

Her mother-in-law hesitated, then shrugged. 'Julian has always lived in his brother's shadow, you know that. It was nothing to do with Rowe. From the time they were both small boys, Julian hero-worshipped Rowland. He relied on Rowe for most things because it made life so

22

much easier. Julian has never liked hard work. He likes a good time, to take things easy. And if there is always someone to whom you can turn, someone who will pull you out of scrapes, put things right when you make mistakes, then of course you can drift along with the minimum of fuss.'

'And now Rowe isn't there any more.'

'Exactly. Rowe isn't there for Julian to rely on. And, to make matters worse, he suddenly finds himself head of Saxelby's, with responsibility for all the day-to-day running of the bank on his shoulders and no elder brother to advise him. Julian's bound to make some less-than-perfect decisions to begin with. That's excusable. He's still coping with his grief, as we are. People might be prepared to make allowances for a month or so.' Colette's eyes were fixed abstractedly on the portrait of Sir John Saxelby, who had started the building of the house in 1539, which hung above the marble mantelpiece. 'But the real trouble is that they don't trust him in the same way they trusted Rowland. Rowe was a very astute man. His business instincts were sound. I suspect that, at the moment, there is some doubt in the City about how far Julian's judgement can be counted on. The bank shares have fallen quite sharply.'

'I don't suppose Sophie's behaviour helps much.' Christine spread jam on her piece of croissant and valiantly took a bite. Her mother-in-law was right. She mustn't make herself ill; that would be stupid.

Colette grimaced, pulling down the corners of the thin mobile mouth which Rowland had inherited.

'Oh, I don't think Sophie has any influence. She and Julian have been separated for so many years now. Perhaps they should get a divorce. It would be best for both of them.' If Christine was surprised to hear her devoutly Catholic mother-in-law advocating something to which her faith was so totally opposed, she made no comment. Colette went on: 'No, if anything's bothering people, it's that attempted takeover by Bérenger's earlier this year.' The brown eyes flashed. 'I shall never forgive Lucien for that. He wanted to do something spectacular before retiring. His swan-song. To go out on a cloud of glory. Instead, all he achieved was to kill his own nephew! I'm sure it was the worry of that which contributed to Rowland's death.'

She sounded vindictive, but Christine knew her mother-in-law well enough to suspect that beneath her justifiable anger Colette admired her brother and took a secret pride in the Bérenger bid to take over Saxelby's. The daughter of one successful merchant banker, married to another, the mother, sister and aunt of three more, Colette was too steeped in the world of high finance to consider such an attempt unethical, or to resent the high price it had cost her, for very long.

'Will things settle down again?' Christine asked. 'At the bank, I mean.'

'If Julian keeps his head and does nothing foolish. If nothing else happens to rock the boat.'

'Could it?'

'Who knows? Now that Giles is in charge, it is impossible to forecast what Bérenger's will do. Whether or not they seek to acquire more shares in Saxelby's is up to him.'

'Could they gain outright control?' Christine abandoned her half-hearted attempt at eating and passed her cup for a refill. Colette picked up the coffee-pot.

'Not unless you or Patrick, Julian or myself were to sell them our shares. Between us, we have the majority holding. But any one of us could upset the apple-cart.'

'Well, that isn't very likely to happen, surely?' Christine took her cup and stirred in a liberal spoonful of sugar. Colette tut-tutted and shook her head.

'Even brown sugar is bad for you,' she chided. 'And it's no substitute for food. I shall expect to see you eat a good meal at lunch-time.' She tilted her head to one side in a characteristic gesture. 'Didn't Rowland tell

24

you that it was Pat's shares Lucien was negotiating to buy last March?'

'Rowland rarely talked to me about his work,' Christine answered bitterly. 'When did he have the time? And he certainly would never have told me anything that reflected badly on Pat. You know how loyal he always was to him. How guilty he felt about not knowing of his existence until Pat was ten years old. So what happened?'

'Oh, Rowland discovered what was going on and persuaded Pat to see reason. I don't know all the details, but I do know that Pat got a promotion at the bank just about then, which entailed quite a substantial rise in salary.'

'Damn!' Christine put down her cup so violently that the coffee slopped into the saucer. 'Isn't it silly? I've never really trusted Pat, but I can't help being fond of him. I hate hearing anything that confirms my worst fears.'

Colette nodded. 'I know. I'm exactly the same. Like you, I can't help liking him, although all my instincts tell me he's a rogue. I wish he didn't remind me so much of Rowland.'

'Everyone says that.' Christine shook her head. 'Whenever I look at him, I can only see his mother.'

'Of course, I never saw Lucy Brennan.' Colette frowned. 'She must have had similar colouring to Rowland, then.'

'Yes, she did, except for the eyes. Black hair, olive skin, but those very startlingly Irish blue eyes that Pat has. I suppose that's why he makes me think of Lucy.'

'What are you doing this morning?' Colette asked, abruptly changing the subject. She could read the distress signals in her daughter-in-law's face. Christine had never liked talking about Lucy Brennan.

The younger woman shrugged. 'I ought to write some more replies to all those letters of condolence. There was such an avalanche of mail, I've only managed to get through half of it so far.'

'Pooh! Leave them.' Colette waved a dismissive hand. 'They'll keep. On a lovely morning like this, you ought to have some fresh air. I'm going into the village to get a few things. You can come with me. It will do you far more good than sitting cooped up indoors.'

Christine hesitated, then smiled her acceptance. 'You're quite right,' she said. 'I will come.'

When she returned to her bedroom to fetch her handbag, one of the daily girls was there, making the bed. She glanced awkwardly at Christine, obviously wanting to say something, but not quite liking to. Christine gave her an encouraging smile and tried to remember her name.

'Sharon, isn't it?'

'That's right. Sharon Coombs. Mum and Dad keep the newsagent's on the Green.'

'Yes, of course. Stupid of me. I should have known.'

The girl answered shyly: 'That's OK. 'Spect you've got other things on your mind. I just wanted to say . . . that is, me and the other girls wanted to say how very sorry we are about Mr Saxelby.' Tears started in the hazel eyes. 'He was a lovely man. The whole village was real upset to hear he'd died. Mum and Dad wanted to go up to London for the funeral, but they couldn't leave the shop.'

'That's perfectly understandable,' Christine said in a restricted voice. 'And . . . and thank you for saying what you did, just now.'

'That's all right.' The tears brimmed over and ran down Sharon's face, leaving two long streaks of mascara. She put up a hand and smudged them away. Her thin body began to shake with sobs. 'He really was a lovely man. That wasn't just something to say. Everyone liked him. I never heard a bad word said about him in all my life.'

Christine gave a wry smile, holding her own tears in check.

'Thank you,' she said again.

The girl nodded, sniffed and turned back to finish making the bed. She was very fond of Mrs Christine Saxelby. Most people in the village were, although she had once heard her mother remark to a neighbour: 'Of course, she isn't anybody really, you know. She was a clerk in the labour exchange in Weston before she got married.' But Mrs Coombs hadn't enlarged on the subject. There wasn't the same resentment of Christine nowadays as there had been some years earlier. The Swinging Sixties had altered a lot of attitudes.

But it was Rowland the villagers had really cared for, particularly the women.

'He's a real charmer,' old Mrs Pearson from Rose Cottage had confided in Christine many years ago. 'A *real* charmer.' Her misshapen arthritic hand had patted the younger woman's arm. 'He's genuine, you see. He likes people. He's not pretending. When he asks you how you are, he really wants to know. Mr Julian, now, he's always just as polite, but it's all on the surface. With him, it's just words.'

Christine picked up her handbag from the chair where she had left it and hitched it over one shoulder. Her reflection stared back at her from the long wall-mirror. She looked cool and elegant in the pale apple-green linen suit.

The bitterness welled up inside her again. She had shared Rowland with so many people. Everyone had wanted a stake in his affections. That wouldn't have mattered if he had just once told her that he loved her best. She wouldn't have minded the sharing then. She had never expected to be the centre of his world.

But he hadn't. He hadn't even told her that he loved her. And now he never would. It was a reality she had to accept and live with if she were not to become permanently twisted and embittered.

She said goodbye to Sharon and went downstairs. Colette was waiting impatiently for her in the hall.

27

CHAPTER THREE

BEFORE THE CONQUEST, the village of Hinton had been nothing more than a collection of wattle-and-daub huts sheltering in the lee of the hill which gave it its name, Hengist's Dun. After Hastings, however, William I had given it and the neighbouring stretch of valley to the Sieur Raoul d'Harcourt, an ambitious young man who, by dint of some hard fighting, had managed to bring himself to the conqueror's notice during the battle. Raoul had built himself a castle on top of the hill and pastured his animals in the surrounding fields.

It had not taken him long to realize that the grazing was poor, the grass stunted and sour. Disillusioned, he had returned to Normandy, leaving his steward, an indolent good-natured man, to run things for him. Life for the peasants continued much as usual, except that, before he went, Raoul d'Harcourt had added the strange new name of Malsherbes to the original one of Hinton and, struggle as they might, the Saxons had never managed to wrap their tongues around so alien a word, 'Mallerby' being the best they could come up with. So, over the centuries, Hinton Malsherbes had become known as Hinton Mallerby, creating one of those English discrepancies between spelling and pronunciation so confusing to natives and foreigners alike.

At the beginning of the fourteenth century, a descendant of Raoul d'Harcourt had made a gift of the land to the Augustinian Canons for the founding of a religious community on the lines of those already established at Ashridge and Edington, known as the

Order of the Bonshommes. The new monastery had been built in the valley, using for the foundations most of the stone from the deserted and crumbling castle. By the time of Henry VIII's break with Rome, two hundred and fifty years later, it was a rich and flourishing house; so rich and flourishing that it became one of the king's prime targets in his quest for monastic gold.

John Saxelby, a young man on the make and in a hurry, was the son of a Bristol soap merchant. By the age of forty, he had made his fortune by trading with the newly discovered West Indies, becoming a member of the Joint Stock Company, the Merchant Adventurers of England for the Discovery of Lands, Territories, Isles, Dominions and Seignories Unknown, and, with Sebastian Cabot, had directed his energies towards the search for a north-east passage to Cathay. Between these events, he had come out strongly on the side of the king in the controversy over Henry's divorce and remarriage, and had been given the signal honour of lending his sovereign several large sums of money, none of which he expected to see again. As a result, in 1540 he not only received a knighthood, but was also given the manor and lands of Hinton Malsherbes.

The house of the Bonshommes was razed to the ground and Mallerby House begun in its place. No conscious decision to anglicize the spelling of Malsherbes had been taken either by Sir John or by his descendants; it was something which had simply happened. So Mallerby House in the village of Hinton Malsherbes had gradually taken shape to become not only one of Somerset's chief tourist attractions – the house was open for public viewing every Tuesday and Thursday – but also that fairly rare phenomenon by modern standards, a stately home still occupied by the same family after more than four centuries.

* * *

'We'll walk,' Colette said firmly, as they stepped out on to the gravel sweep facing the main drive, flanked by its two straight rows of limes. The strong sunlight filtered through the pale green leaves, laying a quivering pattern of shadows along the ground.

'Are you sure?' Christine was solicitous. 'You wouldn't rather take the Mini?'

'For a ten-minute walk?' Colette was snappish. 'What do you think I am – an invalid?'

'No. But there's the return journey and going round the shops. Won't it be too much for you?'

'I'm sixty-eight, not ninety,' Colette returned fiercely, daring her daughter-in-law to breathe the word 'arthritis'. Arthritis was for old people: the twinges of pain she felt now and then in her left hip, and which she had foolishly made public, were occasioned by nothing more than tiredness, which women over a certain age were bound to experience once in a while.

'All right.' Christine shrugged resignedly. 'If you say so.' She took a step backwards, in the direction of the porch. 'At least take a walking-stick.'

But this, it appeared, was an even more insulting suggestion than going by car. Colette did not deign to reply. With a kind of strangled snort, indicative of outrage, she swung on her heel and started up the drive at such a pace that Christine had to run to catch up with her.

'I'm sorry,' Christine said contritely, as she came abreast.

'So you should be.' Then, with a glinting smile, Colette relented. 'You could give me your arm.'

By the time they turned out of Harcourt Lane, which ran past Mallerby's main gates, into the High Street, Colette was leaning so heavily on Christine's arm that Christine was wishing she had insisted on bringing the car. Fortunately, it was not far from the turning to the village green and the shops which clustered along its western edge. After they had visited the newsagent's and the butcher's, and after Colette had had a long argument with Geoff Pollard of the general stores concerning the freshness, or otherwise, of his tomatoes, Christine suggested a cup of coffee.

'The café or the pub?' she asked in a voice tinged with exhaustion.

Colette, considerably revived by the recent altercation, replied without hesitation: 'Oh, the Feathers, of course. We shall only be subjected to more condolences if we go to the Spinning Wheel. You know what Miss Lathbury and her sister are like. They shed tears at the drop of a hat, and I can't stand any more of it this morning. Besides, the coffee's disgusting.'

This was a slight exaggeration, but in general Christine agreed with her mother-in-law. She, too, felt that she could stand no more condolences, however well intentioned and sincerely meant. Too many people had stopped them already to express sorrow at their bereavement. It made Christine wonder if she and Colette had been wise to come down to Mallerby so soon after Rowland's death; but London had been getting them down and, when Julian suggested it, it had seemed the sensible thing to do.

'It'll be quieter there,' he had said. At Inglebatch House the phone rarely seemed to stop ringing with calls from anxious friends.

So they had telephoned Mrs James, instructed Marie and Françoise, the two current au pairs, to pack their bags, and all four of them had travelled down to Somerset the previous weekend. This was their first real foray into the village.

The Three Feathers stood at one corner of the green, an oblong of much-trodden grass, surrounded on three sides by cottages and shops, the fourth side opening on to the High Street and, across the road, the long stretch of wall skirting the Mallerby estate. Behind the pub's car park and garden lay the recently completed Harcourt Housing Complex, its brash newness in stark contrast to the older cottages. The inn-sign, swinging above the saloon-bar door, displayed the three Prince of Wales feathers and the motto *Ich Dien*, both, as Colette was never tired of reminding people, stolen by the Black Prince from the dead John of Bohemia after Crécy.

The landlord, Colin Dando, a big placid-looking man, was in the lounge-bar, and he looked up, smiling, as Christine and Colette came in. The pub had not long opened and was still fairly devoid of customers.

'What can I get you, Mrs Saxelby?' he asked respectfully, coming out from behind the counter and shaking hands. He turned to Christine. 'Joan and I were very sorry to hear of your husband's death,' he added matter-of-factly. 'Now, what's it to be?'

'Just coffee, please, Colin.' Christine was grateful for his reticence. 'And is there a corner table where we won't be too readily seen?'

Colin Dando nodded understandingly. 'Have the table in the ingle-nook. People have been known to go missing in there for days.'

They both laughed and took a seat behind the worn and ringed table in the deep embrasure to one side of the big stone fireplace. And the coffee which Colin presently brought them was at least drinkable according to Colette.

'Though why the English have never bothered to learn how to make coffee properly, I'll never understand.'

'How is your hip?' Christine enquired, changing the subject.

'Fine. Why? What should be wrong with it?' Colette raised her eyebrows, demurely peeping over the rim of her cup.

Christine laughed and stretched out her legs under the table.

'I give up. You're the most obstinate woman I know.' She drank some coffee and sighed with pleasure. 'I'm beginning to feel almost human again.'

Colette eyed her daughter-in-law thoughtfully. 'Christine,' she said at last, 'what are you going to do?'

'Do? How do you mean?'

'With your life. Now that Rowland's dead. Now there's nothing more to wait and hope for.'

Christine coloured painfully. 'I'm not sure I follow you,' she lied.

'Yes, you do.' Colette replaced her cup in its saucer, twisting it round and round between her hands. 'You've spent the last twenty years waiting for something which – forgive me – didn't happen. Now, at last, you're free of Rowland. Free to pursue your own life.'

Christine said nothing, but sat, staring before her, all her recent contentment suddenly vanished. Colette was right, of course. She was free now of that crippling emotion, hope; free to begin all over again; free, perhaps, to find someone who really could love her. She thought fleetingly of Russell Jennings, but dismissed the idea. Their friendship, renewed so unexpectedly ten years ago, had at least taught her one thing: that she had no very deep affection for him, and never would have. She found it difficult, in any case, to consider any other man in that particular way. Rowland had filled her heart, her life, her entire vision for so long that it was impossible to imagine anyone displacing him.

Reading her thoughts, Colette insisted: 'Rowe is dead.' She laid a delicate blue-veined hand on Christine's arm and shook it urgently. '*Chérie*, it is time to make a fresh start.'

Christine shook her head obstinately. 'It's too soon.' The pub was beginning to fill up with the pre-lunch crowd, mostly elderly and retired people who had driven out from the neighbouring towns to sample Joan Dando's cooking. 'Besides, what would I do?'

'Something. Anything. You are an intelligent good-looking woman. You are rich. Comparatively young.' Colette's voice, warming to her theme, had risen excitedly. One or two curious heads were turned in their direction, and she continued with more restraint: 'Women can do anything they put their mind to nowadays, if they want something badly enough. What I'm trying to say is don't let the memory of Rowland turn you to stone. Ah!' She banged the edge of the table in frustration. 'I am not putting this very well.'

'Yes, you are.' Christine forced a smile. 'I know exactly what you're getting at. It's only what I've told myself a hundred times during the past two months. But it's as though . . . Oh, I don't know! As though I'm living in a dream world and daren't let myself wake up. If I do, I shall have to face the fact that there was never any chance that Rowe might fall in love with me. And I can't cope with that at the moment.'

Colette sighed, and her hands slipped back into her lap. Merde! Merde! Merde! Why had Rowland had to die before realizing the true state of his feelings for his wife? He was a fool, Colette thought furiously, wasting his affections on those other women, unable to appreciate what was under his nose. But was that strictly true? He had appreciated Christine, her unswerving love and devotion, and in return she had received his unstintingly loyal support. You couldn't, after all, command love. It was something which had to come as naturally as breathing.

The noise in the pub was reaching a crescendo and, to add to the clamour, the phone had started to ring. Christine saw Colin Dando answer it, then glance briefly in their direction. He listened carefully for a moment or two, nodded and hung up. Opening the counter-flap, he squeezed through the crowd around the bar and crossed to where they were sitting.

'That was your housekeeper, Mrs Saxelby,' he said, addressing them both impartially. 'Says she's been ringing round everywhere to try to find you. Wants you to go home at once. There's been a very urgent phone call from Mr Julian.'

'Julian? I'm sorry we were out when you called earlier. Christine and I have been shopping in the village. Is anything wrong?'

Colette was telephoning from her bedroom, an airy first-floor apartment at the front of the house, overlooking the drive and the avenue of limes. Carpet, curtains, bedspread were all in her favourite blue. On the bedside table was a cluster of silver-framed photographs: a large one of herself and Noel Saxelby on their wedding day in 1937; smaller ones of Rowland and Julian as boys, adolescents and men; and one of Vivien and Patrick together as children. Christine, curled up in a floral-patterned armchair, noticed with amusement that the snapshot of them together when they were older had been removed, the frame refilled with a picture of herself taken at Château Bérenger last year. Colette evidently did not like to be reminded ...

The bay windows were open, and the curtains stirred in a freshening breeze. Christine could hear Julian's muffled tones at the other end of the line, his voice rising and falling in agitation. Whatever the reason for his call, it was evidently not good news. Colette interrupted him.

'Julian! Tais-toi! Tais-toi! Calm down. I cannot make head or tail of what you are saying! *Why* is it necessary that Christine and I return to London? We have only been here four days, just long enough for our mail to begin getting through. Now you want us to disrupt our lives again and return to Inglebatch House. Why?' There was another burst of sound from Julian's end of the line and, once again, his mother was forced to cut across it. '*Why* can't you tell me over the phone? Is it something to do with the bank? "Yes and no." What does that mean?' There was another pause,

35

then Colette said sharply: 'Are you saying it has something to do with Patrick? Well, *what*, for heaven's sake? Julian, you are beginning to try my patience.'

Christine had raised her head at the mention of her step-son's name, looking enquiringly at her mother-in-law. Colette grimaced and made a despairing gesture with her free hand before slamming down the receiver.

'What was that about?' Christine uncurled her legs and sat forward in the chair, her hands gripping its arms.

'I wish I knew.' Colette stared defeatedly at the now silent telephone. 'Apart from the fact that Julian demands our immediate return to London, I'm no wiser than you are. It has something to do with Patrick, that's all I know. But you know how easily Julian panics.'

'Perhaps your nephew has made another approach to Pat with a view to buying his shares. Could that be it?'

Colette shrugged. 'Maybe. More than likely, I should think. All the same,' Colette continued in exasperation, 'Julian should be capable of dealing with something like that without running to me for advice. He is the head of the bank now! And he was most insistent that you come with me. Come to think of it, he did say at one point that it concerned you as well.'

'Me?' Christine considered this. 'Well, I suppose it would, indirectly, if your family were to gain control of Saxelby's.'

'Ye-es.' Colette sounded doubtful. She sat down on the edge of the bed and looked at Christine with troubled eyes. 'And yet somehow I don't really think that was it.'

'So do we return to London or not?'

The older woman hesitated a moment, then nodded. 'Yes. We'll take the Peugeot and drive up this afternoon. If we start immediately after lunch, we should be there by tea-time. Marie and Françoise can follow tomorrow, if necessary, in the Mini. They should be all right if Marie can remember to drive on the left-hand side of the road. Now, would you mind asking Mrs James to bring lunch forward half an hour, while I pack an overnight bag?'

CHAPTER FOUR

INGLEBATCH HOUSE was one of a terrace of Regency houses not far from the Heath, and from its attic it was possible to catch a glimpse of Hampstead Ponds and Parliament Hill beyond. Years ago, the attic floor had been converted into a self-contained flat, inhabited at various times by different members of the family, and by Julian since the break-up of his marriage to Sophie Lennox. But he was not at home when Christine and Colette climbed stiffly out of the car late that same afternoon.

Mrs Johnson, the 'daily', met the two women in the hall, wearing her outdoor clothes and ready to leave. She seemed surprised to see them.

'Didn't Mr Saxelby tell you he'd asked us to come back?' Colette enquired.

Mrs Johnson shook her head. 'Went off to the bank as normal this morning. 'E must 'ave phoned from there.'

'You saw him before he left?'

This time Mrs Johnson nodded, the bird in the hat she wore, with no concession to the weather, bobbing up and down in sympathy.

'Did he seem all right?' Christine lowered the overnight bag she was holding to the floor. 'Not upset in any way?'

'Well, now you come to mention it, 'e did seem a bit out of sorts. And 'e didn't touch the bit of supper what I left for 'im las' night. Mind, 'e's bin workin' that 'ard since you left, I didn't think anythink of it. Jus' thought 'e was tired. 'E ain't ill, is 'e, and didn't like to tell me?'

'No, no. Nothing like that.' Colette smiled. 'He didn't give a reason, but I don't suppose it's anything serious. Thank you, Mrs Johnson. Don't let us keep you.'

Mrs Johnson grunted, managing to imply that, whatever was going on, it had nothing to do with her, hitched her mauve woollen cardigan more securely around her shoulders and went past them to the front door. As she opened it, Christine asked as casually as possible: 'Have you seen anything of Mr Brennan lately?'

'No. Not likely, is it? 'E's at work at the bank when I'm workin' 'ere.' Mrs Johnson paused with her hand on the latch, her plump features narrowing suddenly. Beyond the open front door, the sun-dappled street was quiet with the brooding stillness of early evening. 'Come to think of it, though, 'e must've bin 'ere las' night because there were two stubs of those cigarettes 'e smokes in one of the ashtrays this morning. Well, I'll be off, then. Got to get me old man 'is meal.' She let herself out and slammed the front door behind her.

Christine glanced at Colette with raised eyebrows.

'It seems Pat has been here, then. Oh, well, we'll just have to wait for Julian to come home. I'll take the bags upstairs if you'll make some tea. We can unpack later.'

She went up to the second floor in the lift which Noel Saxelby had had installed just after the Second World War. The bedroom at the front of the house, which she had shared with Rowland, looked exactly the same as when she had left it at the end of last week. Christine summoned up a wry smile. What had she expected, for heaven's sake? That it would have altered in appearance during the past few days?

She suppressed the real reason behind the thought: that it would somehow look less desolate, less bereft of Rowland's presence, less empty of hopes and dreams. She lifted her zip-top bag on to the bed and glanced around at the William Morris wallpaper, at the

Morgan & Sanders bedroom cupboard with the sham drawers that pulled out to form a table-top, at the Sheraton dressing-table and washbasin-stand and at the Regency cheval mirror. Nothing had altered. The two wardrobes still stood side by side against the far wall, the gentleman's still containing Rowland's clothes, like the one at Mallerby. Christine knew that she should start getting rid of some of his things, but she could not bring herself to do it. Not yet.

She went down one flight of stairs and left Colette's case in her sitting-room, overlooking the narrow walled garden, then descended to the basement, where she found her mother-in-law in the process of making tea, cups and saucers laid ready on the table. Unlike the rest of the house, the kitchen and laundry-room, which occupied most of the basement area, were miracles of modern technology and Mrs Johnson's pride and joy. Five days a week, between the hours of nine and six, she ruled over them with a proprietorial zeal.

'No sign of Julian?' Christine dropped thankfully into a chair. The journey had depressed and tired her. The traffic had been heavy, although it would get far worse once the summer season was properly underway and holiday-makers began converging on the West Country.

Colette poured out two cups of tea, taking her own with a slice of lemon and watching in disapproval as Christine added both milk and sugar to hers.

'They are very bad for the heart,' she reproved, then paused, stricken, remembering Rowland. After a moment, however, she shrugged. She couldn't go through life watching every word she said. She went on: 'I telephoned the bank while you were upstairs and told Julian we'd arrived. He's coming home at once. Perhaps then we can clear up this mystery.'

Christine shivered, suddenly cold. The sunlight filtering down the area steps and in through the top of the basement windows gave very little heat, in spite of the warmth of the evening. She was glad that she had kept on her jacket. She remembered sitting here with Rowland, the night before he died, companionably drinking hot milk laced with rum. He had been unable to sleep – perhaps he had already been feeling unwell – and had come down to the kitchen in search of food. Christine, following him, had persuaded him to have the milk instead. The rum had been his own idea. She couldn't recall what they had talked about; nothing of any importance. At last, at one o'clock, he had risen from the kitchen table, stretching and yawning. She had taken the mugs over to the sink to wash them, and at the door he had suddenly stopped, come back and kissed her.

'There's a letter I want to write before I turn in,' he had said. 'You go on up to bed. I'll be along later.'

Strangely moved by the unexpected gesture of affection, Christine had tried to stay awake until he came. But he must have been some time, because when he did finally come upstairs she was asleep. And the following morning she overslept, arriving down to breakfast just as he was finishing his bacon and eggs. Colette and Julian had also been present, and he had made no reference to the previous night. He and his brother had left together for the bank. Less than an hour later, he was dead.

Christine looked across the table at Colette and said in a hard brittle voice: 'Did you know that, the day after Rowland died, Garrard's rang us to say that the brooch he had ordered was ready? A true-lover's knot in sapphires and diamonds.'

There was silence for several moments. A car drew up outside and stopped. Colette asked quietly: 'Who was it for? Do you know?'

Christine smiled mirthlessly. 'Who do you suppose it was for?'

'Faith Malyon?'

41

'Who else? I guess that's who he was writing to, the night before.'

A key rattled in the front door on the floor above them. Julian's voice called: 'Maman! Chris! Where are you?' But before they could reply he must have seen the open door leading to the basement, and his footsteps sounded on the stairs.

'What do you mean, he's claiming to be Rowe's legitimate son? How can that be possible?'

Quarter of an hour had passed since Julian Saxelby's arrival and, at his request, they had gone up to the drawing-room on the first floor. It was evident that he considered the kitchen unsuitable for the momentous information he had to impart.

The two women were sitting together on the long couch which stretched almost the length of one wall, Christine's apple-green suit pale against the rich ruby-red of the upholstery. Julian was standing in front of the empty fireplace. In answer to his mother's question, he replied unhappily: 'Pat claims he once saw a marriage certificate showing that Rowe and Lucy Brennan were married when he was born. He says he's the rightful heir to Mallerby and all of Rowe's estate.'

It took Colette and Christine a moment or two to assimilate the full enormity of the claim, then they both began to speak at once.

'What utter nonsense!'

'How *dare* he?'

'How stupid does he think we are?'

'I've never heard such rubbish in all my life!'

The voices faltered and died while they both drew breath and tried to marshal their thoughts. Julian took the opportunity to say in a troubled voice: 'He seemed in deadly earnest to me.'

'Rowe would never have done such a thing!' Christine exclaimed hotly. 'He wouldn't base the whole of his married life on a lie! Besides,' she went on, unintentionally weakening her argument, 'Pat hasn't seen his mother since he was ten years old.'

Without being conscious of his actions, Julian rubbed his sweating palms against the legs of his trousers.

'Oh, he admits it was a long time ago. Says he was about six or seven. Came across it one day when Lucy had given him a box of stuff to play with, to keep him quiet. Apparently, he asked her what it was. Swears she said it was a certificate of her marriage to his father. Stuck in his mind, he says. Never forgot it.'

Colette sat up straighter. 'Then, where is it,' she demanded, 'this precious certificate of his?'

Julian shrugged. 'Lucy Brennan still has it, presumably. Wherever *she* is.'

'You mean there is no actual proof of this cock-and-bull story?' Christine was outraged. 'It rests entirely on Pat's word? Oh, come on, Julian! It's a hoax. It must be. Why are you getting into a state about nothing?'

'Exactly!' Colette gave a crow of triumph. 'Of course it's a hoax! How could you let yourself believe him? Quelle bêtise! How could Patrick remember so precisely what he saw and what was said to him when he was seven? All of seventeen years ago.'

Julian demurred, angered by their attempts to make him look a fool.

'I can remember things that happened when I was seven. Younger, in fact. So can everyone if the incidents made enough impression at the time.'

There was another silence. Christine suddenly had a vivid picture of herself sitting up in a hospital bed. She had just had her tonsils out and was feeling sorry for herself, grizzling for her mother. An overworked young probationer leaned over her and said sharply: 'Can't you shut up! You're not the only pebble on the beach, you know.' It was the first time Christine had consciously registered that particular expression. It had appealed to her and, as a result, she recollected the whole incident quite clearly. How old would she have

43

been? Five? Certainly not more than six. She could still smell the scent of the hospital disinfectant. And that had happened a lot longer than seventeen years ago.

'But, if Pat doesn't have any actual proof, what does it matter?' Colette was asking.

'It matters', Julian retorted grimly, 'because, if it should happen to be true, I'm doing Pat out of his rights. Mallerby is entailed to the next male heir. And it matters to Christine because – again, if it's true – she was never married to Rowe. She was just another of his women!'

There was a pregnant pause while Christine felt the very foundation of her life shift and sway. Just another of Rowland's women. Please God, not that! Being his wife had been the one solid fact she had had to cling to all these years.

Colette was on her feet, angrily facing her son. 'If Pat has no proof, then he has no case, for heaven's sake! And don't start giving me all that jolly-good-British-sportsman nonsense! We're not talking about a game of cricket. Tell him either to substantiate this ridiculous claim of his or to shut up. That's the only sensible line to take.'

'Does he have any idea where Lucy might be?' Christine asked her brother-in-law in a strained voice.

Julian shook his head. 'None at all, as far as I can gather. You're right. He hasn't seen or heard of her since he was ten, when she dumped him in that hotel in Paris and disappeared.'

'She was always a nomad. One of life's drifters.' Christine put a hand to her forehead, trying to stave off a headache. 'She hated to be tied down to anyone or anything. I can't believe that she would ever, under any circumstances, get married.'

'There you are, then!' Colette swung round with a dramatically outflung arm. 'The whole story's a bag of moonshine. A joke in the worst possible taste, just to get Julian wound up. You and Pat have never really got on,' she added, turning back to her son. 'When he was young, it was always you he picked on to be the butt of his practical jokes. This is just another of them. Tomorrow he'll admit it, you'll see. Although I, for one, shall not be laughing.'

Julian asked coldly: 'Have you seen this morning's papers?'

'Only the *Financial Times*. That and Mrs James's *Sun* are the only ones delivered on a regular basis at Mallerby.'

Julian moved over to a small sofa-table and picked up the *Daily Telegraph*, turning to an inside page. He folded it roughly and handed it to his mother, pointing to an item near the bottom.

'Pat hasn't been slow in spreading the story around. Just wait until the tabloids get wind of it. Their coverage won't be nearly so brief or so discreet.'

Christine got up and read the few lines of newsprint over her mother-in-law's shoulder.

'There is a rumour in the city that Patrick Brennan, son of the late Rowland Saxelby, of Saxelby's Bank in Gresham Street, is claiming to be Mr Saxelby's legitimate offspring. If the claim is valid, as his father's only child it would make him sole heir to the estate. So far, however, Mr Brennan appears to have produced no evidence to back an assertion which could prove highly embarrassing for the rest of the family.'

'Highly embarrassing!' Colette tossed the paper aside. 'The English gift for understatement!'

Christine sat down again. In spite of the warmth of the room, she suddenly felt icy cold. Whatever the eventual outcome, unless Patrick retracted his claim very soon, it was going to be too late to prevent a scandal. It was just the kind of sensational story the tabloids loved, and if there was one thing Saxelby's had no need of at the present moment it was adverse publicity. If Pat stuck to his guns, there would have to be some attempt to trace Lucy Brennan, and that could take months or even years. God alone knew where she was at the moment. Probably in some remote village in Tibet or a jungle settlement on the upper reaches of the Congo. Another, more devastating thought occurred to her. How did anyone know Lucy was still alive?

Of course, the claim was absolutely absurd! Rowe would never have done a thing like that. He would never have married her, knowing he was married already. He simply wasn't the type to commit bigamy. But, then, what *was* the type? How well had she really known him all those years?

Now, don't start that, she told herself sharply. He may have had other women, but he was neither a fool nor a criminal. You would have known if he had been. You wouldn't have loved him. Dear God! That was a fallacious argument if ever she'd heard one. Women had fallen in love with rogues since the dawn of time. All right! All right! But all her instincts told her that Rowe was sound.

And how many women had been led astray by their instincts? How many others had been blinded by love? The arguments clashed backwards and forwards in her brain. The incipient ache in her temples became a red-hot pain; an iron band clamped around her head. She felt sick, but resolutely fought down the rising nausea.

She drew a deep breath and glanced up at Colette, who was regarding her anxiously. It had been a long day since that first desolate moment of waking, soon after dawn. Breakfast at Mallerby, coffee at the Feathers seemed to have happened weeks rather than hours ago. But the day was not over yet.

Colette, too, was looking drawn, reminding them both of her age. Christine got up and put a comforting arm around her mother-in-law's shoulders, feeling the slight bones beneath the thin flesh.

'You stay here with Julian,' she said. 'Julian, fetch your mother a brandy. See that she rests.'

'Where are you going?' For a brief moment, Colette clung to her hand, acknowledging weakness.

'To Half Moon Street. To see Patrick.' Christine looked across at her brother-in-law. 'He'll be in by now, will he? From the bank?'

Julian consulted the long-case clock in a corner of the room. 'Half-past six. I should think so. No reason why he should be working late.'

'If he's not there, I'll wait.' Christine picked up her handbag. 'I'll be back just as soon as I can.'

CHAPTER FIVE

CHRISTINE FOUND an empty parking-meter in Piccadilly and walked the remaining short distance to Half
Moon Street. When she rang the bell of Patrick's flat,
his voice issued promptly from the little microphone
beside it.

'Who is it?'

'It's me. Christine. Can I come up?'

There was the slightest hesitation before he replied:
'Yes, of course. I was sort of expecting you.'

I bet you were, she thought grimly and pushed open
the heavy front door.

Patrick's flat was on the second floor. It had been
a twenty-first-birthday present from Rowland. Unnecessarily extravagant, Colette had called it, but her
son had disagreed.

'The boy needs to be on his own, to spread his
wings. It's not healthy the way this family lives in one
another's pocket.'

Patrick met Christine at the top of the stairs, looking handsomer than ever. The pale olive skin glowed
with health, and there was not a surplus ounce of fat
on the lean rangy body. The black hair gave him an
almost Mediterranean appearance, belied only by the
very Irish blue eyes. He had always been fairly self-
possessed, but today there was a new air of confidence
about him which made Christine uneasy. He stooped
to kiss her, and she thought of Judas. He led the way
into the flat, then politely stood aside as he ushered her
into the sitting-room.

'When I said I was expecting you, I didn't think it
would be just yet. I thought you were down at Mallerby.

I'm afraid the place is rather a mess.' He indicated the remains of his morning's breakfast, still on the table by the window, his squash-racket and sports-bag thrown down on a sofa already cluttered with several copies of magazines, and his jacket tossed over the back of a chair. 'Do please sit down. Let me get you a drink while I put some of this stuff away.'

Christine sank into one of the two leather-upholstered armchairs and said briskly: 'A whisky and water, please. And then I want to talk. I can ignore the untidiness if you can.'

Patrick gave her a sidelong glance and went over to the drinks-cabinet in a corner of the room. He returned with the whisky in a Waterford tumbler and the water in an old cracked jug. It was the sort of inconsistency that Rowland would have shown; a kind of arrogant disregard for appearances. There was no doubt that Patrick had a lot of his father's ways.

'Aren't you drinking?' Christine asked, as he cleared a place for himself on the sofa and sat down.

'If you'll excuse me, no. I'm going out later this evening and I want to arrive with a clear head.'

'You know why I'm here, of course, so let's waive the preliminaries and find out where we stand.' Christine added a generous dash of water to the spirit in her glass and sipped it sparingly, recollecting with a sense of surprise that she had not eaten since lunch-time. She ought to be hungry, but she wasn't.

Patrick leaned forward, clasping his hands loosely between his knees. 'Uncle Julian's told you and Grandmother, I take it.'

'You take it correctly,' she retorted, then wished she hadn't. It sounded silly and slick. 'Yes, naturally he's told us. He telephoned Mallerby this morning and asked us to come back. We drove up after lunch. Now, for heaven's sake, Pat, what is all this nonsense about Lucy and Rowe having been married?'

'It isn't nonsense. There was definitely a marriage

certificate. I remember it clearly. What's more, it was a British marriage certificate. It was printed in English.'

'Australia, New Zealand, Canada, the whole of the United States all speak and write in English.'

Patrick shook his head. 'It had a shield at the top with the royal quarterings, surmounted by a crown and enclosed by the Garter. If you looked at the Garter very closely, you could just make out the words *Honi soit qui mal y pense.* I remember Mum telling me what they meant, and the story of Edward III and Joan of Kent. That's what fixed it in my memory.'

Christine's hand tightened around the tumbler to stop it from shaking. 'What else do you remember?'

'Not a lot. Just asking Mum what the paper was and her reply. "That's the proof of my marriage to your father." We were on a train somewhere – in Eastern Europe, I think – with a lot of smelly people sitting on hard wooden seats. I seem to recall that there was a goat in the carriage, an evil-looking brute with yellow eyes and great curving horns. We'd been on this train for ages – at least, it seemed like ages to me – and I was getting very bored and bad-tempered. Mum gave me her handbag to play with. Well, it wasn't really a handbag. It was one of those old leather school-satchels that children used to carry before duffel and roller bags became common.'

With a jolt of recognition, Christine remembered it, the old battered satchel that Lucy had worn slung carelessly over one shoulder. One day, at the camp-site, she had emptied it out, looking for something; passport, money, bits of paper, old tickets, a couple of gold rings and what might have been a diamond brooch all jumbled together on the grass. Had there been anything remotely resembling a marriage certificate among the contents? Christine shut her eyes in an effort of concentration, but after a quarter of a century the picture was blurred. She took another sip of the whisky and gulped down more than she had intended, coughed and was forced to struggle for breath. Patrick was beside her in an instant, slapping her on the back.

'Thank you,' she gasped, and felt absurdly angry at having to be grateful to him for anything. 'I'm all right now. I'm fine.' Patrick returned to his seat on the sofa and gave her a wide sympathetic smile. She could cheerfully have killed him. She tried another tack. 'Did you ever confront your father with this story?'

'No, of course not.' He looked hurt, as though she had accused him of insensitivity beyond belief.

'Why not, for goodness' sake? According to you, he was . . . living a lie.' She could not bring herself to utter the words 'a bigamist'. There was something criminal and sleazy about it which bore no relation to the man she had been in love with for so many years.

Patrick gave her an injured stare. 'I didn't want to hurt him. Surely that's obvious. I loved him.'

The Irish influence was strong in her step-son, Christine reflected. There had always been an un-English freedom in the open expression of his affections.

'But, according to you, he was deliberately doing you out of your rights.'

'Yes. But I knew him well enough, what sort of a person he really was, to feel sure he'd tell me the truth sooner or later. He couldn't admit it openly, I could see that, or he'd have been ruined. Sent to prison. But I was positive that at some point he'd adopt me legally; give me his name. Everyone knew I was his son, after all. It would have seemed perfectly natural. What neither he nor I foresaw was that he would die so suddenly and so comparatively young.'

Christine mulled this over, sipping her drink and staring at an eighteenth-century sporting print on the opposite wall. That, too, like almost everything else in the flat, had been a present from Rowland.

51

Conscience money? Ridiculous! She looked directly at Patrick.

'Let's suppose for a moment that what you are claiming is true. And let me stress that as far as I am concerned it is only supposition. Why, in that case, didn't Rowe adopt you fourteen years ago, when he brought you home from Paris? As you say, no one would have thought it odd. It was common knowledge that I couldn't have any more children. And suddenly Rowe discovers that he has a son. I expected that he would want to make you his legal heir. So did your grandmother and your Uncle Julian. But he didn't. He didn't even change your name to his by deed poll. I even went so far as to suggest it to him, but Rowe was adamant that you retained the name Brennan.'

She was pleased to note that Patrick looked a little disconcerted. His air of confidence momentarily slipped. In spite of his earlier excuse, he now got up and poured himself a drink, returning to his place on the sofa with a vodka and tonic which he proceeded to drink in three quick gulps. When he had finished, he put the glass on the floor and wiped his mouth with the back of his hand; but the procedure had given him time to think.

'That was probably a natural reaction,' he argued, leaning forward again in the confidential manner he always used towards Christine. 'At the time, the news of my existence was a shock to him. Until then, his deception had involved no one else except my mother, and he knew she didn't care, or she'd have done something about it long before. But then, out of the blue, he suddenly discovers that there was a child of the marriage. His legal heir. Isn't it natural that, at first, he should want to continue to deny everything? He must nearly have forgotten about it after all those years, and then Fate, Nemesis or whatever takes a hand. So his first reaction is to go on rejecting the past. He shut his mind to it; pretended it had never happened. And one of the best ways of doing that was to insist that I was really Patrick Brennan.'

There was a feasibility about the argument which made Christine start to sweat. She would have preferred to describe it as specious or plausible, but found she couldn't. She was beginning to concede that, whether or not the story was true, Patrick really believed it. There was something about the directness of his gaze which convinced her of his sincerity. He was quite capable of lying, she had no doubt whatsoever about that, but in this instance she accepted that he had seen something all those years ago which Lucy had told him was the certificate of her marriage to Rowland. But why would she have done that? Perhaps it had already been in her mind that one day Patrick would prove to be too much of a hindrance to her chosen way of life and that she would abandon him to the care of his father.

'Are you absolutely certain what it was you saw?' Christine asked at last. 'You were only seven.'

She noticed the momentary gleam of triumph in the deep blue eyes and realized that Patrick had been quick to recognize the implication of her words.

'You do believe me, then!' he shot at her.

'I think you might have seen something which your mother, for reasons of her own, pretended was a wedding certificate. But I do not accept for one moment that it really was.'

'But why should she have told me a deliberate lie?'

Christine got up abruptly and went over to the partially opened window. She needed fresh air.

'God knows!' she snapped in answer to her step-son's question. 'Your mother never needed a reason. She was a law unto herself. She made up her own rules as she went along.'

'It *was* a marriage certificate,' Patrick assured her earnestly. 'I've seen enough since to be sure I'm right.

53

My memory isn't playing me tricks, if that's what you're thinking.'

'You were only seven,' she repeated.

They were going round in circles, achieving nothing. Christine returned to her chair and sat down again. She finished her whisky and placed the tumbler on an adjacent table with unnecessary violence.

'Let's get to the real point, Pat. Where's your proof? Have you checked with St Catherine's House?'

His eyes clouded. 'Ye-es,' he admitted, after a pause. Christine raised her eyebrows enquiringly, and he went on: 'They can't find anything. But', he added defiantly, 'records do get mislaid, and I know what I saw. So I'm going to try to trace my mother.'

He was that sure, then, of the truth of his assertions.

'Have you any idea where your mother could be?'

He shook his head despairingly. 'That's the trouble. She's never contacted me once in the last fourteen years. Dad never heard from her, either, after that letter she left for him in Paris. She might be anywhere in the world. Tracking her down will probably cost an awful lot of money.'

'Ah!' Christine eyed him shrewdly. 'You're hoping Julian or I will stump up.'

'Well, it would be in your interests to find out whether or not I'm lying.'

'Meantime', Christine replied acidly, 'you're going to spread the word about as much as possible. One of your journalist friends has already managed a small paragraph for you in the *Telegraph*.'

'I'm sorry about that.' He tried to look shamefaced, but couldn't quite make it. 'It's just as well', he added defensively, 'that people should be properly prepared.'

'At whatever the cost to the rest of us? You don't have any qualms about destroying our peace of mind?'

54

'I'm sorry,' he said again, 'but I have to look out for my own interests, now that my father is no longer here to protect them.'

'And does looking out for your interests include doing private deals with Bérenger's in order to undermine the stability of the bank? Or was that merely a ruse to squeeze a rise and new office and a better position out of Rowland?' Christine stared across at Patrick, her eyes suddenly hard, her temper flaring. 'Or is that the point of this whole seedy exercise? A scheme hatched between you and Giles de Bérenger to erode Rowe's credibility and, as a consequence, Saxelby's as a company. The City's already a bit jittery where Julian's concerned, and something like this could really rock the boat. What has Giles promised you? A directorship if Bérenger's gain control?'

Patrick was on his feet, the colour rising in a tide beneath the olive skin.

'Of course not! If that was all I wanted, I'd just go ahead and sell Cousin Giles my shares. Do you think I'd risk bringing my father's name into disrepute for such a cheapjack reason? I never really intended selling to Giles before. OK! So I did string him along, hoping to get something out of it. I don't see anything very dreadful about that. It's all part and parcel of business. Of looking after Number One. Dad understood that. He knew I wouldn't really have sold.'

Christine felt deflated. Just for a moment there, she had been sure she was on to something. But Patrick's show of sincerity was very compelling, and she had never questioned the genuineness of his affection for his father. She was exhausted, unable to think or even see straight. The day had been the longest of her life: all she wanted was her bed and oblivion. She clutched her handbag and got up.

'I must go,' she murmured. It was nearly eight o'clock, and Patrick had said that he was going out. She wondered uneasily who he was meeting.

He smiled at her, the same smile he used to give her when he was a boy and was trying, against all inclination, to be ingratiating and apologetic.

'You do see, don't you, Chris, that I can't just let things slide? I owe it to myself. While Dad was alive, I wouldn't have lifted a finger to harm him. And if he hadn't died so suddenly I'd have had it out with him one day in private. But things have changed now he's dead. I can't simply pass up my inheritance.'

'If it *is* your inheritance,' she answered wearily. She moved towards the door.

Patrick followed her. 'Don't think I don't realize what it means to *you*, and don't imagine that I didn't consider that aspect of the matter very carefully.'

She didn't believe that for a single instant, but she was too tired to argue any further. She said: 'I shan't worry about that until I know the truth. *If* we ever know the truth. The important thing to me is that I feel like Rowe's wife and always shall do. Don't come down. I'll see myself out.'

Christine walked briskly along Half Moon Street and turned into Piccadilly. Banks of cloud were building on the horizon, the glorious day already threatening to be as isolated an occurrence as all the other fine days this very wet summer. In spite of the sunshine, there were not many people about and traffic was light. She felt marooned in the silence.

She got behind the driver's wheel of the Peugeot and shut the door. The car was hot and stuffy. She wound down the window. A traffic warden sauntered by, eyeing up the meter, but the money had not yet run out. She gave Christine a nod of acknowledgement and continued along the pavement.

Christine closed her eyes for a moment and leaned back against the head-rest. Her body was almost numb with fatigue, but her mind was hyperactive. Her thoughts were all over the place, continually racing up and down blind alleys. In vain she tried to bring them under control, but in the end gave up the struggle. She opened her eyes again, settled herself more comfortably behind the steering-wheel, turned the key in the ignition and slowly engaged the clutch.

CHAPTER SIX

BY THE TIME Christine reached Inglebatch House again, the sky was completely overcast and a few drops of rain spat against the Peugeot's windscreen. Being June, it was still light, but the roads were grey and empty, in contrast to the brilliance of the day. She garaged the car in one of the lock-ups at the rear of the terrace and made her way along the narrow lane which separated it from the parallel street. Like so many eighteenth-century dwellings, the façade was everything. The backs were ungainly, ugly even, as though built by entirely different hands.

'We're down here,' her brother-in-law called, as she closed the front door behind her.

In her absence, Colette and Julian had descended again to the kitchen, where Colette had made coffee and cooked omelettes, which they were eating standing up, propped against the kitchen units. As Christine entered, her mother-in-law put down her plate and began cracking eggs into a basin, turning up the heat under the omelette-pan.

'Sit down,' Colette ordered. 'You must be worn out. And you've had no food since lunch-time. Don't say a word until you've eaten. Julian, pour her some coffee.'

Julian had changed his office suit for silk pyjamas and a yellow silk dressing-gown. He looked strangely dated, like a character from a 1930s Noël Coward play, and in spite of her tiredness and the nagging worry at the back of her mind Christine had a job to stop herself laughing.

Yellow was Julian's favourite colour. He drove a distinctive canary-coloured Porsche and had a number of ties, shirts and pullovers in varying shades of buttercup and primrose. Christine remembered reading somewhere that in the Middle Ages yellow was the colour of hostility: blue meant fidelity, green a new love, but yellow was indicative of hatred. She had often wondered how much aggression there was piled up behind Julian's placid, somewhat bovine exterior. He had less of his mother's dark French colouring than Rowland had done. The hair was much lighter, not so much black as a deep milk chocolate, and the eyes were a far paler shade of brown. They lacked the rich velvety depths of his mother's and brother's. His skin, too, was fairer, although still dark by English standards. But it was his general attitude to life which marked him out as more of an Anglo-Saxon. He seemed to have none of Colette's fiery Gallic temperament or Rowland's bursts of rage, as swiftly over as a summer storm. The general impression which he gave was of an even-tempered hail-fellow-well-met man, difficult to rouse, repressed in his emotions; which, Christine thought, would have been all right if, like his father, he had been completely English. But the spear and distaff sides of his family-tree must be as much at war in him as they had been in Rowland. To suppress the Gallic half of himself so entirely in favour of the Anglo-Saxon must create tensions tantamount to corking a genie in a bottle. One day, surely, the genie must escape.

She ate the omelette which Colette placed before her – pale gold, crisping to amber at the edges – and drank a whole cup of her mother-in-law's excellent coffee before feeling equal to answering their questions. Julian fidgeted around the kitchen picking things up, putting them down, but allowing Christine to finish her meal in silence. Taking pity on him at last, she gave a sigh of repletion and pushed her chair back from the table.

'Thank you,' she said to Colette. 'That was delicious.'

'And now do you feel up to telling us what happened between you and Patrick?' Julian approached the table and sat down opposite her, trying to keep his voice level and controlled.

Christine shrugged. 'He's quite serious in what he says. Whether or not he can prove it is another matter. According to him, St Catherine's House have no record of the marriage but, as he pointed out, documents do presumably go astray. And he's so certain of what he saw that he's out to make trouble. He intends trying to trace his mother.'

'But, if there is no official record, that's all there is to it,' Colette declared flatly.

Julian was still gloomy. 'There's always the possibility that, if they wanted to keep the marriage secret, they might not have used their real names. Rumour and speculation will persist. We must try to find Lucy Brennan ourselves.'

'Why?' Colette looked baffled. 'We know the truth. We know that Rowland would never have married Christine if he had already been married. Why should we waste our money doing Patrick's dirty work for him?'

'Because,' Julian explained patiently, 'if we don't make any effort to find out the truth, we can't be certain that we're not living a lie.'

Bafflement changed to anger in his mother's face. 'I have never heard such nonsense! Patrick has made the claim. The onus of proof is on him. Surely that is the English law?'

The late-June dusk had come, bringing shadows. Christine got up and switched on the light. The area and steps beyond the windows were immediately blotted out, leaving only a reflection of the shining blue and white surfaces of the kitchen and a swath of blackness above the basement railings. She resumed her seat, saying to Colette: 'I want to know the truth, even if you don't. Can't you see that until I do I have no idea

60

who I really am? This time yesterday I was Christine Saxelby, Rowe's wife. His widow. But today . . . who knows? If Patrick is correct, I might still be Christine Chandos.'

'Besides,' Julian interrupted, nervously twisting the signet ring on the little finger of his left hand, 'what do you think all this uncertainty will do to the bank? Chris is right, Maman. She and I are the ones affected. It doesn't really matter to you, because you're not directly involved.'

Colette's anger exploded. She jumped to her feet, oblivious of the sharp stab of pain in her left hip as she forced it to take too much weight.

'I am not involved? In the honour of my own son? How can you say anything so foolish! How can any mother not be involved, not be concerned, when she is suddenly told that she might not have known her child at all? That he might be a complete and unrecognizable stranger?' She was beating rhythmically on the table-top, her wedding- and engagement-rings clattering hollowly against the pine surface. The tattoo was getting on Julian's already overstretched nerves.

'Please, Maman,' he said, trying to remain calm, but speaking through clenched teeth, 'sit down and let's hear exactly what Christine has to tell us.' He glanced appealingly at his sister-in-law. 'I'd like to know everything – or as much as you can remember – that Pat said to you this evening.'

Christine got up once more and poured herself another cup of coffee. 'I'll do my best,' she promised, pushing her hair back from her clammy forehead. Returning to her place at the table, she kicked off her shoes and removed her jacket, hanging it over the back of her chair. It would be a long time before she could face wearing the apple-green suit again.

She repeated as much of her conversation with Patrick as she could recollect, occasionally able to reproduce whole sentences verbatim. While she did so, she tried to put her own thoughts in order and sort out her impressions. When she came to the part where she had accused her step-son of concocting the story with the help of Giles de Bérenger, Colette struck her hands together in excitement.

'But of course that's it! That is the solution!'

Julian shook his head. 'Doesn't make sense, Maman. All Pat need do is sell Giles his shares.'

Christine nodded. 'Exactly what Pat said. No, he's after bigger game than merely being dependent on his cousin's goodwill. Which is what he would be, once Giles gained control. Pat's after Mallerby and this place and the chairmanship of the board. Chief director. He's always been very ambitious, and now I understand why. He believes these things are his by right.'

'Vraiment?' Colette's gaze was fiercely direct, holding Christine's eyes with her own; dark brown and bright light blue. 'You really, truly believe that Pat believes in what he's saying?'

Christine sipped her coffee to gain some time. Then she said at last: 'In my own mind, I'm almost certain. There's no other reason that I can see why he would tell such a story unless he thought there was some possibility of proving it. I should love to think there was, but there isn't.'

'You said "almost certain".' Colette swiftly picked up on her daughter-in-law's momentary doubt. 'That means you're not certain. Why not?'

Christine sighed. 'How can I possibly be a hundred per cent sure in a case like this? There's too much at stake. I can't even be a hundred per cent certain of Rowland any more.' Tears stung her eyelids, and she blinked rapidly to get rid of them. 'All right! I'll stick my neck out and say yes, I'm positive Pat saw something, when he was young, which he remembers, rightly or wrongly, his mother telling him was her and his father's marriage certificate. He recalls details which may be what he saw at the time or might be an accretion of facts and memories with which he has unwittingly embroidered the incident.' She replaced her cup in its saucer and looked helplessly from Julian to Colette. 'What it all boils down to is that, in this instance, I believe Patrick to be genuine, whether the facts are or not.'

Julian grimaced. 'So we can expect more trouble?'

'I don't think you can rely on Pat keeping his mouth shut, if that's what you mean. He's always had a lot of friends – he was off out to meet someone this evening – and one or two of them are journalists. One at least is a reporter for one of the tabloids.'

Colette looked dismayed. Julian swore softly under his breath. 'So what do we do?' he asked presently, but answered his own question almost at once. 'We'll have to try to find Lucy Brennan, whatever it costs.'

Christine nodded her agreement.

'You are both fools!' Colette exclaimed hotly. 'You have a very good English proverb: "Let sleeping dogs lie." Ignore Patrick. Without proof he can do nothing. And tracing Lucy Brennan is going to be a very expensive business.'

Julian got up and put an arm around his mother's shoulders, stooping to kiss her cheek.

'It's no good, Maman. The advice you're offering is no doubt extremely sound, but I can't accept it, and neither can Chris.' Christine smiled faintly at him. She had never been over-fond of her brother-in-law, but at the moment he had all her support. He also had her sympathy, what little she could spare from herself. Julian straightened up and went on: 'I grant you that searching for Lucy Brennan is probably worse than looking for a needle in a haystack, but it'll have to be done. It will most likely entail employing detective agencies all over the world, and without any sure prospect of finding her. However, I'll set things in motion first thing tomorrow. I'll consult Barrett's, near the

Haymarket. I've used them before and always found them very reliable and discreet. They'll have contacts in other countries. I'll ask to see Seamus Barrett personally. He'll advise me what to do for the best.'

Colette admitted defeat. 'I'll phone Mallerby in the morning,' she said, rising from the table and beginning to stack the dirty dishes. 'Marie and Françoise can come up in the Mini and bring the rest of our things.'

'No, don't do that,' Christine was surprised to hear herself answer. Until that moment, she had fully intended remaining in London, but now, suddenly, she had changed her mind. 'I'm going back to Mallerby as soon as I can.' She glanced at their enquiring faces and stumbled over her explanation. 'I want . . . I want to be quiet. To think. To . . . to . . .' What was it exactly that she wanted to do?

She wanted to go back over the events of the last twenty-five years; to try to sort out her impressions of that summer of 1960 when she had first met Rowland and Lucy Brennan at the camp-site in Devon. Had they been married? Could they have been? It was impossible! But nothing was impossible, and she knew that what she really wanted was a chance to be alone with her memories before someone – some faceless someone – told her that she had not, after all, been Rowland's wife, but just another of the many women in his life.

Colette asked dubiously: 'Do you wish me to come with you?'

Christine smiled. 'Yes. Please.' She did not add, as she would normally have done: 'But only if you want to.' She needed her mother-in-law's bracing presence to take her out of herself every now and again, when the memories became too painful.

Colette's eyes lit up, but all she said was: 'Bon! I'm glad.'

Julian asked: 'How long will you stay down there? You'll keep in touch?'

'We'll telephone every evening,' his mother promised, running hot water into the sink and drawing on a pair of bright blue rubber gloves. Her precious omelette-pan, which no one else was permitted to touch, had already been carefully wiped and put away.

'And, if you need us, we'll be up at once.' Christine laid a reassuring hand on her brother-in-law's arm. 'I just want time to sort out my thoughts. Sift through the past. See if there is anything at all, any hint, the slightest clue to the truth that I can remember.'

Julian nodded. 'Good idea. I'll set things in motion here. And I'll have a look through all Rowe's personal papers.'

'No need.' Christine picked up a tea-towel and began wiping the dishes Colette had washed. 'I did it in the weeks following the funeral. There was nothing out of the ordinary. Nothing at all.'

Colette said: 'Julian! What do you intend to do about Patrick in the mean time? You do intend to let him go on working at the bank, don't you? Promise me you won't ask him to leave, or anything foolish like that. You must be seen to be treating his claim as a joke. For now, you must play the indulgent uncle.'

Julian looked sullen. In the harsh strip-lighting of the kitchen, he appeared older than his forty-four years.

'I don't know what I shall do,' he answered. 'I haven't yet made up my mind.'

It was raining again. The formal gardens at Mallerby looked dismal in the miserable light. Only the green of the lawns, bright and close-cut, glowed through the blanketing greyness. Beyond the wall of honey-coloured Ham Hill stone, the parkland stretched southwards in the direction of the A30, its trees – oak, ash, beech, chestnut, with still, here and there, one or two dead arthritic elms – islanded in the mist.

Nearer the house, the rows of clipped Irish yews stood like sentinels between bushes of shrub roses: the *Rosa gallica officinalis*, the Lancastrian badge, and the *Rosa alba* of York.

The drawing-room overlooked both back and side terraces, and was furnished for comfort rather than for style. The two deep chintz-covered settees and the four armchairs had been bought from Harrods in the 1950s and re-covered at least once since. But there were some showpieces, among them a George I walnut card-table, a set of Hepplewhite chairs, a mahogany breakfront bookcase, a pair of giltwood side-tables and two Chinese porcelain Dogs of Fo. These items and others were the reason why the drawing-room was one of the family rooms open to the public every Tuesday and Thursday. One wall, however, was taken up completely with a stereo system and stacks of records.

After breakfast on Saturday morning, Colette drove into the village with Françoise and Marie, both of whom were bitterly disappointed at not having been recalled to London. Christine went into the drawing-room and stood looking out of the windows at the rain. After a little while of staring, but seeing nothing, she gave herself a mental shake and crossed the room to the record-shelves. Mozart, Beethoven, Haydn received no more than a passing glance. She went instinctively to the 'R's and the music of Rameau. She had never heard of Jean-Philippe Rameau before Rowland had introduced her to him, but she had, over the years, developed almost as great a passion as her husband for his work. She hesitated now between *La Princesse de Navarre* and *Les Indes Galantes*, then changed her mind and took down *Hippolyte et Aricie*. Minutes later, the room was filled with rich vibrant sound.

She returned to her place near the window, curling up in one of the all-enveloping armchairs. She leaned back, closing her eyes, letting the music wash over her; letting it evoke, as nothing else could do, Rowland's presence. And suddenly she could see him clearly just as he had been that distant summer on the South Hams: a charming young man with beautiful manners, tall and beanpole-thin, as though he had outgrown his strength, and skin the colour of a gypsy's . . .

PART TWO
1960

CHAPTER SEVEN

THE CAMP-SITE overlooked Start Bay. The field, starred in this week of early August with speedwells and butter-cups and the white of daisies, was high on the cliff, not far from the steep descent-road leading to Slapton and Torcross.

Christine, wriggling free of her sleeping-bag, glanced at the small gold watch on its black silk strap which her parents had given her two years before, on her eighteenth birthday. It was six o'clock, and already the sun was so bright that it made the inside of the orange canvas tent glow like a beacon. The heat was almost palpable, and she found it impossible to go back to sleep. She dragged off the two-layered nylon Marks & Spencer nightdress and made a grab for her blue cotton shorts and blouse. Five minutes later, she crawled free of the tent's stifling interior and stood upright, barefoot, on the grass, drawing in lungfuls of the clean sea-air.

All around her, the fields were green and lush with pasture, the sun shone in a cloudless sky and, below, the water glittered with points of light. From the marshes on the opposite side of the coastal road, alive in these summer months with reed and sedge warblers, a gull rose, screeching noisily in its quest for food, wheeled and arrowed out to sea. The miles of Slapton Sands, visible at this height as a golden arc, were almost deserted at this hour of the morning. A couple of early risers were braving the sea; two distant pygmies capering at the edge of the waves. Everything looked so calm and still, it was impossible to believe that tragedy could ever strike in such a place. Yet

71

it was only sixteen years since American troops had practised here for the D-Day landings, when hundreds of them had been drowned during a night of muddled orders and terrible storm. Nor was that the area's only connection with the horrors of war. A mile inland, in the village of Slapton itself, stood the ruined chantry of Sir Guy de Brian, who had carried the English standard at Crécy.

Christine glanced at the larger tent beside her own. There was no sign of life, no indication that Russell was even stirring, and a moment later she heard the muffled sound of his snores. She hesitated, wondering whether or not to wake him, then decided against it. Russell disliked the early morning. She dived inside her tent again, put on a pair of rope-soled canvas shoes, seized her sponge-bag with its pattern of carmine roses on a pale pink ground, and headed towards the neighbouring caravan-park and the ladies' lavatories.

She and Russell had been here two days now, at the start of a fortnight's holiday, and yesterday evening he had asked her to marry him. She had known he would, of course, at some time. Her parents, who thought him a reliable steady young man, marked down for rapid promotion in the civil service, were banking on it, or they would never have allowed her to come away with him on a camping holiday. As it was, they had insisted that, for sleeping purposes, she had her own tent. Her father had bought her a single-sized one from a shop in Weston.

'We trust you,' he had said, giving her a straight look from under his bushy eyebrows.

'We trust you and Russell,' her mother had added.

The grass was still wet, soaking through the canvas of her shoes. Was she going to marry Russell Jennings? Until the moment he proposed, she would have said that her acceptance was a certainty. But, perversely, when he did 'pop the question' as her mother would no doubt call it, she had been beset by doubts. She was fond of Russell – at least, she liked him better than any other boy she had been out with – but was that a sufficient basis for marriage? Most of her friends would have said yes, with few reservations. Most girls of her age were level-headed enough to keep passion and romance for the cinema and books. The most you could hope for from real life, her best friend, Lois Hartman, had once said to her, was a rich man who would be generous with his money and not too demanding about fidelity. Admittedly, Lois, a year older than Christine, was something of a cynic and what Gwen Chandos termed 'hard-boiled'.

'I wish you'd find a nicer friend,' her mother had complained at regular intervals for the past fifteen years, ever since Christine and Lois had sat next to one another on their first day at infants' school.

In spite of everything, however, Christine had surprised herself and Russell by asking for time to consider the matter.

'Only a day or two. You've taken me by surprise,' she lied.

He had been affronted and, later, angered by her prevarication. She realized now that he had been as sure of her answer as she had been herself, and the knowledge irritated her. She disliked the idea that he had taken her for granted.

But what did she hope to gain from a few days? What would alter between now and the end of the week, when he was almost certain to ask her again? Her future, on this brilliant August morning, seemed as clearly mapped out for her as the last two years, since leaving school with a respectable seven O levels and three A levels to her credit.

'The civil service,' her father had advised her, speaking as a civil servant himself. 'Decent hours, good holidays and, more important, job security.' So she had gone for the necessary interviews and, in due course, had become a Grade 6 Clerical Officer in the Ministry of Labour and National Service, in the employment exchange in her home town of Weston-super-Mare, alongside fellow Grade 6 Officer Russell Jennings. Not that Russell was likely to remain in that grade for long; everyone said he was a 'blue-eyed boy', almost certain to get his Grade 5 at the next promotions panel.

Russell was, literally, blue-eyed, with a thatch of dark brown hair at odds with the fairness of his skin. It meant that he had to shave at least twice a day to avoid a permanent 'five o'clock shadow'. But he was a good-looking young man, a shade too thin for his height, which was nearly six feet, and more than a little conscious of his own worth and career prospects. There were plenty of girls in the exchange in particular and in Weston in general who would have been pleased to be asked out by him, and even more delighted to consider themselves his regular date. That honour, however, had fallen to Christine, although some of her more envious friends had professed themselves unable to understand why.

'She's all right, I suppose. Not bad-looking,' Christine had once overheard one of them grudgingly remark to another, 'but she's not exactly Sophia Loren.'

'Mind you,' a third girl had chipped in, 'she's got the bust for it.'

And it was those deep, generous, well-developed breasts which, as Christine admitted to herself, had always been her chief attraction for the opposite sex. Or as Lois Hartman had so succinctly put it: 'Forget your brains, Chris. It's your tits they're after.' All of which she found faintly depressing.

When she got there, the lavatories had only just been opened by a bleary-eyed employee of the company which owned both the caravan-park and the camp-site. Christine said a cheery 'Good morning' and was answered by an incomprehensible grunt.

The women's lavatory, like the men's adjacent to it, was a forbidding-looking concrete building; but inside, besides the row of washbasins, it did boast three cubicles for showers – all, surprisingly enough, in good working order. Christine, who had never used a shower before – very few English houses were equipped with this American-style novelty – found it refreshing. Afterwards, she cleaned her teeth at one of the basins, put on a little make-up, with the aid of a cracked and fly-blown mirror on the wall above, put on her shoes again and picked up her sponge-bag. Outside it was getting hotter by the minute. It was going to be a lovely day.

Unnoticed by Christine, a loose stone from the edge of the field had found its way on to the asphalt apron in front of the lavatories. Stepping on it, she twisted her ankle and almost fell; would have fallen if a man coming from the next-door lavatory had not made a grab for her and steadied her with his arm.

('Can you believe it?' she said weeks later to Lois Hartman. 'Can you really believe such a corny situation as that?'

'Hardly a romantic setting, though,' Lois answered, wrinkling her nose fastidiously.)

'Are you all right?' he asked. 'Ankle OK?' He stooped, picked up the stone and flung it into some bushes. Then he turned and offered her his arm. 'Let me help you back to your tent. I think yours is pitched next to ours.'

He was tall and very thin and looked like a gypsy. It was not the clothes – the grey flannel trousers and open-necked shirt, both of which looked as though they could do with a wash and smelt a bit. The few gypsies Christine had ever met were scrupulously clean. It was his appearance: his black hair, lank and greasy and far too long, his very dark eyes, a rich, deep, velvety brown, and his swarthy skin. He had at least made the effort to shave, as she could see by the still-bleeding cut on his chin. Oddly enough, he reminded her strongly of Russell, except that Russell was much less disreputable in appearance and far less self-assured in manner.

'I'm all right, thank you,' she said. 'I'm perfectly capable of walking without assistance.'

Most men of her acquaintance would, at that point, either have insisted on supporting her or have made some condescendingly jocular remark about independence. This man did neither. He merely accepted her word without argument and fell in beside her as they returned, through the gap in the fence, to the camping-field.

He said: 'I love the early morning. It's my favourite time of day.'

She regarded him curiously. 'I don't remember you being camped next to us. I don't recall seeing you yesterday.'

'We arrived late last night. You and your friend were cooking your supper while we were pitching our tent.'

Christine did recollect vaguely some new arrivals while she and Russell were frying sausages and bacon over the camp-stove: a Morris Minor bucketing down the slope of the field and the unloading of a tent and some gear. She had not taken much notice at the time, being too intent on not burning the food. Russell disliked anything overdone. He had made some snide remark about the newcomers not being real campers.

'The equipment's not their own. It's all stuff you can hire from the shop near the caravan-park.'

Christine had made no comment. She was not sure that she was a 'real camper', a fact which made her say now: 'I just couldn't go back to sleep, once I'd woken up. I'm not usually an early bird. I like my bed too much. It was the sheer discomfort of a sleeping-bag which got me up this morning.'

Even as she spoke, she reflected that if she married Russell she would probably be expected to go camping

76

every year, hardly an exciting prospect for someone who had fought her mother tooth and nail *not* to become either a Brownie or a Girl Guide.

The camp-site was still fairly quiet, and there was no sign of movement from Russell's tent or from the neighbouring one. Christine wondered who was the other half of the 'we' referred to by her companion. A girl? Oh, yes, definitely a girl. She recalled a vague impression last night of skirts and long hair. But there was also something about the man beside her which told her that he would almost certainly be travelling with a woman. There was a strong emanation of sexuality which, however, neither alarmed nor disturbed her. Christine was unable to define it at that moment, but later realized that it stemmed from his genuine and wholehearted liking for women, not simply as sexual partners, but as people; a rarer emotion in men than was generally imagined.

He said: 'Let's walk along the cliff-path. Lucy and your friend don't seem to be awake yet.'

He neither leered at her nor asked her coyly if her friend would mind. She wondered why he assumed she wasn't married, then remembered the separate tents and her ringless wedding-finger. It was on the tip of her tongue to refuse, on the grounds that Russell wouldn't like it, then she realized that such a refusal presumed too much. She had a sudden vision of the understanding, slightly mocking smile he would give her.

'Yes. OK,' she agreed. 'Just let me drop this inside my tent.' And she indicated the sponge-bag she was still clutching.

The cliff-path was a narrow grassy track, bordered by tufts of coarser grass and clumps of samphire, the greenish-white flowers gleaming palely among the thick, smooth, fleshy leaves. A straggling patch of scarlet pimpernel, the 'poor man's weather-glass', was already opening its petals to the light, a sure sign that it was going to be a fine hot day, and a bush of sea-holly, its stem stout and erect, spread glossy bluish spikes to protect the spiny blossoms in its midst. After a few yards, her companion left the path and, turning to give Christine his hand, helped her down to a natural seat of grass and rocks. When they were settled, he produced a battered packet of cigarettes, together with a box of matches, from his trouser pocket and offered her one.

Christine shook her head. 'I don't smoke, thank you.' She felt silly and unsophisticated. Everyone smoked. All her friends did as soon as they reached the age of eighteen, and many of them had started younger than that. There was a camaraderie about smoking. It got you through awkward social moments. It was a universal habit, and non-smokers were widely looked upon as killjoys or freaks. Christine wished that she could enjoy it, but she hated the taste of tobacco and the lingering sour scent of the smoke. To divert attention from this lack in her, she asked abruptly: 'What's your name?'

'Rowe. Rowe Saxelby.'

'Rowe?' She wasn't quite sure how it was spelled.

'R-O-W-E. Short for Rowland. The English, not the French spelling.'

'It's an unusual name.' Unusual, at least, among the Leslies and Peters, Bobs and Mikes of her acquaintance. Less common even than Russell, a name which had enjoyed a vogue since the pianist Russ Conway had shot to television fame on 'The Billy Cotton Band Show'. Although, as Russell Jennings was quick to point out, his christening predated that event by some twenty years. She added: 'Are you married?'

Rowland finished lighting a cigarette, flicking the spent match over the cliff-edge towards the sparkling sea. A thin ribbon of smoke coiled from between his fingers. He smiled and shook his head. 'No. I'm still up at Oxford. In my second year.'

A small frown creased her forehead. She guessed him to be all of twenty-two or -three. Then enlightenment dawned. 'You did your National Service first.'

He turned to look admiringly at her. 'How did you know that? It doesn't occur to most people.'

She was pleased out of all proportion to the implied compliment, but was forced to admit: 'I can't take any credit, I'm afraid, not even for an inspired guess. I work for the Ministry of Labour and National Service. I know all about call-up and deferment and postponement. I used to be in the military recruitment section of Weston employment exchange. Weston-super-Mare,' she added by way of elucidation. 'In Somerset.'

'Oh, I know Weston-on-the-Mud,' he answered with a grin. 'When I was little, my nanny used to kid me that, at low tide, you could walk all the way to South Wales.'

It never for a moment occurred to Christine that in this context the word 'nanny' referred to a nursemaid. She assumed he was speaking of his grandmother, in the same way that she called her mother's mother 'Nanna' in order to distinguish her from her paternal grandmother.

'Do you live in Weston?' she asked curiously, but with the feeling that, if he did, she would surely have been aware of the fact. In spite of his scruffy appearance, there was something about him which set him apart, made him stand out from the ruck.

Once again, he shook his head. 'No, but I do live in Somerset and I went to school in Bristol. Clifton College.'

That did make her lift her eyebrows, but all she said was: 'I've often wondered what it must be like there in the hot weather, right next to the zoo.'

He gave a shout of laughter. 'It's a bit niffy, I must admit, when the wind's in the wrong quarter and the monkey temple's smelling a bit high.'

Christine was laughing, too. From behind them, a girl's voice with an Irish brogue asked: 'What's the joke? Jesus, Rowe! I don't know how you can be so wide awake this unearthly hour of the morning!'

79

CHAPTER EIGHT

THAT WAS THE FIRST TIME Christine set eyes on Lucy Brennan.

Lucy picked her way carefully down the slope and dropped on to the turf beside them, spreading her thin brown legs out in front of her and lifting her face to the rising sun. She was wearing a black Indian cotton skirt, reaching almost to her ankles, a black cotton blouse, thonged leather sandals and a frayed red-and-white-checked headband to keep the profusion of waist-length dark curly hair out of her eyes. By the end of the decade, it would be as commonplace a uniform amongst the nation's female young as dirndl skirts and bobby-sox were to the present generation, and as twin sets and pearls had been to their mothers. But in 1960 it set Lucy apart, making people turn to stare at her in the street, as though she were some wandering tinker who might have fleas, or worse still, a contagious disease.

Neither was the rest of her appearance reassuring. Christine had thought that Rowland looked gypsyish, but there was an indefinable aura of respectability about him, which neither the long unwashed hair, the grimy fingernails nor the scruffy clothes could conceal. Lucy, on the other hand, looked to be a genuine Romany, with gold-hooped earrings swinging from little ears neatly set on either side of the delicate pointed face, the cascade of jet-black curls and the pale olive skin. Only the startlingly blue eyes, instead of the deep liquid brown that Christine had expected, belied that first impression.

'Did I wake you, getting up?' Rowland asked, smiling at her. 'I'm sorry. I didn't mean to.'

'Ah, think nothing of it! It does me good to be up and about early now and again.' Lucy glanced across at Christine, evidently not in the least put out by finding Rowland alone with another girl at six-thirty in the morning, and quite obviously enjoying her company. 'Hello,' she said, in the strong accent which Christine was insufficiently conversant with to tell if it came from the north or the south of Ireland. 'I'm Lucy Brennan. Who are you?'

'Yes, who are you?' Rowland added. 'How very remiss of me. I forgot to ask your name.'

'Christine Chandos.'

'Indeed.' His eyes danced, and he answered unpredictably: 'I know your ancestor, Sir John.'

Christine was mystified. 'I'm sorry,' she said. 'I don't understand.'

Lucy Brennan crowed with laughter. 'You're not the only one. He's always making cryptic utterances which completely throw people. Go on!' She poked a sharp little elbow into Rowland's ribs. 'Tell the girl what you mean.'

'Sir John Chandos', he explained, 'was seneschal of Poitou in the fourteenth century. He was killed in a skirmish with the Dauphin's troops on New Year's Day 1370. Although he was an enemy – he fought at both Crécy and Poitiers – the French admired him enormously. There's a monument to him at the place where he fell near Lussac-les-Châteaux.'

'He's no ancestor of mine!' Christine disclaimed emphatically. 'Neither of my parents would aspire to anyone so grand.'

Rowland Saxelby made no comment, but continued to look at her; a look in which amusement was mixed with faint irritation.

Lucy Brennan asked: 'How do we know who our ancestors were? By the time you reach back as far as the fourteenth century, you must have thousands of the buggers.' It was the first time Christine had ever heard a young woman – indeed, any woman – use that word, and it gave her the same sort of jolt as when Lucy had said 'Jesus!' earlier on. The most she and her friends ever swore was 'damn' or, if they wanted to be extremely daring, a very occasional 'bloody'. Russell, like most other men of her acquaintance, would have been shocked and horrified, but Rowland seemed to find it perfectly normal. Lucy went on scornfully: 'That's why I think all this ancestor worship is so stupid. What's the point of claiming to be descended from this or that particular grain of sand on a beach?'

Rowland grinned appreciatively and said: 'I know when I'm being got at.' He didn't explain to Christine what he meant, and she felt a spurt of totally unjustifiable resentment at being excluded from his and Lucy's little joke.

'What were you laughing at just now?' Lucy enquired, but idly, not as though she had any right to know. Rowland told her, and she tossed back her head, sending the black curls flicking out like Medusa's snakes. 'Don't talk to me about schools!' she exclaimed. 'Not ever! I hated all mine and ran away from every one I was ever sent to.'

Christine was curious. 'Did you go to many?'

Lucy shrugged. 'Five. Maybe six. I lost count after a while. My parents did, too. In the end, it was difficult for them to find a school in Ireland that'd have me. Once I reached my eighteenth birthday, they washed their hands of me. My father arranged for me to have the twenty thousand pounds my Grandmother Brennan had left me, and virtually said: "Disappear!" So I did. We parted without rancour and with mutual relief two years ago and we've never set eyes on each other since.'

Christine's ideas about Lucy Brennan did a somersault. Twenty thousand pounds was an enormous sum of money. She drew a deep breath.

'What . . . what do you do, then?'

'Do?' Lucy looked vague, as though the idea of a settled occupation was completely new to her. 'I travel.' She waved an airy hand.

'All the time?' Christine tried hard not to sound too incredulous. 'Where?'

'Everywhere.'

That was certainly comprehensive, but Christine was no wiser. 'Europe?' she hazarded.

'Europe, North Africa, the States, anywhere the fancy takes me. Rowe and I met in Algiers six weeks ago.'

So they hadn't known one another that long! 'But how do you manage for money?' Christine asked.

She realized she was being intrusive, but the idea of anyone travelling the world in this nomadic fashion was alien to her. The people she knew who went abroad – her mother's aunts, a couple of her friends – ventured no further than Switzerland or France. The majority of people, however, took their holidays within the British Isles. The great annual migration in search of the sun had not yet started. Christine herself had never been out of England.

Lucy looked surprised. 'I just ring my bankers in Rome and tell them where I am. They arrange for money to be sent to me.' She spoke as though telephoning one's bankers from odd corners of the globe was a normal everyday occurrence, and Christine's ideas rearranged themselves yet again. Lucy had obviously been used to money, and a very great deal of money at that, from the day she was born. Christine could make neither head nor tail of her. Ten years later, she would have dubbed her a dropout and left it at that, but in 1960 no one had heard of the expression.

Rowland got up in his leisurely fashion, stretching his arms above his head until the bones cracked. Then he reached down a hand to each of the girls, helping them to their feet. 'I'm hungry,' he said. 'Time we were thinking of breakfast.'

'I'm not cooking for you!' Lucy said, laughing. 'And I don't eat breakfast. You'll have to get your own.'

'You can share ours,' Christine offered quickly, not giving herself time to consider Russell's reactions. She added, more to convince herself than them: 'I'm sure my friend won't mind.'

As it happened, Russell didn't mind too much in the beginning. It never occurred to him that this none-too-clean scarecrow of a young man could possibly pose any sort of threat to him where Christine was concerned, and she could see that he rather fancied Lucy Brennan. Lucy's slightly exotic, raffish appearance was a challenge to his manhood. He wanted her as a conquest, another scalp beneath his belt. Christine could imagine him boasting to his friends.

'There was this really weird bird we met down in Devon. Looked like a gypsy. Went overboard for me in a big way.'

The trouble was that Lucy played up to him. From that first morning, she strung him along. Nor, Christine reflected, was he very difficult to dupe. He thought too much of himself. He had a lot of self-confidence, but none of it of the right kind. The rights and wrongs of self-confidence was a subject Christine had never considered before, but meeting Rowland Saxelby had changed a lot of things. It had changed her whole life; she realized that after a very few days. It took her a little longer to accept that she was in love with him, but by the end of twenty-four hours she knew that she would never marry Russell Jennings.

They became an unlikely foursome, sunbathing together on Slapton beach, swimming in the bay and sharing meals, most of which Christine cooked single-handed over the primus stove, with, now and then, some help from Rowland. Lucy didn't know how to cook and had no intention of learning, and Russell would never have dreamed of giving Christine a hand. To him, men's and women's work had always been separate and clearly defined.

It was really the meals, Christine suspected, which kept Lucy and Rowland in tow; filling, nourishing meals which cost them nothing. Neither of them appeared to have any money. Whatever Lucy's arrangements were with her bankers in Rome, they seemed to have broken down for the moment, or else she hadn't bothered to make contact. One morning, sitting on the cliff-top, they were trying to raise the four and sixpence to buy a gallon of petrol for the hired Morris Minor to get them into Plymouth. Russell could easily have offered to take them in his car, but he wasn't going to. He was just beginning to be aware of Christine's interest in Rowland Saxelby, and was conscious of the first twinges of jealousy. So he said nothing, staring out to sea and ignoring what was going on around him.

Lucy had emptied her handbag. It was not really a handbag, but an old brown leather school-satchel, which she carried slung over one shoulder. The contents now lay spilled across the grass: her passport, two gold rings, some pieces of paper, old train and bus tickets, a glittering brooch which might be real diamonds or best Woolworth paste – you never could tell with Lucy – some foreign notes, French by the look of them, nothing in the way of English money.

'Oh, well,' she said, giving a fatalistic shrug, 'that's that, then. We'll just have to hitch a lift.' She began pushing everything back into the satchel. One of the pieces of paper, lifted by a sudden breath of wind, went scurrying across the grass.

Rowland made a grab at it and returned it to her. 'You want to take care of that,' he advised lazily. 'It's the hire agreement for the car.' Lucy glanced at it, laughed and shoved it into the satchel along with everything else. Rowland got up with his characteristic stretching action. 'I don't feel like

85

hitching lifts today. I'm going for a walk. Anyone coming?'

Lucy shook her head. 'No, I'd rather stay here and sunbathe.' She seemed in no way put out by this abrupt change of plan.

'OK.' Rowland glanced at the other two. 'Anyone else want to come?'

'No, thanks.' Russell lay back on the grass, linking his hands behind his head. 'I may go swimming later if it stays this warm.'

'Christine?' Rowland smiled at her in his easy open fashion. If she went, he would be pleased, but would be just as happy to go alone. She could never pretend to herself, even for a second, that he showed any interest in her beyond that of friendship; and a very temporary holiday friendship at that.

She had made up her mind to refuse if he should ask her. There was no point in deliberately making herself miserable by being more in his company than she had to be; by rubbing salt into the wound. She told herself that such crushes were not uncommon on holiday, when the everyday world receded and everything became a little unreal. She would, she insisted, forget all about Rowland Saxelby within a week of returning home, and tried hard to ignore the persistent voice at the back of her mind which told her this was not true. She opened her mouth to decline the invitation, but Russell forestalled her, shooting out a hand and grabbing her wrist.

'Chris is staying with me,' he said shortly.

Gently, she freed her arm and stood up. 'Yes, I'll come with you, Rowland. Where were you thinking of going?'

Russell sat up. 'You said you wanted to swim,' he accused her.

'I've changed my mind. I need some exercise.' She relented. 'Why don't you come, too?'

Russell's face set in familiar stubborn lines. A tide of colour stained the fair skin, and he pushed back a lock of dark hair, which had fallen forward over his eyes, with an angry gesture.

'I've already said I don't want to come. I like to make plans and stick to them. I thought you did, too.'

Christine tried to pass off the growing unpleasantness with a laugh. 'Not that rigidly. Honestly, Russ, talk about the civil service mind!'

As soon as the words were out, she knew she couldn't have said anything which would annoy him more.

His lips folded together until they were nearly invisible. 'There's nothing wrong with the civil service mind, and you should have more loyalty than to make remarks like that in front of outsiders.' Bad temper was making him pompous. 'Now, sit down again, there's a good girl.'

Rowland made a little sucking noise under his breath, and his eyes had a glazed look, as though he were trying not to laugh. Lucy was regarding them both with the detached interest of a biologist, examining two rare specimens of a different breed.

Christine stooped and picked up her cardigan from the grass.

'I'm ready if you are,' she said to Rowland.

Russell's handsome face was a picture of conflicting emotions: anger, astonishment, disbelief. 'I forbid you to go,' he said uncertainly.

Christine made no reply, but turned and scrambled back up the cliff. Rowland followed her in a silence which remained unbroken until they were free of the camp-site and walking briskly along the main road.

'Slow down,' he advised, putting a restraining hand on her shoulder. 'He isn't following us. It's too warm to keep up this sort of pace.'

Christine stopped, uncomfortably aware of the perspiration running down her face. She wiped it away with her handkerchief.

'Sorry,' she apologized. 'And I'm sorry, too, about that little scene back there. It was my fault. But there are times when Russ gets right under my skin.'

'Stop taking the blame for everything,' Rowland replied gently. 'You mustn't let him make you feel guilty all the time.' He smiled. 'Just because you're a woman, it doesn't mean you're automatically in the wrong.'

'No. I suppose not.' She tried to relax.

'That's better,' he encouraged. 'We'll walk as far as Torcross. On the way, if you like, we can go into Slapton village and look at what's left of Sir Guy de Brian's chantry.'

She noticed that he pronounced the name in the French way and thought how much nicer it sounded than the English.

'Are you interested in history?' she asked.

They were moving again, descending the hill, part of the coastal road which led down to the long stretch of Slapton beach and, at the end, where the road turned inland once more, the village of Torcross.

'It's a difficult subject to ignore,' he answered lightly.

'You knew all about Sir John Chandos,' she persisted.

'Ah! But, then, you see, my grandmother – my French grandmother – lives near Lussac-les-Châteaux. I've seen the monument and its inscription many times.'

'You're half-French!' she exclaimed, surprised; although why she found the information surprising she did not know. It explained his black hair, dark brown eyes and olive-tinted skin.

'My mother's French. A very formidable lady.' He did not enlarge any further.

'Do you have any brothers or sisters?' Getting information from him was like squeezing the proverbial blood from a stone.

'A younger brother. Julian. He's nineteen and has just finished his first year at Balliol. Unlike me, he sensibly decided to wait before doing his National Service. Rumour is that it's coming to an end. National Service, I mean. It's on the cards he'll never have to do it.' He looked at her enquiringly, as though she might know.

'You're probably right,' she admitted. 'They're beginning to run down the military recruitment sections in the exchanges and at regional offices. The idea of compulsory military service has never been popular in this country. Which branch of the forces were you in?'

'The RAF.' He added, after a pause: 'And I hated it. Padgate must be the last place God made.'

She laughed, and the conversation flagged. They were on the flat now, and to their left the sea stretched for mile after sparkling mile. Overhead, the gulls wheeled and screeched. Christine's thoughts harked back guiltily to Russell.

'I hope Russ is OK.'

Her companion chuckled. 'Don't worry. Lucy will look after him. She won't let a handsome man go to waste.'

CHAPTER NINE

'YOU HAVEN'T KNOWN Lucy very long, then,' Christine said.

They had walked to Torcross and eaten ice-creams topped with thick yellow Devonshire cream. They had gone into Slapton village to see the chantry ruins and now they were seated on the beach, Christine with her arms hugging her up-raised knees, Rowland sprawled on the sand, idly sifting it through his fingers. Sunlight played on the water, and behind them the South Hams were clear of mist. The sea lapped and sucked and lapped again, filling the air with murmurs. A summer idyll; one of those rare, almost perfect days to be saved up and cherished in the memory during the long dark winter months.

For a moment, she thought he would not reply, or would fob her off with a dry monosyllable. She had discovered that he talked freely and openly about most things, except his relationship with Lucy Brennan. Christine, normally oversensitive to people's feelings, found it impossible in this case to keep off the forbidden topic. She steeled herself for a rebuff, but for once Rowland was more expansive.

'No, not long. We met about six weeks ago, in Algiers.'

'Of course. I remember Lucy saying.' She had not really forgotten and wondered if he knew that. 'Isn't Algeria pretty dangerous nowadays?'

He shrugged. 'It's quieter since de Gaulle began talks with Ben Bella. Needless to say, the French settlers don't like it. They're still giving trouble.'

'Why did you go there?' She turned her head and looked at him, feeling a sudden rush of love. Her hands began to tremble, and she clasped them more tightly together around her knees.

'One of my mother's aunts lives there. I'd been hitch-hiking around Europe with a party of friends, but when we got to Gibraltar I decided I'd had enough of their company and decided to go it alone. I decided I might as well go across and visit Tante Eloïse.'

'And that's when you met Lucy.' How she kept harping on that theme.

'That's when I met Lucy,' he agreed.

'You didn't stay long with your great-aunt, then?' Stop it, she told herself. For God's sake, stop it! Whatever was the matter with her? The emotion of jealousy was new, but she was beginning to recognize its little green eyes.

'No.' His voice was cool. 'I got a little tired of her non-stop diatribe against the monstrous betrayal of Algeria by de Gaulle. Algérie Française! So, after a week, I said my adieus and left.'

'With Lucy.'

'Yes.' He sat up, dusting his hands free of sand, and smiled at her. 'The colour of that dress suits you. You should wear it more often.'

Christine turned her head away quickly, feeling the blood stain her cheeks in a painful blush. She knew that the frock, a simple sleeveless cotton in a pale shade of burned orange, looked well on her and that the compliment was deserved. The trouble with Rowland was that, at least as far as she was concerned, he did not pay compliments; he merely stated facts. The remark was not a prelude to an attempt to kiss her or to hold her hand, as it would have been with some other men she knew. He told her the dress suited her with the detached interest of a friend. And that, of course, was all she was to him, because he had this ability of disinterested friendship with women.

He got up and helped her to her feet. 'Thank you for coming with me,' he said. 'I've enjoyed this morning.'

They made the return journey to the camp-site almost in silence, as though they had no more to say to one another. And what does it matter? she reasoned with herself. I shan't be seeing him after the end of this week. I don't suppose we shall ever meet again, once this holiday is over.

Russell was lying on the grass outside his tent, wearing nothing but his swimming-shorts. His fair exposed skin had turned a mottled shade of red. There was no sign of Lucy Brennan. Christine glanced guiltily at her watch and saw that it was one o'clock. She and Rowland had been gone nearly three hours. She expected Russell to be reproachful, but all he said was: 'Have a good walk?'

'Yes. Fine, thanks.' She dropped on to the grass beside him.

Rowland had disappeared inside the tent he shared with Lucy. After a moment or two, he emerged and asked Russell casually: 'Any idea where she's gone?'

Russell opened one eye, squinting up at him. 'Hitched a lift into Plymouth with some people from the caravan-park about fifteen minutes ago. Said she was going to pick up some funds.'

Rowland nodded. He seemed quite conversant with Lucy's mysterious financial arrangements. As he made to re-enter the tent, Christine called after him: 'Do you want something to eat? It's only cheese and salad rolls, I'm afraid. It's too hot to cook, but you're welcome to share them.'

He hesitated, then shook his head. 'Do you mind if I don't? I'm tired. I think I'll sleep for a while.'

She forced a smile. 'Of course not. All the more for Russ and me.' But she did mind. She minded very much. Every hour now which deprived her of his company seemed time wasted. Precious moments lost which would never come again.

She and Russell took the rolls, some fruit and a flask of tea down to the cliff-top and settled in their usual spot, the little natural amphitheatre of ground where she had sat with Rowland on the morning of their first meeting. Only just over a week ago, she thought to herself; but it seemed to her now as though he had always been a part of her life, the most important thing in it.

Russell was quieter than usual, and she wondered if he were sulking. He had put an old white shirt on over the swimming-trunks, his bony wrists sticking out of the sleeves like those of an overgrown schoolboy. All at once, he seemed vulnerable. She felt guilty, thinking of the pain she was bound to inflict on him when she told him, at the end of this holiday, that they were through. And was it fair to wait until the end of the holiday? Wasn't she using him, because it was more convenient to wait until they were back in Weston? And because, if she went now, not only would she have to arrange her own transport, but she would also forfeit Rowland's company for these last few days.

They ate without speaking. The sweep of cliff in front of them was like a lush terraced lawn. It was less hot than it had been that morning. The sunshine was patchier, and the deep azure of the water had faded to gentler blue. A faint breeze ruffled the golden petals of a horned poppy which had seeded itself in a fissure of sand. What was she going to do with her life, Christine wondered, when she had broken with Russell? Her plans for the future had centred around him for some time now, so why was she doing this? Letting him go for a dream. Was it because Rowland had shown her just how little she really cared for Russell? That marriage with him would be a mistake? Or was it because, even then, after so brief a time, she knew she would never love anyone but Rowland? That she would rather remain single all her life than accept second-best? So much had been written by so many on the subject of love, but one quotation above all the rest stuck in Christine's memory. 'They that love beyond the world cannot be separated by it. Death is but crossing the world, as friends do the seas; they live in one another still.' She knew that she would love Rowland Saxelby until the day she died. And beyond. Beyond the world.

Her mother would call such sentiments claptrap. Lois would say that she'd been reading too many romantic novels. No one would attempt to excuse her. And she could not blame them. She did not understand, herself, what had happened over the past seven or eight days. At the same time, she felt angry. Why was she being so negative in her approach? Rowland liked her; he might possibly get to like her better. There was no reason why she should just let him fade out of her life. Lucy Brennan didn't own him. He had only known her for six weeks. Presumably, they would part company as casually as they had joined it, when Rowland returned to Oxford for the Michaelmas Term. And he lived in Somerset. Why should she be afraid to contact him? She promised herself to find out where he lived.

As though he knew exactly what had been passing through her mind, Russell turned to look at her and said: 'Lucy's been telling me all about Rowland Saxelby. And there's quite a lot to tell.'

'Really?' Christine tried to sound casual. She reached for the flask and poured tea into two red Bakelite cups. 'Drink this', she advised, handing one to Russell, 'before it gets cold.'

'Yes, really.' He sipped the scalding liquid and grimaced, putting the cup down on the turf beside him. 'Did he mention that his mother was French?'

'Yes, he did. Nothing wrong with that, is there? Lots of people have foreign parents, especially since the war.'

Russell smiled. 'But did he tell you that his mother's family is very wealthy? They own a château in Poitou and a house in Paris, and claim descent from some

94

French king. Don't ask me which one. History was never my strong point. They are', he finished with a flourish, 'merchant bankers. One of the most important financial houses in France.' Christine felt as though she had been sandbagged, and the feeling must have shown in her face, prompting Russell to finish triumphantly: 'But, more than that, his father's people are merchant bankers, too. Saxelby's in Gresham Street. And do you know whereabouts they live in Somerset? Mallerby House at Hinton Malsherbes. You wouldn't think it, would you, to look at Rowe? He looks like a tramp.'

Christine found she was shivering, in spite of the warmth of the day. She could not really take it in all at once. She only knew that her dream was dissolving, fading into nothingness in the cold light of reality. After a moment, aware that some comment was expected of her, she asked: 'You mean Rowe's father is head of a merchant bank?'

'No. He's dead. Died before the war apparently, when he was still quite young. Rowe will be head of the bank as soon as he's taken his degree. Until then, his mother and the board of directors, or whatever, run things for him.'

'He must be very rich,' she said dully, trying desperately to adjust to this idea.

Russell nodded. 'And not only that. He's very well connected both in this country and in France. Out of our league altogether.'

She could see that for herself, and also how much pleasure Russell was getting from rubbing it in. Little things, which had vaguely puzzled her, began to fall into place. Clifton College. Oxford. The nanny, who, in light of present knowledge, was so obviously not Rowland's grandmother. And Lucy's attraction for him. They were two of a kind; two young people born into wealth and position, who – in Rowland's case temporarily, in Lucy's permanently – were enjoying looking at life from the other side of the fence, 'bumming' around Europe, as the Americans would term it; yet not even really doing that. Hired Morris Minors, tatty unwashed clothes, the search for the price of a gallon of petrol were nothing but the components of a game. The cushion of wealth was always there to protect them from harsh realities. They were secure in the knowledge that someone, somewhere, could always be relied upon to bail them out of trouble.

'You and Lucy seem to have got on very well together for her to tell you all this,' Christine said.

Russell looked smug. 'I think she fancies me. In fact I'm sure she does.' Christine had seen no evidence of this, but she let the claim pass. Russell went on: 'We got talking after you two left. She told me about herself and Rowe. I could see then why she wasn't worried.'

'What about?' Christine's tone was puzzled, but she knew perfectly well what he meant.

'About you and Rowe going off together. She knew you could never be a threat.'

'Good heavens!' Christine gave a tight-lipped smile. 'One walk with a man hardly makes me a *threat*, as you call it. Rowe's never given any hint of regarding me in that sort of light at all.'

If Russell noticed the significance of her phrasing, he made no comment, and she began gathering together the remains of their picnic, pushing the cups and flask into the carrier-bag along with all the rubbish. The scraps of left-over food she threw to the gulls.

'What do you want to do?' he enquired affably. 'Go swimming? A drive somewhere? We could go along to Blackpool Cove or further afield. Dartmouth. Totnes.'

'No, thanks.' She scrambled to her feet, her one desire now to be alone, to come to terms with this new information. 'I'm tired after that walk this morning, and the sun has given me a headache. I'm going to lie down for a while.'

She left him there, staring out to sea and looking pleased with himself. She threaded her way between the other tents and people cooking their midday meals over camp-stoves. She saw Rowland emerge from the tent next to theirs, stretching his arms and glancing about him. As she approached, he grinned lazily and said: 'Hello, Chris.'

'Lucy told Russ you're descended from one of the French kings,' she remarked acidly, adding pettishly, and despising herself for it: 'If I'd known before, I'd have accorded you more respect.'

Not in the least put out, and seemingly unconscious of her bad temper, he replied easily: 'Oh, that! My mother's family claim descent from Henry of Navarre. I only told Lucy because I thought it might amuse her, but for some inexplicable reason it seems to have got under her skin. You heard her, the other day, going on about grains of sand.'

Christine, recalling the conversation, said irritably, 'Well, she was right,' and plunged inside the larger of the two tents to leave the picnic things. The flask and cups could be washed up later when Russell had replenished their supply of water from the tap outside the lavatories. Emerging again, she made for her own tent, but Rowland barred her path.

'What's wrong, Chris? Have I done something to offend you?'

'Good heavens, no!' she retorted lightly, dodging round him and wriggling through the low flap of the orange tent.

She longed for him to detain her, demand an explanation, but she should have known by now that that was not his way. Throwing herself down on the camp-bed, covered with her quilted sleeping-bag, she saw his shadow, silhouetted against the tent wall, recede as he moved away.

Well, that was that, she thought. The idea of being able to contact him later, of renewing their friendship when the holiday was over, was a pipe-dream. A castle in Spain. Once they resumed their normal lives, he would be out of her reach. She was English. She knew her place in the strictly ordered social scheme of things. Money, or aristocratic connections, or, as in this case, both, erected barriers as strong as those preserving the Royal Enclosure at Ascot. Rowland would lead his life, she would lead hers, and never the twain should meet. But the knowledge had not altered anything as far as she was concerned. She still had no intention of marrying Russell Jennings.

She wanted to cry, but found instead that she was falling asleep. She really was tired. A jingle, learned long ago during French lessons at school, and forgotten until now, kept spinning round and round inside her head.

> Vive Henri Quatre,
> Vive ce roi vaillant!
> Ce diable au quatre
> Qui eut le triple talent,
> De boire et de battre
> Et d'être Vert Gallant!

Lucy came back from Plymouth, but Christine did not see her. She had taken Russell up on his offer of a drive to Dartmouth, and they had stayed there for an evening meal. It was late when they returned to the camp-site, and there was no sign of the others.

Christine overslept the following morning, and when she finally awoke at nine o'clock the patch of grass next to her tent was empty. Lucy Brennan and Rowland Saxelby had gone. She stared stupidly at the vacant space.

'Pushed off around seven this morning,' a near neighbour volunteered, returning from the lavatories with two large buckets of water, which he now deposited thankfully on the grass. 'I saw 'em loading the car.'

He went on disgustedly: 'Didn't bother taking the tent down, though, or returning the equipment. The Warden and a mate had to come down from the camp-site office and do it after they'd gone. Some people have no consideration for anyone but themselves.'

'Typical of that sort,' his wife sniffed, overhearing his remarks and poking her head through the tent-flap. 'Looked like gypsies, the pair of them. It's a wonder to me the Warden let them in in the first place.'

Russell appeared. He had washed his hair and was now towelling it dry. It stood up all over his head in short dark spikes, like a hedgehog.

'Yes, it's amazing what riff-raff you meet at these places nowadays,' he said, with a wink at Christine.

She made no response, not even aware of what anyone was saying. All she could think about was that Rowland had gone without a word; without even waiting to say goodbye.

CHAPTER TEN

BOTH HER PARENTS were distressed, as she had known they would be, by the news that she and Russell were no longer thinking of getting married. Or, to be more precise, by the news that she was no longer thinking of marrying Russell.

'But I thought that that was what this holiday was all about,' Gwen Chandos said with a certain amount of annoyance. 'For you to make up your mind.'

'I made up my mind, Mum,' Christine answered patiently. 'That's what I'm telling you.'

'I can't understand you.' Her mother sounded near to tears. 'He's such a nice boy. I don't see why you've turned him down.'

They were having tea, the three of them, Christine and her parents, in the bay window of the first-floor flat overlooking Clarence Park. They often had meals there during the summer months, preferring the bright sunny drawing-room to the more sombre dining-room at the side of the house. The house itself was a solid gabled Victorian mansion built towards the end of the previous century by a wealthy Bristol merchant, who had made his pile and retired to the seaside to enjoy it. Rooms originally intended for a substantial family and the requisite number of servants to cater for their wants were now divided into three flats – four, if you counted the basement maisonette. Robert Chandos had bought the middle one ten years ago, shortly after his promotion to area district manager by the insurance company for which he worked. The rise in salary had permitted the move from the terraced house, where Christine had been born, to this spacious apartment close to the sea-front. The lack of garden had not been felt because of the park immediately opposite.

The journey from Devon in Russell's Triumph Herald, earlier in the day, had been accomplished in almost total silence, broken only by the minimum of stilted conversation. The previous evening, walking along Slapton Sands, and in spite of all Christine's attempts to prevent him, Russell had again asked her to marry him, completely confident this time of his answer. Rowland's departure, without even according her the courtesy of a goodbye, must, Russell felt, have killed stone dead any burgeoning affection Christine might have entertained for him. Not that Russell really believed she had any, although he had known one or two uneasy moments. But, then, he had rather fancied Lucy Brennan. He did not, however, fall into the trap of mistaking it for love or anything remotely like it. This sort of thing could happen on holiday, and he paid Christine the compliment of thinking her sensible enough, and level-headed enough, to accept that fact.

Her second rejection, therefore, came as an even greater shock than the first, because this was a decided refusal, not a plea for more time to think things over. He had recognized the note of finality in her voice, and had too much pride to try to persuade her to change her mind. But he had asked her coldly for her reason, and had been given roughly the same explanation as she now gave her mother.

'I'm not in love with him, Mum. I can't marry someone I'm not in love with.'

'Well, no, perhaps not,' Gwen Chandos said unhappily, pouring her husband a second cup of tea. 'But love isn't everything, you know, Chris. I mean,' she added hastily, with a quick glance at Robert, who, however, seemed to find nothing amiss with this remark, 'there are other things to be looked for in a marriage. Reliability. A steady wage. Job security. Someone who'll be a good provider.'

Robert Chandos nodded in agreement. 'Russ is a good steady bloke, Chris. Not too many of his kind around. I think you ought to think again.'

Christine said: 'It wouldn't do any good. Knowing Russ, he wouldn't have me back now, even if I begged him. And I'm not going to. I meant what I said. This holiday convinced me that he and I just aren't suited. Maybe I shall never get married.'

Her mother was horrified. 'What sort of talk is that? Of course you'll get married one day. You don't want to be an old maid. You don't want to end up like my sister Hilda, at the beck and call of all the family.'

Christine looked at her parents with exasperated affection. They meant well, both of them. They had her best interests at heart, but their outlook was dated and conventional. Women married for children and security, men to have someone to look after them. She could not help wondering if love had ever been an issue for either her mother or her father. Gwen Chandos's faded air of gentility and careful pretensions had always been at odds with her husband's louder, more careless approach to life, just as her colourless appearance – pale skin, soft blue eyes and mousy brown hair – had contrasted, to his advantage, with his large florid features and general air of confidence and well-being.

Suddenly Christine felt too tired to cope any more at present with their dismay and disapproval; although *disapproval* was perhaps too strong a word to use. They were eager for her happiness, but on their terms, not hers. She had said nothing about the meeting with Rowland Saxelby and Lucy Brennan. After all, what was there to say? 'I've fallen in love, completely and for ever, with a man who doesn't care whether I'm alive or dead'? She could imagine their reaction to that.

102

'I think I'll go and unpack,' she said. She smiled apologetically at her mother. 'I'm afraid there's rather a lot of washing.'

Gwen Chandos shrugged. 'I was expecting that. Drop it all in the dirty-linen basket. I'll put it through the machine later this evening.' There was a touch of resentment in her tone, and Christine had the impression that what would have been a labour of love had now become a chore. Oh, well, she couldn't help it! She wasn't going to marry Russell Jennings just to please her parents.

Christine's bedroom was at the back of the house, looking out over the brick-walled garden. Over the bed, with its virginal white counterpane, dominating the entire room, was a life-sized poster of Elvis Presley. For some reason, it suddenly irritated her and, standing on the dressing-table stool, she peeled it carefully off the wall, trying not to damage the green floral wallpaper. She screwed it into a ball, which she crammed into the wastepaper-basket, then opened the heavy sash window at the bottom, leaning out and resting her hands on the stone sill.

None of the other inmates of the flats was anywhere to be seen. The little garden, with its crazy-paving path and straggling rose-bushes, was hushed and expectant in the lull of late afternoon. In the distance, she could hear the roar of the surf and the muted hum of the traffic as it purred to and fro along Beach Road.

Christine recalled her mood of well-being and optimism when she had closed the door on this room two weeks ago. Now she felt tired and depressed, as though she were in the grip of a serious illness. She wondered where Rowland was, what he was doing, if he were still with Lucy Brennan. But it was no use thinking about him, trying to guess where he was. They would probably never meet again. She was condemned to live the rest of her life without him. She felt the tears begin to sting her eyelids and, with an impatient

103

gesture, turned back into the room and started to do her unpacking.

Colette Saxelby took a final look at herself in the cheval-glass, placed close to the bedroom window so that it would catch most of the light, and was satisfied with her appearance. The H-line Dior dress was over a year old, but the dropped waistline suited her and made her seem taller. The colour and fabric, too – the delicate pale blue silk – were ideal for her small-boned, somewhat ethereal figure. And, in any case, this was not an important dinner-party; just Julian, Cecil Lennox and his daughter Sophie, and Matthew and Lisle Ingram, who were spending a few days in London before flying on to Paris.

At the thought of Matthew Ingram, Colette hesitated, wondering if, after all, she was looking her best. Then she made a face at herself in the mirror and laughed. For God's sake, she admonished herself, don't be such a fool! He's only two years older than Rowland, he's just married a gorgeous nineteen-year-old redhead, and you, my dear, are forty-three years of age. Added to all that, there isn't a woman on any of the racing-circuits of the world who wouldn't be willing to go to bed with him if he so much as crooked his little finger.

She went downstairs to the first-floor drawing-room, where pre-dinner drinks had been set out. Julian was already there, looking sulky. He had made arrangements to go out with friends that evening, but had been prevented at the last minute by his mother, who wanted him as a dinner partner for Sophie Lennox. Julian had never seen Sophie, but he was acquainted with her father, who was the bank's chief accountant; a dull, rather boring, heavy-jowled man who no doubt had a dull, rather boring, pudding-faced daughter. He wished his mother did not feel it her duty to entertain the more senior members of staff from time to time, or that he had the courage to refuse when she interfered so high-handedly with his arrangements. But he was dependent on Colette for the very handsome allowance he received while at university, and dared not risk the autocratic temper which would have no compunction in withholding it if he failed to comply with her demands.

His mother gave him a radiant smile and gently removed the glass of whisky and soda from his hands.

'I don't want you drunk, Julian, before our guests get here. I want you to be nice to Sophie.'

She spoke in French, as she sometimes did when alone with her sons; but Julian, as always, answered her in English, and his tone was surly.

'I don't know the girl from Adam and, what's more, I don't want to. We were going to see *The Mousetrap*, and now my ticket will be wasted.'

'Is that still running?' Colette asked lightly. 'Anyway, I'm sure your friends have found someone else to go with them.'

Julian made no reply, but flung himself down on the couch and stared moodily out of the window at the line of roof-tops on the other side of the street. Colette reflected that, with all his faults, Rowland was much easier to handle than this younger son of hers. At nineteen, Julian gave the impression of being younger, his handsome face drawn in the lines of a petulant schoolboy. She had hoped that university would make him grow up, but his first year had so far produced very little alteration in character. She sometimes wished he would show more interest in women, although, God knew, she had had enough trouble with Rowland in that respect. *His* interest in the opposite sex had started at ten years old, when she had caught him trying to look up the skirts of one of the Mallerby housemaids. And it had progressed from there. Since he was twelve, she had never known Rowland without a girl-friend in tow. Julian, on the other hand, she was ready to swear, was a virgin, a dangerous thing to be for a young man approaching twenty. When he did finally fall for a woman, he was much more likely to make a fool of himself.

Colette sighed, pouring herself a gin and tonic. It had not been easy bringing up two boys on her own. She thought of Noel, whose portrait hung here, in the dining-room of Inglebatch House. She had been so much in love with him when she married him, thirty-three years ago. A lot of people had thought it simply a dynastic marriage between two great banking houses, but they had been wrong. After she met Noel Saxelby, while she was still a student at the Sorbonne, there had been no one else for her, ever. With his polite English manners and handsome face, he had ousted all the opposition. And with that magnificent athlete's physique of his, which had made him an Oxford rowing blue and given him a Rugby cap for England, who could have expected him to die of a heart-attack when he was only forty-one? And Colette, who was nine years his junior, had been left to pick up the pieces of her shattered life and bring up their two little boys.

Had she done such a good job of it? she wondered now, eyeing Julian's slumped rebellious figure. And what was Rowland up to, spending his summer hitch-hiking all over Europe, living, no doubt, like a tramp and never bothering to write her a letter to reassure her of his safety?

'Have you heard from Rowe?' she asked Julian, as the doorbell rang downstairs to signal the arrival of the first of their guests.

Julian shook his head, slouching reluctantly to his feet as the drawing-room door opened and Hester, the house-parlourmaid, announced: 'Mr Lennox. Miss Lennox.' His mother was already advancing with hand outstretched, saying in her silkiest tones: 'Cecil, I'm so glad you and Sophie could come.' And then Cecil

Lennox was in the room and, behind him, a ravishing, tall and leggy blonde.

From the first moment of seeing her, Julian had eyes for no one but Sophie Lennox. Not even the beautiful Lisle Ingram, whose face had adorned the cover of practically every fashion magazine on both sides of the Atlantic, and who had all the glamour of an ex-model married to a famous racing driver, could attract Julian's attention away from his dinner partner. Thank God, he thought devoutly, he hadn't gone to see *The Mousetrap*. Had he done so, he would have missed meeting this gorgeous creature.

Sophie Lennox was certainly impressive. Three years older than Julian, she was, at twenty-two, very tall, very blonde, very blue-eyed, with an hour-glass figure, smooth fair skin and a wide sensuous mouth. It was the mouth, Colette decided, watching Sophie across the dinner-table, which stopped her looking like one of those big bland English china dolls, sold in their dozens by the toy departments of shops such as Harrods. The mouth and the eyes, she amended during the second course, when she had an opportunity of studying the girl for a longer period. The eyes, with their fringe of black mascara-coated lashes, were neither as vacant nor as limpid as first impressions suggested. There was a hard calculating look at the back of them; a what's-in-it-for-me expression, which Colette found alienating and unpleasant. She noted, too, that Sophie's conversation, such as it was, revolved almost entirely around herself.

Lisle Ingram, on the other hand, was not only beautiful, but also intelligent. She contributed usefully to a brief discussion about Gary Powers and the U2 incident of the previous May, and to a more protracted conversation about the negro riots and sit-ins currently rocking America. In fact Colette thought her far brighter intellectually than her husband, whose knowledge of life tended to be limited to the racing-track. All the same, Matthew Ingram appeared to be very proud of his wife and listened politely when she was speaking. He was, Colette guessed, by the time the sweet course was on the table, fonder of her than she was of him. She had probably married him for his name and his money.

After dinner, when the gentlemen joined the ladies in the drawing-room for coffee, Julian made a bee-line for Sophie Lennox and sat beside her on the couch. Her short green satin evening dress looked as though it had been moulded on to her figure, and her fleshy shoulders rose whitely out of the strapless top. She gave Julian a quick appraising glance before settling back in her corner and accepting his offer of a drink.

'Vodka and bitter lemon,' she said in a voice that was surprisingly high and thin. When Julian had first been introduced he had expected it to be deep and sultry.

He poured the drink and took his place beside her, ignoring his mother and the other three guests.

'Are you . . . are you doing anything for lunch tomorrow?' he stammered.

She smiled at him sleepily. 'Not that I know of. Why?'

'I . . . I wondered if you'd have lunch with me,' he suggested eagerly, but hesitantly, as though he expected her to refuse. 'I thought maybe Simpson's. One o'clock.'

She laughed, showing small, even, white teeth. 'Now, how did you guess that I like red meat? OK. Simpson's. But make it twelve-thirty. I'm a working girl, and my lunch-hour is half-past twelve to half-past one.'

It had not occurred to him that of course she had to earn a living. 'Where do you work?' he enquired with interest.

'I'm secretary to a firm of brokers. Their offices are just off the Strand, so Simpson's will be very convenient.'

'Good. I'm still up at Oxford,' he volunteered. 'But I shall be going into the bank as soon as I've passed my finals.'

'Yes, I know,' Sophie answered languidly, but before she could say any more there was a diversion. The drawing-room door opened, and an unkempt figure in grey flannel trousers torn at the knee and an open-necked shirt badly in need of a wash came in and dropped a rucksack on to the floor.

Colette gave a little shriek and flew up out of her chair.

'Rowland! Chéri! Where have you been? Why didn't you let me know that you were coming?'

She clung to him, straining up to kiss his mouth, at the same time wrinkling her nose at his unpleasant smell.

He laughed. 'All right, I know I need a bath. My apologies. I let myself in and I had no idea that you were entertaining this evening. Ladies and gentlemen, please forgive me. I shan't inflict my presence on you any longer until I've bathed and changed.'

Across his mother's head, his eyes met those of Lisle Ingram. He thought her quite the most beautiful woman he had ever seen. They smiled at one another, and she winked. He gave an answering wink, picked up his rucksack and left the room. Mounting the stairs to the second floor, he began to whistle.

CHAPTER ELEVEN

WORKING IN THE SAME BUILDING as Russell, Christine found it difficult to avoid him altogether. Only that morning, Friday, he had been paying out benefit money, and she had been his entry clerk. But, except in the line of duty, they had not spoken; and even during an untoward incident, when a claimant had hurled a chair through one of the exchange windows and the police had been called, he had made no comment.

'You've wounded his pride,' Lois Hartman said that evening, when she called at the Chandoses' flat, 'and he won't forgive you for that in a hurry. You see,' she added, sitting down on Christine's bed and examining her friend's purchase of the latest Roy Orbison single, 'Russ was unwise enough to tell a lot of people that you were getting engaged on holiday. So when you came back so obviously estranged it made him look rather foolish.' She turned the record over in her hands. 'You know, I think "Only the Lonely" is probably Roy Orbison's best.'

Christine was sitting in the basketwork chair near her bedroom window, but the pale pink curtains were already drawn against the October dusk. Outside, rainclouds swept across a granite sky, threatening and low, and every now and then a gust of wind spattered the rain against the glass. The protracted spell of warm weather had at last vanished in autumnal mists, and today had been more like winter.

Christine sipped from her mug of instant coffee and frowned. 'It's over two months now since that blasted holiday. I thought Russ would have got over things by now. It isn't as though he's short on girl-friends.' She replaced her mug on top of the wickerwork table, on which reposed her childhood collection of shells, and held out her hand for the record. 'Do you want to hear that?'

'Love to,' Lois said, 'if you're sure it won't disturb your parents.'

Christine shook her head. 'These old houses have very thick walls. And, anyway, I'll keep the volume down.'

She got up and went across to the record-player in a corner of the room and put the record on the turntable. A few seconds later, the rich mellifluous voice of Roy Orbison flooded the room. She returned to her chair. Lois kicked off her shoes and stretched out on the bed, propped up by the counterpane-shrouded pillows. It was some time since they had had a girls' night in like this, and it was something which neither had anticipated happening again after the announcement of Christine's engagement. Now, however, there was no engagement and, if Christine were to be believed, there never would be.

'I had lunch with Russ today,' Lois volunteered after a moment or two, when a quieter passage of the song enabled her to speak without straining her voice. 'He told me he's taking another fortnight of his annual leave next month and going up to the Lake District.'

'In November?'

'My words exactly. But he says he needs to get away somewhere completely different.' Lois giggled. 'I think it's Russ's version of big-game hunting or the Foreign Legion. He fancies he's nursing a broken heart.'

They both laughed at that, then looked guilty and fell silent. 'I suppose,' Christine said, after a moment's silence, 'he'll go fell-walking, or whatever it is they do up there. Striding out across the hills.' The suggestion was too much for their gravity, and she and Lois started to giggle again.

The record came to an end, and silence returned to the room. Christine got up and lifted the record carefully from the turntable, substituting in its place the Shadows playing 'Apache', which had occupied the number one spot in the hit parade during August.

'Any more coffee?' she asked before going back to her seat.

Lois shook her head. 'No, thanks. Chris, you're not serious, are you, when you say you're not going to marry anyone except this Rowland Saxelby? I mean . . . well, the whole thing does sound a bit . . .'

'Georgette Heyer?'

Lois snorted. 'I wouldn't insult such an eminently sane and sensible woman. Denise Robins was the lady I had in mind. According to you, you might as well be hankering after Prince Charles.'

'Have a heart!' Christine protested with a self-conscious laugh. 'Charles isn't twelve years old yet.'

'Don't split hairs.' Lois sat forward, bending her knees and resting her elbows on top of them. 'Are you serious?' she repeated.

'Yes.' Christine pulled aside a corner of one of the curtains and peered outside. The sky was a wrack of flying cloud. Every now and then, the moon appeared, topping the trees in the neighbouring gardens. The winking lights of the houses pierced the darkness. 'At least,' she went on, 'I'm serious now. I don't suppose, at twenty, any decision lasts for ever.'

'It's something for you to admit that much,' Lois conceded. 'It shows you haven't completely lost your marbles. But you and Russ splitting up for such a reason seems so futile somehow.' She sounded disappointed in her friend.

Christine sat down again and finished her coffee, now lukewarm and skimming over. She felt permanently tired nowadays; the tiredness which came from being the recipient of almost universal disapproval. Nothing would make her change her mind, but she had realized that it was no good arguing. She could not explain her love for Rowland Saxelby to herself, let alone to other people. It was a riddle without an answer.

On the other hand . . . She murmured softly: ' "Who ever loved that loved not at first sight?" '

'Yes, well,' Lois said drily, swinging her feet to the floor and looking around for her handbag, 'I don't know that Marlowe is all that much of an authority when it comes to heterosexual love. Do you think I can phone my father and ask him to fetch me? It sounds like a nasty night.'

Christine led the way into the hall and, leaving her friend alone to make the necessary call, joined her parents in the drawing-room. Lois poked her head around the door a few moments later.

'Dad's on his way,' she said. 'He won't be more than a couple of minutes. Thank you for a lovely evening.'

'Have you been able to make Christine see sense?' Gwen Chandos asked hopefully, proffering a bag of marshmallows.

Lois took one. 'Afraid not,' she answered, 'but not for the want of trying.'

Gwen looked resigned. Her husband said cheerfully: 'Don't worry about it, my dear. Mr Right will come along one day, won't he, Chris?'

'I've already told you', she replied quietly, 'that he already has, but no one will believe me.' The flat's front-door bell rang. 'That'll be Mr Hartman. I'll just see Lois out.'

It was nearly nine o'clock. Rowland had at last cleared his room of self-invited guests, and the college quadrangle was finally quiet. With a sigh, he returned to his abandoned essay, which had to be finished in time for his afternoon tutorial the following day. He stared at the sheet of ruled paper, half-filled with his

113

sprawling handwriting, and tried to concentrate on the financial upheavals caused in Europe by the Near East crises subsequent to 1871. His mind, however, was as blank as the remainder of the page. All he could see, interposed between himself and his work, was the face of Lisle Ingram.

He had wasted very little time in getting to know her better after their first meeting at Inglebatch House in August. Within a few days of that meeting, they had gone to bed together, and she had been as eager as he was. She had managed, with apparent ease, to get out of accompanying her husband to Paris.

'Oh, Matthew and I don't live in one another's pocket,' she had said lightly, when Rowland had questioned her. 'I don't interfere in his affairs, so why should he interfere in mine?'

Rowland had taken her down to Mallerby House for the last few days of August. They had spent most of the time in bed, appearing downstairs only for meals. The kitchens and housekeeper's room were buzzing with gossip.

'Have there been many of these affairs?' Rowland enquired casually, propping himself on one elbow and reaching for his cigarettes.

She gave him a slanting look from eyes which, however much fashion writers might mistakenly describe them as blue, were definitely green. Lisle had only to put on a green dress to prove the fact, but at the moment she was wearing a gold identity-bracelet and nothing else.

'One or two,' she had acknowledged. 'How about you?'

'Like you, one or two.' He lit the cigarette with the flame of his lighter. 'But, then, I'm three years older than you.'

'And you're a man,' she had added ironically. She rolled over on to her stomach, tracing an imaginary

114

pattern on his bare chest with an index finger. 'Anything serious?'

He had hesitated fractionally before replying. 'No. Nothing. What about you?'

She had laughed at that. 'You ask me that! A married woman!' She was even more beautiful when she laughed, as photographers all over the world had discovered.

He had grinned, but made no comment. He was of the opinion that Lisle Ingram had never loved, and would never love, anyone but herself.

Nevertheless, there was no denying that she was a most stimulating lover and companion. He thought of her now as he tried to write his essay, and discovered that he had substituted her Christian name for Bismarck's. Irritated, he made the correction.

There was a knock on the door. He tried to ignore this further interruption, but the knock came again, more insistent this time. Then Julian's voice said: 'Rowe, let me in. I've got to talk to you. It's urgent.'

Rowland capped his fountain pen and said resignedly: 'OK. Come in.'

It would never have occurred to him to turn his brother away. He had been pulling him out of scrapes, standing between him and their mother's wrath, almost since Julian was out of nappies. He was fond of his brother, and failed to see that it was this protective attitude of his which was partly responsible for Julian's reluctance to face up to the consequences of his actions.

Julian slithered around the door, and Rowland at once recognized his expression: a familiar look, compound of guilt, defiance and bravado. It was immediately obvious to Rowland that his brother had been up to something of which their mother would almost certainly not approve. She was the only person whose anger and disapprobation Julian feared. Even their redoubtable grandmother de Bérenger had a soft spot for this particular grandson. She might try to lay down the law to Rowland and his cousin Giles, but Julian could always twist her around his little finger and managed to escape the greater part of her censure during family holidays in France.

Rowland waved his brother to an empty chair and, with a sigh, put aside his books. 'Coffee?' he asked hospitably.

Julian shook his head. 'Rowe,' he said urgently, 'I've got to talk to you.'

'So I gather. What have you done?'

Julian looked guiltier than ever. The bravado and defiance had all but disappeared. He said in a rush, as though not knowing any other way to get it out: 'Sophie Lennox and I were married this afternoon by special licence.'

A deep hush descended on the room, and for several moments Rowland did not stir. Then he said slowly: 'You bloody stupid fool.'

A little of Julian's courage returned, and he stuck out his chin aggressively. 'I love her,' he protested, 'and she loves me.'

Rowland raised his eyebrows. 'Then, why the secrecy?'

'You know damn well why.' Julian spoke truculently, his face suffused with colour. 'Because Maman won't approve of our marriage, that's why. And I'm still under age.'

'Ah!' Rowland smiled cynically. 'You mean Sophie may not love you enough to take you without the proverbial shilling.'

'She's not like that!' Julian retorted hotly. 'I told you, we love one another.'

'So you did,' his brother responded drily. 'But I fail to see how you've improved matters by a secret marriage. Why didn't you simply go to Maman and tell her the truth? She might have kicked up a hell of a fuss, but I was only joking just now about the money. There's no way she can cut you out of Father's will, even if she wanted to, and I'm damn sure she'd never do it if she could.'

'No, I dare say not.' Julian looked sulky. 'But she would have done her best to break Sophie and me up. She'd have moved heaven and earth, you know she would. She'd have made things bloody uncomfortable for both of us. She'd have enlisted the help of Cecil Lennox, because he doesn't approve of Sophie and me seeing one another, either. He's got some antiquated notion about knowing his place. Staff and the bosses shouldn't mix – at least, not when it comes to marriage – or some such crap. He has some really antediluvian ideas. He's been having a go at Sophie ever since August, when we first started going out together. And Maman's been having the odd dig at me, except that she hasn't really thought it was serious. I mean, she doesn't care tuppence so long as she thinks Sophie's just my mistress, but if I'd hinted that we wanted to get engaged she'd have raised the roof.'

Rowland frowned. 'I don't follow your reasoning, Jules. It's going to be a damned sight worse when you tell her you and Sophie Lennox are married.'

'Ah, well . . .' Julian put on his best wheedling smile. 'I thought perhaps if *you* told her – you know, sort of got her used to the idea of a *fait accompli* before we saw her – it might be better all round.'

Rowland, who had foreseen what was coming ever since his brother had revealed the reason for his visit, pretended to be taken aback.

'I don't know what you mean by "better all round",' he protested. 'It certainly won't be better for me, and I'm not sure it will be for you.'

'But don't you see,' Julian argued, leaning forward with an earnest expression, 'it's what Sophie says? Now that we're actually married, Maman will have to accept it. You know how dead set she is against divorce. She's bound to make a fuss and be unpleasant to Sophie to

117

begin with, but Sophie's confident she can handle all that.'

Rowland regarded his brother thoughtfully. He felt sure that Sophie Lennox, having achieved her aim of marrying into the wealthy Saxelby family, could cope with any repercussions. He admitted to himself that he might be biased: he had not liked Sophie on the one occasion he had met her, that first evening of his return from his summer vacation. She had drunk too much, talked too much and too loudly, and had obviously resented the presence of Lisle Ingram. Rowland guessed her to be the sort of woman who would always resent not being the undivided centre of attention. She had made a play for him, when he had returned to the drawing-room, bathed and changed, but he had made it plain that she did not interest him. He had had eyes only for Lisle. After that, Sophie had devoted herself exclusively to Julian for the rest of the evening.

Rowland said now: 'I wish to God you'd come to me, Jules, before you did anything so stupid as getting married. I could have pointed out a few of the pitfalls. Besides, you hardly know the girl.'

Julian refuted this hotly. 'We've been going out together for over two months. Long enough for me to know that she's the only woman I want to spend the rest of my life with.'

There was silence for several moments. The gas-fire, which Rowland had lit earlier, hissed and spluttered. Presently he asked: 'Was Sophie your mistress?'

'No!' Julian contrived to look somehow outraged and sheepish at one and the same time. 'Sophie isn't like that. She thinks sex is something to be kept until after marriage.'

Rowland smiled sceptically. So that was how she'd done it! She had summed up Julian easily enough: a little gullible, more than a little naïve. And now, as ever, Julian was running to his brother to pull him out

118

of yet another scrape, this time not altogether of his own making.

'You're a fool, Jules,' he said again. 'You know that, don't you?'

'If that's your attitude,' his brother answered, stumbling clumsily to his feet, 'I'll be going.'

Rowland sighed. 'Oh, sit down again, for God's sake. All right. I'll tell Maman for you.' He grinned wryly. 'I suppose it's the least I can do. But I don't suppose I'm doing either of us, or Sophie, any favours.'

Julian gave him a radiant smile. 'Thanks, Rowe. I knew I could count on you not to let me down.' He got up again. 'I must go and phone Sophie and tell her the good news. She said if anyone can bring Maman round it's you.'

After Julian had gone, Rowland sat looking thoughtfully at the door, before eventually forcing himself to return to his essay.

CHAPTER TWELVE

THE LAKE DISTRICT in November had been a mistake. Since Russell's arrival at the little family hotel in Windermere, the days had been cold and grey, the mist shrouding the mountain-tops from sight. The air had been clammy cold, and the rain almost incessant. Then, at the end of his first week, he awoke on Friday morning to what seemed at first to be a beautiful day.

After breakfast, he walked down to Bowness and strolled along the promenade, looking out over the lake to Belle Isle, where a flock of birds rose high above the trees, quivering in the sky like blown petals. Then, as they turned, cawing and wheeling towards Claife Heights on the farther shore, the pale sunlight caught the tips of their wings, turning them to glittering metal. The leaves of the trees on both sides of the lake were red and gold and beaten copper, and the distant fells were burnished with brakes of dying bracken. A steamer was leaving one of the jetties, bound for Ambleside. Russell pulled up the hood of his duffel coat, feeling cold. He also felt very alone and very miserable.

After a while, he retraced his steps to a lakeside café, where he found a seat by the window and ordered coffee and biscuits. The place was nearly empty. There were few visitors at this time of the year. He stirred the sugar in his cup absent-mindedly and selected a biscuit at random. A girl hurried past the plate-glass window, wearing a navy-blue gabardine mac, her brown hair blown across her eyes by the wind. There was something about her, the way she moved, the sudden irritated toss of the head, which reminded him vividly of Christine and the reason why he was here, trying to forget.

At least, 'trying to forget' was the way Russell liked to think of it. The truth was he was angry and bitter at having been made, as he saw it, to appear a fool rather than heart-broken. Coming to the Lake District in November had been more of a dramatic gesture for the benefit of other people than something he had felt himself impelled to do. He did not really much care for either Westmorland or Cumberland: he was essentially a man of the south, of soft rolling hills, gentle streams and lush water-meadows. But he had once spent a holiday in the Lakes with his parents and had remembered the scenery as sufficiently dramatic to be consonant with his present mood; or, rather, with what he wanted it to be thought was his present mood. Christine and Lois, half-mocking, half-serious, had pictured him striding out across the fells, trying to put back together the pieces of his life. It was precisely the impression he had hoped to create.

In actual fact, Russell had done very little walking, except for one morning when he had gone as far as Waterhead. Apart from that, however, he had mooched around the hotel, gone once by bus to Keswick and, on another occasion, to Kendal, and spent his evenings drinking in the bar with the reps who made up the bulk of the hotel's clientele at this time of year. His chief emotion was boredom, but pride prevented him from admitting as much. His doting parents and family, his legion of adoring fans all imagined him recovering from an unfortunate affair. It made him interesting, and since childhood Russell had been used to being the centre of attention.

He got up and went across to the cash-desk to pay for his coffee, wondering how on earth he was going to fill in another week. He wouldn't be here, he thought angrily, but for Christine and her unlooked-for rejection of him. He still found it difficult to believe, even after all these months, and had spent weeks after their return from Devon expecting her to ring to say that it had all been a terrible mistake, and would he forgive her? In his mind, he had rehearsed his answer; cool and distant at first, keeping her on tenterhooks while he dated other girls; then, gradually, allowing her back into his life, gracious, magnanimous, but making it plain that such a thing must never happen again.

Only, of course, it had not happened. Christine, inexplicably, showed no sign of wanting to renew their former friendship. He felt he had been made to look a bigger fool than ever, in spite of the many girls who had offered to console him. By now, his feelings for Christine were ambivalent, to say the least, and for Rowland Saxelby he felt nothing but hatred.

The light was fading when he left the café, rain-clouds swirling in across the lake. The contour of the land, in this world of ever changing landscapes, had altered once again. The distant horizon was blotted out as the sunlight disappeared, the colour of the trees fading to a uniform grey. It was very silent on the hills, and out of the silence came the whine of the strengthening wind. A moment later, the first drops of rain began to fall; big round drops, each one seemingly separate from the others, splattering on to the roads and pavements. Rain in the Lakes was like no rain Russell had ever encountered elsewhere. If he did not take cover, he would soon be soaking. He plunged into the recessed doorway of a shop selling Lake District souvenirs and once more raised the hood of his duffel jacket.

The rain increased, putting any attempt to make a dash for the hotel out of the question. Russell turned and went into the shop, which had a desolate out-of-season air. The ashtrays and vases and china birds and dogs, all proclaiming themselves presents from Lake Windermere, looked dusty and forsaken. Apart from the owner, who was seated behind the counter, reading a paperback edition of Robert Graves's *Collected Poems*, there was only one other occupant besides himself: a girl, whose back was towards him as she idly inspected the shelves.

There was something familiar about her, even though Russell was unable to see her face. For a moment, he could not think what it was, then he recognized the long black cotton skirt, now bedraggled by rain, trailing some inches below an army greatcoat several times too large for its wearer. A woollen shawl was draped peasant-wise around the girl's head, and over her left shoulder hung an old brown leather school-satchel.

Russell went up behind her and laid a hand on her arm.

'Lucy?' he asked disbelievingly.

She turned and stared up at him, but without surprise.

'Hello, Russell,' said Lucy Brennan with a smile.

'How long', Colette asked with admirable restraint, 'have you known about this marriage?'

'Two, perhaps three, weeks. Maybe more.' Rowland was ashamed of himself for the prevarication. It was more than five weeks now since Julian had confided in him and requested his help; and, having promised it, he had delayed doing anything about it. Finally, two days ago, his conscience troubling him and under pressure from his brother, he had telephoned Colette and asked her to come to Oxford to see him.

He had met her at the station that morning, cutting a lecture to do so, and taken her to the Mitre for lunch. Afterwards they had gone back to his rooms. He had tried to lead up gently to the subject of Julian's marriage, but had not found it easy. His usual tact and diplomacy seemed, on this occasion, to have deserted him. In the end, he had simply blurted it out.

His mother held an elegantly shod foot towards the fire, which had been lit in her honour, in the very small grate. She looked, as always, extremely smart and had obviously dressed with extra care for this visit to her favourite son. The dark-blue Dior baratbea suit was piped around the lapels with red and grey binding, the red being echoed by the ruby studs in her ears. The grey foulard silk blouse was tied in a big artist's bow at the neck, softening the severe lines of the jacket. She sat so quietly that if Rowland had not known her better he would have thought her impervious to his news. But he recognized the tell-tale signs: the thinned lips, which had all but disappeared, and the white gleam of her knuckles as she gripped the chair-arms.

After a few moments' silence, she forced a laugh and shrugged her shoulders. 'He'll live to regret it,' she said.

Rowland was faintly alarmed. 'Maman, you wouldn't . . . you wouldn't do anything to harm Jules, would you?' His tone was anxious.

Colette smiled mockingly. 'Oh, don't worry! I don't intend cutting his allowance or forbidding him and his . . . his *wife*' – the scorn slashed through her voice like a knife – 'the house or anything dramatic like that. No, all I meant was that any fool can see just what sort of a girl Sophie Lennox is.' They had been speaking in French, but now Colette lapsed into English. 'A money-grubbing little tart!'

Rowland chuckled and also switched to English. 'Have a heart, Maman. I think that's coming it a bit too strong. We don't know that much about her. She might be devoted to Julian.'

Colette snorted, suddenly abandoning her tranquil pose and jumping to her feet. When she spoke again, her voice rose dangerously high, and Rowland sensed that hysteria was not far from the surface.

'I seem to be singularly unfortunate in both my sons. One is an idiot and the other a libertine.'

124

She turned her back on him, staring down into the deserted quadrangle. It had been a fine crisp morning with frost on the ground, but now the frost had thawed and turned to water. The square of grass in the centre of the surrounding buildings was soft and yellow from the autumn rains.

Rowland got up and joined her at the window, putting an arm about her shoulders in an effort to defuse the situation.

'Do I presume correctly in thinking that the word *libertine* refers to me?'

Colette hunched her thin shoulders in an effort to slough off the embrace. Then she relaxed and gave a little laugh.

'You and your women,' she said. 'All the same, I wish you'd leave the married ones alone.'

'Like Lisle Ingram, you mean. You know, Maman, I'd never force my attentions on any woman. They're all of them willing.'

'*All* of them?' She glanced up at him over her shoulder. She had never been able to understand how two such small people as herself and Noel had produced two such very tall sons. 'That sounds formidable.'

He gave her a hug. 'Maman, I spent two years in the Royal Air Force doing my National Service. We none of us lived like monks. We had to do something to pass the time.'

That made her laugh, and she returned to her seat by the fire. 'You never needed any excuse for chasing women. You were born with the urge in your blood.'

'Ah!' Rowland murmured, the dark eyes amused. 'Our beloved ancestor, Henri Quatre. A chicken in every pot and a bun in every oven. He's a gentleman who has a lot to answer for.'

'You may scoff,' Colette answered coldly, 'but he was one of the greatest kings France ever produced. You should be proud to count him among your forebears.'

125

'Oh, I am,' Rowland reassured her with a solemnity belied by the twinkle in his eyes. 'He is my favourite grain of sand.'

Colette eyed him suspiciously. 'I don't understand.'

'It's nothing.' Rowland, suddenly restless, his good humour gone, moved about the room. 'It's only something someone once said to me. A silly joke, not worth repeating.'

His mother shrugged and let it go. She had never been the sort of woman who demanded explanations. She returned abruptly to the subject of Julian and Sophie.

'What on earth made him do it, Rowe? Why marry her? Couldn't he just have taken her for his mistress?'

Rowland's good humour reasserted itself, and he sat down opposite her once again. 'Really, Maman, your logic defeats me. I'm a libertine because I sleep with women but don't get married.' He hesitated fractionally, before going on: 'Jules, on the other hand, is a fool because he does the decent thing.'

'You know very well what I mean,' Colette protested angrily. 'You're just trying to confuse me. To have girl-friends – mistresses, if you like – is quite *comme il faut*, but not to play around with married women.'

'Now you've completely lost me,' Rowland laughed. 'All the world's most eminent mistresses were married. It saves such a lot of complications.'

Colette regarded her elder son curiously. 'Have you never been out with a single woman?'

'Heavens, yes! Dozens, I dare say. The girl I met on holiday, while I was in Algiers visiting Tante Eloïse, was single. But, as I said, things can get complicated with unattached women. They think they're in love and want to get married. Not that Lucy Brennan was in that category,' he added hurriedly.

'But somebody else was?' His mother looked at him shrewdly.

126

'What? No, no. There wasn't anyone else. I didn't mean it like that.' But, even as he spoke, Rowland had a vivid mental picture of Christine's face and the way she had looked at him. He had seen the look too often in women's eyes to be mistaken as to its meaning. A nice girl, Christine Chandos – pretty, too, in a strong-featured English sort of way – but not his type. He was attracted by the unusual, like Lucy Brennan, or the exotic, such as Lisle Ingram. Christine would never qualify for either description.

He became aware that Colette was speaking. 'You should be thinking seriously, you know, darling, of getting married. You're well over twenty-two.'

' "Fall'n into the sere, the yellow leaf," ' he quoted, grinning. 'Come off it, Maman. There's no urgency.'

'I don't want to be too old to enjoy my grandchildren,' his mother told him frankly. 'Besides, there's the Saxelby name to think of.'

'Well, there you are, then. Julian's marriage is clearly a blessing in disguise. I'm sure he and Sophie will be only too happy to oblige you.'

'I am not interested in Sophie Lennox's children,' Colette said nastily, glancing at the clock on the mantelpiece. She rose to her feet. 'I really must go or I shall miss my train. Claud is taking me to the cinema this evening. *The Entertainer* with Laurence Olivier.'

'You really ought to marry Claud, Maman,' Rowland said mischievously, helping her on with her coat. 'It would put him out of his misery and distract your mind from other things, like Jules's married state and my lack of it.'

His mother ignored this remark, carefully adjusting her hat, a smart red felt adorned with a grey quill feather, in front of the mirror above the fireplace.

Claud Laing was something of a joke to both her children. A contemporary and close friend of her husband, he had been head over heels in love with her ever since Noel had first brought her to England. At fifty-two, he was still single – a fact which was generally blamed on his passion for Colette, if indeed the word *passion* could be attributed to so reserved and prosaic a character. For Claud was the archetypal Englishman; the incarnation of Colonel Blimp. A former Guards officer and, later, 'something in the City', he was short and stocky with a military bearing, very short grey hair and a toothbrush moustache, endlessly polite and secure in his conviction that all women were fragile beings in need of constant male protection. 'A stick and a bore,' Rowland had once unkindly called him when in his teens, but since those days, although he had not really changed his opinion, he had come to appreciate Claud Laing's sterling qualities. And it made no difference to Claud that Colette was as much in love with her husband eleven years after his death as she had been in Noel's lifetime. He accepted the fact with dignity, even with something like pride, and continued to provide her with an escort whenever she had need of one.

Colette gave Rowland a kiss, and he noticed that there were dark shadows under her eyes which had not been there earlier in the day.

'Try not to worry, Maman,' he urged, giving her a hug which made her frail bones crack. 'Things will work out for Jules, you'll see. After all, he must have considered what he was doing.'

'Do you think so?' Colette was doubtful. 'Julian acts first and considers the consequences later.' She patted Rowland's cheek. 'And you shouldn't agree to do his dirty work for him. You should make him stand on his own two feet. He'll never grow up and accept his responsibilities while he has you to do it for him.'

Rowland sighed. 'No, I know, but it became a habit when we were young, and now I find it hard to break. I suppose it used to flatter me, the way he followed me around and thought that everything I did and said was wonderful. I've never had the heart to disillusion him.

128

I have to go on being the big brother who can make everything turn out right.'

'Well, if he thinks that just because you've spoken to me I'm not going to be very angry with him when I see him, he has another think coming,' Colette replied grimly. 'And don't tell me why he didn't come to me in the first place, because, yes, he's right, I should have tried to persuade him not to marry Sophie. I shudder to think what Cecil's going to say when I give him the news.'

Rowland nodded. 'He'll probably take it far worse than you.'

He escorted his mother to the station and saw her settled in a first-class carriage on the London-bound train.

'See you soon,' he said, kissing her, 'at Mallerby for Christmas.'

'I suppose we'll have to have that Sophie creature there as well,' Colette remarked viciously. 'However, I shan't let it get me down. She won't get the better of me.'

That made Rowland laugh. 'No one's ever got the better of you, Maman,' he said, preparing to leave the compartment as the guard started slamming carriage-doors. 'Except, of course, Gran'mère. But, then, she's every bit as wily as you are and has taught you all her tricks.'

He got out of the train before she could reply, and stood watching it depart from the platform. Things hadn't been so bad after all: the day might have been very much worse. Slowly, as the train disappeared from view, he turned and left the station.

CHAPTER THIRTEEN

'SO, WHAT HAPPENED TO YOU and Rowland, then, after you left the camp-site?'

Russell and Lucy Brennan were sitting at the same table, in the same café, where he had had his morning coffee. They were eating fried eggs, sausages and chips, awash with fat and tomato ketchup. To follow, Lucy had ordered a Knickerbocker Glory. Outside, the weather had improved again, and from where they sat they could see the sun-splashed lines of one of the jetties.

Lucy did not answer for a moment; she was too busy eating. After she had cleared her mouth, however, she said: 'We went back to London to return the hire car. We mooched around for a day or two, sleeping in Salvation Army hostels. Then I decided to hitch my way up to Scotland, but Rowe had had enough and thought it was time to go home. His people have a house in London.'

Russell nodded. That figured: those sort of people had houses everywhere.

'So you didn't stay together long after you left. Why did you leave in such a hurry?'

'Did we?' Lucy looked vague and smothered her few remaining chips with more sauce. 'I don't remember. We were probably fed up with the place. I don't like to stay put very long.'

Russell laid his knife and fork together on his empty plate and watched while Lucy soaked up the last of the fat with a piece of bread. 'So where is Rowland now?' he asked.

'Back at Oxford, I suppose.' Lucy seemed unconcerned. She gave a little giggle. 'Back in the bosom of his family.'

A waitress came to take away the dirty plates, then brought Lucy's ice-cream and Russell's coffee. The café was beginning to fill up now, although there were still a number of empty tables. Russell guessed that in summer, at the height of the holiday season, it would be packed to the doors.

He was feeling a little piqued that, so far, Lucy had evinced no interest in either himself or his movements since they had last met. She had not even enquired what he was doing in the Lake District.

He spooned sugar into his coffee and said: 'Chris and I have split up, you know. We decided we wouldn't suit.'

Without glancing up from the serious business of eating, Lucy grunted: 'Rowe has that effect on women.'

Russell felt the blood creep up under his skin. He had tried to make it sound as if the split had been a mutual decision, but Lucy had not been deceived for a minute. He said stiffly: 'Not on you apparently.'

'Oh, me!' Lucy laughed. 'I'm different.'

'How different?'

She shrugged, scraping the last bit of ice-cream from the tall glass and laying down her spoon with a sigh of repletion. 'I get bored easily. That's why I lead the sort of life I do. Nothing holds my attention for very long.'

He asked: 'What are you doing here in Windermere?'

'Nothing special. I went all round Scotland, the Highlands and Islands, and now I'm on my way south again. I'm working my way down to Plymouth, and from there I'll probably cross to Brittany. After that, I may go to Spain or to Eastern Europe. I'd like to see something of the Iron Curtain countries. I've always fancied Russia.'

'You're mad,' Russell said with conviction. 'How long is all this going to take?'

'How do I know? It depends what else crops up along the way. But, in any case, what does it matter? I have a whole lifetime ahead of me.'

The waitress arrived with the bill, which she gave to Russell. He put the necessary money on the table, noting with a little flick of irritation that Lucy made no attempt to pay her share.

'Don't you ever intend to settle down?' he asked, as they got up to leave.

Once again, she gave that dismissive lift of her shoulders. 'Perhaps, when I'm old. Or perhaps tomorrow, if I feel like it. I just don't know. It depends on how the fancy takes me.'

They walked along Bowness Promenade again, wrapping their coats more tightly around them. It had turned very cold. Lucy told Russell that she was staying in Ambleside for a few days, at the home of an old school-friend, who had recently married an Englishman and come to live in Westmorland. He wondered vaguely how, with her kind of life, she managed to keep in touch with anyone, but supposed she had her ways and means, just as she kept herself supplied with money.

He said: 'I'm here for another week. Shall we see each other again? Or are you thinking of moving on?'

'Not for a day or two. Bridget says I can stay as long as I like.' She chuckled. 'I don't think Des – that's her husband – shares those sentiments. I see him looking at me sometimes, wondering what this weird Irish bog-woman is doing in his nice clean English house. He'll be glad to see the back of me, I dare say, but I'll go when I'm ready.' Suddenly, quite unexpectedly, she took his arm, pressing into his side to protect herself from the wind. 'Russ, let's go and get a cup of tea somewhere. I know we've only just eaten, but anywhere to get out of this cold.' She turned her face up to his, dark curly tendrils of hair escaping from beneath the knitted shawl, the little pointed features pinched and raw, the eyes very big and blue. 'There's something I want to tell you. I hadn't intended saying anything to anyone, but I can't keep it to myself any longer.'

It was dark just after four o'clock, and Regent Street was glittering with Christmas lights. Some were strung across the street like diamond necklaces, others seemed to be suspended in the air in clusters of amber stars. The Christmas tree in Swan & Edgar's window shimmered with a cascade of crystal drops, and in Dickins & Jones Santa Claus sat, red and jovial, in his sleigh, driving his team of reindeer.

There was still almost a week before Christmas day, but the pavement crowds were thick. Christine and Lois, struggling along in the direction of Oxford Circus and the tube, were nearly swept off their feet in the crush. They had come up for a day's shopping, catching the early-morning excursion-train from Weston-super-Mare. Now, exhausted and with aching feet, they decided they had had enough, and were heading for Paddington and the return journey home.

'I could do with a cup of tea,' Lois grumbled, but Christine hardened her heart. She just wanted to get out of the crush.

'We'll get one at the station,' she promised, 'but I can't face pushing my way up and down escalators with all these parcels. I hope people appreciate all I've gone through to get their presents this year.'

Lois snorted, making a dive for a Selfridge's carrier-bag which was in imminent danger of getting away from her. 'I doubt it. They'll probably think you bought them all in Weston.'

The crowds were getting even thicker now as a few early office-leavers joined the shoppers in the street. Lois suddenly stopped, with a cry of delight, to look in the window of Garrard's, the jewellers, at the blaze of gems: rubies, sapphires, emeralds, diamonds, not one of which she would ever be able to afford.

'Look at that necklace,' she breathed in awe. 'And those rings. And that bracelet.'

'Oh, do come on!' Christine exclaimed irritably. 'My feet are killing me. I shall be glad to sit down.'

She forged ahead, forcing Lois to follow her at a run, pushing a way between the people and almost dropping her parcels. After a moment or two, Christine stopped and said contritely: 'I'm sorry. It's simply that I'm so over at the knees I'm getting bad-tempered.'

Her apology was impatiently brushed aside as her friend gasped: 'Did you see who that was?'

'Who what was? Where?'

Lois shunted her into the nearest shop-doorway as passers-by began making pointed remarks about people who blocked the pavement.

'That man who crossed the road just then. Didn't you notice him? I'm sure it was Russ.'

'Russ Jennings?'

'Well, of course Russ Jennings! What other Russ do we know?'

Christine shrugged. 'This *is* London after all. It might have been Russ Conway. Anyway, what would Russell be doing here?'

'The same thing as we are, I suppose. Christmas shopping.'

Christine remained unconvinced. 'I didn't see him.'

'You wouldn't, would you? You were rushing ahead as though all the hounds of hell were at your heels.'

'Did he tell you he was coming up to London this Saturday?'

Lois shook her head. 'He doesn't confide in me any more. I'm *your* friend, remember? He's become very reserved and secretive lately. Several people in the exchange have remarked on it. Miss Linley said his fortnight in the Lake District didn't do him any good. She thinks you ought to be boiled in oil.'

Christine smiled bitterly. 'Oh, I know a lot of people think that. I'm growing used to being ostracized.' She managed to twist her arm so that she could see her watch. 'Look, it's nearly quarter to five. The early excursion-train goes at six-thirty, so we ought to get a move on if we want a cup of tea first.'

'We could always catch the later excursion,' Lois suggested.

'We-ll ... If you really want to do some more shopping ...'

A man came out of the store behind them and said politely: 'Excuse me, could you move your parcels? I'm afraid I'll do some damage if I try to push through.'

Christine and Lois turned, flustered, offering apologies, making a concerted dive for carrier-bags and boxes. The young man smiled his thanks. His eyes met Christine's.

'Good God!' Rowland Saxelby exclaimed. 'It's – er – you,' he finished lamely.

'Christine Chandos,' she said in a voice which sounded totally unlike her own.

'Of course. I should have remembered. Sir John and the battle of Lussac-les-Châteaux.' He laughed. 'How pleasant to see you again. No need to ask what you're doing in town.'

Self-consciously, Christine clutched the mound of parcels in her arms. 'We're only up for the day. This is my friend, Lois Hartman. Lois, this is Rowland Saxelby, the young man I met on holiday in Devon.'

The words seemed trite and foolish; inadequate for what they conveyed and all that she was feeling. Her paramount thought was that he had forgotten her name. Four short months, and he could not even remember what she was called. That ought to tell her something. She wondered what Lois was thinking.

Lois was shaking hands with Rowland; or, at least, was attempting to shake hands, encumbered as she was by her purchases. She murmured conventionally: 'Chris has told me all about you.'

The black eyebrows were raised in amusement, but he forbore to make any comment. Instead he said: 'Are you in a hurry? Can I take you both somewhere for tea?'

'Thank you, we'd like that very much,' Christine said, avoiding Lois's eyes. 'Our train doesn't leave until half-past seven.' She was aware of sounding slightly breathless and swore inwardly.

'Hold on, then,' he instructed, 'while I find a taxi.'

He did this with surprising ease. One of the big black London cabs just seemed to materialize at the kerb side the moment he raised his arm. Luck, of course, but Christine could see that Lois was impressed.

He took them to Brown's Hotel in Dover Street. The softly lit interior, the hushed voices, the thick carpets and the deep well-padded armchairs and settees gave it the appearance of a gentleman's club. And the food was lavish; sandwiches, toasted buns, scones and butter and an infinite variety of cakes were too much even for Lois, who loved eating and was, at twenty-one, already showing signs of putting on weight.

To begin with, the conversation was forced and a little uneasy, but the combination of Rowland and Lois ensured that it would not stay that way for long. Both were apparently easy-going extroverts, although Christine suspected that Rowland had a secretive side to his nature. People, especially women, might be deluded into believing that they knew him well, only to discover that they had never really known him at all.

While he and Lois chatted, she took covert stock of him. He was smarter, sleeker than when she had last seen him, in August. He was wearing a dark suit beneath his raincoat, and a shirt and tie. He might have been a City businessman rather than an Oxford undergraduate. But then she recollected that he was, of course, old enough to be working for his living, had he not chosen to do his National Service first.

He turned to her with his charming smile. 'You're not saying much, Chris. I haven't offended you in any way, have I?'

It was on the tip of her tongue to reproach him for having left the camp-site without a word, but she restrained herself. Why give him the satisfaction of thinking that she cared? Instead she asked: 'What's happened to Lucy Brennan?'

'Oh, Lucy and I split up not long after we returned to London, and I haven't seen her since. We parted by mutual consent. She wasn't the type to stay with one man long. Lucy's the most restless person I've ever known. A born nomad. She'll never settle down. When we first met, she thought it might be fun to try, but I shouldn't have let myself be fooled. I realized after a very short space of time that it would be like trying to cage a wild bird.' He grinned in self-deprecation. 'Now, there's a cliché-ridden description for you.'

'So you're footloose and fancy-free,' Lois remarked, making her own hackneyed contribution.

Christine felt herself blushing, and wished that her friend would not be so obvious. She saw the wary look which sprang into Rowland's dark eyes. She wanted to say something offhand, laconic, to show that his answer was a matter of supreme indifference to her, but her mind was blank as she waited for his inevitable snub.

He did it politely by simply ignoring the question and asking a passing waiter for a second pot of tea. The richness of the food had made them all thirsty.

Christine saw Lois open her mouth to repeat the question, and managed to catch her eye just in time, giving a tiny, barely perceptible shake of her head. Lois made a moue of frustration, but held her tongue, to the great relief of her friend. Christine glanced at her watch and said that they should be going: it had

137

gone six o'clock. It would take them a while to get to Paddington in the rush-hour, and she didn't want a last-minute scramble.

'I'll order you a taxi,' Rowland said, getting up from the table.

Christine and Lois exchanged startled glances, each mentally reviewing her financial situation, but neither liked to confess that the taking of taxis was not, for them, a normal everyday occurrence.

A tall girl, expensively dressed in a pale green coat with mink collar and cuffs, a curtain of red hair half-concealing her beautiful face, was being shown to a seat at a neighbouring table. Attracted by Rowland's sudden movement, she turned her head.

'Darling!' she exclaimed delightedly and came across to kiss him. 'Darling,' she repeated, 'this *is* a surprise. What are you doing here? I didn't think I should see you until this evening.'

Christine recognized her immediately from the glossy magazines: ex-model Lisle Talbot, who had married the racing driver Matthew Ingram. It was apparent at once what her relationship was with Rowland. Lois grimaced at her friend with a look of sympathetic understanding.

'Lisle!' Rowland seemed equally pleased to see her and not at all abashed at being found with two other women. Christine supposed bitterly that only a complete fool would see them as any sort of competition for Lisle Ingram.

Rowland made the introductions, describing her as 'a girl I met at a camp-site in Devon'. Which just about summed her up, Christine thought. Lisle Ingram extended a gracious hand.

'I shan't be long,' Rowland assured her. 'I'm just going to see – er – Christine and her friend into a taxi. I'll be right back. Don't go away.'

An hour or so later, as the excursion-train pulled slowly out of Paddington station, Christine leaned back against the seat of the third-class railway compartment and closed her eyes. She had eaten too much tea and felt slightly sick. Her head ached and her throat hurt with the effort of suppressed emotion. This meeting with Rowland, far from curing her of a hopelessly silly romantic attachment, had only confirmed what she already knew: that she loved him and would always love him; that, for her, there could never be anyone else. Marriage, or an affair, with someone different would merely be a compromise, a making-do with second best. It might have to come to that one day, she supposed: no one could live with an empty dream for ever. But not yet. Not yet . . .

Lois, who was sitting in the opposite corner, leaned over and squeezed her hand. Outside, the lights of passing houses hung for a transitory moment amidst the winter darkness, then slipped sideways and vanished. 'He's a very nice man,' she said. 'Everything you told me about him is true. He has that sort of charm . . .' She broke off, not knowing quite how to go on.

Christine opened her eyes and smiled wryly. 'It's all right, Lois. You don't have to say any more. I realize I don't exist for him. He couldn't even recollect my name to begin with, and even after I'd told him he had difficulty remembering it. But it doesn't make the slightest bit of difference to my feelings for him.'

Lois looked as though she were about to say something further, then decided against it. It was strange, she reflected, how alike Rowland Saxelby and Russell Jennings were in looks; the same type, tall and dark and lean. But there was a sweetness in Rowland, totally lacking in the other man. She could see why Christine was in love with him. She could quite easily fall for him herself.

With a sigh, she leaned back in her seat and opened a magazine.

PART THREE
1964 – 5

CHAPTER FOURTEEN

IT WAS one of the longest, hottest summers anyone could remember, and by the bank holiday, at the beginning of August, the fine weather looked set to continue well into the autumn.

Lois's little three-wheeled Bond rattled along the Shaftesbury-to-Sherborne road, the noise so great that Christine had to raise her voice to make herself heard.

'Next time, don't bother fetching me. I'll come by bus.'

Lois grinned. 'These things have motor-bike engines. That's why they're so noisy. I did warn you, but you said you didn't mind.'

'I hadn't had the experience then. No, seriously' – Christine's voice resumed its normal level as the Bond came to a halt outside a modern red-tiled bungalow a little way out of the town – 'I'm very grateful. Weston to Shaftesbury isn't the easiest journey in the world, in spite of the fact they're only about sixty miles apart.'

'I know,' Lois said. 'And as I'd asked you down for the weekend I thought the only decent thing was to give you a lift. Besides, it gave me the chance to visit my parents. Barry gets a bit jealous if I go to see them too often. You know what husbands are.'

'Not really,' Christine answered gently. 'Only second-hand.'

Lois climbed out. 'Come on,' she said. 'Let's extricate you and your luggage from this old tin-can. Barry won't let me drive the Austin any more. Heaven knows why! That accident I had in it was the merest scratch. But I had to have something to get about in. I ask you! We're

143

quite a way outside the town, and I'm not walking or waiting for a bus every time I want to get to the High Street.'

She lifted Christine's overnight case from the bench seat at the back of the car and carried it up the drive to the front door. She nodded towards the Bond, still parked on the road. 'I have to leave it there until Barry gets home. His precious Austin, naturally, goes in the garage. The rattletrap stands out in all weathers. It's a miracle that it goes at all.' Lois unlocked the door and led the way into the bungalow. In the narrow hall, she put the case on the floor and turned to face her friend. 'I'm glad you could come, Chris. It's lovely to see you again. I miss our girlish heart-to-hearts. Letters and the phone are never the same.'

'And I'm glad to be here. I was lucky to be able to get today and Tuesday off. With tomorrow, Sunday and Bank Holiday Monday, it makes a decent break.' She regarded Lois affectionately, noting that married life agreed with her, if her additional weight was anything to judge by. 'I can't believe it's nearly four months since the wedding.'

'Nor me. It feels more like forty. No, no,' Lois added, laughing. 'I mustn't say things like that. If Barry ever heard me, he might think I was serious. The poor darling has no sense of humour.'

'But you are happy?' Christine wanted to know.

'We have our moments,' Lois replied crisply. 'Now, come into the kitchen and we'll have a cup of tea. I bet you could do with one after that extremely noisy journey.'

'Yes, I could,' Christine admitted.

The bungalow's kitchen looked out on the steeply rising back garden. It was bright and cheerfully modern, with blue Formica-topped units, blue-and-white checked curtains, a large poster on one wall of a 1930s Colman's mustard advertisement and a pine table, with two pine stools, in the centre of the

144

linoleum-covered floor. At the moment, the room was in shadow, the bungalow being west-facing so that the front of the building caught the afternoon sun.

Lois pulled out one of the stools from under the table for Christine to sit on, then filled the electric kettle with water and plugged it in. Reaching up to a shelf, she brought down a biscuit-tin and started to arrange chocolate biscuits on a dark red melamine plate. After that, she moved to the refrigerator and took out a cold cooked chicken and a salad-basket full of salad. She looked competent and easy, a woman at home in her own house. In four months, she had adjusted well to married life. It was just over two years since Lois had met Barry Aylward, who was on holiday at the time in Weston. Short and stocky, with a round fresh face peppered with freckles and hair that was definitely ginger, Christine had never considered him Lois's type. But when she had said as much her friend had shrugged.

'What is my type? I'm not waiting around like you, Chris, for an impossible dream. Barry is a nice man, has a good job' – he was a dispenser for a Shaftesbury chemist – 'and we get on well together. What more can I ask for?'

'Love?' Christine had suggested.

But Lois had been dismissive, and Christine remembered that when they had read *Pride and Prejudice* as a set school-book Lois had stoutly defended Charlotte Lucas's decision to marry Mr Collins. Watching her now, it was plain that she liked the domestic side of marriage perhaps rather more than the romantic or the physical. Christine reflected that Lois had always been very prosaic.

Lois made the tea, arranged cups and saucers, milk-jug and sugar-bowl on the table, and sat down opposite her friend. 'So how are things?' she asked, offering the plate of biscuits. 'Are you and Russ still speaking?'

'Of course. Why on earth shouldn't we be? Four years is a long time to bear a grudge, even for him.'

'You're being unfair again,' Lois protested. 'It was understandable that he should have been upset at the time. But since that office Christmas party, when you asked him if he'd enjoyed his day in London – remember? – he's been perfectly friendly. It only needed that overture from you to break the ice. And he hasn't married, either, has he? Though I must admit I fully expected him to have done so by now.'

Christine helped herself to another chocolate biscuit. 'You're incorrigible, do you know that? You're still hoping that Russ and I will get back together again. You're as bad as my parents. But it won't happen, Lois. It's far too late, for Russ as well as for me.'

'Still carrying the torch?' Lois asked gently.

Christine made an effort to smile and answered flippantly: 'I'm stuck with the damn thing, like the Statue of Liberty.'

Lois poured the tea and pushed a cup towards her friend. 'In that case,' she said, 'I won't mention the subject again. And I promise, while you're here, not to introduce you to any eligible men. You're here to relax and enjoy yourself, and that's just what you're going to do.'

Breakfast at Mallerby, particularly at holiday-times, was always a haphazard affair and tended to linger on until well past eleven, much to the annoyance of the housekeeper, Mrs Renshaw.

'It's all very well for them,' she grumbled to the new housemaid, Rose James, 'but I was brought up to get breakfast cleared away before I started preparing lunch. They come straggling down in ones and twos and then start ringing for fresh toast or coffee. Mr Julian, he's the worst. He can never get up in the morning.'

Rose, a thin-faced local girl with a high-bridged nose and sharp bright eyes, was peeling potatoes at the kitchen sink. She had been at Mallerby House exactly three weeks, but it was already her ambition, one day, to be housekeeper. She knew that her parents had hoped for better things for her than domestic service: she had shown academic promise at school, and the Youth Employment Officer had tried to persuade her to take a job in a solicitor's office in Yeovil. But she had always wanted to work 'up at the big house', and no arguments would move her.

'*Mrs* Julian's down,' she volunteered. 'She wanted tea instead of coffee. I took it in to her just now. Mrs Saxelby came in while I was there. But nobody else has put in an appearance.'

Mrs Renshaw sniffed. 'And won't, neither, not for an hour or two. That friend' – she gave the word a wealth of meaning – 'of Mr Rowland's, that there Lisle, or whatever she calls herself – damn silly name for a woman, if you ask me – she won't bestir herself till lunch-time. Didn't show her face yesterday until nearly one.' Mrs Renshaw took a deep disapproving breath and scowled. 'Where's her husband, that's what I want to know. He never comes down here with her. Oh no! Always just her and Mr Rowland. It's been going on now for over three years. I wonder Madam doesn't put a stop to it.'

Rose James giggled. 'Don't s'pose she can. Mr Rowland's twenty-six.'

'That's as maybe,' the housekeeper snapped, 'but Mallerby's still Madam's home, even though it might legally belong to him. He ought to have more consideration for his mother. Carrying on his affairs in "fragrant delicto" as the saying is, though to my mind there's nothing fragrant about it. Howsoever, the hussy won't be able to lie in all hours on Monday. She'll have to be up and about bright and early, like the rest of them. That'll learn her.'

'Why? What's happening Monday?'

147

Mrs Renshaw began gathering together her pastry-making things on the big well-scrubbed deal table.

'It's Bank Holiday Monday, that's what, and they always open the house to the public on Bank Holiday Mondays. Normally, the opening-days are Tuesday and Thursday, but bank holidays they open on Monday as well. You're from the village. You ought to know that.'

'I'd forgotten,' Rose said. 'Does that mean', she enquired anxiously, 'that I have to work?'

'No, not you. But I shall be here, of course,' Mrs Renshaw added grandly. 'They have special people in to do the conducted tours.'

Rose James nodded as the internal telephone buzzed. The row of metal bells between the top of the kitchen door and the old-fashioned room-indicator board were silent nowadays, a relic of the past. Mrs Renshaw lifted the black receiver from its cradle.

'They want some coffee in the breakfast-parlour,' she said. 'Mr Julian's just come down.'

By the time Rose entered the room, Colette had finished her croissants and jam and disappeared. Only Julian and Sophie were still seated at the table. Rose put down the coffee-pot she was carrying and removed the cold one hurriedly. It was obvious that another row was brewing.

As the door closed behind her, Julian said sulkily: 'Why do you have to go back to town this morning?'

Sophie poured herself another cup of tea and cradled her hands, with their vivid red finger-nails, around the delicate china.

'Because I'm bored, darling,' she said. 'Bloody bored and fed up. You know how I hate these old mausoleums. They give me the creeps.'

'Maman will be very upset if you do. And Mallerby is not a mausoleum.'

Sophie ignored the rider and yawned. 'Your mother won't care tuppence if I'm here or not, provided I leave

148

you and Vivien behind. Her precious son and her darling little grand-daughter. She's never liked me from
the moment we were married.'

'She's always been all right to you,' Julian protested
lamely. 'You can't pretend she hasn't.'

'If, by "all right",' Sophie retorted acidly, 'you mean
she's never actually called me a gold-digger to my face,
or accused me of seducing her innocent child, I would
agree with you. On the other hand, if you mean she
has treated me as she would a perfect stranger, never
making me welcome or feel a part of the family, then
you're wrong. I don't know why I consented to come
down here this weekend in the first place. But after
twenty-four hours I'm just about climbing the walls.
Vivien'll be OK. Miss Trim looks after her better
than I do.'

'Viv's only two and a half years old,' Julian protested.
'A child of that age needs her mother.'

'Codswallop.' Sophie got up from the table and
studied her reflection carefully in the mirror above
the mantelpiece. The blonde hair, once so long and
flowing, had now been cut by Vidal Sassoon into a
shining cap, shaped close to the head. The skirt of her
smart print frock was at least an inch above the knee,
and she wore very pointed, low-heeled shoes. 'And don't
pretend you'll miss me, either,' she went on. 'You know
damn well you're happier when I'm not around.'

'That's not true,' Julian said half-heartedly.

'Yes, it is. Our marriage was a mistake, at least as
far as you were concerned. I got what I wanted out of
it: the Saxelby name and the Saxelby money. So don't
ask me for a divorce, darling, because you won't get it.
And don't try for one on the grounds of my adultery,
because I'll fight you every inch of the way for the
custody of Vivien. But, apart from that, you're free to
do as you like. I shan't interfere with your pleasures.'

'You're a bitch!' Julian exclaimed angrily. 'What the
hell did I ever see in you? I must have been mad.'

149

Sophie laughed and, coming up behind his chair, dropped a mocking kiss on the top of his head.

'You did it to annoy Mummy. Sorry – Maman! To assert your independence of the maternal apron-strings. You wanted to prove that you were as big a dog with the ladies as your brother, only when it came to the point you got cold feet and agreed to marry me, in case I got away and left you looking foolish. Poor little Julian! You don't have much self-confidence, do you? Still running to big brother whenever anything goes wrong.'

'Shut up!' Julian shouted, getting up with such violence that his chair overturned on the floor. He grabbed her by the shoulders and started to shake her. 'Shut up, you silly bitch! Shut up!'

The door opened, and Rowland sauntered in, just as the long-case clock in one corner of the room struck eleven.

'For God's sake, you two, lower your voices. You can be heard all over the house. Unless, of course, you enjoy washing your dirty linen in public.'

Sophie twisted free of her husband's hands. 'If we're talking about dirty linen,' she sneered, 'there's the little matter of that whore you keep bringing down to Mallerby. At least Julian and I are not openly committing adultery.'

Rowland's mouth set in a thin hard line, but he refused to rise to the bait. He sat down at the table and poured himself some coffee. Seeing that she was not going to provoke any reaction, Sophie said to Julian: 'I'm off to pack. I'll take the car, if that's all right by you. Rowland can give you a lift back to town. I expect your mother will want Vivien and Miss Trim to stay on for a day or two after the bank holiday.'

She went out, closing the door with a decided snap behind her. Rowland raised his eyebrows at his brother.

150

'It's none of my business, I suppose, but don't you think you'd be better off without her?'

'Oh, mind your own business,' Julian snapped and rushed from the room, almost colliding with Lisle Ingram as he did so.

'What was that about?' she asked, joining Rowland at the table.

'Just another skirmish in his and Sophie's perpetual state of war.' He smiled at her. 'Did you sleep well?'

'When I finally got back to my own bed at five this morning, like a log.' Her answering smile was reminiscent. 'What else would you expect after all that nocturnal activity?'

Rowland made no reply, but was uneasily aware that one was expected of him; a gallant reference, perhaps, to joys past or an allusion to pleasures to come. The truth was, however, that he was getting a little tired of Lisle Ingram. Their affair had lasted for four years and was beginning to shows signs of wear and tear. He no longer felt excited at the prospect of making love to her, and suspected that, although she might not be ready yet to admit it, she felt much the same way about him. Perhaps when he went with the rest of the family on their annual holiday to France in September he would be able to make the break. The one place he could never take Lisle was his grandmother's house in Poitou. Marie de Bérenger would be outraged if he ever dared to bring a married woman-friend beneath her roof. As it was, she would lecture him endlessly as to why he was not yet married.

He took one of Lisle's hands in his and kissed it, but it was an empty gesture and he wondered if she knew.

'The toast's cold,' he said and, getting up, went over to the internal phone. As he lifted the receiver, he grimaced and added: 'Mrs Renshaw won't be pleased. She'll be in the middle of preparing lunch. Never mind. Live dangerously, that's my motto.'

CHAPTER FIFTEEN

CHRISTINE AND LOIS emerged from Shaftesbury Abbey ruins on to the wide promenade known as Park Walk, high above the town. Below them, the houses nestling at the foot of Gold Hill basked in the morning sunshine. In the distance, the green Dorset uplands shimmered in a summer haze.

'Let's get some coffee,' Lois said briskly. 'My feet are killing me. I shouldn't have worn these new sandals.'

Christine felt guilty. She had accompanied her friend into the town to do the weekend shopping, and it had been her suggestion that they visit the Ancient Monument which comprised a small museum and the scanty remains of the once great nunnery, founded by King Alfred. The body of Edward the Martyr had been interred beside the high altar in 979; King Cnut had died there in 1035. Christine, an indefatigable visitor to ancient places, had felt she could not miss it. It had just been unfortunate that Lois was improperly shod for stumbling about amongst the ruins.

They found a small café in the High Street and sank thankfully into the wheelback chairs at a polished oak table, which were a part of the general aura of 'olde worlde' charm. A waitress in a blue-and-white checked gingham dress and mob-cap took their order for coffee and biscuits. Lois surreptitiously eased off the offending shoes.

'That's better,' she sighed. 'You and your passion for old buildings!'

'Sorry,' Christine grinned. 'I promise I'll try not to let it happen again.'

Lois shook her head reprovingly. 'You shouldn't make promises you're not going to keep. Here, take a look at this.' She rummaged around in the bottom of her capacious shoulder-bag and eventually produced a printed sheet of bright pink paper, which she pushed across the table to her friend. 'I picked it up from the desk in the entrance-lobby of the Abbey ruins.'

At the top of the sheet was a line drawing of a large Tudor mansion, and beneath it the legend 'South façade of Mallerby House, Hinton Malsherbes, Somerset'. And under that again, in bold black type: 'Open August Bank Holiday Monday between 2.00 p.m. and 6.00 p.m. Adults 2/6. Children half-price. Dogs not allowed.'

'Well?' Lois demanded, as Christine made no comment. The waitress returned with their order, and for a moment conversation was suspended. When she had gone, however, Lois repeated eagerly: 'Well?'

Christine raised her eyes slowly. 'I'd love to go and see it, of course, but you and Barry don't want to spend your bank holiday wandering round Mallerby House.'

'Barry will do as he's told,' Barry's wife answered crisply, completely ruining her effect by adding: 'He's playing cricket anyway. And this will give me a good excuse not to have to go and watch. I know it's supposed to be a part of our national culture – the sound of leather on willow and all that jazz – but if there's one game that bores me silly it's cricket. So what do you say? Shall we go? I might persuade him to let me take the Austin if I take a solemn oath to be very careful and drive at no more than thirty miles an hour all the way there and back. But at least we shall be spared the horrors of the Bond and stand a good chance of getting there in one piece.'

'We-ell . . .' Christine hesitated, then gave an answering grin. 'Of course, I'd love to go. Is it far?'

'About twenty miles the other side of the Somerset border. We can have an early lunch with Barry first and still be there easily by half-past two. That'll give us plenty of time to look around at our leisure. The gardens are supposed to be very fine. If this weather holds, it should be lovely.' Lois helped herself to another chocolate biscuit. 'Wouldn't it be a lark if we bumped into Rowland Saxelby?'

Christine quickly suppressed the faint hope which Lois's words had raised.

'I don't suppose for one moment that the family's in residence,' she said. 'They'd hardly open up the house if they were staying there.'

Lois sucked the chocolate from her fingers, then, almost absent-mindedly, started on a cream-filled wafer. 'The house is open twice a week from the beginning of April until the end of October. They're bound to be there some time during that period, surely.'

Christine concentrated on stirring her coffee. She wasn't sure how she felt about the prospect of encountering Rowland again after all these years. Time and distance had only added enchantment to her memories of him. Would she be disappointed if they met once more? And, even if she were, wouldn't that be the very best thing that could happen? But of course they weren't going to meet. The chances of Rowland's being at Mallerby on Monday were remote.

She glanced up at Lois's eager face, watching her intently from the other side of the table.

'I thought we weren't going to mention the subject of Rowland Saxelby again while I was here. No, don't apologize, you fool! And, even if we did accidentally run into him, he probably wouldn't even remember my name. Now, if we're going to finish the shopping by lunch-time, stop stuffing yourself with biscuits and let's get going. And this is my treat, so put away your money.' She signalled to the waitress for the bill.

'What time', Colette enquired over lunch, 'do we open the doors to the *canaille*?'

154

Rowland made a gesture of protest and hurriedly emptied his mouth of cold beef and salad.

'Maman! I've asked you before not to make that sort of remark. One day you'll forget yourself and say something in public, and then the takings on the door will be drastically down.'

Colette smiled cynically. 'I don't suppose any of your English clodhoppers would even know what the word *canaille* means.'

'There you go again!' her elder son protested, with still greater vehemence. 'I do wish, Maman, that you'd guard your tongue.'

His mother, having achieved her object of becoming the focus of attention, merely smiled and continued demurely with her meal, making a mental note to tell Mrs Renshaw that open days were no excuse for serving up inferior food. Lettuce and tomatoes without any kind of dressing did not, in Colette's book, constitute a salad. Nor did stewed fruit and that most hideous of English culinary inventions, custard made from tinned powder, merit the name of pudding.

Julian remarked irritably: 'To hear you talk, Rowe, anyone would think that this afternoon's takings were of vital importance to our financial survival.' It was not often that he criticized his brother, but Sophie's departure had left him feeling unexpectedly lonely, and the continued presence of Lisle Ingram kept Rowland occupied and unable to spend much time with other members of the family. Julian was suffering from the pangs of jealousy.

'Never undervalue any source of income, Jules my boy,' Rowland advised sententiously. 'Not if you want to make a banker.' He pushed aside his empty plate and, rising, went to the sideboard, where he helped himself liberally to stewed fruit and custard, much to the horror of his mother. Noticing her expression, he smiled, pausing by her chair to stoop and kiss her. 'It's no good frowning, Maman. You shouldn't have subjected us to the rigours of English nursery fare when we were little if you wanted us to grow up with discriminating palates. It's powdered custard, soggy boiled cabbage and cold rice pudding that's made the English what we are today.'

'I had hoped', Colette retorted acidly, 'that the French half of you and Julian would have predominated and given you both natural good taste.'

Lisle Ingram laughed and asked: 'Are we expected to mingle with the *canaille*, as you call them, Mrs Saxelby? Or do we stay behind the scenes in select seclusion?'

Colette looked horrified. 'Of course we stay behind the scenes. Some of the village ladies take it in turns, on open days, to man the cash-desk, conduct the guided tours and make sure that no one strays into the private apartments.'

Rowland shouted with laughter. 'Maman! You're incorrigible. You make it sound like Woburn or Longleat, with you as the gracious chatelaine, which it isn't at all.' He added for Lisle's benefit: 'The village ladies get well paid for anything they do, and sometimes, if we're here, Jules and I help with the cream teas, served in the conservatory at the side of the house. Maman's idea, and a fairly lucrative source of income, as it turns out, although I must confess that I was against it in the beginning.'

Lisle Ingram pushed aside her plate, still more than half-full of food, at which she had only picked, and asked permission to light a cigarette. She was aware of Rowland's flagging interest but, contrary to his suspicions, she was not yet ready to end the affair. Somehow she doubted that she ever would be and foresaw unhappiness ahead. She had already, secretly, asked her husband for a divorce, knowing that she could never return to Matthew now, however much he still wanted her. Rowland Saxelby, she thought despairingly, did that to women: he spoilt them for other men. And he had no idea how potent his charm was. That, Lisle supposed with an inward sigh, was the basis of his fascination.

She had taken particular care with her appearance today, brushing the red hair into one of the new bouffant styles which suited her better than they did most women, and emphasizing her eyes with green eye-shadow and kohl pencil, close to the obligatory false eyelashes. Her cotton dress, too, was green, worn well above the knee, displaying her elegant legs to advantage. She nevertheless had the feeling that her efforts had been wasted as far as Rowland was concerned. It was Julian who was giving her the admiring glances, whenever he forgot to resent her.

Lisle drew on her cigarette, then stubbed it out, only half-finished, in the ashtray. She knew that Colette did not really approve of smoking at table, although everyone did it, even between courses. But, then, in many ways, Rowland's mother was surprisingly conservative and old-fashioned; surprisingly because Lisle had the mistaken idea that all Frenchwomen were racy and broad-minded and ultra-modern. She had never believed Rowland when he had excused himself from taking her to France each September on the grounds that his grandmother would strongly disappprove of his involvement with a married woman.

Colette, having satisfied herself that everyone had finished, pushed back her chair and rose from the table.

'You are all free to do what you like this afternoon. Tea will be served at four-thirty promptly in the drawing-room. I am going upstairs to see my granddaughter and to let Miss Trim have a well-earned rest. Have you seen Vivien today, Julian?' And she gave a little snort as she said the name. The English habit of giving girls French boys' names never ceased to irritate Colette.

'I'll be up later,' Julian promised and turned to his brother.

157

'How about it, Rowe? Are we going to help with the teas, or do you have something else planned?'

'And this is the Crimson Bedroom, used today as a guest-room for family friends.' The quiet cultured tones of the vicar's wife ushered the party of sightseers into a rather dark room, the chief feature of which was a profusely carved seventeenth-century oak bedstead with decidedly modern coverings in various shades of red. 'You will note', the Vicar's wife continued, 'that the headboard bears the coat of arms of James I and the date 1612. That was the year which saw the death of James's eldest son, Henry, Prince of Wales, during the wedding festivities of his sister, the Princess Elizabeth, and Frederick, Elector Palatine. The succession then devolved upon the younger son, Charles, who became, of course, King Charles I. At the foot of the bed, you will note the oak chest, *circa* 1500, with arched plank top and peg hinges . . .'

Lois hissed in Christine's ear: 'Nasty little room, this. I hope they don't give it to us if ever they invite us to stay.'

'Be quiet,' Christine mumbled, conscious of the Vicar's wife's disapproving eyes fixed on them.

Half an hour later, they emerged from a side-door which led from the old kitchens, that small area carefully preserved in all its Victorian splendour – 'or squalor', Lois had remarked, just a trifle too loudly – into the gardens. The Vicar's wife, looking tired and harassed, informed them all that they were free to wander the grounds, provided that they kept to the paths, and that cream teas were available in the conservatory on the south-facing side of the house. Then she turned wearily back to collect the next party of visitors who were already gathering at the main entrance.

158

'Well, what did you think of it?' Lois asked as they dutifully set off for the Elizabethan garden, with its raised walks, pond and circular mount.

Christine glanced back at the symmetrical façade of honey-coloured stone with its hundreds of windows, all glittering in the afternoon sun. 'It's beautiful,' she answered simply. 'You can't imagine people really live here.'

Lois said prosaically: 'Who cleans all those acres of glass? That's what I want to know.'

'You're impossible!' Christine protested, laughing. 'For God's sake, let's go and have tea before you burst my lovely bubble completely.'

The makeshift tea-room, when they found it, was extremely hot, in spite of all the doors and windows having been left open. Small white wrought-iron tables had been set out between the potted ferns and palms, with collapsible wooden chairs as seats. Three or four young girls from the village were plying their way from kitchen to conservatory and back again with laden trays. One of them was just loading her tray with dirty crockery left by the previous visitors when Lois and Christine sat down.

'Hold on a minute,' she told them cheerfully. 'I'll just get this lot out to the kitchen and then I'll take your order.'

She whisked away on sturdy bare brown legs after giving a half-hearted swipe at the table-top with the cloth she was carrying. Lois brushed a few stray remaining crumbs on to the floor.

'They're not terribly well organized,' she complained.

'What on earth do you expect?' Christine demanded indignantly. 'This isn't a professional operation.'

'Sorry, sorry!' Lois held up both hands in mock surrender. 'I confess that I have committed heresy in daring to criticize the Saxelbys.'

'Oh, shut up and stop playing the fool!' Christine's tone was more acerbic than she had intended, but the afternoon had tired her, emotionally as well as physically. In one of the rooms there had been some framed photographs of two young boys, one of whom was unmistakably Rowland. He must have been about twelve when the picture was taken; already tall and very thin, outgrowing his strength, a gangling adolescent, gauche and very vulnerable. Her heart had twisted in her chest: she wanted to reach out and protect him.

She knew she was being stupid; that that young boy had never been in need of outside protection. He had been cocooned by a loving family and everything that money could, and could not, buy since the day that he was born, and the knowledge made her despise herself even more. But she was as unable to control her feelings for him now as she had been at the time of their first meeting. It was something she would have to live with.

There was a crash from the direction of the kitchens, followed by raised voices and a girl's high-pitched wail: 'It was an *accident*, Mrs Renshaw!' The protest evidently fell on deaf ears, because the scolding continued. A few moments later, there was the sound of noisy sobbing, and the same high-pitched voice, now choked with tears, said angrily: 'I'm going! You can stuff your rotten holiday job! The pay's lousy anyway!'

The visitors were by now craning their necks in an effort to see what was going on, and the other girls waiting at table were giggling self-consciously and looking sheepish.

Lois sighed. 'I rather think that's our waitress who has just quit. Shall we hope for the best or make a strategic move to another table?'

Christine's head was beginning to ache. 'Let's call it a day,' she suggested. 'We can probably find somewhere open for tea in the village.' She picked up her handbag and unhooked her cardigan from the back of her chair. Lois followed suit.

Someone was standing over them. A well-remembered voice urged: 'Please don't go, ladies. A slight contretemps in the kitchen, nothing more. I'm here instead to take your order.'

Christine raised her head slowly, deliberately, forcing herself to appear and sound calm. 'Hello, Rowland,' she said. 'Fancy seeing you again after all these years.'

CHAPTER SIXTEEN

A RED SILK ROPE, with brass fittings at either end, had
been hooked across a narrow passageway leading to
the western side of the house. Rowland lifted one of the
hooks from its eye, screwed into the wall, and motioned
Christine and Lois through. Christine just had time to
register the look of astonishment on the face of the lady
who had shown them round the house, and who was
now conducting another party of eager sightseers into
the Great Hall – nowadays a comfortable sitting-room
– before Rowland opened a door on his left and ushered
the two women inside.

Christine's first jumbled impressions were of a large
room with deep embrasured windows on two sides, of
sunlight flooding the dark blue carpet, of a plethora
of modern chintz-covered settees and armchairs, of
a carved marble surround to the enormous fireplace
and of a number of other, smaller pieces of furniture
and ornaments, which, having seen something of the
rest of the house, she rightly guessed to be valuable
antiques. It was only after a few moments that she
noticed the woman and child seated at a table in one
of the window-bays, and a second, younger woman – a
very beautiful woman, whom she remembered having
seen in Brown's Hotel, four years before – sitting on the
window-seat, balancing a plate containing scone and
butter on her lap. Lisle Talbot. Mrs Matthew Ingram.
So she and Rowland were still friends.

'We shouldn't be here,' she muttered, tugging unhappily at the sleeve of Rowland's shirt.

'Nonsense!' he answered robustly. 'You're an old
friend. Besides, on normal visiting-days, this room is

open to the public. It's just on Bank Holiday Mondays we keep it closed. So, you see, you have every right to be here.' He led the way across what seemed to be an endless stretch of carpet, saying: 'Maman! This is a friend of mine, Christine Chandos. We met some years ago, in Devon. And this is her friend, Mrs . . .?'

'Aylward. Lois Aylward.' Lois, looking for once a little overawed, held out her hand.

Rowland continued: 'My mother, Colette Saxelby. My niece, Vivien. And the lady over there is Lisle Ingram.' He had no recollection that she and Christine and Lois had already met. Christine had already had to prompt his memory about the London meeting. ('Good Lord!' he had said. 'So we did! It was Christmas.' But he had recalled no more than that.)

Lisle Ingram gave no sign of recognition, either, but Christine had the feeling that on her part the lapse of memory was deliberate. Colette shook hands, genuinely bewildered. Where had these two friends of Rowland sprung from?

Rowland gave a pithy description of the circumstances surrounding today's encounter. 'But don't worry, Maman. Julian has calmed Mrs Renshaw down and, although it was a whole tray of crockery which was dropped, there wasn't nearly as much broken as was first suspected. Jules is helping with the teas, in place of the girl who left.'

Colette wiped her grand-daughter's jam-smeared mouth with a table napkin. 'I do so dislike these unpleasantnesses,' she frowned. 'I know some of the girls are inclined to be careless, but Mrs Renshaw should have more patience with them. They do their best.'

'Like you, Maman,' her son agreed dulcetly. 'We all know what a model of patience you can be.' He placed two more chairs at the small circular table and invited Christine and Lois to sit down.

'There is no need to be sarcastic,' Colette reproached him. She smiled distantly at Christine. 'You have not, then, had your tea?'

'That's why I've invited them in here,' Rowland said, before either Christine or Lois could reply. 'I don't think I dare ring at the moment for Mrs Renshaw, so if you'll excuse me I'll just pop along to the kitchens and get what's necessary.'

Once he had gone, there was an awkward silence. Lisle Ingram had withdrawn even deeper into the window-embrasure and was staring idly out into the gardens, completely divorced from the proceedings. Christine suspected that she resented Rowland's display of friendship towards herself. Colette seemed at a loss for something to say. Eventually she murmured: 'How did you come to meet my son in Devon, Miss – er – Chandos? Is that correct?'

'We met at a camping-site four years ago. I was there on holiday with a . . . a friend, and Rowland's tent was pitched next to ours. He was with a girl called Lucy Brennan.'

Colette nodded. 'Ah, yes. Lucy Brennan. Now, that is a name I have heard him mention.' She cast a rather spiteful look at Lisle Ingram. 'He still keeps a photograph of her. Most unusual for Rowland, as I'm sure Lisle here will agree. He keeps it in the drawer of his bedside-table at Inglebatch House. I came across it one day when I was looking for some aspirin,' she added by way of a somewhat lame excuse. After another brief silence, she asked: 'Do you live near here?'

Christine swallowed. Her mouth felt dry. For some reason, she found this little bird-like woman intimidating.

'I live in Weston, but I'm spending the holiday weekend with Lois at Shaftesbury,' she explained. She stumbled on: 'We – er – we saw that the house – I mean Mallerby House – was open today, so . . . well, as I knew Rowland slightly, I . . . we . . . thought it would be interesting to look around.' She glanced desperately at Lois for support, but her friend seemed to be as bereft of ideas for conversation as she was herself. To her great relief, Rowland returned at that moment, carrying a tray on which were plates, cups, saucers, the necessary cutlery and a fresh pot of tea. He put his burden down on a convenient side-table of polished rosewood.

It had been a mistake, Christine thought, to yield to his invitation to take tea with him and his family. She was sure that he had only offered out of politeness, but the temptation had been too great to withstand. Lois, by various grimaces and under-the-table kicks, had tried hard to dissuade her, and she had, of course, been right. The situation was fraught with embarrassment from the very beginning. Nevertheless, Christine could not entirely regret her decision. Here she was, in Rowland's own home, having tea with him and his mother. It would be something to remember in the years ahead.

Rowland, having unloaded his tray and made the necessary dispositions of crockery, drew up another chair and squeezed in between her and Lois. He had begun to regret his impulsive invitation, and on his way back from the kitchen had been wondering how soon he could rid himself of his guests. Now, however, noting Lisle's cold withdrawal and his mother's expression of faint disdain, his anger was aroused. Neither his mother nor his mistress had any business to judge his friends. Whoever he chose to bring into his own house had every right to expect to be treated with courtesy and on their own merits. It was time both women were taught a salutary lesson. He turned to Christine.

'Have you had your holidays this year?'

The question struck none of his hearers as anything more than trite; a gallant attempt at promoting conversation.

'I went to Norfolk for a week in May. Some friends and I hired a boat on the Broads, but so far that's all.'

165

She took a cucumber sandwich and bit into it cautiously. She was very hungry, but afraid of appearing too ravenous.

'You must have a lot of leave left, then,' Rowland said, recollection suddenly, and for no definable reason, becoming total. He explained to his mother: 'Christine works in the employment exchange in Weston. Or, at least, she used to.'

'I still do,' Christine admitted, blushing fiercely as she noted the look of incredulity on Lisle Ingram's lovely face. Even Colette had raised her eyebrows, as though loath to believe that any friend of her son could possibly be a lower-rank civil servant. Rowland, too, noticed the two women's expressions. His resolve hardened.

He asked: 'You haven't been abroad, then?'

Christine laughed. 'I've never been abroad, although I do own a passport. I was going to go to France last year, but in the end it didn't come to anything.'

Rowland drank some tea before replacing his cup in its saucer. 'Then, here's your chance. Take a couple of weeks of that leave you have left and come to Poitou with me and the rest of my family next month.' He ignored his mother's outraged gasp, the way in which Lisle Ingram suddenly sat forward, tense with anger, on the window-seat, Christine's own stunned expression, and continued: 'I think I told you that my French grandmother has a house near Lussac-les-Châteaux. Remember the story about Sir John Chandos?'

'Yes.' Of course she did: she remembered in detail almost every conversation they had ever had. 'B-But I couldn't. I mean . . . Well, I couldn't.'

'Why not?' They might have been alone in the room for all the notice he was taking of the others. 'If you're worried about my grandmother's reactions, don't be. Any friend of mine will be welcomed.' He did not add: 'Provided she isn't married and we sleep in separate rooms.' But in this case that proviso could be taken for granted. Christine's eyes flitted to Colette's face, but Rowland laid a hand on her wrist, compelling her attention. 'No, don't look at my mother. It's nothing to do with her. I'm asking you as *my* guest.'

Christine's mind was whirling, but she was too shrewd not to guess at some of the underlying reasons for this amazing invitation. A love-affair of which he was growing tired was probably the main one. What better or more efficient way to cut it short than to ask another woman, however innocuous the circumstances, to go away with him? But what was she going to reply? What possible answer was there but a polite refusal?

But she did not want to refuse. Understanding his motives, recognizing all the hazards, she still wanted to go. She glanced at Lois, who had suspended mastication and was seated like a statue, her mouth slightly open. No help was to be found there; her friend was, for once, as incapable of making a decision for her as she was herself. Lois could not believe what was happening, either.

A voice inside her head warned: If you don't take this opportunity, you'll regret it for the rest of your life. So she took a deep breath and said unsteadily: 'Th-thank you. I'd . . . I'd very much like to go, if your grandmother really wouldn't mind.'

Rowland smiled. 'Leave Gran'mère to me. We go on September the twelfth. Let me have your address and phone number, and I'll be in touch.' He was already uncomfortably conscious of a sense of deflation. He had scored a victory at the expense of his mother and Lisle, but he had saddled himself with the responsibility of a girl whom he hardly knew, and for whom he felt nothing, for both weeks of the family holiday. Moreover, his mother would probably sulk for the entire fortnight. Perhaps he could placate her with what was partly the truth: that it was a quick, clean, if ruthless, way out of his liaison with Lisle Ingram, of which Colette had

167

never approved. But in the main he was beginning to think that he had scored a Pyrrhic victory. When he was younger, his mother had often warned him against this propensity of his, of acting first and thinking second. In his business dealings, he was shrewd and cautious, a different being, so why did he let it play havoc with his private life? Why could he not exercise the same control in personal relationships as he did when seated behind his desk at Saxelby's, dealing with the world money-markets? It was a mystery, but he doubted if he would ever change now. Character traits and behaviour patterns were generally set by the age of twenty-six.

'Rowland,' Colette said with admirable restraint, 'perhaps you should check with your grandmother first. It would be . . . well . . . polite.'

She was offering him an escape-route and he knew it. Let Christine go, with the promise to contact her once he had spoken to Madame de Bérenger, and there the matter could rest. He knew, as his mother knew, that Christine would never presume to contact him. She was so obviously not the presumptuous sort. Perversely, he was unable to avail himself of this opportunity. It would be mean, underhand, and would diminish him in his own eyes. He had asked her and he must stick by what he had said, however much he might regret it. There was a simple way to settle things.

'A good idea, Maman,' he said, getting to his feet. 'I'll ring Gran'mère now.' He got up, laying a reassuring hand on Christine's shoulder. 'I shan't be more than a few minutes. I'll telephone from the library.'

This time, his departure left not so much an awkward silence as a deep black pit of embarrassment, into which they were all falling. Christine's cheeks were flushed, and her heart was thumping raggedly. She was racked with guilt, knowing that she should have refused at once Rowland's invitation. She had seen for herself the look in his eyes, the moment he had made

168

his extraordinary offer: a look of mingled astonishment and rueful horror. She was so much in love with him, she felt she knew him well, in spite of the brevity of their actual acquaintance. She had recognized from the first that he had this facility to surprise himself, as well as other people, so she should have said no.

Her friend's glassy-eyed look of disapproval told her that Lois thought the same. Lois was disappointed in her lack of backbone, in her inability to resist making the wrong decision in order to pursue a ridiculous dream. As for Colette Saxelby, she looked not only agitated, but also angry, as well she might be, when the rashness of her son was backed by the insensitivity of his guest. She had a right not to have her family holiday spoiled by this cuckoo in the nest.

I can't help it, Christine thought. I have to take this one heaven-sent chance to get to know him. And perhaps – who knows? – a fortnight in Rowland's company might prove that this is just a stupid infatuation which close proximity will cure. But she did not really believe it. The only real cure for her was never to see him again, so she was simply flying in the face of Providence.

Colette lifted her grand-daughter down from her chair, set her on two sturdy, if as yet unsteady, feet, and said to Lisle Ingram: 'Will you ring the bell for me, please? I think it's time Vivien went back to Miss Trim.'

Lisle uncoiled herself from the window-seat and trod elegantly across to the push-button bell beside the fireplace. She ignored Christine and Lois with a thoroughness that made them invisible. Silence descended once again.

Rowland and Mrs Renshaw, the latter looking hot and flustered, arrived together. Colette requested the attendance of the nanny.

'As soon as you can find her, please, Mrs Renshaw. Vivien's rather tired.'

The housekeeper withdrew, relieved that she had not been hauled over the coals for the row earlier with

Marlene in the kitchen. Rowland advanced into the room.

'Well,' he said, smiling down at Christine, 'that's all fixed. Gran'mère will be delighted to see you.'

'You've done it now,' Lois observed, easing the Austin out of the main gate of Mallerby House and into Harcourt Lane. A few hundred yards along, she carefully negotiated a second turning into Hinton Malsherbes High Street and settled herself more comfortably behind the wheel for the straight run to the A30, the main Shaftesbury road. Irritated by Christine's lack of response, she said again: 'You've really done it. Whatever made you accept?'

'Why shouldn't I?' Christine asked defensively. 'It's a once-in-a-lifetime chance to see not merely a foreign country, but also life as the inhabitants live it, not just the tourists' France. I should have been a fool not to go.'

'Yes, you would, if that was your real reason,' Lois answered tartly. 'But it's not.' She paused for a moment to concentrate on overtaking a cyclist, then went on: 'Chris, what do you think will happen at the end of this visit?' And, without waiting for a reply, added: 'He'll go his way and you'll go yours, back to Weston-on-the-mud and the good old Min of Lab, the difference being that, whereas he won't give you another thought, your torch will be burning brighter than ever. And what hope do you have of leading a normal life while you're still feeling like that?'

Christine laughed shakily. 'What do you call a normal life? Marriage? Children? Lots of women never have either.'

'Only because they don't get the chance.' Lois trod viciously on the accelerator as the road once more stretched clear ahead.

Christine said quietly: 'You're behind the times, love. This is 1964. Things are changing, particularly for women. They're wearing topless dresses in the King's Road, and Maria Bueno wore shocking-pink frilly knickers at Wimbledon this year. And last year there was a good deal more openly expressed sympathy for Christine Keeler than would have been possible a decade ago. Women and domesticity aren't necessarily going to go hand-in-hand in the future.'

'I wouldn't be too sure of that,' Lois retorted. 'Climates of opinion don't alter that drastically. And, anyway, you want nothing more than to be Rowland Saxelby's wife and have his children. All I'm saying, Chris, is don't, for God's sake, go on cutting yourself off from other relationships to pursue a pipe-dream. Accepting this invitation, which anyone could see was made on the spur of the moment, is only prolonging the agony.'

'You were the one', Christine pointed out, 'who said wouldn't it be a lark if we bumped into Rowland. Now, admit it.'

'I know.' Lois slowed down as they approached the major junction with the A30. 'I wonder if there's any insanity in our family? Or in yours?' She eased her way out into the main flow of traffic heading east. 'Chris, if you love me, and to ease my conscience for having suggested this ill-advised trip, as soon as you get home tomorrow, write to Rowland Saxelby and tell him you've changed your mind.'

CHAPTER SEVENTEEN

'BUT WHAT does it have to do with cows?' Christine asked, puzzled.

Rowland laughed. 'Nothing. Plateau de Millevaches doesn't mean the Plateau of a Thousand Cows. In this case, *vaches* is a corruption of an old Celtic word, *batz*, which means a spring. The Plateau of a Thousand Springs. The Creuse, the Vienne and the Vézère are just three of the rivers that originate up there.' And he nodded northward, to the high tableland of granite rocks and dark forbidding pine-forests.

They were standing at one of the viewpoints of the Suc-au-May, the summit of a ring of moorland, the Massif de Monédières. Below them, great carpets of heather and bilberries glowed richly purple in the afternoon light. Rowland glanced at his watch.

'We'll have to be going soon,' he said, 'if we're to get home with comfortable time to shower and change before dinner.'

'Just five more minutes,' Christine pleaded. 'It's so beautiful.'

They had set out early that morning and driven over a hundred kilometres south from Lussac-les-Châteaux, down the N147 and N20, stopping for lunch in Limoges. For Christine, her head full of the Black Prince and the sack of the medieval town by the English in 1370, the modern, rather characterless industrial city was a disappointment. Rowland had said that there was no time to visit the Cathédrale St-Etienne, as he wanted to push on south, but he had insisted on buying her a little silver enamelled brooch, Limoges being as famous for its enamels as for its porcelain. She had wanted to refuse it, but he seemed to regard it as such a slight gift that she was afraid of appearing foolish if she did so.

Christine had been at Château Bérenger for almost a week now, and was enjoying herself as much and as little as she had expected to. She had been extremely disconcerted, on her arrival, to discover that Rowland's grandmother, Madame de Bérenger, an active lively-minded sixty-four-year-old, had completely misread the situation and regarded her as Rowland's future wife. She trusted that, by now, either Rowland or his mother had disabused Madame's mind of the idea. But, even if they had, Madame continued to treat her with courtesy and distinction as though she were a highly important guest.

Colette, on the other hand, was coldly polite, making it plain that Christine was there on sufferance and that the situation would never arise again. Rowland had made a fool of himself by asking her, but he was not stupid enough to make the same mistake twice. At least, that was the message which came across to Christine. It was only what she had anticipated in the light of her own parents' reaction to her news.

'You want to be careful of that sort of man,' her mother had told her anxiously. 'Pots of money, old established names. They think they own the earth, that kind, and everyone on it, especially women. I wish you hadn't said you'd go.'

Her father had endorsed that opinion, although unable to prevent himself boasting to his friends about his daughter's 'aristocratic connections'. Christine had tried to allay their fears by pointing out that it was a family holiday; that there would be others besides herself and Rowland staying at the château.

Quite how many, she had not been prepared for. Apart from Rowland, Colette and Julian Saxelby, with Vivien and Miss Trim in tow, Sophie, for some reason best known to herself, had also elected to come along. Then there were the French relatives: Colette's brother, Lucien, and his wife, Solange, and their three-year-old son, Giles, whose arrival after thirteen years of childless marriage had delighted not only his parents but also his grandmother, who had by then begun to despair of a male heir in the direct Bérenger line. Christine had been a little overwhelmed, particularly as everyone talked colloquial French at break-neck speed, and she found herself in danger of being left out in the cold. This might, indeed, have been the case but for Sophie, who had no intention of ever acquiring the smallest smattering of any foreign language, and the vigilance of both Rowland and his grandmother.

'We will speak English for our guests,' Madame had decreed each night at dinner. 'It will be a good chance for Lucien and Solange to get some practice.'

Madame herself spoke almost faultless English, having had, so she confided to Christine, a succession of Scottish nannies and an English governess. 'A Miss Bryanston. A most formidable lady.'

Rowland had gone out of his way to entertain and protect her, taking her, from day one, on trips around the neighbouring countryside and making certain that she was always seated next to him at meal-times. He watched his mother like a hawk, deflecting her shafts of sarcasm and barbs of wit, intended for Christine, either on to himself or on to his brother. Julian, amiable and uncritical, abetted Rowland as much as he could.

He had, in fact, been quite glad of Christine's presence, once his wife had decided to accompany him. It was someone for Sophie to talk to; someone of her own age and nationality and sex. Why she had made the decision to be with him this year, Julian had no idea, nor did he intend probing too deeply. He knew that there were other men – she made no secret of the fact – and suspected that one of these affairs might have gone wrong.

174

'Why do you put up with her?' Colette had demanded, and he had told her about Sophie's threat regarding Vivien.

'If you want the Saxelby name dragged through the courts and the Sunday newspapers in a nasty legal wrangle, then I don't,' he had retorted.

His mother had said no more.

Sophie, however, had shown no inclination to make a friend of Christine, perhaps because Rowland monopolized Christine's company. Not that there was anything to be made from that, she thought sadly. His whole attitude was entirely brotherly. There had been nothing, during all their expeditions, not one single incident, which could be construed as even remotely lover-like.

They had gone to Poitiers and visited the twelfth-century Eglise Notre-Dame-de-la-Grande, with its elaborate sculpted façade and tympanum of the last Judgement. They had driven out beyond the modern industrial sprawl and made a gallant attempt to retrace the lines of battle, when the English, under the Black Prince, and the Gascons, led by the Captal de Buch, had crashed down through the Maupertuis vineyards to victory over the French.

'And a fat lot of good it did them, in the end,' Christine had observed. 'A hundred years later, they were out of France for ever, and the Angevin empire was finished.'

Rowland had shown her the memorial at Lussac to the man he half-mockingly insisted on calling 'your ancestor, Sir John': Constable John Chandos, seneschal of Poitou. 'The French respect his memory,' he had said. 'They like a man who can fight and who is also a man of honour.'

'Nothing to do with me,' Christine had protested, shaking her head.

Today's trip was the longest they had done together, and she was beginning to feel guilty about taking up so much of Rowland's time. Last night, in the salon after

175

dinner, she had overheard Lucien complaining to his sister that he had hardly seen his nephew at all this week. Her school-girl French had been good enough for that; and, although Colette's answer had been less easy to understand, the tone of voice had interpreted the words for her.

She said now, as the Citroën sped northwards along the N20 towards Limoges: 'Don't you think you should be spending more time with your family? I think I've got the lie of the land around the château, and as long as I don't stray too far I shall be quite all right. I'm perfectly well aware why you invited me in the first place and I've been very grateful for this chance to see France at first hand. But you don't have to feel responsible for me. I'm able to take care of myself.'

Rowland glanced in his driving-mirror at the lorry behind him, whose driver seemed perfectly willing to commit suicide by trying to overtake, accelerated rapidly and asked: 'Has someone been getting at you? Uncle Lucien? Aunt Solange? My mother?'

'No, of course not.' Christine closed her eyes as they fought for right of way with an oil-tanker entering the outskirts of Limoges. She would never get used, she thought, to the French mode of driving, and when he was in France Rowland's Gallic blood gained ascendancy over the Anglo-Saxon. 'For God's sake!' she breathed, as he blithely ignored the tanker's blaring horn. 'I don't think my nerves can stand it.'

Rowland took a quick glance at her face and slowed down, allowing the oil-tanker to pass him and ignoring its driver's two-fingered gesture. 'Sorry,' he said contritely. 'I forget you're not used to all this.'

'If you mean I haven't got a death-wish, yes, you're right.'

They both laughed, and some of the tension which had been between them ever since the start of the holiday suddenly snapped. For the first time since she had known him, Christine felt completely relaxed in his company. We could be good friends, she thought; and if it were all that Fate allowed her she would be willing to settle for that.

Something of the same sort seemed to cross Rowland's mind. He said: 'I like being with you, Chris.' It was the first time he had used the diminutive of her name. 'Nobody's twisting my arm. You're good company, and we like the same things. Take no notice of anything anyone else might say.' He did not mention his mother specifically, but he did not have to. Christine knew who he meant.

'OK,' she answered simply. 'I won't. It's been a lovely six days, and I've enjoyed myself immensely. Thank you. I shall look forward to next week. I'm sure it will be just as much fun.'

Except for Rowland's muttered imprecations at the lack of a bypass, they maintained a companionable silence until he had negotiated Limoges's tangle of streets and they were once more travelling at speed along the N147. Then he started to sing 'Auprès de ma Blonde' at the top of his voice, and Christine joined in. After that, they went in quick succession through 'Frère Jacques', 'Sur le pont d'Avignon' and 'La Normandie', by which time they had exhausted almost their entire repertoire of French songs, learned at school, and were nearing Bellac. Christine had discovered that Rowland had a strong tenor voice, even though he sang slightly off key, and he had found that she was even more fun to be with than he had thought. She was completely unlike any other woman he had ever met, offering him companionship without any of the flirtatiousness displayed by the women he generally encountered. He recalled that he had thought otherwise during that holiday in Devon, and decided that he must have misread the signs. Four years was a long time, and his memory was imperfect. He wondered idly why she had broken with Russell Jennings.

It was nearly seven o'clock when they drove across the bridge at Lussac and past the inn, whose sign was the heraldic device of Sir John Chandos, a red wedge on a white ground. A little further on, Rowland swung the Citroën to the left, along the narrow road which led to Château Bérenger, set on its mound above the surrounding fields and woods. The car came to rest in a cobbled courtyard where horses had once been exercised, but whose stables nowadays housed a different means of family transport, most of them having been converted into garages. Rowland glanced at his watch.

'If we get our skates on, we should be ready by eight.' Without any warning, he leaned across and kissed her lightly on the cheek. 'I'll see you at dinner.'

The room allotted to Christine was on the first floor of one of the three turrets, with their pointed orange-tiled roofs, which decorated the western façade of the château. It looked out on to the sweep of gravel drive which led up the hill to the main door. Château Bérenger had once been heavily fortified, with a moat encompassing the base of the mound, but today it was a peaceful family home, the defensive ditch long since drained and overgrown.

Christine, seated at the dressing-table, waiting for the sound of the gong which would summon her down to dinner, thought about that kiss and wondered what it meant. A sudden excess of brotherly affection? There was no other explanation, and yet . . . and yet . . . There had been a warmth in it which it was not easy to ignore. She stared moodily at her reflection in the mirror.

The face which looked back at her was the same as it had always been: pleasant, open, frank – but unmemorable. The mouth was still a little too wide, the nose too straight for prettiness, the blue eyes fiercely direct beneath thick brows. She had back-combed her hair into a fashionable 'beehive', but the style did not really suit her. She toyed with the idea of brushing it out and leaving it straight, but felt too tired and, strangely, too depressed to bother, although she had at least twenty minutes in hand. She had bathed and changed tonight like an automaton.

There was a knock at her door. She called, 'Come in!' not knowing who to expect, and was surprised when it turned out to be Sophie. They had exchanged so few words, and those had been of such a mundane nature, that the present friendly overture was all the more unexpected.

Sophie said, 'Hi!' – she was addicted to this particular American form of greeting – and perched herself on the end of the bed, swinging long silk-clad legs. Stockings had not yet generally been replaced by tights, and as the skirt of Sophie's short green evening dress was several inches higher than the accepted length – she was always ahead of the current trend – Christine had an uninterrupted view of stocking-top, bare leg and suspender. Sophie went on: 'I hope you had a better day than I did. Darling, this place is the absolute pits. Worse even than Mallerby. At least, there, I can understand the natives.'

'Why did you come, then?' Christine asked, trying to suppress her natural antagonism.

She was answered by a shrug. 'Oh ... a man, darling. What else? His wife found out about our little affair, and things had turned a bit ugly. It seemed wise to get out of London for a while till things cool down.' She laughed at the expression on Christine's face. 'Oh dear! Have I shocked you? Sorry!' There was a moment's silence before she added: 'You're nuts about him, aren't you?'

Christine felt her colour rising. 'What do you mean?' she demanded stiffly.

'Oh, come off it! I'm not a fool! Rowland. You're in love with him, it's obvious.' Sophie tilted her head to one side and regarded Christine shrewdly. 'There's nothing to be ashamed of in that. Most women are, although I must admit I can't see the attraction.' She said this so vehemently that Christine was immediately suspicious that Rowland had, at some time, rejected her advances. The idea of an affair with his brother's wife would repel him. Sophie added pityingly: 'You're not his type, but I guess you know that already. He likes more glamour.' She pursed her lips judiciously. 'Mind you, something could be made of you. More make-up, smarter clothes, different hairstyle.' She slid off the bed and walked across to stand behind Christine, resting her hands lightly on her shoulders and considering her image in the triple bevel-edged mirror.

Christine, feeling like a specimen under a microscope, dutifully submitted to the scrutiny and awaited the verdict, sadly conscious of her shortcomings and wondering if she were beyond all hope. Two firm hands were placed beneath her chin and her head moved up and down, from right to left. The banging of the five-minute warning-gong interrupted Sophie's deliberations.

'No time to do anything now,' she said, 'but if you're game we could come upstairs and try after dinner. The others will only be making up a table for bridge, or something equally boring. What do you say?'

Christine hesitated. She had no particular desire to be made over into a new, more updated model, but there was some truth in Sophie's implication that the evenings dragged. Rowland usually played bridge with his mother, uncle and grandmother, and French television seemed to be comprised mainly of variety programmes and incomprehensible game-shows. 'All right,' she agreed reluctantly. 'If you want to.'

'It'll be fun,' Sophie assured her as the second and final gong sounded. 'Come on. We'll go down together. A united front of blooming English woman-hood.'

* * *

Rowland heard the first gong just as he was slipping into his dinner-jacket, cursing, as he always did, at his grandmother's antiquated rule about dressing formally each evening. When it was only the family, what did it matter? But Marie de Bérenger, born Marie Ducrois, and of an even more ancient lineage than her late husband, lived by a set of rules and regulations which made the laws of the Medes and Persians seem positively effete. Meals were served on time, and latecomers went without; the correct dress was worn, and everyone sat down to table in the big, gloomy and forbidding dining-room. There was none of this lax modern nonsense of lolling around in easy-chairs and eating off laps. Servants were treated with consideration and respect, and there were never any raised voices. Politeness and deference were her watchwords. But the strictest rule of all, deviation from which was denied all pardon, was no copulation beneath Madame's roof, except between man and wife.

It was this enforced celibacy which Rowland found irksome; the one thing which, for him, spoiled the annual family holiday. He had never, for instance, been able to bring Lisle Ingram to the château. His grandmother would have frowned on any liaison of his with a married woman. Madame was neither a fool nor a prude: she knew these things happened and was secretly proud of her eldest grandson's masculinity. But family life and the family home were sacred. What Rowland did elsewhere was his business. Beneath her roof and in the bosom of the family, he played by her rules or not at all.

The second gong sounded. Rowland sighed and made his way downstairs. He was a man who needed women, their love, their company, in bed and out; a certain type of woman, glamorous, intelligent, sophisticated, not too virtuous and preferably married. That way, there could be no awkward talk about weddings.

He sighed again and opened the door to the main salon, where everyone assembled before each meal. Christine, seated on the arm of a brocaded couch, sipping her pre-dinner drink, looked up and smiled. He crossed the room to stand beside her.

182

HE THOUGHT SHE WAS looking rather pale. She seemed to have lost the colour which the day's outing had put into her cheeks, as if something had happened to upset or disturb her. He cast a suspicious glance at his mother, but Colette, extremely elegant in a plain black shift and the famous Saxelby pearls, was deep in conversation with her brother and, judging by their heated exchange, had been so for some time.

'Nonsense!' Lucien was saying. 'France under de Gaulle just gives the impression of being a booming nation. All right, I grant you that this administration has created new industry, modernized farming, and that the per-capita GNP is a quarter higher again than six years ago, before le Vieux came to power, but . . .' His voice rumbled steadily on, clashing now and then with Colette's, as she vigorously contested some point that he was making.

Sophie, seated on the couch beside her husband, yawned with boredom. Rowland looked down at Christine and winked.

'I wish I could understand what they're talking about,' she told him guiltily. 'I feel ashamed that my French is so abysmal.'

'For God's sake, why?' Sophie cut in. 'Everyone knows English is the international language.'

'Everyone', Rowland answered coolly, 'except the French.' He laid a hand on Christine's shoulder. 'You're looking tired. I hope the day hasn't worn you out. Perhaps it was too far to go.'

'No, no!' she said quickly, resisting the impulse to lay one of her hands over his. 'I loved every minute of it. Thank you once again.'

'My pleasure,' he answered, and found that he really meant it, wondering what it was that he felt for this girl who, until this week, had been a comparative stranger.

He wasn't in love with her, but then, if he were truthful, he had never been in love in his life. He thought he was, of course, at the beginning of each new affair, but the feeling did not last, rarely surviving more than a year. Lisle's four-year reign had been exceptional, and had been largely due to her own efforts to keep the relationship going. Rowland recalled kissing his first girl at the age of five, in the playground of the Hinton Malsherbes village school, now threatened with closure. Later, he had gone to prep school and then on to Clifton College. And how he had hated those years spent exclusively in the company of his own sex. For him, women made the world a more exciting place. In that, he was a true Frenchman; a true descendant of Henry of Navarre.

None of which shed any light on his feelings for Christine Chandos; feelings which confused him and therefore made him uneasy. When she looked up and smiled at him, he felt a sudden surge of affection; but precisely what sort of affection, he could not say. He was relieved when the salon door opened and his grandmother made her stately entrance, the signal that dinner was about to be served.

Christine was, as usual, seated next to him, but tonight it was Lucien, not Julian, who was on her other side. Lucien de Bérenger was not normally a very conversable man, except on financial matters, nor was his English of the best, but this evening he seemed to be willing to make an effort, monopolizing Christine's attention and making enquiries about her day. Rowland found himself forced to talk to his Aunt Solange, a rather dull woman with very few interests outside her husband, home and, more recently, her child. In fact her conversation these days was centred almost exclusively on little Giles; his precocity, his winning ways, his undoubtedly brilliant future. Rowland became more and more irritated each time he turned to Christine, only to discover that she was still talking to his uncle.

'Well, I suppose', he heard her saying once, in that earnest way of hers, 'that English history is more bound up with France than French history is with England, if you see what I mean . . .'

And another time, with one of her unexpected mischievous bursts of laughter: 'Oh, I don't think I'd like to do *that*!' Like to do what? he wondered, straining his ears for some sort of clue, but hearing only how his cousin Giles had taken his first tottering steps at nine months old. He dug his fork viciously into his *pompe aux grattons* and silently wished both his aunt and uncle anywhere but where they were.

Family meals at Château Bérenger were kept simple – another of Madame's draconian decrees. Dinner was never more than three courses, ending with either a sweet or cheese. Tonight it was a *poirat*, a pear tart, and as the last mouthful was finished Madame de Bérenger rose to her feet.

'Coffee in the salon,' she said in English. 'The gentlemen have ten minutes, no more. I want my revenge for that defeat at bridge yesterday evening. Colette, this time you and Lucien will play against Rowland and me.' She pushed back her chair, and the rest of the women did the same. No one dreamed of arguing, although Rowland swore under his breath.

As she mounted the main staircase in the wake of her hostess, Colette and Solange de Bérenger, Christine found her arm seized and pinched conspiratorially by Sophie.

'Don't forget,' Sophie hissed in her ear. 'As soon as they start playing bridge and Julian settles down in front of the television, we'll go to my bedroom. It'll be quite an interesting challenge to see what I can do with you. It might make you-know-who sit up and take notice, at least.'

Christine looked doubtfully at her reflection in the long pier-glass in the room which Sophie, to her great disgust, shared with Julian. There were no separate bedrooms for married couples at Château Bérenger, just as there were no double rooms for those unwed.

'Well?' Sophie asked. 'What do you reckon?'

Christine was unsure. She certainly looked different. For a start, she was wearing a very short white chiffon frock by Courrèges and soft white leather boots which, Sophie assured her, were absolutely *de rigueur* in London just at present. Her hair had been brushed out over a wide elasticated band which seemed to Christine to come halfway down her forehead. But it was her face that had suffered the brunt of Sophie's ministrations. Her own pink lipstick had been replaced by one which was almost white, a pale gash in a mask of panstick. Her eyes, beneath heavily blue-shadowed lids, were fringed with thick, false, slightly furry lashes. She barely recognized herself, and her first impulse was to burst out laughing. Clearly, however, this would give offence, so she took refuge in silence.

'Well?' Sophie repeated impatiently. 'Don't you think it's an improvement?'

'I . . . I don't know,' Christine answered uncertainly. 'Do . . . do you think so?'

Sophie raised her eyes to the stuccoed ceiling. 'For God's sake! Yes, of course I do! Why else would I have taken all this trouble? Wait till Rowland sees you. You'll knock his eyes out.' She added with unusual generosity: 'Actually, that dress suits you better than it does me. You're slimmer.'

The bedroom door opened, and Julian walked in. 'Soph! What on earth are you doing up here all this time?' he began. 'Gran'mère has noticed that you're absent ...' He broke off as his gaze alighted on Christine. 'Good heavens!' He pursed his lips and whistled.

'There you are, you see!' Sophie was triumphant. She normally took very little notice of her husband's opinions, but on this occasion he was a man, giving a man's reactions. 'Julian approves, don't you, darling?'

'Ra-ther. Wouldn't have known you, Christine,' he added with an attempt at gallantry which somehow missed its mark.

Christine felt more doubtful than ever. When she looked at Sophie, she had no great faith in Julian's judgement.

'Come on,' Sophie said. 'Let's go downstairs to the salon. Have they finished playing bridge yet?' Her husband nodded. 'Right! Let's go and give them all an eyeful.'

Christine cast another dubious glance at her reflection, then followed Sophie and Julian out of the room. At the top of the main staircase was a huge triptych in oils, depicting Henry IV of France and his two wives: the beautiful dazzling Marguerite de Valois on his right, and the plainer frumpier Marie de Médicis on his left. It had been painted for one of the eighteenth-century Bérengers, proud of his antecedents, and had probably been posed by models, bearing little resemblance to the real people. Nevertheless, it was a striking piece of work, the colours glowing on the canvas and the features seeming almost alive. As she passed it, Christine had the uncomfortable feeling that the eyes of the two women were mocking her, warning her that there was no sure way of harnessing the affection of the Bourbon male.

As Sophie opened the door of the main salon, Christine could hear the low-voiced hum of conversation, confirming Julian's assertion that bridge was over for the evening. When Madame was playing, the television set at the far end of the room had to be turned down as low as possible and all verbal exchanges made in whispers. Sophie pushed the door as wide as possible and announced at the top of her voice: 'Ladies and gentlemen! May I present the new revamped Miss Christine Chandos!'

Christine felt her cheeks go scarlet. If she had had any idea that Sophie intended making such a production of her entrance, she would have refused to accompany her. As it was, she was forced to make the best of a bad job and try to look as unselfconscious as possible.

Reactions were mixed. Lucien looked admiring; Solange nodded in gentle approval, as though Christine had merely changed her dress; Colette raised her eyebrows in astonishment; and Madame de Bérenger peered down her nose.

'I think you looked very nice as you were, my dear,' she commented in her careful, slightly accented English.

Rowland said nothing, his face impassive, as he stared at her from beneath his straight dark brows. He took a cigarette from a silver box on the inlaid marquetry table next to his chair, lit it and exhaled a cloud of smoke. He felt angry – blazingly angry – that Christine had allowed his empty-headed sister-in-law to lure her into this foolish scheme, and needed a moment or two to bring his emotions under control. These were so strong that they left no room for surprise that they should, indeed, be so, or for self-analysis as to the reason why. He only knew that he resented her making an exhibition of herself, on her behalf as well as on his own.

He got abruptly to his feet, stubbing out his half-smoked cigarette in the ashtray next to the cigarette-box, and crossed the room to her side.

'Let's go for a walk in the gardens,' he said. 'It's a very mild night.'

'It's dark,' she protested, sensing his disapproval, in spite of his smiling face, from the rough pressure of his fingers on her arm.

'All the more romantic,' he answered; and, behind his back, Christine saw Sophie's triumphant thumbs-up gesture.

'It's not as mild as you think, Rowland,' Colette intervened hastily. She was looking alarmed.

Her mother overruled her. 'Nonsense! It is a beautiful evening. Take your young lady outside, *mon cher*, but don't be too long.'

As the salon door closed behind Rowland and a reluctant Christine, Colette, lapsing into French, remarked bitterly: 'Will you please rid yourself, Maman, of this ridiculous notion that Christine Chandos is Rowland's young lady – a loaded phrase, if ever I heard one. She is a friend – hardly that, if the truth be told – and nothing more.'

'I like her,' Madame pronounced, holding out her glass imperatively towards her son for another drink. 'And it is high time that Rowland was married. Chandos is a name known and respected in these parts, and love is not always necessary for a successful marriage.' She nodded thoughtfully, sipping her Pernod. 'Christine will suit Rowland very well. She is the right woman for him. She will make him happy, and he'll be a fool if he lets her slip through his fingers.' Madame leaned back in her chair, crossing her still shapely legs. 'But whether or not *he* will make *her* happy is an entirely different matter.'

It was warm in the gardens, although a faint breeze was blowing. The skirt of the white chiffon dress, what there was of it, was pressed against Christine's legs. As soon as they were outside, Rowland had released her arm and was now walking beside her, silent, making no attempt at conversation.

She said, in a desperate effort to break the tension: 'You were right. It is mild. I thought I should need a coat in this dress, but I'm perfectly warm.'

Rowland stopped, swinging round to face her.

'Why the hell did you let her do it?' he demanded furiously. 'Why did you let Sophie make a fool of you like this?'

Christine was suddenly out of her depth, floundering in a sea of emotion. She was puzzled by the violence of his reaction, and was not helped by his own obvious bewilderment. She could hear in the uncertainty of his voice that he had no idea why he was behaving like this.

'It was just a bit of fun,' she said, and was annoyed with herself at the apologetic note she had struck. 'Sophie was bored. She thought – probably with good reason – that I'm a bit old-fashioned in the way I dress. Provincial fashions are never abreast of the London ones. I don't see what harm we've done, to you or to anyone else.' She was doing it again, being defensive, placatory. She tried a change of tack. 'And, anyway, how I dress is my business. My appearance has nothing to do with you. You're not my keeper. Just because you've invited me to your grandmother's home for a holiday doesn't give you the right to criticize me, provided that I do nothing uncivil.' Now she was blustering: she could detect the hectoring tone in her voice. She fell silent, realizing that she could not win; that a quiet, remote, slightly disdainful withdrawal was her most potent weapon, something she was unlikely to achieve. She was too involved with him, cared too much for what he thought, to be sufficiently detached.

But he must have felt the justice of some of her arguments, at least, because he said more gently: 'I'm sorry if I was rude. But you really looked very nice as you were. You don't need a woman like Sophie to take you in hand. You must be able to see for yourself the sort of creature she is. Brash. Vulgar. You're an intelligent person. I hate it', he went on, growing angry again, 'when people are afraid to be themselves.'

She knew she should walk away from him; go back

indoors and leave him to work off his bad temper and his unreasonableness by himself, but she was unable to move. She loved him too much to make any sort of grand gesture, which was ridiculous when she would probably, after this holiday, never see him again. In addition, she was desperately trying to discover what it was that had provoked his outburst. It wasn't as though he cared for her in any sort of way.

Rowland was as confused as she was. His anger seemed totally irrational. He liked Christine; during this past week he had found her fun to be with, but nothing more. Yet, in spite of that knowledge, he had the impulse to kiss her. He leaned towards her, gathering her into his arms, and was startled by the warmth of her response. Her body pressed close to his as she returned his kiss. He could feel her trembling.

The grass was bone-dry after the recent weeks of drought. The trees which were set along the edge of the lawn, although just starting to yellow, had not yet shed their leaves and screened them from the windows of the house. To make love here was, Rowland told himself, foolhardy. What if someone should decide to follow them? His mother, perhaps, or Julian, not noted for his tact. But it was no more than a momentary consideration, before he was lost in the tide of his own sexual needs and passions: carried, for the moment, far beyond caring what anyone might see or think. He was not even aware of Christine's sharp cry of pain, and it was only afterwards, as he rolled clear of her, gasping, on to the grass, that he was shocked to realize that she had been a virgin.

At first, he wouldn't admit it; would not let himself admit something which he found so hard to believe. When he had first met Christine, she had been on holiday with Russell Jennings. She had told him that they were nearly engaged. He had assumed automatically, therefore, that they were lovers. It had not occurred to him, even though they had used separate tents, that they were not sleeping together. He had been to bed with so many girls that he had imagined they were all the same. But he had been mistaken. How could he have been such a fool?

'Why on earth didn't you tell me that I was the first?' he whispered angrily, as she began tidying herself, searching around on the grass for scattered items of clothing. 'Why did you let me do it?'

'I wanted you to,' she answered with simple dignity. 'It isn't your fault I didn't enjoy it as much as I'd expected. No one had told me it would hurt.'

'I shouldn't have done it at all,' he answered quietly. 'God knows, I've no excuse. Can you forgive me?'

'There's nothing to forgive,' she said. 'One word from me, the slightest effort on my part to repulse you, would have stopped you. I know that. But I didn't want to stop you, so I'm just as much to blame for what's happened. And, anyway, there's no harm done. No one gets pregnant at their first attempt, do they?'

'I believe the odds against it are pretty high.' He tried to smile, trying to work out what had come over him, he who was usually so careful about these things. It seemed like a moment of blind madness, brought on by his own bodily needs and Christine's proximity in the dark deserted garden. If only she hadn't allowed Sophie to dress her up in this stupid tarty fashion! If only he hadn't lost his temper and suggested going outside! But it was too late for 'if onlys' now. The damage had been done.

He got to his feet and reached down a hand, helping her up.

'Are you all right?' he asked.

She nodded. 'Yes, I'm fine. We'd better go back into the house. They'll be wondering where we've got to.'

CHAPTER NINETEEN

IT WAS ALREADY DARK when she left work, the November evening closing in early over the town. There was something desolate, Christine thought, about a seaside resort in winter: the shuttered arcades, the deserted promenade, the wind-swept sands. The donkeys, which carried the shrieking delighted children up and down the beach in summer, had gone to their winter quarters; the pier was empty, the ticket-office closed; and, at high tide, the waves crashed against the sea-wall in a flurry of spume. Only the seagulls remained the same, as they screamed their way inland, scavenging for food.

As she hurried along Walliscote Road, buffeted by a sudden squall of rain, she noticed that some of the lighted shop-windows were already displaying Christmas goods. She shivered. She did not want to think about Christmas – at least, not yet. First, she had the present to get through. She rounded the corner into Clarence Road North and was almost knocked off her feet as the wind raced up from the sea-front to meet her. The leafless trees in Clarence Park thrashed the air helplessly with thin arthritic limbs.

She pushed open the wrought-iron garden-gate and made for the outside flight of steps leading to the first-floor flat. As she paused on the stone landing, scrabbling in the depths of her handbag to find her key, she could hear music coming, very faintly, from the flat downstairs. After a moment, she identified it as Sandie Shaw singing 'Always Something There to Remind Me', and for some stupid reason it brought her close to tears. Taking a grip on herself, she inserted her key, turned it and stepped into the lighted hallway.

'You're late,' her mother called from the kitchen. 'Your dad's been home for ten minutes. Hurry up, tea's nearly ready. Don't bother titivating your hair.'

Christine went into her bedroom and took off her coat, hanging it neatly in the wardrobe, and putting away her scarf and gloves. Then she went over to the dressing-table and studied her face carefully in the mirror. She looked pasty, her skin a dirty putty colour in the electric light. She had lost weight, too, which was ironic, considering what lay ahead of her in the coming months. The doctor had said that it was perfectly normal; just the morning sickness taking its toll. She patted her cheeks to bring a little colour into them, before going into the dining-room, where her father was already seated at the table, impatient to begin his meal. The television was on in one corner: BBC News, reporting the outcome of the American presidential election.

'Johnson in again by a mile,' Robert Chandos said with satisfaction. 'That Barry Goldwater never stood a chance.'

Christine smiled without really hearing what he was saying. She had too many other things on her mind.

Her mother bustled in with the evening meal: lamb chops and mint sauce, boiled potatoes and cabbage swimming in gravy.

'There you are,' she said, adding as she did almost every night: 'Get that down you and you won't be doing so badly.' She went back to the kitchen to fetch her own plate. When she returned, she and Christine sat down together.

There was silence for a few moments, except for the droning of the television set and the rattling of the window-frames as they were hit by a gust of wind. Then Gwen Chandos said: 'I phoned you at the office this afternoon, Chris, but you weren't there. The girl who answered told me you'd taken a half-day. Why was that? You didn't mention you were taking time off. I

194

wish you had. I could have met you and we could have had a cup of tea somewhere. I had to go into town to get the meat. And stop messing your food about like that. Your appetite's been poor ever since you came back from France.'

Christine laid down her knife and fork. 'I'm sorry, Mum. I'm just not hungry. And, before you start, it has nothing to do with your cooking. You're a very good cook,' she added diplomatically. She glanced at her father. 'Dad, would you mind if I switched off the television for a while? There's something I have to talk to you and Mum about.'

Robert Chandos looked vaguely surprised, but raised no objection. Christine got up and went over to the set, cutting off short an item concerning the new Labour government's crisis budget. Then she returned to the table, meeting her mother's uneasy gaze.

'I have some rather bad news for you both,' she said. 'At least, you're bound to think it's bad news.'

'Oh, my God!' Gwen Chandos's face had drained of colour. She had had her suspicions for the past few weeks, but had hoped against hope that they were unfounded.

Christine stretched out a hand and laid it over one of her mother's. 'I'm sorry, Mum,' she said.

'Will someone kindly tell me what's going on?' Robert demanded irritably. 'Why are you sorry, Chris? And why does your mother look as though she's been struck by lightning?'

'She's pregnant,' his wife told him, without giving Christine a chance to reply. 'You are, aren't you? It's that Saxelby man. You've been acting strangely ever since you cut short that holiday in France. I wondered why you came home a week before you should have done. He took advantage of you, didn't he?'

Christine flinched, finding the euphemism offensive. But what else could a woman like her mother have said? That generation had never learned to be abrasive.

195

'What do you mean, she's pregnant?' Robert blustered, his mind refusing to accept the enormity of what he had just been told. 'Look at her, woman! She's as thin as a lath!'

'Mum's right, Dad.' Christine pushed away her plate, her meal barely touched. 'You go thin before you start to put on weight.'

'I don't believe it! I don't believe it!' Her father jumped up, hitting his knee against the table-leg as he did so, but not even conscious of the pain. He added furiously, suspending disbelief: 'How could you let yourself down so? How could you let your mother and me down, after the way you've been brought up?' He began striding around the room, his face red and mottled with anger. 'Rich people are all the same! Think they can do as they bloody well like! I always knew no good would come of you breaking with Russell Jennings. A good bloke, Russ! You know where you are with a chap like that. You'll have to have it adopted! You can't manage a baby on your salary.'

Only one clear fact emerged from this diatribe of regret, recrimination and fear of what people might think and say, and that was Robert Chandos's strong desire to dissociate himself from such an embarrassing business. Christine glanced at her mother for support.

'Sit down, Bob,' Gwen said quietly, 'and finish your tea. The damage is done, and there's no point in raking up the past. This Rowland Saxelby will just have to marry her.'

Christine was appalled. She had not foreseen this line of argument, although she supposed she should have done. It was the way her mother's generation thought. If a man had done wrong, he must be made to pay.

'No!' she said forcefully. 'I don't want him told, not ever! Rowland must never know. Can't you see', she went on, forestalling Gwen's attempted protest, 'that

I don't want him on those terms? He's not in love with me; he never has been. And I'm every bit as much to blame for what occurred as he is. More, probably, because I wanted it to happen.' She saw the look on her father's face and added hastily: 'It was only the once, I swear it. It was a sort of . . . accident. It wasn't planned.'

Gwen's grim expression relaxed a little. 'Well, if that's the truth, you've been very unlucky. However, it doesn't alter the facts. The Saxelbys ought to be told. Your precious Rowland's got a right to know that he's going to be a father.'

'I don't want him told,' Christine repeated stubbornly.

Her mother heaved a sigh of exasperation. 'And how, pray, do you imagine that you're going to support a baby on your own?'

Christine shrugged. 'I don't know. I haven't really thought about it. I'll probably have it adopted, as Dad suggested.'

Her mother snorted. 'Don't give me that, Christine. You can't pull the wool over my eyes. I know you too well. You've no intention of having the child adopted. It's a part of *him*. You could never bring yourself to give it up.'

Christine said nothing, suffering the mixture of surprise and resentment that all children feel when they realize that parents have their measure. Her mother's perspicacity annoyed her.

Her father had sat down again and was drumming with his fingers on the table, miserable and out of his depth. 'When's it due?' he asked, calculating the amount of time left before they need begin the uneasy process of concealment. Not for a moment did he share Gwen's sanguine belief that Rowland Saxelby could be made to marry Christine. 'Those sort of people don't marry our sort of people,' was the way he phrased it to himself. But then he brightened a little. They might,

197

however, offer her a substantial sum of money towards the baby's upkeep. Words like 'paternity order' and 'maintenance' floated through his mind.

'Next June. Round about June twenty-first, Doctor Richards says. I went to see him this afternoon. I took an hour off, not a half-day. The girl who answered the phone to you, Mum, must have got the wrong idea. Perhaps it would have been better if I had taken the whole afternoon. Come to think of it, when I said I was going to the doctor's, I did get one or two knowing looks.'

'I thought as much,' Robert Chandos said gloomily. 'People'll be talking and whispering behind our backs before you know it. Your mother's right. The Saxelbys ought to be told.' A sense of self-preservation prevented him mentioning his hopes about the money.

'No!' Christine pushed back her chair and stood up. 'I've told you, I don't want them to know anything about it. I forbid either of you to get in touch with Rowland. I want you to promise. If you don't, I'll leave home and you'll never see me again.' She knew it was a form of moral blackmail, which, in any case, she would probably not have the strength of will to carry through, but she was desperate to obtain their agreement.

'Now, look here, my girl—!' her father was beginning, but Gwen frowned him down.

'All right,' she answered unexpectedly. 'I agree.'

'To what?' Christine looked at her suspiciously.

'To what you've just said. I promise.'

'You do?' Christine tried to remember exactly what it was that she had just said. She felt there was a catch somewhere in her mother's sudden compliance, but felt too tired and too emotionally drained to disentangle her jumbled thoughts. 'Very well, and thank you. Do you mind if I go to my room for a while? We'll discuss things properly tomorrow, but I just can't face doing it tonight.'

'No, that's fine. You run along.' Gwen patted her daughter's hand.

As the door closed behind Christine, Robert demanded angrily: 'What was all that about? Why on earth did you make her that promise?'

His wife smiled, getting up and going to one of the sideboard cupboards, from which she extracted notepaper and envelopes and a ballpoint pen.

'What's that for?' he asked her.

'I'm going to write to Mrs Saxelby,' she said. 'I'll send it to Hinton Malsherbes. If she's in London, someone'll send it on from there.'

Robert rubbed his forehead, conscience troubling him. 'I don't say I think you're wrong, but you did promise Chris you wouldn't say anything. I thought you were making a big mistake.'

'If you'd been listening carefully, you'd have heard her ask us to promise not to tell Rowland. Those were her exact words, and that's why I agreed. I'm not going to tell Rowland. I know it was a slip on her part and it isn't what she meant. But, for Chris's own good, I'm sticking strictly to the letter of what I promised and not the spirit. So here goes.' She cleared a space on the table and began writing.

Robert, abandoning his half-eaten, cold and congealing meal, got up again and lit his pipe. He muttered to himself: 'I bet Machiavelli was really a woman.'

Christine switched on the light, closed the bedroom door behind her and kicked off her shoes, sending them spinning across the floor to land, one on its side under the dressing-table, the other, by some miracle of precision, the right way up beneath the bed, in its accustomed place. Then she sank wearily into the armchair beside the window.

Since the days when she and Lois had listened to records together, the room had been redecorated in shades of pale blue and peach. Christine herself had

199

bought the chair, with its covering of peach-and-blue floral cretonne, in the previous year's January sales, egged on by her mother, who had thought it high time she showed some inclination to furnish her own nest. An armchair was at least a step in the right direction.

It was deep and well upholstered. Christine pushed the cushion into the small of her back, stretched out her legs and thankfully closed her eyes. The worst was over now: she had told her parents, and the secret which had been haunting her for the past few weeks was at last out in the open. Waves of lassitude washed over her. She felt unutterably weary. Yet, in spite of her tiredness, she could not sleep. She could not even doze. Her thoughts kept going round and round in circles, like prisoners on a treadmill. She kept on covering the same old ground.

For the thousandth time, she wondered what Madame de Bérenger, Colette and the others had made of her sudden departure. Had they really believed her story of a telephone call to say that her mother wasn't well? Had Madame ever checked on incoming calls and discovered that it was not true? Or had Rowland managed to cover her tracks? He had done his best to dissuade her from going, from practising the deception, but without much conviction. He could see as well as she could that a whole week spent in one another's company, with so much tension and shared guilt between them, would be unbearable. The friendship and comradeship, which had been growing steadily between them, had been destroyed by those few minutes of mindless passion.

Rowland felt guilty twice over because he had betrayed his grandmother's trust and because he had made the false assumption that Christine was not a virgin. It worried him, she could see, although why, as she had said to him, she was unable to understand. In a climate of increasing sexual freedom for both men and women, it had been a natural enough assumption to make. But he had not liked her trying to find excuses for him and felt that he had made a fool of himself. It was no use her assuring him that his good judgement, usually so acute where women were concerned, had been temporarily blinded by the ridiculous Sophie-inspired outfit she had been wearing. He could not forgive himself so easily.

In the circumstances, therefore, it had been far better that she left. She suspected that Colette might have guessed the real reason for her departure. She had given both Christine and Rowland a penetrating look when they had returned indoors from the garden. But, of course, she had asked no questions: she had been too relieved to see Christine go.

Christine leaned forward so that she could rearrange the cushion, pummelling it into a shape more likely to support her aching back. It had naturally been some time before she had realized that she was pregnant, and even when she had gone six weeks without a period – she who was always so regular that she could count almost to the day – she had at first refused to believe it. Everyone said that pregnancy was nearly impossible after only one attempt. Of course, people added, it *was* just possible, if a woman were *very* unlucky . . .

She had been unlucky. When she missed a second period, she had been forced to accept the fact, and her initial reaction had been one of complete dismay. She tried desperately to recall remedies which she had vaguely heard about: gin, hot baths, pennyroyal. She had an idea that the last was some kind of herb, used to induce the flow of blood, but was insufficiently knowledgeable to risk enquiring at a chemist's if it could be obtained in medicinal form. She had thought of ringing Lois. Barry Aylward would surely know; but in the end she had been too embarrassed at involving him to do so. And by this time she was beginning to want the baby, no matter what hardship was involved in keeping it. It was a part of Rowland, something of him which would belong to her always – 'flesh of flesh,/Bone of my bone thou art, and from thy state/Mine never shall be parted . . .' They had done Milton in the fifth form at school. 'Our state cannot be sever'd; we are one,/One flesh; to lose thee were to lose myself.'

Christine found that the tears were running down her cheeks. Angrily, she brushed them away. She could never have Rowland, but she could have the next-best thing, his child. Her mother had been right; she had no thoughts of adoption. Whatever difficulties lay ahead, she was going to keep her baby. She would manage somehow, with or without her parents' support; although she knew them both well enough to feel certain that, whatever they might say, whatever embarrassments they might suffer, they would stand by her. It was only on their behalf now that she experienced any misgivings. She wanted this baby and she was going to have it.

She felt suddenly at peace. Her whole body relaxed, and she began to feel drowsy. Her back had stopped aching, and the slight feeling of nausea which had persisted all day receded. She settled more comfortably into her chair and was asleep within two minutes.

'There.' Gwen Chandos laid down her pen, read through what she had written and folded the two sheets of notepaper into an envelope. 'That should do the trick, I fancy.'

Robert, struggling with a recalcitrant pipe, glanced up and asked: 'What have you said?'

'Enough.' Gwen sealed the letter and affixed a stamp. She could be very secretive on occasions. She gave the impression of being a submissive woman – it was that which had first attracted Robert to her – but there were times when she got the bit between her teeth and insisted on having her own way. This, he recognized, was one of those times, and he had the good sense to keep quiet.

Gwen got up from the table. 'I'm going out to the post-box right away,' she said. 'And then I'll come back and clear up these dirty things.' She sighed. 'I hate seeing a good meal wasted.'

CHAPTER TWENTY

COLETTE STILL INSISTED on going to the bank each day, occupying the first-floor office which she had used since Noel's death. She had always refused the use of the big ground-floor room, insisting that that was for the managing director only; it was to be kept for her elder son whenever he took over the reins.

Rowland had been installed there now for the past three years, ever since he had graduated from Oxford. It had surprised most people how mature he was, how well he had settled in, how willing to listen to older and more experienced voices. Young men, as Cecil Lennox had been heard to remark, suddenly finding themselves in positions of power, were inclined to let it go to their head. But not Mr Rowland. His two years' National Service had stood him in very good stead. They had taught him, if nothing else, discipline and the need for self-control and self-reliance. It was a pity, many people felt, that Julian, by opting for deferment to go to university first, had missed going in the forces altogether. National Service was now a thing of the past.

Whoever else he relied on to show him the ropes, it was to his mother that Rowland always turned in the first instance for advice and guidance. He respected her judgement and was grateful for the way in which she had safeguarded his interests in the decade and a half since his father's death. By going to the bank for at least part of every working day, she had ensured that she knew exactly what was happening in the board-room. Her flare for making money was instinctive. Even the most reactionary of the directors, who had deeply resented interference by a woman, had finally been forced to admit that she showed an astonishing acumen.

For many years, she had been the first to arrive in the morning, the last to leave at night, but since Rowland's advent Colette had been taking things a little more easily. There were now whole days when she did not put in an appearance at all, and on those when she did she more often than not came late. Her secretary, who was a glutton for work, might complain that things were not like the old days, but Colette knew better than to crowd her elder son, or to make him think that she was reluctant to yield up her place. So on this particular November morning it was almost eleven o'clock when she arrived at the main entrance to Saxelby's. The doorman raised a hand in salute and commented on the extremely cold weather.

Colette smiled. 'Yes, very. But what can you expect at this time of year?' She had lived in England long enough to know all the stock answers and, indeed, to take a very British interest in the weather. 'No, don't call the lift yet, Lindsey. I want to see Mr Rowland before I go upstairs. You wouldn't happen to know if he's free?'

The doorman had no idea, but was flattered, as she had meant him to be, by her assumption that he might know the answer to her question. Colette had her own ways of inspiring loyalty in the bank's employees.

Rowland's secretary, Joyce Crocker, a smart, highly efficient divorcee in her mid-forties, said yes, Mr Rowland was in and was free, but, she added warningly, he had a meeting at eleven-thirty, which it was impossible for him to miss.

Colette smiled sweetly. 'Oh, I shan't keep him that long, I hope.' And without waiting to be announced, she pushed open the door into the inner office.

Rowland was hard at work, the desk-lamp switched on, a little pool of artificial sunshine amidst the

205

November murk and gloom. The big window to his right, facing on to Gresham Street, was double-glazed, and the traffic swished silently by outside, like goldfish in a bowl. The thick-piled fawn carpet was a further barrier to noise, and over everything lay a reverential hush. Colette deliberately let the door bang shut behind her, and Rowland glanced up.

'What—?' he was beginning, in annoyance, then his face relaxed. 'Maman! You're in bright and early. What can I do for you?'

'It's gone eleven,' Colette said tartly. 'If that was meant to be sarcastic . . .' She let the sentence hang, watching the slow grin which spread across his features and lifted the corners of his eyes into a network of tiny wrinkles. How she loved him! So much more than Julian. But it would never do to let anyone know. She continued in the same acerbic tone: 'The post came about half an hour after you left this morning.'

'It usually does,' he answered mildly. 'Maman, I have an important meeting in twenty minutes. I presume there is a point to this visit.'

For reply, Colette took a letter, already opened, out of her handbag and passed it across the desk. Rowland read the superscription and remarked, puzzled: 'This is addressed to you.'

'Read it', she said, 'after your meeting. Then come up to my office and we'll discuss it. I am sure we can find a satisfactory solution.'

He frowned. 'Why the mystery? What's this all about? Why read it *after* the board meeting?'

'Because you'll need a clear head to decide on this new Saudi Arabian loan. If you want my advice,' Colette added, turning to go, 'you'll wait a while, until you see just what sort of a ruler Feisal is going to make. We'd had experience of Saud, but now that he's been deposed . . .' She broke off, shrugging.

Julian came in, looking for his brother. He kissed Colette and held open the door for her as she left. 'Are you ready?' he asked Rowland. 'I thought we might as well go up to the boardroom together.' He glanced curiously at the envelope in Rowland's hand. 'What's that? Something important?'

His brother laid the letter to one side. 'I shan't know until later. Strict instructions from Maman. I'll explain as we go up in the lift.' And without bothering to look at the postmark he got to his feet, gathering up the necessary papers. 'About this Saudi loan – I want it to go through. There will be a lot of opposition, including Maman's, so I'm relying on your support all the way.' He glanced at his watch. 'Come on. We'd better get going.'

Christine was tired to her very bones. She always hated those Fridays when she was pay clerk, handing out unemployment benefit over the counter: the queues, the columns of figures, the worry that the balance would not work out exactly, the arguments with irate clients who insisted that they had signed on for more days than they actually had. It was bad enough at the best of times, but now that she was pregnant far worse. If only she could admit the truth, she might at least get some sympathy, but both her mother and her father had begged her to say nothing for the moment.

Once again, she turned into Clarence Road North, but there was no rush of wind to greet her tonight. The gales of the past week had at last died out, and all that could be heard was the distant hushing of the sea and the sound of home-going traffic. She went slowly up the outside steps, pausing as always on the landing to search for her key. Tonight, the radio from the ground-floor flat was belting out 'Baby Love' by the Supremes.

As she stepped into the lighted hallway, her mother came quickly out of the living-room to greet her, flushed and agitated.

'Chris love! There you are.' She went on hurriedly, before Christine could protest that she was in fact earlier than usual: 'You have a visitor. He's in there. In the sitting-room, with your father.'

Christine looked bewildered. 'Who's in there with Dad? Who are you talking about? What visitor?' She took in her mother's flustered appearance and was suddenly suspicious. She pushed past Gwen and opened the living-room door. Rowland was seated in one of the armchairs near the window and got up to greet her as she entered.

'Chris,' he said, not beating about the bush, 'why didn't you tell me as soon as you knew you were pregnant?'

Christine rounded on her mother. 'You *promised*! You promised you wouldn't say anything! How *could* you?'

'I promised I wouldn't tell Mr Saxelby. Rowland. Well, I didn't. But ... But I did write to his mother.' Gwen looked defiant.

'You're splitting hairs!' Christine had gone extremely white, but her eyes were blazing. 'You broke your promise to me.' For a moment, she was in danger of striking her mother.

Rowland came forward quietly, turning Christine round to face him.

'Your mother did the right thing,' he said sternly. 'She's worried about you, naturally. This isn't the sort of thing you can keep to yourself. Or, indeed, have the right to keep to yourself. The child is mine as much as yours. Do you think I want him to grow up not knowing his father?'

In spite of herself, she smiled. 'It might be a girl,' she answered. The smile faded, and the anger returned. She twisted away from him. 'I don't want your charity or the charity of your family. I'll manage without you.'

'Now, Chris,' her father said, half-rising from his chair, 'don't be hasty. You don't want to do anything foolish.'

'I'm not offering you charity.' Rowland met her eyes steadily. 'I wouldn't insult you. I want to marry you, if you'll have me.'

Gwen Chandos gasped audibly. 'Oh, Chris!' she breathed. 'Of course you'll say yes.'

'You'll be a damn fool if you don't,' her father told her bluntly. 'For the baby's sake as much as your own.'

Rowland interposed swiftly: 'Mrs Chandos, I wonder if you and Mr Chandos would be kind enough to leave us alone.'

'Yes, of course.' Gwen shot her husband a warning look as he seemed disinclined to move. 'Bob! Come and help me lay the table. You'll stay and have a meal with us, I hope?' she added, turning to Rowland.

'I should like to, thank you, if it's not too much trouble.' When they had gone, Robert with extreme reluctance, Rowland looked again at Christine. 'Well? I asked you to marry me. You might at least give me an answer.'

Christine, conscious suddenly that she was still in her outdoor things, removed her coat and scarf, throwing them over the back of a chair. Then she turned to face him once more. She was breathing raggedly, and her voice was not quite steady.

'You don't call that charity?' she asked. 'You don't think that marrying beneath you – as I'm certain your mother and family must regard it – is a charitable deed? How *dare* you come here, offering me your favours and your condescension! Please go away! I never want to see you again.'

He said nothing for a moment, just standing and looking at her beneath frowning brows. But after a while he went across to her, putting one hand on her shoulder and, with the other, forcing up her chin until she met his eyes.

'That's better,' he said. 'Do you really hate me so much?'

Christine gave a shaky laugh. 'Of course I don't hate you. What an absurd notion. Hate implies . . . feeling, and I don't have any feelings for you at all.'

'Well, I do for you,' he answered. 'I like you. You're one of the nicest people I know. You're a good friend. You're fun to be with. I'm very fond of you and I wish you were of me.'

'But you don't love me. You would never have thought of marrying me if it hadn't been for the baby – now, would you? Can you deny it?'

He sighed. 'Why do women always want you to be "in love"? I don't really know the meaning of the phrase. I doubt if many people do, men or women. It's an invention of romantic fiction. I like you, Christine. I want you to be my wife. I've thought about almost nothing else these last few days, since I read your mother's letter, and I know my own mind. All right, perhaps I shouldn't have asked you to marry me if it weren't for the child, but that is because I had no intention of getting married. Knowing about the baby just made me realize that if I *had* to get married I'd rather it was to you than to anyone else I can think of. Does that answer your question?'

Christine stared at him, not knowing what to think. Was he telling her the truth? She wanted desperately to believe him; quite how desperately only she knew.

'What about your mother?' she asked at last. 'I can't imagine that she's pleased by your decision.' She gave a hysterical giggle. 'Your marriage to me would rank as a worse disaster than your brother's to Sophie.'

'Forget Maman,' he said shortly. 'You can leave her to me. Just don't let her bully you, that's all. I'll tell you someone who will be pleased by the news, and that's

210

Grandmother de Bérenger. She's been nagging me to get married for years.'

'But not to a nobody like me!' Christine was bitter.

'You're not a nobody,' he answered angrily. 'Nobody's a nobody. That's to deny the whole spirit of the French Revolution. And whatever you may think, not all my ancestors ended up with the aristocrats on the steps of the guillotine.' She laughed at that, and he smiled encouragingly. 'That's more like it. Now, I'll ask you once again. Will you marry me? And this time you'd better say yes.'

Her head was whirling, and she had the impression of being in a dream. She told herself sternly that if she accepted him it would only be for the sake of their unborn child. She could not possibly do it for any other reason. Oh, the whole thing was preposterous! How on earth would she go on in a place like Mallerby? And there was a London house, too. It was absurd. Ridiculous. She should have married Russell Jennings, or someone like him, and by now she would have had a mortgage on a nice little semi-detached, the statutory two and a half children and, if she were very lucky, a modest savings account with a building society. That was the sort of life she was used to. Any other kind was tempting Fate.

Well, as Montrose had pointed out three centuries earlier, Fate was there to be tempted. She loved Rowland as she had never loved anyone else, never would love anyone else, and she was being given the chance to make him a present of it. Fate had intertwined their lives, and kept on doing it, so let Fate take the consequences. She lifted her head and smiled.

'Yes, I'll marry you,' she said.

It was a register office wedding at Caxton Hall in London. Both Christine's parents were present, as were Lois and Barry Aylward and a couple of her aunts. The groom was supported by his brother and sister-in-law,

211

Sophie insisting on taking credit for the whole affair. Colette did not attend, nor any member of the Bérenger family, but Madame sent a telegram of congratulation and had offered them the use of Château Bérenger for their honeymoon. She herself was going to Paris for a month and would be staying at the Villa Dauphine, the family home in the Avenue Foch, so they would be quite alone except for the servants. She also sent a substantial cheque as a wedding present.

Altogether, it was a very quiet affair, attracting little attention from the press and meriting only a couple of short paragraphs in one or two of the more reputable newspapers. It was how both Christine and Rowland wanted it. After an equally quiet reception at Claridge's, they flew to Paris, where Madame de Bérenger had left the Citroën at Orly Airport for Rowland to collect, and began the long drive south to Poitou.

They stopped for the night at Bonneval, but they were both too tired to do more than eat their dinner and go straight to bed. Rowland was looking very pale and seemed preoccupied, as he had done all day. Christine ventured once to ask him if he were regretting his decision to marry her, and was told tersely not to be so stupid. After that, she held her tongue.

The following morning, however, with a good night's rest behind him, he was in a happier mood. For the rest of the journey, and throughout the time they spent at Château Bérenger, they recaptured some of the comradeship they had known during that earlier week in September. The December weather prevented them from going so far afield, but they found plenty to do indoors, and it was then that Rowland introduced Christine to what was to become a lifelong passion: seventeenth-century music, particularly the work of Jean-Philippe Rameau. He taught her to play bezique, and she showed him how to play canasta, a favourite card game of her mother's. They also talked about anything and everything, but one subject was taboo: Colette and her reaction to their marriage.

Christine longed to know all that had passed between Rowland and his mother, but when she tried to probe he shut up like a clam. He was devoted to Colette, and would never be disloyal to her or talk about her behind her back. In one way, Christine was glad; by the same token, he would never discuss *her* with his mother. He displayed an innate integrity in all his dealings.

They returned to England in time for Christmas, but the confrontation with her mother-in-law, which she had been so dreading, was postponed. During the return flight from Orly, Christine blacked out on the plane. The Saxelby family doctor, hurriedly summoned to Inglebatch House, diagnosed high blood-pressure and ordered her into hospital for immediate rest. It was eight weeks before she was allowed home again, and by that time Colette was in France, spending a month with her brother and his family in Paris. Christine had won another reprieve.

'Take care,' Rowland told her, kissing her goodbye on that first morning after her discharge from hospital.

'I promise,' she said, but failed to mention that she had been feeling dizzy ever since she got up.

Rowland received the telephone call at the bank an hour later; from a hysterical charlady who had arrived, late, at ten o'clock to find Christine unconscious in the hallway at the foot of the stairs. Mrs Floss had dialled 999, and the ambulance was on its way.

By the time Rowland arrived at the hospital, frustrated by traffic delays, it was all over. Christine had recovered consciousness, but had suffered a miscarriage. Furthermore, the doctors informed Rowland, sadly shaking their heads, it had caused such extensive damage to the womb that she would never be able to have another child.

PART FOUR
1971 – 5

CHAPTER TWENTY-ONE

SHE OPENED the narrow red velvet-covered box and regarded the contents with a sinking heart. Lying on the white satin lining was a bracelet, each separate link in the shape of a flower with diamond petals and an emerald centre. Inside the lid was a hastily scribbled note: 'With my love, Rowland.'

After a moment or two, Christine carefully closed the lid, unlocked a drawer in her dressing-table and slid the box inside it, to join others, all bearing the names of famous jewellers, both in London and in Paris. To herself, she called it the 'conscience' drawer; the place where she kept those presents which Rowland gave her when he was feeling guilty about his latest infidelity. She knew perfectly well that this particular gift was because he had recently started an affair with the novelist Maxine Larson, who would be at this evening's party, accompanied by her publisher husband. Christine got up and walked over to the window, staring down into the street.

It would soon be time to get dressed. Colette's fifty-fourth birthday would be marked, as always, by a small family dinner before the arrival of the other guests. Lucien and Solange had flown over from Paris with Giles, now a tall, thin, dark-haired boy of fourteen. Julian and Sophie would be arriving from their Park Lane flat to join Vivien, who had come to Inglebatch House straight from school, bringing her dress for the evening folded up in her case, along with her weekend homework. Only Rowland's movements were as yet uncertain: he had telephoned from the bank twenty minutes earlier to say that he might be delayed. He was waiting for an important call from Toronto.

The July day had run the whole gamut of English weather. An insipid morning had brightened towards noon, turned to rain by three, and now the afternoon was fading imperceptibly into a warm and pleasant evening. It would be possible to have the windows of the drawing-room open, which was always of benefit when there was a crush of people. Christine wondered if the bathroom were free yet. Young Giles, who was occupying one of the spare bedrooms on the second floor, seemed to have been in there for ever. She glanced at the clock on the bedside table and saw that she still had plenty of time. She was just wondering whether or not to read for ten minutes before checking again on the bathroom, when there was a knock at her door. In answer to her 'Come in!' Vivien appeared, in a white silk frock which ended just above her knees. White floral-patterned tights and white flat-heeled shoes completed the outfit.

'Hi, Aunt Chris!' she said. 'Can I talk to you?' And, without waiting for an answer, flopped on to the big double bed, leaning back on her elbows.

Vivien Saxelby was three months past her ninth birthday. Tall for her age, it was difficult to say which parent she most resembled. She had been fair as a baby, but now had Julian's colouring, dark brown hair and warm brown eyes. The wide sensuous mouth, however, was entirely her mother's, as was the small, pointed, very determined chin. Both Sophie and her daughter had a hard calculating streak, but whereas Christine had never liked her sister-in-law she could not help but be fond of Vivien, who was so patently fond of her. Indeed, the child's preference for her aunt could, at times, prove acutely embarrassing.

'What do you want to talk about?' Christine asked, laying aside the book which she had that moment picked up. 'Because if you've come to complain about

218

your mother I'd just as soon that you didn't. Your quarrels with Sophie are not my business.'

'But I can't talk to anyone else,' Vivien wailed. 'If I say anything to Dad, it only makes things worse. He and Mum are rowing all the time as it is. And Grandma isn't really interested. She just says that it serves Dad right, he shouldn't have married a tart like Mummy.'

'Vivien!' Christine tried to sound suitably scandalized and not break into giggles. The child was far too precocious for her age. 'I'm sure your grandmother has never said anything of the kind.'

'Well, not in so many words, perhaps, but I know what she means.' Vivien rolled on to her stomach, propping her chin on her hands, raising the lower half of her legs behind her and crossing her ankles. 'Mum is a tart. She sleeps with heaps of men besides Daddy.'

This time Christine was genuinely shaken. She went across and sat on the opposite side of the bed, facing her niece. 'Darling, I'm sure you're mistaken.'

Vivien shot her an old-fashioned look. She had, Christine thought, grown up far too fast, and her niece's next words confirmed it.

'There's no mistake,' Vivien said calmly. 'Mum told me herself.'

'Told you what, for heaven's sake?' Christine felt as though she were trapped in a quagmire.

'Oh, about men and women and what they do in bed. Lots of girls in school know all about it,' she added airily. 'It's not just me. Mum reckons it's good for me to know anyway. She says schools ought to provide sex education.'

Yes, Christine thought bitterly, she could just hear Sophie saying it. Sophie, who had never wanted children and who, after Vivien, had made sure that she had no more, was probably the world's worst mother. Childhood was important; a real traditional childhood. Her sister-in-law had turned Vivien into a woman, a brittle, sharp-eyed, prurient woman, before she was ten. Why did Fate arrange things so that women like Sophie had children, while she was unable to have any? But she must stop herself thinking that way. Bitterness and resentment were ugly eroding emotions, eating away at the soul.

But after Vivien had gone, after she had said what she had really come to say – 'Look at this frock, Aunt Chris! Isn't it absolutely puke-making? It makes me look about four! She wouldn't buy the one I wanted, you know. She's jealous of me; jealous of the competition' – the bitterness and resentment were still there. She had wanted that child so much. Things between her and Rowland might have been so different had it lived.

There was another knock at her door, and Giles's polite voice, with its attractive French accent, called: 'The bathroom is now free, Cousin Christine.'

She smiled in spite of herself and called back: 'Thank you.' French children were so well behaved. She gathered up her towel and flannel and crossed the corridor to the bathroom she and Rowland normally had to themselves.

She busied herself running water and pouring in her favourite bath oil, trying by activity to blot out unwelcome thoughts. But once she was immersed in the scented water they returned, refusing to be suppressed. Of course a child would have made some difference – she wouldn't, for one thing, have felt such a fraud, and Colette's attitude might have been less antagonistic – but it wouldn't have made Rowland love her in the way that she wanted to be loved. He had never pretended that he was more than fond of her, or that he had married her for any other reason than that she was expecting his child. And there was no doubt that, as the years went by, he increasingly wanted a family.

Not that he ever said so or reproached her in any way. But she could tell by the look in his eyes when they rested on Giles or Vivien, or on any of the sons and

220

daughters of his friends. She knew for a fact, because of a conversation she had once overheard between Rowland and his mother at Mallerby, that Colette had urged him to divorce her and marry someone else. And Christine felt sure that it was not the first or the last time that Colette had tried to persuade him. Her mother-in-law had found it difficult, six years ago, to disguise her relief when she knew that Christine had lost the baby. She had expected it to be the end of what she considered to be a disastrous marriage, but Rowland had refused even to consider the idea.

'Christine is my wife,' he had said. 'She stays that way.'

And when Christine herself had offered him a divorce he had been furious, telling her through lips white with anger that he never wanted to hear the subject raised again. And, although she had, on one or two occasions, defied him, she had always met with the same response. She was his wife. Period. Finish. End.

But his loyalty to her, that loyalty which brought down his wrath on the head of anyone who made a disparaging remark about her in his hearing, did not stop him having numerous affairs. There was always some other woman in his life, and she had forced herself to accept the fact that he was the sort of man who could never resist the charms of the opposite sex. Some men drank heavily; others smoked a hundred or more cigarettes every day; some, in the wake of the Swinging Sixties experimented with drugs. Rowland liked women; not just sex, although it naturally played a large part in any of his relationships, but female companionship. He preferred the company of women to that of men. But, then, she had always known that. She was telling herself nothing that she did not already know, that she had not known from that very first meeting.

Christine got out of the bath, showering water everywhere in a rainbow of iridescent drops. You're a fool,

221

she told herself angrily, to keep going over and over it in your mind. If you want a divorce, get one. You'd be a damn sight better off without him.

But the moment she saw him again she knew that any thought of leaving him was simply bravado. She loved him as much as ever.

He had been forced to miss dinner. The telephone call from Toronto had come through much later than expected, and by the time he reached home guests were already arriving for the party.

'Sorry, Maman,' he had said, kissing Colette's cheek, 'but I'm afraid it was unavoidable.' And he had vanished upstairs to shower and change.

When he next put in an appearance, the party was in full swing. The drawing-room was packed, and people were spilling out on to the landing and down the stairs into the hallway. Colette, looking supremely elegant in a plain black Dior dress, the Saxelby pearls her only ornament, was sipping vodka and lime and moving animatedly amongst her guests. Christine, from her retired corner, where she was perched on the arm of a settee, watched her mother-in-law's almost royal progress.

There were a lot of bank employees – Colette never forgot them on her birthday – and several instantly recognizable faces, politicians and show-business people, with others less well known, whose features stirred a chord in the memory without being able to conjure up a name. Then there were the family and those simply categorized as 'friends'. Maxine and Sebastian Larson were amongst the latter. Christine was not the only person in the room who found herself constantly watching them. A good-looking couple, they drew the eye.

Maxine, whose first novel, *A Sudden Heat Wave*, had hit the bestseller lists three years ago and paved the way for her second, even more successful

222

book, *The White Poplar*, twelve months later, was an extremely striking-looking woman; nearly six feet tall, with short-cut ash-blonde hair, she was wearing a red silk dress and very long gold pendant earrings which brushed her shoulders as she moved. Her husband was an equally striking-looking man, also blond and blue-eyed, as befitted his Swedish ancestry. He was listening attentively to a woman in a green velvet frock when Rowland made his belated entrance, and did not look round. Maxine Larson, on the other hand, broke off abruptly her conversation with one of the MPs and turned a glowing face towards the door.

'Rowe!' she exclaimed, moving in his direction. 'Here you are at last! I thought you were never coming. Whatever kept you?'

There were a number of knowing winks and nudges, and a few raised eyebrows. Someone near Christine giggled. One or two people gave her pitying glances. She could feel her cheeks beginning to burn.

But Rowland ignored Maxine and went straight over to Christine's corner of the room. 'Hello, darling,' he said, and bent to kiss her. Someone had just put an Elvis record on the record-player. He pulled her to her feet. 'Come on,' he said, 'let's dance.'

She began to laugh. 'In this crush? Are you mad?'

'We can pretend we're dancing,' he said. 'Put your arms round me and we'll sway in time to the music. "The Wonder of You" is one of my favourites.'

She did as she was bidden, but asked: 'Don't you think you ought to go and speak to Maxine? You ignored her very rudely just now.'

'Maxine who?' he asked blandly, but she saw the way he looked at the other woman; the smile of apology in his eyes. She saw, too, Maxine's little grimace of understanding as she turned back to the MP. Gently Christine pushed her husband away. 'I don't feel like dancing,' she said. 'Find somebody else.'

'Very well,' he answered equably, but made no attempt to leave her. 'Come and introduce me to some of these people. I swear I don't know half of those here.'

It was a lie, of course. As they pushed through the press of bodies, it was Rowland who greeted people by name. To Christine, most of them were still just faces. She had not found it easy, in this new world of hers, to make friends.

'Why aren't you wearing your new bracelet?' he asked suddenly. They were wedged against the makeshift bar which had been set up opposite the door, and Rowland was pouring himself a whisky and water. 'It would have gone very well with that green dress.'

Christine gave a shrug. 'Oh, you know me,' she answered lightly. 'I've never been one for much jewellery.' She touched the brooch pinned to her right shoulder. 'This is all I need.'

He said nothing, but she knew from his face that he had got the message. The brooch she was wearing was the one he had given her as a wedding present: a small oblong of diamonds with a triangle of rubies in the centre, the blazonry of Chandos. Rowland had had it made specially for her, and because of that it was the most cherished piece of jewellery she possessed. She wore it all the time, while far more valuable items languished in the drawer or in the wall safe of their bedroom.

'Chris—' Rowland began, but was prevented from saying more by Lucien de Bérenger, who had finally managed to struggle through the crowd to his nephew's side. Lucien, as always, and whatever the circumstances, wanted to talk business, and was anxious for Rowland's opinion on the rumour that the United States was proposing to sell its grain surplus to Russia, and on the probable world-wide inflation that this would cause. Oil prices, too, were increasing. He broke into a torrent of French, accompanied by much waving of his arms. Rowland looked resigned, and Christine took the opportunity to slip away.

She found herself in a group which included Julian and Sophie. Vivien, looking heavy-eyed and not a little bored, was leaning against her father, his arm around her shoulders. Sophie, in a skin-tight scarlet gown, was making a play for Sebastian Larson and laughing loudly at everything he said which could remotely be construed as funny. Maxine Larson, Christine noted, had left the others and was making her way determinedly through the crush to the corner where Rowland and Lucien were standing. She turned her head away quickly, not wanting to see her husband's smile of pleasure as the other woman approached. She began talking hurriedly to her neighbour – she fancied he was an actor: she knew his face, but could not place the name – without being at all aware of what she was saying. It must, however, have made sense, for he smiled and nodded and answered.

Three hours later, at one in the morning, Vivien was curled up in a corner of one of the settees, sound asleep, and Christine herself was conscious of a feeling of exhaustion. The crush was thinning out slightly as people left, and there was now space enough for those who wanted to dance in the middle of the room. Sophie, very drunk by this time, was draped around the neck of Sebastian Larson, who was whispering in her ear and holding her far more tightly than was necessary. Rowland and Maxine were also dancing – if the slow sensuous swaying being indulged in by most couples could really be called dancing – their heads close together, their bodied touching. Julian was propping up the bar with several of his friends, but after a while he left them and came across to sit by Christine.

'Why do we put up with it, eh?' he demanded gloomily, nodding towards Sophie and Rowland. 'We're a couple of fools, that's what.' His speech was faintly slurred, the only indication that he was three parts drunk.

'Perhaps because we haven't any choice,' Christine

said, patting his hand affectionately. 'Do you mind very much?'

'Not in the way you do,' he answered, startling her by his percipience. Julian was not usually attuned to other people's thoughts and feelings. 'But I don't like being made to look a fool.'

'Why don't you stop her, then? Or failing that, why not divorce?'

Julian shrugged, slopping some of the whisky in his glass over the arm of the settee. 'I haven't any stomach for rows and scenes, I suppose. As for divorce, I'd prefer Sophie was around while Vivien's still young. A bad mother is better than no mother. Besides,' he added surprisingly, 'although Rowe and I weren't brought up as Catholics – my father insisted on that before he married Maman – I've always had a tendency that way. One of these days, I'll go over to Rome.'

Satisfied that it was not the drink talking, Christine leaned over and kissed her brother-in-law's cheek. 'You do that,' she encouraged him. 'Stand up for what you believe in.'

'And what about you?' he asked, tucking his free hand inside her arm and giving it a squeeze. 'What about your convictions, eh?'

'Mine?' she laughed. 'Oh, I haven't any.'

'Yes, you have.' He kissed her cheek in return. 'You think . . . you think' – he took another deep swig of whisky, becoming drunker by the minute – 'that Rowland's won-der-ful.' He enunciated the last word very carefully. 'So he is. Can't deny it. But got an eye for the ladies.'

Christine sighed as Julian's head dropped on to her shoulder and his eyes began to close. Rowland had that all right. She looked across to where he was still swaying in time to the music with Maxine Larson. She remembered Lisle Ingram. And then, for some inexplicable reason, she thought of Lucy Brennan.

CHAPTER TWENTY-TWO

DESCENDING TO THE BASEMENT in search of coffee halfway through Saturday morning, Christine found only the current daily help, Mrs Jones, pouring herself a second cup of tea from the big brown pot set squarely in the middle of the kitchen table. It was flanked by milk-jug, sugar-bowl and a large plateful of assorted biscuits. The smell of bacon and fried bread still lingered on the air, indicating that Rowland had eaten a full-sized cooked breakfast before leaving for the bank. Just the thought of bacon and eggs made Christine shudder.

She seemed to have drunk far more the previous evening than she had intended, judging by her throbbing head. The light, too, hurt her eyes, and although the obliging Mrs Jones offered to make her some toast she declined it. The only thing she could face was a mug of coffee.

'Got a thick head, have you?' the daily asked sympathetically, rising to put on the kettle. 'Not that I'm surprised, mind you. Judging by the state of that drawing-room this morning, it looked like you'd been having a right old knees-up. Mrs Saxelby enjoy her birthday-party, did she?'

Christine took down a mug from one of the hooks on the dresser and spooned in brown sugar and instant coffee. 'Yes, very much, I think. She was still up when I went to bed at three.'

Rowland had also still been up, although the company had reduced dramatically by then. Julian and Sophie had finally been commanded by Colette to take an exhausted Vivien home, Lucien and Solange

227

had made their apologies and dragged an equally weary Giles off to bed, and many of the guests had left.

Only the inveterate loiterers had remained to wear out their welcome. Not that either of the Larsons appeared to have been trespassing on hospitality. Sebastian had been regaling Colette with a story which she had found highly amusing, and Maxine had been sitting beside Rowland on the floor, her long legs stretched out in front of her. And that was the last sight Christine had had of them before she closed the drawing-room door and went up to bed. It had been an hour later when Rowland eventually followed, and she had pretended to be asleep.

Mrs Jones poured boiling water into the mug and pushed across the milk-jug. Christine smiled and shook her head. 'I'll have it black. It might wake me up a bit,' she said.

The older woman helped herself to another biscuit. 'You and Mr Saxelby shouldn't give these late-night parties, specially not when he's got to work the next day. He looked pretty done in while he was having his breakfast, I'll tell you.' Mrs Jones jerked her thumb in the direction of the ceiling. 'What about them French relations of Mrs Saxelby senior? Will they be wanting any breakfast?'

'I shouldn't imagine so. They were only just moving when I came down. But they'll be here to lunch. They're catching the late-afternoon plane to Paris.'

'Well, I'm not cooking anything fancy,' the daily warned her grimly, starting to empty the tea-pot. 'They can have good wholesome English food and like it. They can keep their nasty frogs' legs and snails to themselves.'

'I'm sure they won't expect anything like that,' Christine told her, suppressing a laugh. It was the first time she had felt remotely amused by anything since she got up that morning.

The lift-doors clashed in the entrance-hall over-head, then footsteps sounded on the basement stairs. A moment later, Colette entered the kitchen, looking as refreshed as she did after a normal night's sleep. Christine wondered enviously how she managed it. Colette greeted Mrs Jones and said: 'Don't worry about luncheon. I'll see to it myself. Something light, perhaps. An omelette *aux fines herbes*. What do you think, Chris?'

If Christine was surprised at being thus appealed to, she gave no sign. 'It sounds good to me,' she answered.

Mrs Jones looked pleased. 'Well, in that case, I'll just wash up these few things and then I'll be off.' Saturday was not one of her usual days: she had only come in this morning to 'oblige'. She whisked away Christine's half-empty mug and started to fill a bowl with hot water. Colette sat down, resting one elbow on the kitchen table and cupping her chin in her hand.

'You don't look well,' she told her daughter-in-law. 'You're very pale this morning.'

'Late nights and too much to drink don't agree with me,' Christine answered.

Colette thought this over. 'I don't really think it's that,' she said after a moment or two. 'It's Rowland, isn't it? And Maxine Larson.'

Christine eyed her mother-in-law warily. It was the first time in all the six years of her marriage that Colette had shown anything approaching sympathy.

'His affairs don't help,' she agreed. 'But it isn't only that. I feel I've cheated him.'

Colette, suddenly aware that Mrs Jones had stopped splashing about at the sink and was standing, quietly listening, said no more. Later, however, she asked Christine to accompany her to the airport, to see Lucien and his family off on the Paris plane. That, too, was something she had never done before. Christine felt even more wary. She accepted, nevertheless. She

229

liked the general tawdriness of airports: the escalators, the vending machines, the self-service restaurants, the noise and bustle. Perhaps, she thought, because it was the world to which she really belonged: concerts at the end of the pier, morning coffee in the Winter Gardens, bank-holiday crowds. Had she ever truly adapted to this new life, even after all these years? But she had other things to occupy her mind. Colette's unexpected friendliness, for example.

She need not have worried, however. It was a long time now since her mother-in-law had felt any dislike for her. In the beginning, it had been different. Rowland's decision to marry Christine had at first stunned and then enraged Colette, who had done her utmost to dissuade him. When she found that her words had no effect, she transferred her anger to her prospective daughter-in-law. Christine was a scheming little gold-digger, who had deliberately seduced Rowland in order to trap him into marriage. The fact that both Julian and her own mother liked Christine and thought the marriage a good idea had only made her more antagonistic.

'It's time Rowland settled down,' Madame de Bérenger had said. 'An infusion of sound bourgeois blood from time to time is just what this family needs. Stops the line running to seed.'

But there was to be no line; at least, not through Rowland. Colette had heard of Christine's miscarriage with guilty relief, hoping that now her elder son would see sense and get a divorce. It was against the teachings of the Catholic church, but in the circumstances she felt it would be morally justified. And, in any case, neither of her children was being brought up as a Catholic, so what did it matter? Rowland, however, had refused even to consider the idea.

'I'm not marrying anyone else, Maman,' he had told her brusquely, 'so forget it. Chris is my wife and she'll remain that way. Don't ever suggest such a thing again.'

Colette had known that it was no use arguing further. There were moments when Rowland was exactly like his father: obstinate to the point of pig-headedness. The set of the lips, the angle of the jaw were Noel all over again. There, of course, the similarity ended. Noel Saxelby had been a small precise man – in their height, both Rowland and Julian took after the Bérengers – devoted to Colette from the moment he first saw her. He had never been tempted to look at another woman, but even if he had he would not have done so. He had been, like so many Englishmen of his generation, a Puritan at heart, and regarded marital infidelity as very bad form. He had tended to regard all Frenchmen as natural-born lechers. What would he have thought of his elder son? Colette often wondered ruefully.

But he would certainly have approved of Rowland's decision to stand by Christine. He had possessed all the romanticism of the Teutonic races and none of the Gallic pragmatism of his wife. In that respect, both Rowland and Julian were their father's sons. So Colette had fought a losing battle over the divorce and had eventually held her tongue, but her dislike of both Christine and Sophie had manifested itself in the coldly formal way she treated her daughters-in-law, in contrast to the effusive warmth extended towards Rowland's and Julian's friends. Sophie could escape, but under the terms of Noel Saxelby's will Mallerby and Inglebatch House, although officially Rowland's after his father's death, were to be Colette's home also until she died. She and Christine were thrown together constantly and spent weeks at a time under the same roof.

It might well have made for an unbearable situation, and for the first two or three years things were not easy. But Colette's initial animosity had begun to fade as she was slowly forced to realize that Christine loved Rowland as much as she did herself. She was compelled to recognize that her elder son's wife had not married him from any motive except one: she was deeply in love, with the sort of passion that very few women were lucky enough to experience. Or unlucky enough. It depended on the man. And over the past few years, almost subconsciously, Colette's sympathies had suffered a sea-change.

She accepted that Rowland had other women; what, in the jargon of the sixties, had come to be known as 'one-night stands'. But since Lisle Ingram there had been no one particular woman in his life. And Colette had never become sufficiently anglicized to feel that occasional and casual infidelity need trouble a wife. But then, four months ago, Rowland had met Maxine Larson, and their friendship had quickly developed into a full-blown affair. And last night, at the party, watching her son and Maxine together, finding so much obvious enjoyment in one another's company, and seeing the hurt in Christine's face, the desperate gallant attempt to pretend she didn't mind, Colette suddenly discovered that she was angry on her daughter-in-law's behalf. She wanted to take Rowland by the shoulders and shake some sense into him; tell him what a blind fool he was. The past, the fact that Christine could have no more children, seemed no longer to matter. And perhaps, Colette had thought guiltily, she had aggravated the situation by her offhand treatment of Christine. From now on she determined that it would change.

'Christine! Christine Chandos!'

Hearing her name called in that peremptory fashion, Christine looked round, startled. She and Colette were about to enter one of Heathrow's multi-storey carparks, where, an hour and a half earlier, they had been lucky enough to find a space. Now, having

232

waved goodbye to Lucien, Solange and young Giles, they were returning to collect the dark blue Simca which Colette drove around London, preferring it to the larger and more unwieldy Daimler, used only for grand occasions.

'Chris!' A man dodged recklessly between two lorries on the busy terminus road and reached the safety of the pavement. 'I thought it was you when I saw you ahead of me on the escalator. How are you after all these years?'

She stared blankly for a moment at the blue eyes smiling into hers, at the thin pale face already showing signs of a 'five o'clock shadow', at the dark hair ruffled by the wind. Then she exclaimed incredulously: 'Russ! Russ Jennings! Well! I'm fine. I'm fine. And you?'

'Yes, I'm fine, too.' The conversation, such as it was, seemed in danger of petering out while they stood looking at one another. They both gave an embarrassed laugh. Colette nipped her daughter-in-law's elbow.

Recalled to a sense of duty, Christine said a trifle breathlessly: 'Oh, I'm sorry. How remiss of me. Colette, this is an old friend of mine, Russell Jennings. Russ, my mother-in-law, Colette Saxelby.' After the conventional exchange of greetings, she went on: 'What are you doing here? Are you just back from holiday or something?'

He smiled. 'Or something. I came to meet a friend, who didn't turn up. Look, could you spare the time to have a cup of coffee? I'd like to hear all your news.'

Christine glanced hesitantly at Colette, who said: 'I'm sorry, but I have to get back. I'm going to the theatre this evening.' A thought struck her. 'Do you live in London, Mr Jennings?' He nodded and she turned to Christine. 'Well, then, why don't I go on, *chérie*, and your friend can bring you home later?'

'A good idea,' Russell approved. 'I seem to recall that it's Hampstead. Not a part of London I know very well, but Chris can direct me.'

'Yes . . . yes, of course.' Christine was still a little dazed by her mother-in-law's term of endearment. Colette had never called her *chérie* before, or shown her such kindness and consideration as she had this afternoon. And yet, looking back, Christine could see that for some time now Colette's manner had been softening towards her.

Russell took Christine's arm and guided her back across the road and into the nearest terminal building. On the first floor, they found two seats at one of the hideous orange plastic tables, and Russell went up to the self-service counter to join the queue of people. After about ten minutes, he returned with a couple of plastic cups full of weak coffee.

'Not exactly the Ritz,' he said, 'but it will have to do.'

'I'm not really thirsty anyhow,' Christine answered. 'Is it true, what you told Colette? You're living in London now?'

He nodded, stirring the contents of his cup with the plastic spoon provided. 'I've a flat in Ealing, in one of those big prewar blocks that survived the Blitz. I've been up here for two years, ever since I got my promotion and was transferred to headquarters.'

'Oh, Russ!' she said, genuinely pleased. 'Congratulations! Promotion's no more than you deserved. Lois always used to say you were going places.'

'How is Lois?' he asked. 'I don't imagine you see much of her nowadays.'

'Not as much as I'd like to, but not for the reason you imagine. Rowe would never stop me seeing my friends. But two small children keep her pretty busy. I always drive over to see her whenever we're at Mallerby House. The elder girl, Cheryl, is my god-daughter.'

Russ laughed. 'Trust Lois to choose a name like Cheryl.'

'It's a diminutive of Charlotte, in case you're interested, and means "little woman". I think it's pretty.' Christine smiled. 'Although I must admit that Cheryl

234

Aylward is not all that euphonious or easy to say. The other little girl, Judith, is much more prosaically named.'

He said quietly: 'I was sorry to hear that you'd lost your baby. Your mother told mine. Also that you couldn't have any more.'

Christine swallowed hard, conscious of tears stinging her eyelids. She sipped the weak liquid in the plastic cup. 'It was a bad time,' she admitted, then forced a smile. 'But it's over now. You're not married yet, so Lois tells me.'

He made no reply for a moment, apparently wrapped in contemplation of a very large lady in extremely tight jeans. When he could eventually tear his eyes away, he smiled a little sadly. 'I've only ever wanted to marry one woman, and as she wouldn't have me . . .' He broke off, making an apologetic grimace. 'Sorry. Didn't mean to bring that up.'

Christine felt a surge of guilt and said uncomfortably: 'Oh, Russ! There were always so many women after you. I can't believe you're still wearing the willow.' Two young children, brother and sister by their looks, were weaving in and out of the tables, their arms outspread, screaming and whining in imitation of aeroplane engines. Their parents looked on indulgently, unconcerned by the disturbance they were causing. 'Why on earth can't people control their children?' she added irritably. 'If they belonged to me . . .' But they would never belong to her. She looked up in time to see the compassion in Russell's eyes. 'Oh damn!' she laughed. 'What a pair we are. The first time we've met in years and all we can do is sit here feeling sorry for ourselves and one another.'

He grinned. 'You're quite right. Let's change the subject. Pick one.'

'OK.' She pushed the plastic mug and its unfinished contents to one side. 'You said you'd come to meet a

235

friend who hadn't turned up. What do you think has happened to him?'

'She,' he said. '*She* hasn't turned up. But when you know who it is you won't find it surprising.' He paused for a second, enjoying her mystification, then added: 'It's Lucy Brennan.'

'Lucy Brennan!' Christine was incredulous. 'But . . . but why? How? I mean . . .' She stopped, lost for words.

'Why would she write to me, d'you mean?' Christine nodded. Russell continued. 'You remember I went up to the Lake District that year that . . . that year that you broke off our engagement?'

'There was never any engagement,' she countered swiftly.

He shrugged. 'All right, if you want to be strictly accurate. But there was an understanding. Anyway, as I said, I went on holiday to the Lakes that October . . . November. I forget exactly when. Some time that autumn. And I met Lucy Brennan again. She was staying with a married friend near Ambleside whose husband didn't approve of her, and I was on my own at the hotel in Windermere, so I suppose it was natural that we should have met once or twice. The upshot being that every now and then she sends me a postcard from wherever she happens to be at the present moment. I had one such card a few days ago, from Hamburg, to say she might just possibly pop over to London on today's afternoon plane. She was on her way down to the south of France for the rest of the summer, but . . . well, you remember Lucy! A detour via London would be all in a day's march to her. But, as I said, she didn't arrive. Something cropped up, no doubt, to change her plans.' Russell pulled down one corner of his mouth. ' "Plans" is probably the wrong word to use. Lucy never has plans. She just drifts.'

'And you came to meet her on the off-chance?' Christine was too surprised to comment further on this revelation that Russell still kept in touch, however infrequently, with Lucy Brennan. She felt a little stab of something that was almost like jealousy and picked up her handbag from the orange-topped table. 'I hope I'm not rushing you,' she said, 'but I ought to go. Rowe and I are dining out later this evening.'

'No, of course you're not rushing me.' But his tone lacked conviction. He fished in his trouser pocket and produced his car keys. 'Right, let's be off, then.'

He took her arm and guided her towards the escalator.

CHAPTER TWENTY-THREE

CHRISTINE HAD HAD HER BATH and was trying to decide what to wear when Rowland came in. He stood in the bedroom doorway, watching her.

'Wear that red thing,' he suggested. 'It suits you. Gives you some colour.'

She jumped and turned. 'Heavens, you gave me a start. I didn't know you were there. And "that red thing", as you call it, cost you a great deal of money. Over three hundred pounds.'

'Old or new currency?' he asked flippantly, coming round the end of the bed to kiss her. 'This decimalization is playing havoc with inflation.'

He looked tired, as he always did when he returned from the bank. He put his arms around her, and she could feel her body take his weight as he sagged against her. She slid her own arms behind his back, supporting him, and they remained like that for a little while, neither of them speaking.

'I need you, Chris,' he said at last. 'You know that, don't you?'

'I'm beginning to,' she answered. 'There was a time when I thought . . . well, that you'd be better off without me, but now I'm not sure that's true. But you're still not in love with me.'

He rocked her gently to and fro, his eyes closed as though he could hardly keep awake. 'I told you years ago,' he murmured, 'love's a myth. It belongs to fairy-tales and Shakespeare. But you're my safe anchorage. My calm at the eye of the storm.'

She could not help laughing, even though her heart was hammering in her chest. 'For a man who doesn't believe in love, you have a very poetic line in conversation.' But she was sober again instantly. 'And what's Maxine Larson?' she asked, knowing full well that she was treading on dangerous ground. Her heart-rate accelerated even faster.

She thought for a moment that he wasn't going to answer. Then he said: 'I like women. After all these years, you should know that.' There was no trace of apology in his voice. 'I don't believe that man was meant to be a monogamous animal. It's something Church and State dreamed up between them for the protection of the family.'

Christine gently released herself from his embrace. 'But we don't have a family – is that what you're saying? My fault, I know. Hadn't you better start getting undressed? You haven't even showered yet. The Semphills are expecting us at eight. Eight for eight-thirty.'

Rowland made no comment, but started shedding his clothes as he moved towards the bathroom. What had got into her? Christine wondered dismally, as the connecting door closed behind him. She had deliberately broken up a moment of tenderness and intimacy; shattered it beyond repair, so that it lay in shining fragments all around her. Why had she done it? Had it been because of that unexpected mention of Lucy Brennan this afternoon, following as it did on the heels of her own unexplained recollection of Lucy the previous evening? Was it some kind of a portent of things to come?

'Now you're being stupid!' she told herself severely. It had been pure coincidence, nothing more. She just wished she could explain to herself why the recollection of Lucy Brennan, the mere sound of her name, always made her so uneasy.

The bathroom door opened, and Rowland reappeared, wrapped in a bath-towel. He looked better; there was more colour in his face, even if it had only been induced by the heat of the water, and the strained expression had left his eyes. He padded across the carpet to where Christine was sitting, on the edge of the bed, still staring unseeingly at the contents of her wardrobe.

'For God's sake,' he laughed softly, 'haven't you made up your mind yet what to wear? Here!' He stepped forward and pulled the red dress off its hanger. 'I've told you. It suits you. You'll be the best-looking woman in the room.' He sat down beside her. 'And another thing. Don't ever let me hear you blame yourself again because we haven't a family. It's not your fault. It's just one of those things.'

'But you wouldn't have married me—' she began, but got no further. He pulled her down on the bed, stopping her mouth with kisses. And for the next half-hour she forgot everything else in the ecstasy of love-making.

But later, seated round the Semphills' dining-table, watching Rowland flirt outrageously with Mollie Semphill, and the way a smile lit his eyes every time he looked across at Maxine Larson, all Christine's doubts and anger came flooding back, and with them the memories and vague anxieties about Lucy Brennan. It was no use now telling herself not to be silly. She could not rid herself of the idea that this afternoon's meeting with Russell and his mention of Lucy had been some kind of omen.

Ridiculous, of course! She was far too rational a woman to believe in omens. Even when it happened, Christine would not allow herself to indulge in such idiotic fancies. It was coincidence, chance, anything she liked to call it except a warning from Fate.

The family – herself, Rowland, Colette, Julian and Vivien, but not Sophie – were at Hinton Malsherbes for the August bank holiday. This had been moved, by arbitrary Whitehall decrees, from the first to the last

240

Monday in the month, and it was not always possible nowadays for Rowland to be present. Late August was much closer to the annual family vacation in France, which was sacrosanct, and on occasions he had found it necessary to work over the bank holiday. This year, however, he had been determined to get to Mallerby for the Monday opening if he could. It was the one day when people really expected to see him. Regular visitors, who remembered and liked him, felt cheated when he was not present. So, to the relief of his fellow-directors, all of whom had plans to play golf, or to 'mess around in boats', or simply to laze in deck-chairs, Rowland had departed for Somerset on Friday evening with the avowed intention of not returning to the bank until Tuesday morning.

Christine was delighted by the decision, and Colette had remarked austerely that, finally, he was showing a bit of sense. He had been overworking lately and was looking strained and tense. There had been family problems, too, with Sophie, whose latest affair had landed her name in the gossip column of one of the more scurrilous national dailies. Julian had been pouring his heart out to his brother.

'One of these days, she'll up and leave me. She'll just go. I can see it coming.'

Rowland had been patient. 'But wouldn't that be the best thing all round?'

'Not if she fights me for custody of Vivien. Besides, I'm still fond of her.' Julian's voice had grown plaintive. 'I wouldn't want to lose her completely.'

'What in heaven's name can you do with him?' Rowland had asked Christine in despair. 'How the hell can anyone, in his right mind, be fond of Sophie?'

Sophie, however, was not at Mallerby this weekend to create dissension. It should, Christine thought, looking out of her bedroom window on the Friday evening, be three whole days of peace and tranquillity. The open parkland, visible beyond the formal gardens, drowsed in the summer warmth, carpeted with buttercups and daisies. The immediate foreground was studded with trees, beeches and once-fine elms – now dead and leafless, victims of Dutch elm disease – planted centuries ago to shelter the house from easterly winds. But in the distance the valley opened out; acres of the thin sour grass which had earned Hinton Malsherbes its name.

Rowland came up behind her and put his hands on her shoulders. 'I'm looking forward to this weekend,' he said, echoing her thoughts. 'I mean to enjoy myself and forget the fact that poor old Ted Heath's economic policies just aren't working. Growth's slow, investment's down and—' But he was allowed to get no further. Christine twisted round and laid a finger against his lips.

'That's quite enough of that. I don't want to hear the words "economic growth", or lack of it, mentioned for the next seventy-six hours. If they are, I shall pack my bags and go straight back to London.'

He laughed. 'Idle threats, my girl. I happen to know you've made arrangements to go over to Shaftesbury tomorrow, and wild horses won't stop you visiting Lois.'

'Won't you come with me?' she asked a little wistfully, but Rowland shook his head.

'Better not. I like Lois a lot, but Barry and I have never got on. He thinks I'm a bloated plutocrat and eyes me with deep suspicion. Whenever I've gone with you in the past, he's worn a bright red tie and had a copy of *Das Kapital* prominently displayed on the coffee-table.'

It was Christine's turn to laugh. 'You liar! He's done nothing of the sort. All the same,' she added more cheerfully, 'I must admit he's pretty far left in his views. Perhaps you would be safer at home.'

'As a matter of fact, in the morning I'm going riding with Julian. And after lunch I shall just browse around the village and renew old friendships. Now, we'd better get showered and changed or we'll be late for dinner, and you know how much store Maman places on punctuality. We don't want to blot our copy-books the very first evening.'

'Right.' Christine made a grab for her dressing-gown. 'Bags I the bathroom first.'

'First come, first served!' yelled Rowland, and a moment later they were both shoving and jostling each other in the bathroom doorway, like a couple of children let out of school. Later that evening, after the telephone call, Christine was to remember how happy she had been.

The call came through just as Mrs Renshaw carried in the summer pudding, the mound of juice-soaked bread sitting in the middle of a blue lustre dish and bursting at the seams with redcurrants and raspberries. As she placed it on the table in front of Christine, flanking it with a jug of rich Devonshire cream, the telephone bell began to ring in the entrance-hall and the library. Several moments passed, then Rose James appeared in the dining-room doorway.

'It's for you, Mr Saxelby,' she said to Rowland. 'A call from Paris. A lady. But it's not Madame de Bérenger, nor Mrs Lucien, either. Her English is about as good as my French, which isn't saying much, as you know, but I did manage to gather that she wants to speak to you. Sounded pretty urgent, too.'

Colette frowned. 'Whoever can that be?'

Rowland got to his feet. 'I'd better go and find out. And don't eat all the pudding before I get back. Summer pudding's my favourite. Mrs Renshaw made that especially for me.'

The housekeeper smirked, and Christine reflected how pleased all members of the staff always were to be singled out by Rowland. Poor Julian. He had never really stood a chance, perpetually overshadowed by his brother. But, then, he seemed to like it that way. She began to dish out the pudding.

243

Colette and her younger son resumed their discussion about the Oz obscenity trial, and the rights and wrongs of gaoling three of the magazine's editors. Christine listened in growing irritation to Julian gradually abandoning his own more liberal stance as he allowed himself to be influenced by his mother's point of view. She was just about to interrupt with a scathing indictment of the judge, plus the hope that the conviction would be quashed on appeal, when Rowland returned. She had only to take one look at his face to realize that something traumatic had happened. All other considerations were immediately forgotten.

'Rowe! Darling! What's the matter?'

The urgency of her tone caught the others' attention, and Colette broke off in mid-sentence to stare at her son. Julian, too, became aware that something was amiss.

'Rowland, what is it?' Colette was half out of her chair, her face suddenly very white. 'Something has happened to the family . . . Oh my God! A car accident! They've all been killed. Maman, Lucien and little Giles!' Even in the midst of her own anxiety, Christine noted with grim amusement that Colette had not named Solange. There had never been a great deal of affection between the two sisters-in-law. They tolerated one another, which was about all one could say. 'For pity's sake, say something!' Colette continued, her voice rising almost to a scream.

'No, no! It's nothing like that.' Rowland sank into his chair, absent-mindedly pushing aside the bowl containing his portion of summer pudding. 'No one's been hurt. No one's been killed. In fact . . . quite the opposite.' He put up a hand and pushed the lank dark hair away from his forehead. There was a dazed expression in his eyes. 'It seems', he added after a moment's charged silence, 'that I have a son.'

The words were at first meaningless to the other three, who continued to stare at him as though waiting for him to speak. Then Colette asked: 'What do you mean?'

Rowland repeated slowly, wonderingly: 'I have a son. He's ten years old.'

'What in hell's name are you talking about?' Julian demanded. 'Have you had too much to drink, old son?'

Christine said nothing, but she could feel the cold clutch of fear in the pit of her stomach. It was as though this was a moment she had seen coming from a long way off, watching it inexorably drawing closer, without being able to define either its nature or its form.

With a great effort, Rowland seemed to collect his thoughts and fixed his gaze on her face. 'I must go back to town tonight and catch the first plane to Paris in the morning. I want you to come with me, Chris. Patrick's going to need you.'

It was the first time she ever heard her step-son's name, but it told her at once all she wanted to know. That and his age. 'He's Lucy Brennan's son, isn't he?' she asked flatly.

Colette banged her fist on the table. 'Will one of you please inform me exactly what is going on? Rowland! I demand an explanation! Who was that on the phone just now?'

Rowland took a deep breath. 'That, Maman, was a Madame Dupont, the owner of a small hotel near the Place du Tertre. Last night, a woman – an Englishwoman, Madame called her, but that's a natural enough mistake – checked in with a young boy. Today, the woman has vanished, leaving the boy behind with a letter addressed to me and a note for Madame, informing her that he is *my* son and asking her to contact me urgently. It's taken the poor woman most of the day to trace me, having first telephoned the bank – the only address Lucy could remember – who put her on to Inglebatch House, where she drew a blank because we'd all left by then. It was only

245

when Mrs Jones arrived there this evening that she finally managed to get through and was given this number.'

'I still don't understand,' Colette protested. 'Do you mean to tell me that when you parted from this Lucy Brennan you had no idea that she was going to have your baby?'

Rowland shook his head. 'I don't suppose she knew herself at that time. She must have discovered she was pregnant later.' Without being at all aware of what he was doing, he pulled the bowl towards him again and began to eat his pudding. Christine mechanically passed him the cream. Her own pudding lay untasted in its dish.

'Are you sure this boy really is your son?' she asked quietly. 'Could he possibly belong to anyone else?'

Her mother-in-law nodded vigorously. 'A very good point. Well, Rowland? What do you say? It seems to me that a woman like this Lucy Brennan might have to do the "eeny-meeny-miny-mo" to decide who she is going to name as the father of her child.'

'I don't think that's very fair, Maman,' Rowland answered levelly, but with an underlying note of anger. 'However, the main reason that I'm going to Paris is to satisfy myself on that point. Thank you, Mrs Renshaw,' he added, as the housekeeper came in with the coffee and started to clear the dirty plates. 'It was an absolutely delicious summer pudding. One of your best.' Christine guessed that he could not even remember tasting it, but on no account would he hurt Mrs Renshaw's feelings.

When they once more had the room to themselves, Julian asked, voicing the thought uppermost in all their minds: 'And if you are satisfied this boy is your son, what then?'

Rowland glanced at his brother, puzzled. 'I shall bring him home, of course.'

* * *

Christine reclined in the front seat of the car, pretending to doze, but really wide awake. She could hear the rush of the tyres against the tarmac; could see, through half-closed lids, the black shapes of trees as they fled past the window; could feel Rowland's excitement as he coaxed a dangerously high speed from the engine over the long deserted stretches of night-time roads. That moment before dinner, when, just for a minute, they had seemed to mean everything to each other, was already a lifetime away. Rowland believed, because he desperately wanted to believe, that this boy, abandoned by Lucy Brennan in the Paris hotel, was his son.

Christine herself had very few doubts that it was so; and even those she had were based on hope rather than on likelihood. If Patrick Brennan was indeed ten years old, that meant he had been born some time in 1961, and if during the first half of the year there was very little possibility of him not being Rowland's child. Rowland and Lucy had been together from June or July of 1960 until the autumn. However many calculations Christine's tired brain did, it always came up with the same answer.

They reached Inglebatch House just after midnight and went straight to bed. Rowland had already booked their seats on the early-morning Paris flight from Heathrow before they left Hinton Malsherbes. As she was falling asleep, Christine felt Rowland's arm steal round her waist, cuddling her against him.

'Thanks, Chris,' he whispered.

'What for?' she mumbled.

'Oh . . . just for everything. For being you. Not making a fuss. Taking me as I am.' His voice grew fainter as he drifted towards unconsciousness. 'You'll make a good mother, you know. For Patrick.'

A good mother for Lucy Brennan's bastard. Yes, that was her. Good old Chris! She stared unseeingly into the darkness.

CHAPTER TWENTY-FOUR

THE HÔTEL VILLETTE was in a side-street off the Place du Tertre, where already, because it promised to be another fine day, people were gathering at tables set out on the cobbles beneath coloured umbrellas. Through the tracery of trees could be seen the gleaming white dome of the Sacré-Cœur, and a number of young artists were hard at work painting the view or offering to sketch a portrait. One youth, with long black hair and an engaging smile, accosted Christine, but Rowland waved him aside with an impatient hand and a terse French phrase.

Christine protested. 'Did you have to be quite so rude?'

Her husband shrugged. 'Je m'en fiche!' Then he paused and turned to face her, looking rueful. 'Sorry. I'm just nervous, I suppose, at the thought of seeing Patrick.'

She nodded understandingly. 'Of course you are. Let's get on, then. I think this must be the street.'

The Hôtel Villette was halfway along the narrow cobbled alley, a tall thin building, three storeys high, with green shuttered windows. Inside, it was very dark and smelt of garlic. Christine's immediate impression was of a welter of potted palms and red plush velvet. The reception-desk was deserted, so Rowland pressed the bell.

Madame Dupont, when she arrived, a little breathless, from a room at the back, proved to be as tall and thin and shabby as her hotel. The hawk-like nose in a deeply lined face supported a pince-nez, and the grey hair was twisted into the nape of her neck in an untidy bun.

'Monsieur?' she queried, somewhat intimidated by Rowland's air of affluence and authority.

There followed a protracted exchange in French, far too rapid for Christine to make head or tail of. She waited patiently, studying her surroundings, until such time as Rowland could translate for her. It seemed exactly the sort of place that Lucy Brennan would choose: cheap, rather seedy and none too clean. Christine's head and feet ached, and she longed for another cup of coffee. She had drunk two on the plane with her breakfast, but her mouth still felt dry. She supposed it was due to nerves.

Today, Saturday, she should have been in Shaftesbury with Lois and her family, taking the children to the park, or driving out somewhere into the country – Sherborne, perhaps, or Wardour Castle. Instead she was in Paris to meet Lucy Brennan's son. She had at least been able to telephone Lois before they left for the airport that morning.

Lucy Brennan's son. Rowland's son? Undoubtedly.

A sudden thought struck Christine. Did Russell Jennings know that Lucy had a child? According to him, he had met her only once since the holiday in Devon; in the Lake District during the autumn of 1960. October or November, he had said, in which case, depending on the time of conception, Lucy might not have looked pregnant, even though she certainly must have been. Had she confided in him? Unlikely, Christine thought, or surely he would have mentioned the fact. Nevertheless, as soon as she returned to London she would telephone and ask him. It would give her an excuse to get in touch with him again.

Before she had time to analyse her motive for wanting to contact Russell, Rowland was claiming her attention.

'This way,' he said. 'The boy's upstairs.' He added with a laugh: 'Lucy absconded without paying her bill. Typical! However, I've promised Madame that I'll settle the whole account.'

The child was in a second-floor bedroom at the back of the hotel, lying supine on the bed, reading a book. He looked as though he had recently been crying. As they entered, he laid the book aside and sat bolt upright, a look of apprehension on his face.

'Are you my father?' he asked Rowland with a pronounced Irish accent.

Rowland went over and sat on the edge of the bed. 'That's what I'm here to find out,' he answered gently.

The boy blinked nervously. He was a very thin child, tall for his age, with a strong look of his mother about him. But he also bore, surely, a resemblance to Rowland. The colour of his eyes, that deep startling blue, was, of course, Lucy's, but the dark, almost black hair and thin mobile mouth reminded Christine at once of her husband. The skin was paler, olive-tinted, but that, again, Patrick Brennan inherited from his mother. Judging by appearance alone, there could be little doubt about his parentage.

Madame Dupont, who had left them for a few minutes, returned clutching a cheap foolscap manila envelope, which she handed to Rowland.

'The ... the letter', she said, making an effort to speak in English for Christine's benefit, 'is inside with his ... his ... *acte de naissance,*' she finished, not knowing the correct expression.

'Birth certificate. Merci, Madame.' Rowland smiled a dismissal.

When she had reluctantly withdrawn, he opened the envelope and shook the contents on to the bed. There was an official-looking document and a thin sheet of foreign notepaper covered in Lucy's scrawling hand. Rowland first picked up the birth certificate and read it.

250

'Born Madrid, on the eleventh of May 1961,' he said and handed it to Christine. 'The dates fit at any rate.'

'Did you think they wouldn't?' She was unable to prevent a sour note creeping into her voice, but he did not seem to notice.

'No, not really.' He turned his attention to the letter. 'Lucy's writing hasn't improved, that much is certain.'

While he skimmed through it, Christine went to the other side of the bed and looked down at Patrick. 'Hello,' she said. 'What are you reading?'

'*Treasure Island.*' He made a face. 'I don't like it much. I'd rather have science fiction.'

She laughed. 'I dare say you would, but I expect this is better for you.'

'That's what my mother said, but I don't see why.' But at the mention of Lucy his thin mouth quivered.

Christine sat down and cradled him in her arms. 'Don't cry,' she said. 'We'll look after you.'

He made no objection to her embrace as many boys of his age would have done, but he did mutter rebelliously: 'I don't see why I have to go to school and get an education. I'm all right as I am. I don't see what's so all-fired important about it. I don't know why Mummy had to go away and leave me.' And he burst into tears.

'Hush. Hush,' Christine murmured inadequately, smoothing his hair. 'I expect your mother thought she was doing the right thing, you know. Children do need a proper education, and it can't have been much fun for you never staying in one place for very long. You can't have made any friends.'

'I don't need friends!' he exclaimed fiercely, pushing her away and wiping his eyes and nose with the back of his hand. 'It was all right, just Mum and me. I don't want to live in just one place.'

'You won't have to,' Rowland answered cheerfully, ignoring the child's pathetic heart-rending sniff. 'Sometimes we'll live in London, sometimes in the country. And, later on, you'll be going away to school. You'll enjoy it,' he added positively. 'There will be so much to do, you won't have time to miss your mother.'

'Have a heart,' Christine muttered, horrified by these ruthless tactics, but Rowland only gave her a warning shake of the head.

And she had to admit that his methods seemed to be justified. Patrick had stopped crying and was regarding Rowland with a calculating look in his bright blue eyes. 'Shall I have my own bedroom?' he asked.

'Of course.'

'Lots of clothes?'

'As many as are necessary.'

'And can I have a dog and a bicycle and a horse?'

Rowland grinned and leaned across to ruffle the dark hair. 'We'll have to wait and see about that little lot, but, yes, probably. All in good time. Now, be a good chap and start getting your things together. Christine will help you.' He got off the bed. 'I'll be downstairs in the foyer. I have to settle up with Madame.'

'Where are you taking me?' Patrick asked, with a return of his former uneasiness.

Rowland smiled reassuringly. 'For the rest of today, to my uncle's house in the Avenue Foch. Then, tomorrow, you'll be coming home with us, to England.'

The Villa Dauphine was at the western end of the Avenue Foch, not far from the Porte Dauphine. A square stuccoed building, it stood a little way back from the road, behind a low wall and some elegantly decorative railings. It had been the Bérenger Paris home now for over a hundred years.

Patrick, worn out by excitement and the trauma of the last two days, was packed off to bed as soon as

252

dinner was over, barely able to keep awake. Giles, too, retired to his room, but the four adults were served coffee and brandy in the Yellow Salon at the front of the house, Lucien taking this, the first real opportunity he had had since returning home that evening from the bank, to speak his mind.

'You're a fool,' he told his nephew roundly. 'Accepting this boy as your son on nothing more than a woman's say-so! Absolute madness! What do you say, eh, Christine?'

Tight-lipped, Rowland translated for her. She placed the delicate Sèvres coffee-cup on the spindle-legged table beside her and glanced from her husband to Lucien.

'I don't think there's any doubt that Patrick is Rowland's son,' she said quietly. 'So it's only natural that he should want to give him a home. I only hope we can make the child happy, and that he doesn't find a conventional upbringing too restricting after the nomadic life he must have led with his mother.'

Lucien, who could follow English much better than he was able to speak it, snorted disparagingly, but Rowland gave Christine a grateful smile and squeezed her hand. Solange continued placidly with her embroidery.

'What does your mother have to say about it?' Lucien demanded after a moment's silence, unwilling to let the subject drop.

Rowland frowned into his brandy, swirling the amber liquid around the sides of his glass. He raised a pugnacious chin and stared coldly at his uncle.

'Maman won't interfere. Whatever she thinks, she'll have the good sense to keep it to herself.'

Lucien gave a bark of laughter. 'That doesn't sound like my big sister. Colette could never keep a still tongue in her head.'

'Perhaps she's more anglicized than she used to be. We English believe in minding our own business.'

Christine, who had understood most of the conversation, realized that a quarrel was brewing. If only her spoken French were better, she might be able to avert it; and she resolved to start learning the language properly as soon as she returned home. School-book French was no good. She needed to be able to speak it colloquially, idiomatically, as Rowland did. Meantime, she would have to find another means of preventing a row between Rowland and his uncle.

She got up gracefully and went across to where Lucien was standing, feet aggressively apart, in front of the empty fireplace. She slipped a hand through his arm and kissed his cheek.

'There really isn't any doubt', she said, 'that Patrick is Rowland's son. The dates fit. No one else could be his father. You, of all people, surely wouldn't want to deprive a man of his son.'

Lucien, without comprehending all she said, nevertheless got the gist of it. He was pleased, too, by her gesture of affection. He had always thought his elder nephew's wife a handsome woman, had admired her from afar, but had always been slightly intimidated by her cool English reserve. Now, however, he took the liberty of putting an arm about her waist and kissing her resoundingly full on the lips.

'You have a wife in a thousand here,' he told Rowland severely, but there was a twinkle in his eye. The awkward moment had passed.

'I know it. I know it,' Rowland agreed, laughing and holding out his hands to Christine.

She returned to sit beside him on the sofa and drink her coffee. Solange beamed placidly at them from her corner and selected a strand of emerald embroidery silk from the little pile on her work-table.

'A bit of a diplomat, too,' Lucien added.

'I know that also.' Rowland smiled at his wife, and, as always when he did that, Christine felt weak with love.

She glanced up to see such a look of sympathy in Lucien's eyes that the colour burned in her cheeks. It was a look she had seen far too often on people's faces, and one which she was almost bound to see even more frequently in the future, now that Patrick was to become a part of her and Rowland's lives. She could hear the whispers, the sly innuendoes.

'My dear! What next? Now he's saddled her with one of his bastards.'

'More fool her, then, to let him do it.'

And they would be right. But how could you explain to people who had never been in love what the real thing was like? Apart from anything else, Rowland was the nicest person she had ever met; kind, gentle, considerate; good with animals and children ... Christine suppressed a grin. Damn it all! It sounded as though she were giving him a reference. And she wasn't the only woman who had fallen for him hook, line and sinker. She was just the lucky one whom he had married. The point was she didn't feel put upon or used or taken advantage of, and it wasn't her fault if other people saw her that way. It was their misfortune not to understand that true love, even if it were unrequited, could lift them up among the stars ... 'A penny for them,' Rowland said, and she jumped.

'What? Oh, sorry. I was miles away.'

Rowland got to his feet. 'You're tired,' he said. 'It's been a long day. Aunt Solange and Uncle Lucien won't mind if we turn in. We have an early start in the morning.'

Solange smiled calmly, when the situation was explained to her, and wished them 'Bonne nuit'. Lucien gave Christine another smacking kiss and whispered 'Bonne chance!' in her ear. This time, she was able to smile back at him with perfect equanimity.

'I had all the good luck I ever needed when I married Rowe.'

Rowland laughed and clapped his uncle on the shoulder. 'There's an English expression', he said, 'which goes "Stick that in your pipe and smoke it"!'

But later, when they were finally in bed, listening, through the open window, to the muted sounds of Paris by night, he took her in his arms and held her close.

'I don't deserve you,' he whispered, 'but, then, I've told you that before. Thank you for putting up with me.'

She stroked his face, feeling the hollows beneath the cheek-bones. 'There's nothing to thank me for. I love you because you're you. I shouldn't have fallen in love with you if you'd been different. You wouldn't have been the same person.'

'I can't change, you know. It wouldn't be fair to pretend that I can. I shall go on seeing Maxine.'

'I know that. It doesn't matter.'

'Doesn't it?' He held her tighter. You think, he mocked himself, that because you're honest, with yourself and with her, that it makes everything all right. And you're never utterly, entirely, completely honest. There are times, quite rightly, when you don't like yourself: when you at least have the courage to admit that you're a cheat.

Christine kissed him lightly on the mouth. 'No,' she said, 'it doesn't. My love for you is an integral part of me. Without it, I'd be a poorer person. That's what matters.'

They made love, and afterwards slept in each other's arms. Or, rather, Rowland slept. Christine lay awake for a long time, thinking about Patrick and Lucy Brennan, and about the holiday in Devon all those years ago. Something stirred at the edges of her memory: a tiny nagging recollection which raised a ghostly head, then vanished again and would not resurface, however hard she tried to coax it back. But it left behind a ripple of disturbance; a feeling that there was something she ought to remember and couldn't . . . Finally she, too, fell asleep.

'And this is your grandmother,' Rowland said. 'Maman, meet your grandson.'

They had gone straight from the airport to Hinton Malsherbes, with Patrick wide-eyed and excited in the back of the car. He had talked almost non-stop all the way from Paris, asking a hundred questions without waiting for a single answer. Neither Christine nor Rowland had attempted to check him, accepting that it was a reaction to the nervous tension which had him in its grip. His young life, secure in its very insecurity, had been rudely torn asunder; arbitrarily broken in two by his mother's decision to be rid of him. And that fact was something he still had to come to terms with.

Now, however, faced with this unknown grandmother, not to mention an uncle and a cousin, the latter only a year younger than himself, his tongue and his composure both deserted him. He backed against Christine, groping for her hand, and burst into a flood of tears.

'Well,' said Colette, raising her eyebrows, 'not what you'd call an auspicious start.' She regarded Patrick consideringly. 'All the same, he looks like a Saxelby, I'll give you that. There's a touch of the Bérengers about him, too.' She held out her hand peremptorily. 'Come here, *mon cher*. Stop behaving like a silly child and kiss your grandmother.'

Standing beside her husband, Christine could almost feel Rowland's relief. He had accepted Patrick as his son, and it was vital for his peace of mind that his mother did, too. Gently Christine released her stepson's hand and once again pushed him towards Colette. Reluctantly this time Patrick went, still sniffing. Colette gave him a handkerchief and told him to blow

257

his nose. Then she enfolded him in a warm scented embrace.

It had all been too easy, Christine thought. Only one little hitch with Lucien and even that, thanks to her, had been smoothed over. Patrick Brennan, Lucy Brennan's son, had come home.

CHAPTER TWENTY-FIVE

IN THE ENSUING MONTHS, learning how to become an adequate mother to a ten-year-old boy – a boy, moreover, who had led such an unconventional life – Christine forgot about Russell Jennings. That, perhaps, was not quite true; but she certainly pushed all thought of him to the back of her mind, concentrating on Patrick, trying to control his more excessive demands and attempting to put a brake on Rowland's spending. Given his head, her husband would have showered Patrick with everything he asked for: it was only Christine's forceful and repeated representations that prevented Patrick's rooms at both Inglebatch and Mallerby House from being overrun with all the latest toys.

As it was, he got most of the things he asked for; the shiny lightweight bicycle, with continental hubs, was followed by Crab, the mongrel, chosen with loving care from Battersea Dogs' Home and named after Launce's dog in *The Two Gentlemen of Verona*. (One thing Lucy seemed not to have neglected, somewhat surprisingly, was her son's introduction to the classics.) A grey Welsh mountain pony, called, this time with less imagination, Snowy, short for Snowdonia, graced the stables at Mallerby.

'You're spoiling that child,' Colette said crossly, adding her protest to Christine's. But she was just as bad herself, particularly as Christmas approached, ransacking the toy department at Harrods and haunting Hamleys.

Julian, on the other hand, ignored his nephew's existence as much as possible, jealous on his daughter's behalf, but also, Christine suspected, on his own. There was no doubt that Rowland had less time for his brother now that he had a son to claim his attention. And with his marriage going from bad to worse, with Sophie's name constantly in the gossip columns, Julian needed Rowland's sympathetic ear and advice. He had always been able to count on them in the past. Nowadays, however, he found Rowland preoccupied and less willing to listen.

Christine liked Patrick. He had all his father's charm and his mother's happy-go-lucky nature. But she refused to let herself be blinded. Her step-son, she discovered, could be both selfish and greedy; no more, perhaps, than other children of his age, but less blatantly so. He got his way by cunning rather than by tantrums; and she was inclined to agree with Julian's assessment of Patrick, that he manipulated people. With more charity than her brother-in-law, she ascribed this tendency to the life the boy had led since birth, the people he had mixed with. He was old for his age, and she thought it would have been better for him if he had been sent to school immediately, rather than taught at home by private tutors.

'Look,' Rowland said, defending this decision, 'he's led a footloose life with Lucy and it's only fair to break him in gently. Besides, if he's to get a place at Clifton, he needs to concentrate. He's a hell of a lot of leeway to make up. He needs a crammer.'

Christine disagreed, but thought it wisest to hold her tongue. Rowland's temper was short these past few weeks. He was working long hours at the bank as the building boom of the sixties began to collapse, taking whole companies with it, and the bank was forced to call in loans. Ted Heath's Tory government had reduced spending and lowered taxes in an effort to encourage investment, but the policies had failed to produce the necessary economic growth.

The affair with Maxine Larson was not progressing satisfactorily, either. Christine suspected that the lady was becoming too possessive, too demanding. Sooner or later, the various women in Rowland's life mentioned the word 'divorce', their own and his, with a view to stabilizing their relationship, completely misreading the situation. In the end, they were forced to accept the *status quo*, but only after months of wrangling, which Rowland hated. Christine knew from long experience when one of these crises had been reached: he was unnaturally touchy and bad-tempered.

It was to avoid quarrelling with him and saying things which she might later regret that she went Christmas shopping one afternoon towards the end of December – the last Saturday before they all went down to Hinton Malsherbes for the holiday. She still had to buy a present for Colette, and was in Bond Street, looking in the windows of Asprey's, when someone touched her lightly on the shoulder.

'Hello, Chris.' It was Russell Jennings, looking with wry amusement from her to the window-display of leather goods, gold and silver jewellery and rare antiques. 'How the rich live, eh? Don't let me stop you if you were just going in.'

'Russ!' She ignored his comments and gripped his arm. 'I'm glad we've bumped into one another. There's something I want to ask you. Come on! We'll go and have tea in John Lewis's.'

'You don't have to slum it just because I'm with you,' he taunted her, but once again she took no notice. Firmly she guided him back the way she had come, towards Oxford Street.

When they were comfortably settled at a table in the restaurant, and had ordered tea and assorted cakes, Christine came straight to the point.

'Did you have any idea', she asked, 'that Lucy Brennan had a child? Rowland's child?'

Russell stirred his tea, then glanced up, smiling. 'I'll say this for you, Chris, you don't waste time on preliminaries. "How are you, Russ?" "How nice to see

261

you again, Russ." "What have you been doing with yourself in the months since we last met?" No silly nonsense of that kind. Just straight in with your latest problem about dear Rowland.'

She regarded him narrowly. 'You did know, didn't you? That information didn't surprise you at all. So how did you know? Come on. Tell me!'

'As I said, no finesse. All right. I'll play ball. Yes, I did know about Patrick Brennan. I gather *you* now know as well. How did that happen?'

Christine shook her head. 'That can wait for a minute. You first.'

Russell shrugged and made a careful inspection of the plate of cakes. 'I told you, when we met back in the summer, that Lucy and I have kept in touch, albeit very infrequently and only by post, since our encounter in the Lakes eleven years ago.' He selected a cream slice and bit into it, the cream oozing like a white beard over his chin. Carefully he wiped it off with his napkin. 'As a matter of fact, that's when she told me she was pregnant. Said she felt like confiding in someone. I asked her, I remember, if she intended to get in touch with Rowland, and she said no. It was all over between them: her decision. They'd split up before she realized she was pregnant, and she was glad. The child would be hers and no one else's. Rowland had no idea and wasn't to know. However' – Russell eyed Christine speculatively – 'I surmise that that situation has now altered.'

Christine explained. Russell said nothing for several seconds, staring at the remainder of his cake, at the wreck of pastry, cream and gooey icing on his plate. Then he looked up, eyes and voice both hostile. 'You mean he's saddled you with his and Lucy Brennan's bastard?'

'I'm not "saddled" as you call it,' Christine responded just a shade too quickly. 'And what else could Rowland do, could either of us do, when Lucy disappeared, abandoning the child like that? We couldn't possibly leave a ten-year-old boy on his own in Paris.'

'Didn't she leave any address where she could be contacted?'

'Not a hint. She just took off somewhere during the night, when Pat was asleep, leaving a letter for Rowe and a note for the proprietress of the hotel, giving her the address of the bank. She didn't even pay her bill.'

Russell snorted disgustedly. 'Typically Lucy! She's never thought of anyone but herself in the whole of her life. So ... What's happening, then? Is Rowland adopting young Patrick?'

Christine looked faintly surprised, as though this idea was new to her. 'He hasn't mentioned *legal* adoption. I don't suppose he feels there's any need. Pat is his son. He was named as father on the birth certificate. There were certain formalities to complete with the Spanish authorities, because Pat was born in Madrid. Although he travelled on Lucy's passport, which I imagine is Irish. It's been a bit messy, but it's all sorted out at last. I don't know a lot about it. Only the bits that Rowe has told me.'

Russell regarded her shrewdly. He suspected, although he did not say, that she did not want to know more; that beneath her complaisant exterior Christine was finding it harder than she would admit, even to herself, to accept the idea of being a loving, caring step-mother to Lucy Brennan's son. He leaned towards her across the table and squeezed her arm.

'I think you're a brick,' he said.

That made her laugh. 'What a very dated expression. "Ace" is more the slang nowadays surely. And, anyway, what rubbish! I'm only doing what any woman would do in the circumstances. I can't give Rowland children, so what a dog in the manger I should be if I begrudged him the son he has.'

'I'd be interested to see the boy some time,' Russell said. 'I feel a sort of proprietorial interest in him,

263

having known of his existence since before he was born.'

'Of course. That could be arranged. I'll give you a ring when we get back to town after the New Year. You gave me your address and telephone number when we met before. I'm sorry I haven't got in touch, as I promised, but now you know why. This business blew up so soon afterwards. Anyway' – she smiled warmly at him – 'tell me all that you've been doing.'

It was well into the New Year before she and Russell met again; a cold raw Saturday afternoon in February, when the whole country was in the grip of the fuel crisis which accompanied the miners' strike. Rowland was once again spending most of his weekends at the bank, trying to get as much work done as possible in those periods between power-cuts when both lighting and heating failed. Colette was out, playing bridge, and Christine found herself with only Patrick for company.

Patrick, who had enjoyed the freedom of Mallerby House and its surrounding acres over Christmas, had been reluctant to return to London and Mr Bryce, his tutor. He disliked the restrictions of lessons and ordered days; was irked by the narrower confines of Inglebatch House. He submitted to all three with a grace surprising in one so young, but Christine suspected that it was not merely gratitude and a desire to please herself and Rowland that motivated him entirely. He also had self-interest at heart. He had seen enough of the world that the Saxelbys inhabited to want his share of it, and understood that, before he could enter, certain standards of behaviour and education would be expected of him. In later years, Christine realized that, for a child of his tender years, Patrick Brennan had picked up remarkably quickly the fine gradations of the English class system, its totems and shibboleths. He meant, from the first, to belong.

Nevertheless, by the weekends, he was ready, like any normal boy, to have fun and be entertained. More than anything else, he wanted Rowland with him, and was inclined to resent it when his father was unavailable. He was fond of Christine, but she discovered early on that he preferred male company. Women tended to bore him. In that way, he was not at all like his father. So, on this particular Saturday, she had the sudden notion of getting in touch with Russell. She had promised him a meeting with Patrick before Christmas, but so far had had no chance to make her promise good. She went to the telephone and dialled the number of the Ealing flat.

He answered almost at once, and was delighted to accept her invitation.

'Where are you thinking of going?' he asked.

'The Tower. Pat hasn't seen it yet. We'll meet you outside the main entrance, in front of the Middle Tower.'

'What time? I believe it closes at four o'clock in the winter.'

They arranged to meet as soon after one-thirty as possible and, in the event, they were all three early. Patrick shook hands solemnly with this unknown man, then said: 'Christine tells me you know my mother.'

'She writes to me from time to time. She sent me a snapshot of you once, when you were a little boy. I think you were about three when it was taken.'

Patrick frowned. 'Did she? I can't remember that. I don't think Mummy could have taken it. She didn't have a camera.'

'Oh, well, I expect someone else took it for her.' Russell smiled at Christine. 'Shall we get going? It's a damnably cold afternoon.'

He insisted on paying the entrance fee for the three of them, and looked offended when Christine proffered the money. Patrick scampered excitedly ahead of them, across the stone causeway leading to the Byward Tower.

'And what do you think of him?' Christine asked after a few minutes' silence. 'Do you think he looks like Rowland?'

Russell turned up the collar of his sheepskin coat. 'He certainly has a look of him,' he conceded at last. 'But to me Patrick resembles Lucy too closely to be very much like anyone else. I suppose it's the eyes.'

She nodded, but would not let it rest there. 'Oh, those Irish blue eyes are his mother's all right. But the dark hair, the height, the thinness are all Rowe's. Surely you must agree to that.'

Russell laughed. 'OK! OK! If it's that important to you! He's his father's son. Now, are you satisfied?'

They had a splendid afternoon, in spite of the weather and the general air of gloom which hung over everyone and everything during those difficult weeks when a state of emergency prevailed and before the Government finally gave in to the miners' demands. Patrick was indefatigable, wanting to see it all, asking a thousand questions, staring with sadistic relish at the axe and block, preserved in the Bloody Tower, and at the scaffold site between the Chapel and Tower Green. He jumped with fright when one of the ravens, strutting about the Green, screamed and flapped its great clipped wings. He goggled, round-eyed, at the Crown Jewels, removed five years previously from the Wakefield Tower to the vaults beneath the Waterloo Barracks, and was disappointed to be told that most of them dated only from the reign of Charles II, the original regalia having been melted down during the Commonwealth, on the orders of Cromwell. He was fascinated by the grim portal of Traitors' Gate and by the cannon on Tower Wharf. Eventually, just when Christine was about to expostulate that she could not possibly go another step, he, too, decided that he had had enough.

'Thank God for that,' she said to Russell. 'My feet are killing me. Is there anywhere we can get a cup of tea?'

'Look . . .' He hesitated, then went on: 'Why don't you and Patrick come and have tea at my place? I take it you came by Underground? Right. We can get the District Line from Tower Hill to Ealing. What do you say?'

It was Christine's turn to hesitate, but not for long. Neither Rowland nor Colette would be in until late, and the prospect of some company other than that of a ten-year-old boy was too pleasant to refuse. Besides, Russell Jennings was such a very old friend.

She smiled her acceptance. 'Yes, why not?' she said. 'Thank you. That would be very nice indeed.'

'It's a beautiful flat.' Christine stood by the uncurtained window, looking out at the stretch of green on the other side of the road, illuminated fitfully by one street-lamp in three, the others extinguished because of the power crisis. After a moment, she turned back into the room, where Russell, assisted by Patrick, was busy laying the table for a meal. 'You really ought to get married, Russ. Why don't you?'

'I've already told you,' he answered lightly. 'There's only ever been one woman for me.'

'Who's that?' Patrick asked curiously, emerging from the kitchen with a plate of bread and butter. His bright eyes darted from one to the other. He had obviously been following the conversation with careful attention. 'Why aren't you married, Mr Jennings?'

'I think you'd better just call me Russ,' Russell said swiftly, before Christine could let rip with a sharp reprimand. He added: 'I think if you look in the fridge you'll find some ice-cream in the ice-making compartment at the top. I know it's winter, but boys like ice-cream at any time of the year, don't they?'

'You bet!' Patrick, delighted at this unexpected sign of intelligence in an adult, returned to the kitchen, his attention successfully diverted.

Russell pulled a face. 'Little pitchers et cetera. Living alone, I forget how much children have in common with Kipling's elephant's child.'

Christine laughed. 'Insatiable curiosity. Yes, one does forget. I'm not really used to having a child about the house, either.'

Russell finished arranging the plates and cutlery and turned to look at her. 'You make a good mother, though,' he said quietly. 'A damn sight better one, I'd like to bet, than Lucy Brennan.'

'Oh, I don't know.' Christine approached the table and sat down on one of the chairs. 'I've been surprised. She hasn't done a bad job at all. And that's being patronizing. If I'm truthful, she hasn't neglected his education. I imagine he learned most of what he knows from her, and his maths is practically nonexistent. That's why Rowe has got him this crammer. But his general knowledge and his knowledge of English literature are extremely good.'

Russell stood looking down at her, saying nothing. Then, without warning, he stooped and kissed her cheek. For a moment, she thought she must have imagined it, the brush of his lips against her skin had been so light, so transitory. And when she glanced up he had turned away and was calling to Patrick in the kitchen.

'Hurry up with that ice-cream! Haven't you found it yet?'

But she knew she had not made a mistake. Russell had kissed her. And, what was even more disturbing, she had quite liked it. She would never be in love with him – Rowland had all her heart – but she had found the embrace enjoyable. Even exciting.

CHAPTER TWENTY-SIX

THE SANDS looked washed and clean and peaceful in the early-morning light, and the long green finger of Brean Down, pointing seawards, was shrouded with low-flying cloud. It was cold, even for late March, although Christine had noticed plenty of crocuses and daffodils in bloom on the rockeries as she and her mother walked down to the beach.

Both women were in black, Christine out of deference to Gwen's wishes rather than from any natural inclination to prolong the wearing of mourning. She had worn it yesterday for her father's funeral, but when she had appeared this morning in fawn slacks and a bright red anorak her mother had been upset.

'Couldn't you put on something darker?' she had asked. 'Supposing we meet someone we know? Whatever will they think?'

It was on the tip of Christine's tongue to argue the point; to say that no one attached much significance to mourning nowadays. And, anyway, whom did they know who would be out walking on the sands at seven-thirty in the morning? It was only because neither of them had slept well, because they had both converged on the kitchen at six to make themselves a cup of tea, that they had decided some exercise would do them good. It had been Christine's suggestion that they go to the beach.

'Remember how Dad used to take me down when I was little? He loved the sands before there was anyone about.'

The news, six months ago, that Robert had cancer had come as a shock to Christine. She had never been really close to her father, and in recent years, since her marriage, they had grown even further apart. Robert had never been comfortable in the presence of the Saxelbys, and had declined most invitations to stay with them in London or at Mallerby House. He had been proud of Christine and the way things had turned out for her, talked constantly about her to his friends and acquaintances, but preferred to keep his distance. 'Not our sort,' he would say to Gwen, who would secretly agree, while telling him to his face what an inverted snob he was. But, in spite of the fact that their paths had so infrequently crossed, Christine had been devastated by his death. When relations and friends had returned to the flat yesterday, after the funeral, someone had asked Gwen what she intended to have carved on the gravestone.

'Oh, just his name and dates,' she had said. ' "Robert Chandos, 1913 to 1973." '

It had hit Christine then, with a deep and rankling bitterness, that her father had only been sixty. It was far too young to die.

She said now to her mother: 'How can you go on believing in God, or at least a God of love, when you've seen someone you're fond of die comparatively young and in such pain?'

Gwen looked shocked. She was of a generation who went to Sunday school and who never questioned the tenets of the Christian faith. 'God knows what's best for us,' she answered simply, adding inconsequentially: 'I was so sorry Rowland couldn't come.'

'He was sorry, too. But he is a very busy man.'

Too busy to attend his father-in-law's funeral? Or was it because Patrick was ill with a particularly virulent attack of measles? Because Rowland felt that one of them ought to remain in London in case he took a turn for the worse? Wasn't it true that Patrick had become all-important to his father over these past eighteen months? The Maxine Larson affair had dwindled and died, in spite of all the lady's desperate attempts to keep the spark alive. There seemed no room in Rowland's life now for other women.

Christine supposed she should be grateful for the fact, but she hadn't wanted it to happen that way. She didn't want to have to be grateful to Patrick. She linked her arm through her mother's and stared sombrely at the wide expanse of sand and sky. Her father's death, the first death of anyone close to her, had brought home the fact of her own mortality.

'What on earth am I doing with my life, Mum?' she asked suddenly, stopping in her tracks and gazing out to sea. At their feet was a rock-pool, left behind by the receding tide, and in it floated long brown tentacles of seaweed. 'I shall be thirty-three at the end of July, and I lead a completely aimless existence.'

Gwen protested. 'What about all your committees? Your charity work? Raising all those funds? Dr Barnardo's. The Red Cross. St John Ambulance Brigade. None of them can function without money.'

Christine snorted. 'Coffee mornings. Charity balls and matinées. How can anyone brought up on the Methodist work ethic, as I was, ever think that stuffing my face in order to raise money for the starving is either moral or desirable? Answer me that!'

Gwen couldn't. She thought for a moment or two before offering tentatively: 'You have Patrick to look after.'

'Ah, yes. Patrick. Another woman's son. Oh, don't misunderstand me, Mum.' They moved on, towards the pier, along the palely glistening, closely packed stretch of sand. 'I'm fond of him. He's a lovable boy in many ways.' If Gwen noticed the qualification, she made no comment, and Christine continued: 'But, in any case, he'll be going away to boarding school next year. And if I weren't there, as I'm not now, there's always someone to look after him. My presence isn't vital, as yours was to me when I was small. I remember once, when we

271

both had flu together, Dad had to take leave from the office to look after us.'

Her mother laughed. 'I never saw him so thankful to get back to work as he was that time. So! What sort of thing do you want to do with your life? Do you have any secret plans?'

'I'd like to go into the bank and learn the business,' Christine replied with such promptness that Gwen realized she must have been thinking about it for a very long time. 'Like Colette did after Rowland's father died.'

'But wasn't that rather different? I mean, she was protecting her sons' interests. Besides, didn't you tell me her people are merchant bankers? It was a world she was brought up in. As she grew up, she must have heard those sort of matters discussed.'

'And *I've* heard them discussed, endlessly, for the past eight years. I'm not as green as I was when I first married Rowe.'

By mutual consent, they turned to retrace their steps, both of them suddenly hungry. 'Have you told Rowland how you feel?' Gwen asked quietly. Christine shook her head. 'Then, don't you think you should?'

It was a question Christine had asked herself many times, without ever coming up with a satisfactory answer. What was she afraid of? A snub? That slightly mocking smile Rowland wore in order to depress pretension? Or was it that she was afraid of her own ability to learn? Of making a fool of herself? The civil service clerk who fancied herself in the world of high finance! And there was more to it than that. She had married Rowland almost by accident; a misalliance which he and his family had grown to accept, but of which she herself was still acutely conscious.

She despised herself for such feelings, but in moments of honesty was forced to admit that she was less at ease with any of the Saxelbys than she was with, say, Lois and Barry Alyward. Or with Russell Jennings.

272

She had seen a lot of Russ over the past thirteen months, since that day at the Tower of London. She had not been lying when she told her mother that Rowland had been working hard. Late nights and busy weekends had become almost a way of life for him and Julian. During the past year, both the pound and the franc had been floated by the British and French governments in an effort to bolster the two countries' ailing economies, but the United States was still selling its surplus grain to the Russians and oil prices continued to soar. Inflation went on rising. Sometimes she did not see Rowland properly for weeks on end. He was out of the house before she was up in the morning, and at night all he wanted was just to crawl into bed.

'You'll kill yourself,' his mother warned him, but he merely shrugged.

'We're going through a sticky patch, Maman,' was his only answer.

Colette had almost given up going to the bank nowadays. Her sons were capable of managing without her, consulted her less and less, and she was not the sort of woman who hung around to be ignored. She was therefore able to indulge her passion for bridge, to spend more time in her beloved France, either in Paris or at Château Bérenger with her mother, and to keep up with her many friends in the hectic social whirl she loved so much. What Christine did with her time, she did not enquire, not from indifference but because she deemed it bad manners to be too intrusive. And it occurred to Christine now, as she and her mother returned to the flat opposite Clarence Park to cook themselves breakfast, that probably neither Colette nor Rowland knew much about her meetings with Russell Jennings. If, that was, they knew of them at all.

Not that there was anything to conceal about them. Since that afternoon in his flat, over a year ago, Russell

273

had made no further attempt at anything remotely approaching an intimate embrace. For one thing, he must sense that Christine would not allow it and, for another, more often than not on their excursions together Patrick was with them. And, on reflection, that was odd, Christine decided, as she drove back to London the following morning along the busy A4. Why did Pat not mention these meetings to his father and grandmother?

She asked him, two days later, sitting beside his bed and reading to him from one of Arthur C. Clarke's novels. She had found him much better on her return, but his eyes were still very weak, and the doctor had advised resting them for a few more days.

'Don't you ever say anything to Daddy or Grandma about our outings with Russ?' she asked curiously. He shook his head. 'Why not?'

He gave her a slanting look. 'It's nice to have secrets, don't you think?'

She was taken aback. 'Well, perhaps ... Sometimes,' honesty compelled her to admit. 'But, as a general rule, I don't think it's a good idea. Do you have many secrets?'

He looked smug. 'I do have one. A big one.'

Christine began to feel uneasy. 'Is it something your father or I ought to know?'

He prevaricated. 'I don't know. Maybe.'

She shifted her position on the bed so that she could see him better. His face was bland, the blue eyes wide and innocent. She was unable to decide whether or not he was pulling her leg, simply trying to make himself interesting. Or was he really concealing something of importance from herself and Rowland? He had already demonstrated that he was capable of keeping things to himself in a fairly unchildlike way. But, if she made an issue of it, she was playing into his hands. She could not force him to tell her his secret, whatever it was; and if it were really nothing, which was what she suspected, then she was laying herself open to further teasing on the subject. She decided to ignore the ploy.

'Oh, well,' she said, once more picking up the book and searching for her place, 'I don't suppose it's anything. Now, where were we? Page one hundred and three, I think.'

But later that day, eating the cold supper which Mrs Jones had left for her, alone in the kitchen of Inglebatch House, her mind reverted once again to her conversation with Patrick. All children had secrets – she certainly had when she was young – but there was something about her step-son which made her uneasy. There was a hint of slyness in his character that worried her. Yet she could not get away from the fact that she herself had said nothing to Rowland about her meetings with Russell Jennings. Why not? And it was no use trying to kid herself that it was simply because she saw so little of her husband these days. There were still sufficient opportunities for conversation to mention the fact. But she and Rowland had virtually stopped communicating except on the most superficial level, and it was as much her fault as his. She was as passionately in love with him as ever, but lately that love had become clouded by resentment.

The house suddenly seemed very quiet. She had taken Patrick's supper up to him an hour ago, and he was now fast asleep. Crab, the mongrel, who had spent most of the cold March day dozing by the nearest convenient radiator, was now sprawled across the foot of his master's bed, apparently worn out by the exigencies of this exhausting life. He was, as Christine frequently informed him, quite the laziest dog it had ever been her misfortune to meet. For answer, he would open one eye a slit and thump his tail good-naturedly on the carpet.

She carried her dirty crockery over to the sink and, in spite of Colette's oft-repeated exhortations to her to 'leave it all for Mrs Jones in the morning', began

275

washing up. When she had finished, she went upstairs to the drawing-room and did something she very rarely permitted herself the luxury of doing: she telephoned Rowland at the bank.

'Darling, how long are you going to be?' she asked, when Marcia Corby, the new and highly efficient successor to Joyce Crocker, was persuaded to put her through.

He sounded bemused at this almost unprecedented interruption.

'Is something the matter?' he asked. His voice took on a sharper note. 'Is it Pat? Has he taken a turn for the worse?'

'No.' She kept her voice level with a determined effort. 'I was just hoping you could come home earlier tonight. I'd like to see something of you sometimes.'

He was immediately contrite. 'I'm sorry. There's just been so much to do these past months. Look, I'll finish what I'm doing, and then I'll leave. Expect me in about an hour.'

He was good as his word, walking into the drawing-room at Inglebatch House just before nine o'clock. He looked grey with fatigue, and Christine poured him a stiff whisky. 'Have you eaten?' she asked.

'Marcia and I had something sent in about seven.' He grinned ruefully. 'Don't ask me what, because I don't remember.' He took a long pull at his drink, then set it down and took her in his arms. 'I've been a selfish brute, haven't I? Letting you cope with your father's death all on your own. Not even coming to the funeral. Leaving you by yourself so much.' He released her, glancing around him. 'Where's Maman this evening?'

'Gone to the cinema with that bridge partner of hers, Major Risely. A Woody Allen film. You know how much she likes Woody Allen.'

Rowland frowned, dropping on to one of the sofas and drawing Christine down to sit beside him. 'That's

276

all very well, but she might give you the opportunity to get out sometimes.'

It was on the tip of her tongue to point out that she was not his mother's responsibility, but she desisted. Instead she answered lightly: 'Oh, I get out quite a lot, especially at weekends. Pat and I have been doing a lot of sight-seeing.'

'Good. I'm glad. Glad, too, that you and he seem to be getting on together so well.' Rowland passed a weary hand across his forehead.

She said quietly: 'It – er – it isn't always just the two of us on these excursions. I . . . That is, I've been seeing quite a lot of Russell Jennings.' She went on hurriedly, suddenly flustered for some unknown reason: 'We met up again about two years ago, at Heathrow airport. Colette and I had gone to see Lucien and Solange off, that time they came over for her birthday, and I bumped into Russ. It sort of went on from there. He works in London now. He has a flat in Ealing. He's not married, no family, and I think he's rather lonely. He's taken to Pat in a big way. Likes showing him around. And he's such an old friend. That's all there is to it really.' She stopped, aware that she was starting to sound defensive.

'Why haven't you told me this before?' Rowland was frowning.

'I don't know. The opportunity never seemed to arise. It isn't as though Russ and I go out every week, or even once a month. Only now and then. Pat likes male company. He doesn't think very highly of women, and you haven't been very accessible these past twelve months. Oh, I know you've been around at holiday times, but children need a lot of attention. Pat and Russ like each other. They get on well together.'

Rowland got up abruptly and turned to face her. Behind him, the long red velvet curtains glowed gently in the light from the big chinese lamp placed on a seventeeth-century gate-leg table. For several seconds, there was silence, but when he did finally speak his words and the intensity of his emotion astonished Christine.

'I want you to stop seeing Russell Jennings.'

'But I've told you, he's just a good friend. He simply escorts Pat and me to places like the Zoo or Kew Gardens, Hampton Court or the Tower. It's educational for Pat and company for me.' She felt bewildered by Rowland's reaction; but, at the same time, her heart was beginning to pound excitedly. He was jealous. That was the only explanation.

Rowland's voice was cold. 'I just want it to stop.' He took a deep breath. 'All right, I admit I'm largely to blame. I've left you and Pat far too much on your own. I realize Maman is away much more than she used to be, but I thought you had plenty to occupy your time. I thought you and Pat were sufficient company for one another.'

He knew, even as he spoke, that he had had no right to make such assumptions; that he had been neglectful and, worse, insensitive; that he was in the wrong. If she had been angry, he would not have been surprised, nor felt it any more than he deserved; but, astonishingly, she wasn't.

'Of course I won't see Russ again if you don't want me to.' She was smiling at him. 'I honestly didn't think you'd mind.'

'Well, naturally I mind,' he answered. 'Pat's my son. I'm the one who ought to be doing all those sort of things with him. I promise you' – he sat down again beside her, taking her hands in his – 'that in future I'll make more time to be a better father.'

And then she understood. The jealousy was not on her behalf, but on Patrick's. What a fool! What an utterly besotted blind fool she had been! She pulled her hands free of his and half-ran, half-stumbled from the room.

CHAPTER TWENTY-SEVEN

SHE RAN UPSTAIRS to their room, slamming the door behind her, not caring if she woke Patrick, who had been given one of the two spare bedrooms on that floor for his use. She flung herself face downwards on the bed, beating impotently against the coverlet with her fists, indulging in a bout of hot angry tears. Damn Rowland! Damn Patrick! Damn Russell! In fact damn all men! *Sigh no more, ladies, sigh no more, Men were deceivers ever* . . . But the trouble with Rowland was that he wasn't a deceiver. He was so transparently honest.

She was aware that he had come into the room and was standing by the bed, looking down at her. She sensed his distress and, for once, hardened her heart. She felt that he deserved it. The bed-springs gave as he sat down beside her and gently stroked her hair.

'I'm sorry,' he said finally, when her sobs grew less. 'I'm very conscious of the fact that I have no right to object to any male friendships you might see fit to make; that I'm the last man on earth who deserves consideration in that respect. I suppose I'm just jealous of another man usurping my place with Pat. I feel guilty, too. As I said, *I'm* the one who ought to have been doing all those things with him—'

Christine did not let him finish. She jerked herself into a sitting position, her face ugly and blotched with crying. 'Pat!' she exclaimed thickly and furiously. 'Is he the only person you can think of? What about *me*? Don't you think I'd like a share in some of that jealousy? It would be nice to think that you cared just a little bit that I'd been seeing another man, however innocent the relationship. All right! I know I've no right to expect it.

You've never been in love with me, you've made that quite plain. You married me because of the child, and I'm grateful. And I'm grateful, too, that you've refused to divorce me since. But I've kept my side of the bargain as well. I haven't made a fuss about Maxine Larson or any of your other women, and I've ignored the fact that other people laugh and talk about me behind my back. And not so very much behind my back, either, because I've heard and seen them. And I've let you foist Pat on me and I haven't complained. So, in view of all that'—she found her handkerchief and blew her nose defiantly—'I should think you might have the courtesy to be just a little jealous of me.' And once again she burst into tears.

Rowland put his arms round her. 'Oh, Chris! Chris!' She could feel him shaking.

Indignantly she pulled away. 'You're laughing!' she accused him. 'You're bloody well laughing at me!'

'I can't help it,' he gasped. He drew her back against him, kissing her between the eyes. 'You're the only woman of my acquaintance who would dream of complaining because her husband wasn't jealous enough about her relationship with another man.'

'That doesn't surprise me at all,' she answered waspishly, searching around on the coverlet for her by now sodden handkerchief. 'The women you know aren't in love with their husbands.' She found the wet scrap of cambric and, with difficulty on account of Rowland's all-enveloping embrace, once again blew her nose. 'Anyway, Russ and I don't have a relationship. At least, not the sort you mean. We're just friends.'

'You mean the fool has never made a pass at you?'

'N-no. Well, he did once, sort of. But I didn't encourage him, and he hasn't repeated the experiment.'

'He must be an even bigger fool than I thought,' Rowland said, gently pushing her down on the bed and starting to kiss her eyes and lips and throat. His fingers manipulated the buttons of her blouse and the zip of her skirt. Her senses were swimming.

He had made love to her many times before, but never quite like this; not with such a mixture of tenderness and passion; not as though it were the beginning of something new in their life together; not as though he really, truly, deeply cared . . . But later, as she wallowed in a long hot bath, while he went down to the kitchen to rifle the refrigerator, and with the promise to look in on Patrick before he returned, Christine realized with painful clarity that Rowland had still not said he loved her. Nothing had really changed.

And yet, for the next couple of years, it seemed as though it might have done. As far as Christine could tell, no one else had appeared to take Maxine Larson's place, and she began to have hopes that, at last, even if he were not in love with her, she and Patrick together could keep Rowland happy. Other women, she told herself, half-believing it, had become an irrelevance in his life.

She felt guilty, though, about Russell. He had been upset when she had told him that she and Pat would not be seeing him again; so upset in fact, that she realized she must mean more to him than she had suspected. She had been inclined not to take him seriously when he informed her that she was the reason he hadn't married, but perhaps she had been wrong to do so. Maybe he had always loved her, as he said. But she kept to her unspoken promise not to see him any more, in spite of Patrick's barrage of questions about what had happened to 'Uncle' Russ.

These, in any case, soon petered out as Rowland began to play a bigger part in the life of his son. He forced himself to make time for all those activities which in recent years he had neglected: riding, cycling, walking, watching cricket in the summer and Rugby in the winter, until Patrick went away to school. Even then, holidays were sacrosanct.

'I don't know what's got into Rowe,' Julian complained tetchily. 'He's becoming such a family man.'

'And a good thing, too,' his mother responded tartly. 'A pity things haven't worked out that way for you.'

Colette and her younger son were seated on the terrace at Mallerby House one warm July weekend. In the distance, Rowland and Christine were playing French cricket with Patrick and Vivien, the sound of their laughter carrying clearly on the hot still air. The following day would be Colette's birthday once again, and Lucien, Solange and the now eighteen-year-old Giles had been expected to be present. But 1975 had, so far, not been an easy year for the French economy. There were over a million unemployed, industrial production had fallen by more than ten per cent in one year, and economics professor Raymond Barre had replaced Jacques Chirac as Prime Minister. Lucien had regretfully telephoned his sister to say his presence was needed at the bank. He would, unfortunately, be working.

Julian stared moodily in front of him. His long legs, in their pale fawn slacks, stretched almost to the end of the sun-lounger. His arms were crossed defensively in front of him, pale brown against the vivid yellow of his short-sleeved cotton shirt.

He said suddenly: 'I'm leaving Sophie. I've had enough of her. Do you think Rowe would agree to turn the top floor of Inglebatch House into a self-contained flat for Vivien and me? I know there was some talk at one time of doing it for you, only you said you preferred the suite of rooms on the first floor, where you've been since Father died.'

'Are you thinking of divorce?' Colette asked slowly.

Julian shook his head. 'I'm being received into the Roman Catholic church soon, Maman. I've been having instruction.'

His mother appeared neither particularly surprised nor gratified by this information. Julian had often

282

noticed that French Catholics were neither so fervent nor so proselytizing as their English counterparts.

'Well, then, is Sophie thinking of divorce?' she asked him.

'I shouldn't think so. She likes being Mrs Julian Saxelby. She can run up more and bigger bills that way. Besides, she doesn't want to get married again.' Julian added contemptuously: 'She just wants a good time.'

Colette nodded. 'It's high time Vivien was removed from Sophie's influence. Some of her conversation is not suitable for a thirteen-year-old girl. I caught her and Patrick last night whispering and giggling together in a corner. Their manner was most unseemly. I can't say that boy has improved since he went away to school. Children of that age need parents. If Vivien is living at Inglebatch House, Christine and I can keep an eye on her. I'll have a word with Rowland this evening.'

And, in mid-September, as Patrick packed his school-bags and prepared to return for the autumn term at Clifton College, Julian and his daughter moved into the newly converted flat on the third floor of the Hampstead house.

'So here I go again,' Christine complained to Lois, during one of her long weekly telephone calls. 'Surrogate mother to Vivien. Fortunately, she's always liked me.'

Lois's reaction was predictable. 'You're a fool,' she said, then added with a sigh: 'I'd like a pound note for every time someone's told you that. I bet I'd be a very rich woman. Anyway, how are things going these days between you and Rowe? You sound cheerful enough. No more . . . er . . .' She hesitated tactfully.

Christine finished for her. 'No more women – is that what you're asking? There don't seem to be. Not at the moment. Nothing, at any rate, sufficiently serious for the affair to have reached my ears. And, contrary to popular belief, the wife is not always the last to know.'

'Good,' Lois said. 'Let's hope it stays that way. And I suppose, to give the devil his due' – she was the only woman Christine knew who was able to resist Rowland's charm – 'he's never been really serious about any of them.'

A few weeks later, Christine was to recall Lois's words as a bad omen; a dangerous tempting of fate. That was after they had been to the Festival Hall to hear Faith Malyon play Mozart's Coronation Concerto.

Faith Malyon was nineteen years old, a small doll-like girl with straight fine-spun fair hair and wide cornflower-blue eyes. She looked fragile and vulnerable, as though a breath of wind or a harsh word might break her, and the doll-like appearance was further enhanced by her predilection for Laura Ashley prints, frilled necklines and big puff sleeves. The only child of a London taxi-driver and his schoolteacher wife, neither of whom had shown the slightest talent for music, she had astounded both parents by becoming a child prodigy of the piano. From the time she was given her very first lesson, she displayed not merely an aptitude for the instrument, but positive genius. She had won a scholarship to the Royal College of Music and today was spoken of as one of the brightest up-and-coming stars in the British musical firmament.

This was only her second appearance on the concert-platform, and she could have been forgiven for a display of nerves. She showed instead an admirable aplomb, causing Christine to wonder – although she kept the thought to herself – if Miss Malyon had ahead of her quite as brilliant a career as everyone predicted. In her experience, an iron-clad temperament rarely produced that touch of genius in any member of the performing arts.

It was two weeks after the concert at the Festival Hall that Christine came face to face with Faith Malyon at a party to which she and Rowland had been invited and had only decided to attend at the very last minute. When Rowland arrived home shortly after eight o'clock, Christine discovered that he had forgotten about the engagement.

'What party's that?' he demanded irritably, once she had jogged his memory.

'The Colmers. Holland Park. A nice couple. Their elder daughter is a friend of Julian's.'

'Not that beanpole of a girl and her parents we met him with one night at Covent Garden?'

'The same. And at the time you said Trish Colmer was a very attractive young woman.'

'Temporary insanity,' Rowland pleaded, pouring himself another drink. 'Besides, why are we being invited to a party given by Julian's girl-friend's parents?'

'You obviously made an impression on them as a desirable adjunct to any festive gathering. Look,' she added, laughing at the outraged expression on his face, 'we don't have to go. I did accept the invitation when it arrived last week, but I can always ring up and make some plausible excuse.'

He hesitated, tempted by her offer, a hesitation Christine was to remember later. If only she had been more positive, telephoned the Colmers there and then to say she was unwell, perhaps Rowland would never have met Faith Malyon. But, then, again, Fate being the fickle jade she was, perhaps he would have.

Rowland downed his second whisky. 'No,' he said reluctantly, 'we'd better go if you've already accepted.'

'I did ask you if you wanted to go, and you grunted what I took to be a "yes". I'm sorry if I was mistaken.'

He came and sat beside her on the couch, putting an arm around her shoulders. 'I don't suppose I was even listening. Is Julian going?'

'Naturally. He was home early from the bank and left about half an hour ago. Your mother's staying in to look after Vivien.'

285

'Very noble of her. I happen to know that Claud Risely has tickets for the ballet at Covent Garden this evening.'

'Oh dear!' Christine felt guilty. 'Perhaps, then—'

'No, you don't.' He squeezed her shoulders and got to his feet. 'You look after that child too much. It'll do Maman good to do her fair share. If you've set your heart on going to this party, you shall.'

Christine smiled at him. 'Cinderella shall go to the ball! Rowe?' She paused for a moment, then asked resolutely: 'Have you given any more consideration to the idea of my having a job at the bank?'

It was several weeks now since she had first mooted the idea, and he had promised to think about it, but so far had not given her an answer. He had his back to her, pouring himself a third whisky – he drank far more than he used to, in an effort to unwind – and did not reply immediately.

'Well?' she prompted.

He turned towards her, but did not look at her, his eyes fixed on the contents of his glass. 'I don't think it's a good idea,' he said at last.

'Why not?'

'Look, Chris,' he murmured uncomfortably, 'the wives of men like myself don't go and work in their husbands' businesses in subordinate positions. Maman was different. She took over my father's role, standing in as proxy for me, until I had done my National Service and was through university. You've plenty to keep you occupied with all your committee and charity work. Then there's Pat in the holidays. And now Vivien. Give up this silly idea. Please.'

She came, in that moment, as close to disliking him as it was possible for her to come.

'All right,' she said abruptly, standing up. 'I won't mention it again. I'm sorry to have embarrassed you with my Nonconformist working-class ideas.'

'Chris! I didn't mean that. You're being unfair.'

'Am I? I don't think so. You're selfish, like all your family, like all people born to wealth and position. You consider no one but yourselves. You use me. Oh, I'm good for a few things: the occasional fuck, mother to your bastard by Lucy Brennan, and now as unpaid babysitter for your niece. But as to a life of my own — that's out of the question.'

Rowland put down his drink untasted, and took a deep breath. 'I'm sorry,' he said gently. 'I really didn't know you felt that way. But believe me when I say that you mean far more to me than any of those things you just mentioned.'

She could have caved in then, thrown her arms round his neck and begged his forgiveness. It was what she wanted to do, what every instinct prompted her to do, but something held her back. A feeling that if, at some point, she did not make a stand her all-consuming love for him would turn her into a cipher. Afterwards, she was to wonder what difference it would have made if they had not gone to that party in the throes of a quarrel.

'I'm going upstairs to shower and change,' she said. 'I should be ready about half-past nine.'

'Very well.' He picked up his whisky again.

They got ready in almost complete silence. When Christine put her head round the door of Colette's sitting-room, her mother-in-law waved a cheery hand and said: 'Have a good time. I've told Vivien she can come down and watch TV with me when she's finished her homework.'

'She'll enjoy that, but make sure she really has finished. Colette!'

The other woman glanced up enquiringly. 'Yes?'

'Oh . . . oh, nothing. Good night.'

By the time she and Rowland got to Holland Park, the party was in full swing. The Colmers were flatteringly pleased that they had come, having given them up some half an hour ago. Julian pushed his way to their side, Trish Colmer in tow. 'Hello, you two. You're late. What's the matter? You both look like you've lost the proverbial pound and picked up sixpence.'

'Don't you mean three pee?' Christine asked, with a feeble attempt at a joke.

Trish Colmer gave one of her loud snorting gasps of laughter, one of the many things about her which made Christine wonder what on earth Julian saw in her. But, then, he had never had very good taste in women. It was on a par with his passion for bright canary-coloured pullovers, acid-yellow sports-cars and two-tone shoes.

Mrs Colmer, as round and jolly as her daughter was tall and thin, was making her way towards them, dragging a young woman determinedly by the hand. It was obvious to Christine that Mai Colmer had fallen heavily for Rowland, and, like a mistress presenting a delicate morsel to a favourite pet, had saved especially for him her star guest of the evening.

'Mr Saxelby' – Christine noted ironically that she was not included in the introduction – 'may I present Faith Malyon, the concert pianist? Faith my dear, this is Rowland Saxelby. Julian has told us that he's a great admirer of yours.'

Rowland extended his thin brown hand and took the proffered slender, almost childishly soft and rounded white one.

'How do you do?' he said. 'And my brother's quite right. I am an admirer.'

Faith Malyon smiled; just smiled, as Christine told herself later. But there was an expression on Rowland's face which she had never seen before: a look compounded of tenderness, the desire to protect and something more . . .

It was a little while before she identified that something more as abject and total surrender.

PART FIVE
1980 – 5

CHAPTER TWENTY-EIGHT

'WHAT TIME do you call this?' Colette asked crossly. 'Midday is no hour to come down to breakfast. It's not fair on Mrs Renshaw. It's almost lunch-time.'

Vivien lowered herself into the empty sun-lounger between her grandmother and Christine and stretched long bare brown legs towards the balustrade. Behind her, the honey-coloured façade of Mallerby House glowed golden in the hot August sunshine; before her, the park and gardens shimmered in the noonday heat.

'This is the life,' she said with a sigh of contentment. 'Just think of it! No more school. I don't have to go back again, ever.'

'That's all very well,' Colette answered crisply. 'But what are you going to do with yourself? You've opted out of going to university, which I think is a great pity, and you're much too intelligent to fritter your time away at home.'

Vivien protested. 'Give me a chance, Grandmamma! Term only ended last week. I want a nice long holiday, preferably here at Mallerby, before I start making any decisions. I'm right, aren't I, Christine?'

Christine, who had been resting with her eyes closed, raised one lid a fraction and took covert stock of the niece she had virtually brought up single-handed for the last five years. Six months past her eighteenth birthday, Vivien had grown into a very striking-looking girl. The brown hair of youth and adolescence had darkened until it was nearly the same colour as her father's, and she had always had the deep brown Saxelby eyes. She had lost her former childish plumpness, and the rounded curves of her face had given way to interesting hollows beneath the cheek-bones. But she had her mother's voluptuous figure and wide sensuous mouth; and, as did Sophie, she liked men. Christine had noticed the way Vivien looked at Patrick, now down for the long vacation after his first year at Oxford. And he, in his turn, had been visibly impressed by the little cousin who had suddenly spread her wings and become a swan. Christine could foresee trouble in that quarter.

As though her thoughts had summoned him, Patrick strolled out of the library on to the terrace, dressed American-style in Bermuda shorts and a shirt patterned with cockatoos and rioting purple palm-trees. His grandmother winced and averted her eyes. Patrick leaned over the back of Vivien's chair.

'So you're down at last,' he said. 'A proper little slug-a-bed, aren't you? How about coming for a walk? The exercise will do you good and give you an appetite for lunch.'

Here, again, Christine thought, she had not done such a bad job. Good-looking, well mannered, intelligent, with most of the social graces, her step-son, at nineteen, was a credit to her and to his father. She had grown to like him over the years, although never to love him as she would have wished. But that was Patrick's fault, rather than hers. He never let anyone, not even Rowland, get too close. So far and no further, he seemed to say. It was as though there were some sort of barrier which prevented him giving himself completely to anyone, particularly to members of his family.

Vivien gave a groan, but got up willingly enough out of her chair; too willingly, perhaps, Christine thought. Vivien, too, was wearing shorts, but extremely brief ones, over which was dragged a skimpy, sleeveless, tie-dyed T-shirt in shades of blue and orange.

'I'll walk as far as the Feathers with you,' she said to Patrick. 'You can buy me a drink.'

They disappeared round the side of the house, and silence reigned once more. Christine was just beginning to doze again, when Colette's voice roused her.

'What are you going to do about that Malyon woman?'

Christine sighed inwardly. The last thing she wanted at the moment was a discussion with her mother-in-law on the subject of Faith Malyon. But she appreciated Colette's concern for her, her partisanship, and so overcame her reluctance.

'What can I do?' she asked, as she had asked so many times before.

'Tell him it's her or you.'

Christine smiled faintly. 'I'm too fond of you all to want to leave.'

Colette gave an exasperated snort. 'You're too defeatist. I've told you that before. What makes you think that Rowland wouldn't choose you?'

'Because' – and Christine sounded equally exasperated – 'this time it's different. You must know that, Colette, without me having to spell it out. The others – Lisle Ingram, Maxine Larson and the like – really didn't mean anything to him. But Faith . . . He's in love with her. The man who has always said that he doesn't know what love is has finally found out.'

'Has he told you that?' Colette asked fiercely. 'Has he said so in so many words?'

'He doesn't have to. I can see for myself.' Christine slewed round in her chair until she was facing her mother-in-law. 'Five years this has lasted. And shows no sign of abating even now.'

'Has he mentioned divorce? Has he indicated that he wants to marry the creature?'

'No.' Christine gave a cynical smile. 'But that's because Rowe's needed me for Patrick. Now that neither Pat nor Vivien has need of me any longer, it will be interesting to see what happens.'

'Nonsense!' Colette beat on the arms of her garden-chair in frustration. 'He's infatuated, that's all, with that silly little china-doll face. She gives men the impression that she is *une oie blanche, une pucelle*, but she isn't. I know that type. Une allumeuse! Une pute! Elle a les cuisses légères!'

Christine began to laugh. 'I don't know what that all means, but it's obviously something very rude.'

Her mother-in-law gave an answering smile. 'It is, and it gives me great satisfaction to say it.'

From the first, there had been something about Rowland's friendship with Faith Malyon which had antagonized Colette. She had looked on his previous affairs almost with indulgence, shrugging them aside as of no consequence; the sort of lapses to be expected from any man, especially one who had made an unfortunate marriage. But time had softened and changed her attitude towards her daughter-in-law; she no longer thought of Christine as a misalliance. The two women had become not just fonder of one another, but friends. But this fact did not entirely account for Colette's dislike of Faith; for her rigid ban on all Faith's records at either Inglebatch or Mallerby House. Early on in the relationship, Rowland had presented his mother with Faith's latest LP; a recording of some of the Chopin Preludes, very much in demand and difficult to buy in the shops. Colette had smashed it in front of his eyes and stalked from the room. They had not spoken to each other for days after, and it was the first time they had ever seriously quarrelled. They made it up, of course; but, from then on, there was a barrier between them, a subject they could not discuss.

Christine herself hated Faith Malyon; hated her because she could bring a light to Rowland's eyes, a look to his face which no one else had ever put there.

'You're in love with her!' she had accused him one day, during one of their now all too frequent rows.

At least, she supposed they were rows. She did all the shouting. Rowland just became more silent and withdrawn.

He had angered her even more on this occasion by continuing to deny it.

'No, I'm not. But ... oh, I don't know what it is, Chris. She holds a fascination for me. I can't explain it, except to say that when she plays I feel ... I feel ... Hell! I don't know what I feel, except that I need her. I can't give her up. Please don't ask me to.'

'Then, I suggest you and I call it a day.' She remembered, even now, the effort it had cost her to say that. 'You can divorce me and marry Faith.'

But he would not hear of it. There was no point in a divorce, he had said, unless she wanted it. He had no intention of marrying Faith. Infuriated as much by her love for him, which made her a prisoner, as by his own apparent dog-in-the-manger attitude, she had slammed out of the drawing-room at Inglebatch House, only to find Patrick outside on the landing. It had been holiday-time – Easter, she fancied – and she had forgotten his presence in the house. She had ignored him and gone up to her bedroom, but later he had knocked on the door.

'What do you want?' she had asked as he came in.

She had been sitting at the dressing-table, repairing her make-up, and he had crossed the room to stand behind her. She could see his face reflected in the mirror.

'Only to tell you that Dad means what he says about not divorcing you. He won't, you can take my word for it. You see, there wouldn't be any point.'

He had refused to enlarge on the subject, and Christine had dismissed it as just another of those cryptic utterances which he came out with from time to time in an attempt to draw attention to himself and appear more interesting.

Nevertheless, recalling the incident now, four years later, she wondered what had made him say it; what motive he could possibly have had apart from the obvious one. She prided herself that Patrick was fond of her, and he did not like Faith Malyon. So why bother to search for a reason other than that?

Her thoughts reverted to Faith, to her own future and what was to become of her life now that her stepson and niece were grown up and no longer needed her. And yet, in spite of the worry nagging away at the back of her mind, the heat proved too much for her. Her eyes began to close again. She could hear Colette speaking to her, but the words had ceased to make sense. By the time her mother-in-law paused for an answer, Christine was fast asleep.

Faith Malyon bad-temperedly pushed aside the bed-clothes and swung her legs over the edge of the bed, presenting Rowland with a view of her back. She was rigid with anger, and her hands gripped the mattress convulsively. Rowland braced himself for the coming storm and, his hands shaking slightly, lit a cigarette. It gave her the opening she needed.

'You smoke far too much,' she said acidly. 'It's a filthy habit, anyway, and extremely bad for your health. It's bad for the people around you as well. If you won't consider yourself, you might at least think of me. But you don't, do you? Ever!' She was getting into her stride now, and jumped up from the bed, starting to search for her clothes, which were scattered across the floor; left anyhow in her eagerness to make love to him. (Or perhaps, a little voice whispered cynically in the back of Rowland's mind, in her eagerness to let him make love to her.) But she was satisfied now, and all her grievances were, as usual, about to surface. 'You're a selfish bastard.'

'Am I?' he asked quietly. 'I'm sorry. I thought I'd been very generous.'

She jerked upright, holding a slip and a pair of tights in one hand. The cornflower-blue eyes were blazing with anger, the straight fine-spun fair hair falling in a curtain across her face. The mouth had thinned to a bloodless line. Gone was the fragile little-girl-lost look that so enchanted the legions of her fans. In place of that vulnerable waif was a harpy. But was that his fault? He was uncomfortably aware that he gave her everything but the one thing she really wanted: his name.

'Oh yes! You give me presents!' she answered scornfully. 'But I'm sure you've given equally generous gifts to many other women in your time. I don't need them. I don't want them, any more than I want to be brought to anonymous hotel bedrooms so that we can make love. Your mother and your son, whenever I come anywhere near them, treat me as though I have the plague. They refuse tickets for my concerts. At that last party I went to at Inglebatch House, even your brother ignored me throughout the entire evening.' She dropped the slip and stockings and came to sit on the edge of the bed once more. 'It's no good, Rowe. I can't go on like this. I want to marry you. I want you to get a divorce.'

'No.' He stubbed out the cigarette in the ashtray which the hotel provided on the bedside table. He turned towards her and stretched out a hand. 'Faith, please. I won't divorce Christine. I made that quite clear at the start of our relationship, and you accepted it as a condition of our friendship.'

'That was five years ago. I was nineteen and still had a lot to accomplish. I'm twenty-four now. I still have a lot to accomplish, but I'm old enough to want a stable background to my life. I do so much travelling, stay in so many faceless hotel bedrooms. Like this one,' she added nastily, waving an expressive all-encompassing hand. 'I need to come back to a home, a husband, a family, not to an empty, echoing, musty-smelling flat. And it's you I want, Rowe. Why don't you want me?'

'I do,' he said passionately, sitting up and trying to draw her into his arms. 'You know how I feel about you.'

She resisted his embraces, struggling free and again beginning to get dressed. 'No, I don't know how you feel about me. That's just what I don't know, and I don't think you do, either. You strike me as a very emotionally confused man. You're searching for something; and, whatever it is, I can't provide it. I think it's probably love.'

'I love *you*,' he said pleadingly, but Faith shook her head.

'No, you don't. After five years, do you think I wouldn't know if that were really true?' She pulled on a navy-blue Laura Ashley dress with a big sailor collar and an enormous white bow. 'Even though I'm free tomorrow, no rehearsals, no engagements, you're still going off to Hinton Malsherbes without me, to be with your wife and family for the weekend.' She tilted her head to one side, regarding him thoughtfully. 'There's something about you that I just can't fathom. A secret inner core that you protect against all comers.' She went to the dressing-table and combed her hair. The sunshine, filtering through the curtains from the dusty London street, turned it into an aureole of pale spun gold. When he made no answer to her accusation, she put away her comb and closed her handbag with a snap. 'By the way,' she added, almost casually, 'I've accepted that concert tour of America. I shall be away for the first three months of next year.' She slipped her bare feet into a pair of strappy white sandals, walked to the door and opened it. 'I'll go on, if you don't mind. I have some shopping to do.' She let herself out.

Rowland made no attempt to stop her. As the door closed, he lit another cigarette and lay back against the pillows, inhaling smoke and expelling it through his nose. He felt desolate, as he always did when she left him, but at the same time relieved. When they were apart, he couldn't hurt her any more, nor she him. Was she right? Was what he felt for her not love? How was he to tell? He had nothing to judge it by. Certainly his feelings for Lisle Ingram and Maxine Larson had been entirely different. When the time came, he had parted from them without a pang.

And Lucy Brennan? But he didn't want to think of Lucy. She should have told him she was pregnant as soon as she knew. She had deprived him of ten years of his son's life. It hadn't been easy to gain the confidence of a boy of ten. Sometimes he felt that Patrick resented him, even now, even after all his efforts to make him feel wanted. Christine had once thrown it in his face that Patrick was just like him: his son, she had said, found it difficult to give himself entirely to anyone.

Christine. Why was he so adamant that he would never divorce her? But, again, he refused to face the truth, shying away from it, closing his mind. He wanted his freedom too badly. The one thing he had always feared all his life was being tied down. A psychologist might have told him that he had suffered, when young, from an over-uxorious father. Noel Saxelby had been so besotted with his wife that he had had little time for his sons. For him, the sun, the moon and the stars had revolved around Colette. His love had amounted almost to an obsession, and had aggravated an already puritanical nature. Rowland recalled having been soundly beaten, when he was about eight, when he was discovered reading a cheap girlie magazine by the light of an electric torch under the bedclothes. It was an insult, his father had told him, to his mother. Rowland, smarting, had made a conscious decision in that moment never to let any woman hold such power over him.

He smoked his cigarette to the end, then got slowly out of the crumpled bed and got dressed. Was Faith serious when she said she was accepting the United States tour? Probably. Why not? It was her bread and butter after all. But three months! Supposing she never came back . . .

He handed the room-key in at the hotel reception-desk and walked to where he had parked the car a couple of streets away. The day was hot, with that sticky London heat, trapped between the walls of the houses. The way was punctuated with openings and alleyways, but the slight currents of air were stale and smelt of garbage. As he slid behind the wheel, he found himself thinking with longing of Mallerby.

He drove back to Gresham Street, but did not immediately enter the bank. Instead he sat in the car for several minutes, listening to the subsiding tick of the cooling engine. He had been forty-two years old on his last birthday in May. Wasn't it time that he took stock of his life and decided what it was he really wanted? But, again, he shied from the thought like a nervous horse, got out and slammed the car door with unnecessary violence.

'Have you had a proper lunch?' Marcia Corby asked severely, as he passed through the office. He nodded, but she looked sceptical. 'There's someone waiting to see you,' she said. 'She's been waiting quite some time.' As he paused enquiringly, one hand on the doorknob of his own room, his secretary finished with a certain amount of relish: 'It's your wife.'

TWENTY-NINE

'WHAT ARE YOU DOING HERE?' he asked. 'You're supposed to be at Mallerby. I'm coming down to join you tomorrow.'

Christine smiled. 'I'm glad you're pleased to see me,' she said.

She was looking attractive and cool in a plain pale-blue Dior dress which Colette had made her buy the previous year, during their annual trip to Paris. Its only ornamentation was a row of large mother-of-pearl buttons down the front, and it had a simplicity and elegance which contrasted sharply with Faith's love of fussy clothes. Rowland resented the comparison which sprang unbidden to his mind.

He resented, too, the little display of sarcasm, but at the same time knew that he deserved it. He stooped and kissed her cheek, smelling the slightly musky scent she always wore.

'I'm sorry,' he apologized. 'Let's start again. I'm pleased to see you.' And, suddenly, he realized he *was* pleased to see her. He was always pleased to see her: she was such an old friend. They had been together for fifteen years. 'But that doesn't explain why you're here.'

'I want to talk to you.'

Rowland raised his eyebrows. 'Couldn't it have waited until the weekend?'

'No. I have to say it while I have the courage, so I drove up to town this morning and came straight here. Rowland, I need to work. I need to do something. I want a job.'

He sighed, suppressing his annoyance. 'We've been

301

over this ground before. Has Maman been getting at you again?'

'We talked yesterday afternoon, yes, but not about that.' She paused, giving him time to draw his own conclusions, and had the satisfaction, if she could call it that, of seeing a faint tinge of red stain his sallow cheeks. She went on: 'Vivien and Pat no longer need me. Pat hasn't needed me for quite some time. As for Viv, she's over eighteen now, and surely it's time that Julian began to shoulder his responsibilities. He's no backbone, Rowe, and never will have as long as the rest of us go on shouldering them for him.'

'He's had a bad deal with Sophie,' her husband countered. He looked at her pleadingly. He could do without this, coming as it did on top of the scene with Faith. He was tired, and his liver had taken a lot of punishment recently. As well as smoking heavily, he was drinking too much. He sometimes felt unable to cope with the sort of life he was living. All he wanted some nights was to go to bed and never wake up again. He said, surprising himself: 'If Vivien and Pat don't need you any more, I do. I want to be able to call you any time of the day, here or at Mallerby, and know that you'll be there.'

Christine took a deep breath. She loved him so much it was like a physical pain. But where did it get her? What about Faith?

'If I worked here,' she argued unanswerably, 'you could see me all the time.'

It was the wrong thing to have said; she could see it by his face. He suspected her of wanting to check on him; to supervise his movements. She, in her turn, became suspicious. Where had he been this lunch-time? Had he been with Faith? He had. She could see it by the sudden guarded expression in his eyes. She felt suddenly, furiously angry, but after a moment or two the anger drained away, leaving her with an all too familiar sense of desolation.

She said firmly: 'Then, if you won't give me a job, I must find one for myself. And don't', she added fiercely, 'tell me about the wonderful charity work I'm doing. If I have to sit on another of those stupid committees, I shall scream.'

'But surely—' he began, but got no further before the buzzer sounded on his desk. Annoyed, he depressed the intercom button, and Marcia Corby's incisive tones announced: 'I have a telephone call for you from your mother. She wants either you or Mr Julian, but Mr Julian's not in his office. I've tried. His secretary says he's slipped out for a while and should be back around three.'

Rowland sighed and said: 'Put her through.' At the same time, he raised enquiring eyebrows at Christine, but she shrugged and shook her head. She had no idea why Colette could be calling. She sat back in her chair and waited.

She could hear a gabble of quick-fire French at the other end of the line, and Rowland answered in the same language. A frown appeared between his brows, and he sounded angry. Just before the end of the conversation, he reverted to English.

'Don't worry, Maman. We'll be there some time this evening. As soon as I can get hold of Jules, we'll make a start. We'll have to go home and pack first, but we shan't wait until tomorrow. Christine's here. She'll be returning with us.'

As he replaced the receiver, she asked: 'What was that about? Everything was all right at Mallerby when I left this morning.'

But Rowland was already making arrangements with Marcia Corby to cancel the one meeting he had that afternoon, and issuing instructions for Julian to be found immediately. Christine resigned herself to patience until he was able to give her his full attention.

* * *

303

Vivien had watched her aunt's Renault disappear that morning along the avenue of limes, before going in search of her grandmother.

'Where's Christine gone in such an almighty hurry?'

'To London, to see your uncle. She made up her mind suddenly at breakfast. Which', Colette added severely, 'you would have known, had you been present, instead of still in bed.'

'Sorry.' Vivien tired hard to sound apologetic. 'Why did she do that? Uncle Rowe and Dad are coming down tomorrow.'

'I don't know. I didn't ask.' Colette regarded her grand-daughter austerely. 'I don't pry into other people's business. Anyway,' she went on, getting to her feet, 'you and Patrick will have to amuse yourselves this morning. I'm going into Yeovil to do some shopping.'

'So there you are,' Vivien announced half an hour later, when her cousin finally put in an appearance, 'it's just you and me, babe.' She hooked one leg over the arm of her chair and looked at him from beneath half-closed lids. 'What shall we do? Do you have any suggestions?'

They were in the drawing-room, a freshening breeze making the terrace and gardens uncomfortable for the moment, even though it was still very hot. Pat, lounging in one of the armchairs, regarded Vivien thoughtfully. She was looking very pretty this morning in a fuchsia-pink cotton sun-dress which complemented her dark colouring and olive-tinted skin. It was not a shade which everyone could wear, but on Vivien it looked dramatic, and he could tell that she agreed with him.

When Patrick had first come to live with his father, Vivien had been nine, eleven months his junior. He hadn't thought much of her then, in either sense of the phrase. She had just been a silly coltish girl with whom he was expected to play whenever she visited

Hampstead in the company of her father, or during holidays at Mallerby. Later, when she and Julian came to live permanently on the top floor of Inglebatch House, he was away most of the time at school, and managed adroitly to avoid her somehow or other when he was not. It had not been until this past week that he had really become conscious of her as a person.

Seeing her again, when she had arrived at Mallerby House for the summer vacation, he had experienced a pleasant shock. His cousin had blossomed into a very attractive young woman, but there was more to it than that. He had recognized instantly that Vivien was a kindred spirit; that there was a substratum of malice in her nature which corresponded to the one in his. Was *malice* too strong a word? Perhaps. But they both of them liked to stir things a little; to make mischief, Colette would have said. And there was a sexual attraction between them as well. They had each felt it as soon as they met. The only wonder was that they had not been made aware of it before.

Patrick said: 'Aren't there some attics at Mallerby? I don't think I've ever seen them.'

'They're not attics exactly.' Vivien unhooked her leg from the arm of her chair and smiled. 'It's a very long gallery with one or two small rooms and recesses opening off it. In the old days, I think, it was used for taking exercise during the winter months. Do you want to see it? I'll take you.'

Her cousin shrugged. 'Why not? If nothing else, it should be nice and quiet up there.' He avoided looking her directly in the eyes.

Vivien had no such inhibitions. She got up and crossed the room, to stand behind his chair. She leaned forward, slipping her arms around his neck.

'It should be very quiet,' she agreed. 'I don't think the servants go up there, except once a week to vacuum. Come on. I'll lead the way.'

He followed her up the main staircase to the first-floor landing, then through a door which led to the back of the house. Another door opened on to an uncarpeted flight of stairs which spiralled upwards to an archway, a corridor and, finally, a third door, giving on to a long, empty, echoing gallery which stretched almost the entire width of the house. Uncurtained windows let in the bright July sunshine for the length of one wall; but, at either end, heavy oak doors indicated the existence of secondary rooms, used, Vivien informed her cousin, as supper-rooms in the days when the gallery had been the venue for Saxelby dances and grand county balls. Now they were as empty as the gallery itself.

'Not quite,' Patrick contradicted her, pushing wide one of the two doors. 'This room at least has a carpet.'

Vivien came to stand beside him, staring thoughtfully at the thick fawn druggeting which here covered the ancient uneven floorboards. Her eyes met his in a long speculative glance, then she stepped inside the little room, pulled him in after her and closed the door. She unzipped the fuchsia sun-dress and let it fall to the floor. She was wearing nothing underneath.

Startled, Patrick caught his breath. Vivien had a beautiful body, very like her mother's. She was indeed far more like the erring Sophie than he, or any of the rest of her family, gave her credit for. He felt the excitement surge along his veins. With fingers which felt like thumbs, he hurriedly undressed, hoping to heaven that this was the first time for her as it was for him, and that she would not realize how inexperienced he really was.

The druggeting was hard, and Vivien squirmed a little as it chafed her back. Patrick sweated and heaved on top of her, and she was conscious of a sharp stab of pain which made her cry out. She was also conscious of grave disappointment. Was this rather uncomfortable process what the girls at school had whispered and giggled about in corners? What they had enthused and boasted about, so that she had been forced to invent her own sexual experiences in order not to be left out? And the anticipation had been so pleasurable, had produced such exciting sensations in the pit of her stomach, that the sense of a let-down was even more acute. Patrick, on the other hand, seemed, most annoyingly, to be enjoying himself.

They were both too preoccupied with their different emotions to hear any noise outside the room. Consequently, Mrs James, manhandling her vacuum cleaner across the gallery, already bad-tempered because one of the girls from the village was sick this morning and she was saddled with extra work, almost tripped over their recumbent figures as she flung open the door. She gave a horrified squawk before hurriedly withdrawing, her cheeks hot and flushed with embarrassment. What on earth were the young coming to nowadays? It was disgusting! It was an outrage! Madame should hear about this just as soon as she got home!

The thought uppermost in Patrick's mind was that, if Vivien had known the gallery was cleaned once a week, she might at least have taken the trouble to find out which day. As it was, her carelessness had let them both in, first, for a ridiculous scene with Colette and, second, for the present even more highly charged confrontation with his father and Uncle Julian, who had been summoned at top speed from London. Patrick really couldn't see what all the fuss was about. Sexual promiscuity had been acceptable ever since the Swinging Sixties. If friends and fellow-undergraduates were to be believed, he had really been rather abstinent. Not that you'd think it, the way everyone was carrying on; even his father, who, God knew, had no grounds for taking any sort of moral stand.

'Look,' he said at last, when he could make his voice heard, 'don't you think this is all a bit over the top? All right, so Viv and I are cousins. That doesn't make it incest!'

'It means that we should have been able to trust you!' Julian retorted hotly. 'I didn't expect my daughter to be raped by a member of her own family!'

There was a stir of protest from Rowland, who said: 'Oh, come on, Jules! That's overstating it a trifle. No one is suggesting that Vivien's been raped.'

Julian spun round angrily to face his brother. 'What are you suggesting, then? That Vivien's a whore, like her mother?'

There was a brief shocked silence, broken by Patrick. 'So that's it, is it?' he sneered. 'That's what's behind all the fuss and bother! Not paternal indignation at the deflowering of his little daughter. Oh no! Just naked fear that Viv's going to turn out to be another Aunt Sophie.'

Rowland snapped, with more hostility than Christine had ever heard him use towards his son: 'Shut up, Patrick! You've done enough damage, so just keep your mouth shut.'

At the same moment, Vivien bounced up out of her armchair and shouted: 'Will you all please stop talking about me as though I'm not here!' She glared at her father, who was straddled in front of the empty drawing-room fireplace. 'As for being like Mother, I hardly think you have any right to censure either my conduct or hers. And especially not Uncle Rowe! His affairs are every bit as much of a scandal as my mother's.'

There was another silence. Colette murmured: 'Out of the mouths of babes and sucklings . . .'

Christine, who had contributed nothing to the scene, looked with interest at her husband to see how he would wriggle out of that. But she should have known better than to imagine, even for an instant, that Rowland would try to excuse himself.

He said gently: 'No, you're quite right. But, Vivien my dear, I'm sure your mother would agree with me that no parent wants to see a child make the same mistakes as he or she has done. To tread the same path to perdition.' The phrase, with its slightly biblical ring, brought Colette's head round sharply, and she and Christine exchanged glances. Rowland went on: 'And, however hypocritical my intervention may seem to you and Pat, I agree with your father, the family should be sacrosanct. If you wanted to marry one another, it would be different. But I assume that's not the case?'

'Good God, no!' Patrick exclaimed ungallantly. 'I mean,' he added hurriedly, in answer to his cousin's indignant stare, 'we're both far too young. And it isn't likely to happen again, not after all this furore.'

'That's not the point!' Julian yelled, banging his fist on the mantelpiece. 'How do you know Viv's not pregnant? I don't suppose you thought to take any precautions.'

'No, I didn't,' Patrick replied hotly, his face set in sullen angry lines. 'You talk as though the whole thing were my idea, when actually it was your daughter's. Anyway, who gets pregnant at a first attempt?'

Colette and Julian looked distressed. Christine said quietly: 'I did.'

The fact that she had had a child was plainly news to both her niece and her step-son, but before they could ask embarrassing questions Julian once more stepped in.

'The point is I don't trust you, Pat. I don't trust either of you,' he amended a shade too swiftly. Patrick looked at him with hatred. 'So I suggest, Maman,' Julian continued, turning towards his mother, 'that, if you'll arrange it, Vivien goes to stay with Gran'mère for a while. After all, she's nothing planned. She's just loafing around here, getting into mischief. Gran'mère will keep a stricter eye on her than we can.'

Patrick regarded his cousin. 'You don't have to go,' he said to Vivien. 'You're eighteen. They can't make you. This isn't the bloody Dark Ages. Tell your father to go take a running jump.'

'That will do, Pat!' Rowland exclaimed sternly. 'I will not tolerate rudeness.'

Vivien hesitated, tempted to follow her cousin's advice. She deeply resented her father's attitude and this public humiliation. It would be a very long time, if ever, before she forgave him. He had made her look a fool in front of everyone, treating her like a child. But the thought of going to live with her grandmother de Bérenger for a while was extremely appealing. She liked Gran'mère, and had always been able to twist the old lady around her finger, the only member of the family who could do so, except Uncle Rowland. They need not stay at Château Bérenger. She would persuade her grandmother to take her to Paris. Great-Uncle Lucien and Great-Aunt Solange had always been favourites of hers, and she was fond of Giles, now a man of twenty-three. She conjured up a mental picture of Giles's dark good looks, and decided that there was even more to be said for an extended holiday in France than she had at first imagined.

'OK,' she agreed, leaning back in her chair and crossing her shapely legs. 'I'll go and stay with Gran'mère.' She gave her father a hostile look. 'It'll be better than staying here with you lot. Not you, Aunt Christine. I'm sorry for you. But I'll be delighted to get shot of the rest of you. The sooner I go, the happier I shall be. And if I were you, Patrick, I wouldn't stay, either.'

CHAPTER THIRTY

PATRICK, however, did not follow Vivien's advice.

'He knows which side his bread is buttered,' Christine said to Lois. She was seated in Lois's living-room, watching her friend take down the Christmas decorations.

Lois and Barry Aylward lived in a bigger house than formerly, nearer to the town centre of Shaftesbury. During term-time, the two girls, Cheryl and Judith, were away at boarding school, but on this particular afternoon during the first week of January 1982 they were out visiting friends.

'They'll be sorry to have missed you,' Lois had said, when Christine arrived unexpectedly on her doorstep just after lunch-time. 'I wish you'd let me know that you were coming.'

'Sorry.' Christine had been glad to get indoors, out of the biting wind. 'I hadn't intended coming until tomorrow, but it looks like snow and blizzards are threatened. I believe they've already started in the north. I thought I'd better drive over from Mallerby while I was still able. I did try to phone you before I left, but there was no answer. You must have been out.'

'We were shopping. The girls wanted to spend their Christmas money. Thank you and Rowland for your more than generous gifts, by the way.'

Christine cocked a wary eyebrow. Did she detect a note of resentment? She must be careful not to overdo her presents in the future. It was so easy to appear patronizing, even to old friends.

'Cheryl is my god-daughter,' she pleaded in extenuation.

311

Lois had laughed, a little shamefaced. 'Did I sound churlish? Then, it's my turn to apologize.' And amity had been restored.

Over the years, Lois had grown, if not fat, then certainly to matronly proportions. She had acquired, too, the country habit of wearing comfortable serviceable clothes. She paid little attention to fashion these days; and sometimes, meeting her again after a lapse of months, Christine felt that this large, placid, rather dowdy woman had nothing in common with the Lois of old. But then she would say something, make some caustic observation, and Christine would immediately be transported back to their younger days. She was still the same old Lois.

When Lois had made tea, and brought it in on a tray, together with slices of Christmas cake, she excused herself and continued to take down the decorations. 'I like to get rid of them well before Twelfth Night. Once New Year is over, I think they always look so sad and out of place. You don't mind, do you?'

'Good heavens, no.' The house was very warm. Christine kicked off her shoes, tucking her feet up beneath her. 'We go back too far to stand on ceremony with one another.'

Lois smiled. 'I know. Comfortable, isn't it? Like a pair of old well-worn shoes.'

They began, as always, by asking after one another's family. Barry was well and thriving and also putting on weight. The girls were turning into a pair of proper little madams. Lois's parents had come down from Weston to join them and Barry's mother and father over Christmas, but had returned earlier than intended because of the adverse weather forecast. Gwen Chandos, who had spent the holiday at Mallerby, had done the same for similar reasons.

'Although I don't think it was really the weather forecast that sent Mum scurrying home,' Christine admitted with a sigh, sipping her tea from an earthen-ware mug. 'She still feels awkward, out of her depth there, even after all these years.'

'I know exactly how she feels,' Lois answered cheer-fully, rolling up yards of silver-red tinsel and packing it away in its box. 'That one time Barry and I came over was enough for me. I've never been tempted to repeat the experience. All those miles of corridor and priceless antiques! I either got lost or was afraid to move. So tell me your news. What about that job you were once so keen on getting?'

Christine tried hard not to look sheepish. 'Oh . . . I decided to wait a while longer after all. But one of these days I'll surprise you and do it.'

'Humph.' Lois, having stripped the Christmas tree, started to unhook branches of dried holly from behind the pictures. 'What you mean is that one day you'll wake up and realize that you owe yourself something. A life free from Rowland Saxelby.'

Christine replaced her mug carefully on the tray. 'I wouldn't want that,' she said softly. 'It wouldn't be any life if I didn't have Rowland. You may find this hard to believe, because you're prejudiced against him, but he needs me. He always has, I think. And lately more than ever.'

Lois snorted and maltreated an inoffensive piece of mistletoe. 'You mean since Faith Malyon got married to that American saxophonist, I imagine, and based herself in the States.'

Christine said nothing. She was thinking of that day last spring, when she had read in the newspaper of Faith's wedding to Lloyd Hilder. The press had made much of it, the marriage of a leading classical pianist to one of America's foremost exponents of progressive jazz. There had been no way of keeping it from Rowland, even for a little while; it was too good a story, and even the quality papers made it front-page news, with pictures of the happy couple smiling at one another on the steps of New York's City Hall. She remembered him coming home that night, looking grey and drawn with shock. He had obviously had no idea what was in the wind, in spite of the fact that he had received an airmail letter from Faith only the previous day. He had made no comment, and neither had she, but during the succeeding months she noticed that he smoked more, drank more, and worked harder than ever.

His dependence on Christine grew. He liked to have her near him; to know that she was there in the evenings when he got home from the bank; to see her sitting opposite him when they stayed home, listening to music and quietly reading, or if they went out to dine. 'You're my best friend,' he had told her more than once, 'you know that, don't you? There's no one can ever take your place.' And with that she had to be content. Was content. As someone had once said – or nearly said – in some film, if you have the stars, why ask for the moon? But love like hers for Rowland was difficult to explain to other people: it was rare. And a damn good thing, too, she thought, finishing her mug of tea.

Fortunately, Lois had too much respect for her privacy to question her more closely on a subject Christine so obviously did not wish to pursue. Instead she said: 'If you want to make yourself useful, come and give me a hand sorting out these Christmas cards. Some of them belong to the girls, and I daren't throw them away without their permission. I expect you'll be able to tell which are which. Barry's and mine are usually staid and rather dull.'

Christine was only too pleased to assist, and they spent the next quarter of an hour giggling over some of the more florid messages received by both Cheryl and Judith and recalling Christmases past.

'Remember that Christmas we went shopping in London and bumped into Rowland?' Lois asked. 'It was the first time I'd seen him, although you'd talked about

314

him so much, and I felt we were already acquainted. He took us to tea at Brown's Hotel.' She waited a moment for some response, then, getting none, added: 'Chris! Did you hear what I said?'

'What? I'm sorry. Yes. I did.' Christine frowned. 'It's just that when I think of that afternoon there's something I feel I ought to remember about it. Something that happened ... No, I just can't call to mind what it is.'

'What sort of thing?' Lois asked curiously, picking up her daughters' pile of cards and snapping them into a rubber band.

Christine shook her head. 'If I could answer that, I might know what it is I'm on about. Sometimes I seem very close to resolving the riddle, but I never do. Like now. Something almost surfaced a second or two ago, but sank again before I had time to catch it. Ah well! I'll remember one day.' The front door slammed, and there was the sound of raised voices in the hall. She smiled. 'It seems as though the girls are home early. I shall be able to see them before I go after all.'

The weather had deteriorated by the time she returned to Hinton Malsherbes. The High Street was already covered by a thin coating of snow. The sky was leaden and visibility poor, but many of the shop-windows were still brightly lit, still gleaming with tinsel and the bright shiny green of holly. The butcher, on the other side of the green, had 'A Happy Christmas to All Our Customers' picked out in glittering red letters all across the expanse of plate glass. Beyond the walls of the Feathers, lights from the Harcourt housing estate starred the encroaching darkness. As she passed the turning to Church Street, Christine could see a subdued glow inside St Mary's and heard faintly the strains of 'All Things Bright and Beautiful'. Mr Gerard, the organist, was practising for the children's service on Sunday morning. She swung the car right into Harcourt Lane, then right again down the long avenue leading to the front of Mallerby House.

Colette was waiting for her in the hall, having seen the approach of the Renault from an upstairs window.

'There you are!' she exclaimed, when Christine, having garaged the car, eventually arrived indoors, her head and shoulders powdered with snow.

'I came back earlier than I intended,' Christine said. 'I could see we were in for some pretty bad weather. I'm sorry if you've been worried.'

'Oh, my darling, it's not that,' Rowland said, strolling into the hall and kissing her cold lips. '*I'm* the one who's been worried, not Maman. She's just dying to tell you the news.'

'What news?' Christine asked, shedding her coat and shaking it free of melting snowflakes.

'Of course I've been concerned for you, out in this horrible weather,' Colette protested, pained. 'But, *chérie*, you're such a good careful driver, and I really can't see the point of worrying myself unnecessarily.' Having delivered herself of this artless speech, she drew Christine's hand through the crook of her arm and ushered her into the drawing-room.

Julian and Patrick were already there, seated at opposite ends of the room and studiously ignoring one another. There had never been much love lost between them, and this state of affairs had been exacerbated by the incident involving Vivien eighteen months ago. The fact that she had not returned from France, but had settled there with her grandmother, had only made matters worse. Julian blamed Patrick for his daughter's desertion. It never occurred to him that he, too, might be deserving of some blame. Patrick, in his final year at Oxford, returned his uncle's dislike with interest, particularly since he had discovered that Julian strongly opposed Rowland's wish to take his son into the bank later in the year.

316

Both men looked up and smiled as Christine entered. Both were fond of her in their different fashions. Julian got up and ushered her to a seat near the fire. In this sort of weather, central heating alone was insufficient for Mallerby. Rowland followed and sat down beside her on the sofa.

'So what's the news?' Christine asked. 'What's been happening in the short time I've been absent?'

'Viv telephoned from Paris,' Julian was beginning, but his mother interrupted him with a scream.

'Tais-toi! This is *my* story! I shall tell Christine.' She turned to her daughter-in-law triumphantly. 'Vivien is to marry Giles in the autumn. They became engaged on New Year's Eve.'

It took Christine a moment to assimilate the news, it was so entirely unexpected.

'Giles?' she asked at last, pronouncing his name, as she invariably did, in the English fashion. 'But . . . but didn't anyone have any idea that this was going to happen? Julian? Surely Vivien must have given you a hint?'

He shook his head. He was in a surly mood, not certain yet what he thought of his daughter's surprise announcement, and in no mood to join in his mother's wholehearted celebrations.

Colette made no secret of her delight. A wedding – and a wedding, moreover, which linked both the English and French sides of the family – could not fail to please her. She was jubilant and was unable to talk of anything else for the rest of the evening.

'You've been very quiet,' Christine said to Rowland when, very late, they at last managed to escape and go to bed. 'What do you think of the engagement?'

Her husband shrugged, taking off his jacket. 'If it's what Vivien wants, it's what she'll have. She's a very determined young woman. There's nothing to be said against it that I can see. Although Giles is my and Julian's first cousin, he's only five years older than

317

Viv. Uncle Lucien and Aunt Solange were married for thirteen years before he was born. Aunt Solange was thirty-six. I recall the jubilation at his birth very well. I was nineteen and doing my National Service.'

Christine pulled on her nightdress and sat down at the dressing-table to brush her hair. She fancied she could see some grey. She would be forty-two this summer.

'Do you think it's wise for cousins to marry?' she asked.

Again Rowland shrugged. 'Maybe. Maybe not. It depends on the families concerned and their medical histories, I suppose. As far as I know, both the Saxelbys and the Bérengers are sound.' He went over to one of the windows and parted the curtains slightly. Snow was piling up on the narrow stone ledge outside. 'I hope the Council get the snow-ploughs moving early tomorrow morning,' he said. 'I need to be in London by noon!' He turned back into the warmly lighted room. 'How did you get on today?'

Christine laid down her hairbrush. 'If you mean did I enjoy myself, I always do when I visit Lois. We can gossip about old times.'

He laughed and finished undressing, then got into bed. He linked his hands behind his head.

'Maman will have a fine time organizing the wedding. She'll be off to Paris as soon as she can to see Vivien. She'll usurp Sophie's place entirely. Come to think of it, we don't know if Sophie's even been told.'

Christine joined him in bed. 'We don't really know very much at all yet. Are they being married here or in Paris? All we know is the month. October.' She snuggled down beside him, pulling the bed-clothes around her shoulders. 'Julian doesn't seem very pleased.'

'He's annoyed because Vivien asked to speak to Maman when she rang up this afternoon, and not to him. He feels excluded from her life and he's venting his anger on Pat. He's hardly spoken a civil word to him all Christmas.'

'He'll get over it,' Christine said with a good deal more assurance than she felt. But she did not want Rowland worrying over things he could do nothing about. As head of Saxelby's bank, he had enough responsibility. She wondered if he had heard from Faith Malyon over the holiday. A card perhaps. She could imagine Faith making such a sentimental gesture. It went, somehow, with her doll-like looks and frilly dresses. Now I'm being bitchy, she thought. But she found that she was still afraid of Faith Malyon, in spite of the affair being over.

Thinking of Faith made her also think of Lucy Brennan. In spite of the fact that they were apparently two totally dissimilar types, there was, nevertheless, something which linked them. Selfishness. Dedicated ruthless self-interest. Was that what Rowland found so fascinating about the pair of them? About all his women? Did he find her too timid, too tame?

Christine gave herself a mental shake. She had been through this sort of conversation with herself before, and it led nowhere. Human relationships, the things which attracted and repelled, were too complex to be analysed by such simple methods. She was tired after her drive to Shaftesbury and back. She could feel herself drifting off to sleep . . .

She awoke over an hour later to find the bed empty beside her and a soft white light flooding the room. Confused, still drugged with sleep, she sat up abruptly, staring around her like a frightened child. Then she realized that Rowland was standing by the window, where he had drawn back the curtains. The light was the reflection of moon and starlight on the snow outside.

'Rowe,' she asked, 'what's the matter? Are you feeling all right?'

At the sound of her voice, he jumped and turned his

head. After a moment's hesitation, he answered: 'Yes. I'm fine.' He drew the heavy brocade curtains again and came back to bed, taking her in his arms.

She rested her head in the hollow of his shoulder, aware of the bones sharp and protruding beneath the skin. 'Are you sure you're all right?' she asked again. 'You're much too thin.'

'I've always been thin,' he protested. 'One of Pharaoh's lean kine. I burn up energy faster than most.'

'How long', she demanded sleepily, 'since you went to the doctor for a check-up?'

He nuzzled her hair. 'I never go to a doctor unless I'm absolutely bound to, you know that. Stop worrying. I'm fit as a flea.'

She said no more, but she could not help contrasting Rowland with Barry Aylward, who had arrived home from work early that afternoon, just as she was getting into the Renault. He, like Lois, had put on weight, but his skin had the sheen of good health, his eyes bright with happiness and contented living. He was a man who had accepted his limitations and had never tried to push himself beyond them. Not a man who would ever make his fortune or build a commercial empire. But almost certainly a man who would make old bones.

Gently, so as not to disturb Rowland, who was already asleep, Christine laid her hand against his heart, feeling for its beat. It seemed strong enough, steady enough. Reassured – and yet, somewhere, in the depth of her being, not reassured – she also slept.

CHAPTER THIRTY-ONE

AFTER MUCH WRANGLING, it was finally settled that the wedding should be held in Paris, which, suitably enough, was what Vivien wanted. Her grandmother's decision that she should be married at home and the reception be held at Mallerby House was overset by two cogent arguments: first, Hinton Malsherbes had no Catholic church, and Vivien, after instruction, had been accepted into the Roman Catholic faith two weeks before her wedding; second, it was less likely that Sophie would attend or interfere with the arrangements.

Christine suspected that, secretly, her mother-in-law was rather pleased to have an excuse for visiting Paris so often, even though she was piqued to discover that Solange and Madame de Bérenger had made themselves responsible for most of the organization.

'The truth is', Colette confided to Christine after one of these trips, 'Vivien is more concerned with excluding her father, rather than Sophie, in the run-up to the wedding. She really seems to be holding a grudge against him, which I cannot understand. Julian's reaction was only that of any father concerned for his daughter's welfare. I've given that girl a piece of my mind.'

Christine was inclined to think this very unwise, but did not say so. She was in a hurry, having been just about to leave Inglebatch House when Colette emerged from her taxi.

'I have a fitting for my suit for the wedding at two,' she excused herself. 'Tell me all the news this evening.'

She walked to the row of lock-up garages in a neighbouring street and got out the Renault. She

321

remembered, almost with amusement, the shy provincial girl she had once been; a girl who would never have dreamed of driving herself around London. She slipped into the driver's seat and turned the key in the ignition.

It was nearly three before she finished her fitting and emerged once more into the fitful sunlight of the September afternoon. Should she go somewhere for tea, or was it still too early? Too early, she decided, and made her way instead to St James's Park. Today, the autumnal light gave it a magical quality; the tranquillity of the English countryside dropped in the middle of London's turmoil; a green oasis of peace. A slight haze hung like gossamer above the lake, reminding her of the brooding marshy wasteland it had been in the Middle Ages, its only habitation a hospital for female lepers. It was Charles II who had had the land drained and landscaped into formal gardens.

She sat on a seat opposite Duck Island, watching the pelicans patrol its fringes with their customary proprietorial air. The ornamental ducks swam serenely in and out of the weeping willows, giving an occasional quack. Christine felt a sudden surge of relief that everything looked so normal after a spring and summer which had seen British troops involved in fighting for the first time since 1953 and the end of the Korean War. The war in the Falklands had lasted for only a matter of some ten weeks; nevertheless, it had left behind it a feeling of edginess and uncertainty and a sort of dazed disbelief about the future.

Someone sat down beside her, but she took no notice, lost in her own thoughts, until a man's voice said: 'Hello, Chris. We meet once again.' She turned her head quickly. It was Russell Jennings.

'Russ!' She was genuinely pleased to see him. He looked much the same. A little older, a trifle greyer, but still the same man she had known for most of her life. She shifted to face him, so that their knees were almost touching. 'How nice! I haven't seen you for ages. Why don't we run into each other more often?'

He answered with irrefutable logic: 'If we really wanted to keep in touch, there's no reason why we shouldn't.' She looked uncomfortable, as he had intended she should. He went on: 'However, be that as it may, I've been working in Sheffield for the past three years, but I'm back for a while now, so I suppose we might see something of one another. I still have the same flat. I rented it out, furnished, while I was up north.' There was a fractional pause before he asked: 'How's Patrick?'

Christine blushed, feeling guiltier than ever. 'He's fine. He's just graduated from Oxford with a good Second-Class Honours degree. He's on holiday at present, in Italy. Lake Como. Then he's joining Rowland at the bank. I'm sure he'll do excellently. He likes the life, and Rowland has made him a shareholder. Not, I may add, without some opposition from Julian.'

'But not from you, I take it?'

'On what grounds? Patrick is Rowe's son, and Saxelby's is a family business. I don't feel I have any right to object, whatever my feelings.'

Russell looked at her curiously. 'And what are your feelings?'

She shrugged. 'Not what most people imagine. I don't resent Patrick as they seem to think I should. I like him, although I don't altogether trust him . . . Russ,' she added, after a little hesitation, 'I don't think I've ever thanked you properly for your kindness to Pat all those years ago, when he was young. I did appreciate it, and so did he, however it may have appeared subsequently.'

'Oh, I can't say I was surprised.' He smiled, but without warmth. 'I guessed that Rowland would eventually object. He thought I was usurping his place. I suppose that was only natural. I should have felt the same in his shoes.' There was another pause before he asked: 'Has Rowland ever heard, since, from Lucy Brennan?'

'Not a word. How about you?'

Russell shook his head. 'No. The postcards stopped coming after that time she was supposed to meet me at Heathrow; that time I ran into you. I've never had any word of her since.'

'Strange, isn't it?' Christine watched the sunlight gilding the ripples of the lake. 'It's as though, when she abandoned Pat, she abandoned all her past life with him. Nothing we can do about it, though.' She got up. 'I'm going to get some tea. Can you join me? Or are you . . .?' She stopped, confused, realizing that it was a weekday and she had no idea what he was doing there.

Russell laughed. 'I've been at a meeting in Caxton Street. It ended early, and I'm not expected back at the office. The rest of the afternoon is my own.'

'Right,' she said. 'Then, let's get tea, and we can tell one another all our news.'

Over the next few weeks, Christine found herself seeing far more of Russell Jennings than she had expected. Rowland had flown to the States on business, taking Julian with him. Patrick was still in Italy, and Colette had settled, more or less permanently, in France. Until the wedding was over, she intended keeping a close eye on things, determined that neither her mother nor her sister-in-law should have all the glory. She was Vivien's grandmother and, in Sophie's absence, stood *in loco parentis*.

As a result, Christine was very much on her own, and the old restlessness seized her; the feeling that she was wasting her life. She discussed it with Russell one evening, when he took her out to supper. They had been to a concert at the Wigmore Hall, and then Russell had suggested a small Italian restaurant he knew nearby.

'You don't have to get straight home, do you?'

'No, of course not. There's nobody there.'

'It must be lonely for you,' he sympathized later, as they ate their spaghetti Bolognese.

Normally, she would have turned the remark aside, but she was feeling particularly sorry for herself that evening; missing Rowland and wondering if, while he was in New York, he might not meet up with Faith Malyon once again. Silly, of course! Faith was probably away on tour. She was even more popular these days; even more in demand. Nevertheless, Christine could not keep her imagination under control. She knew she was being stupid and self-indulgent but, with Rowland away, she felt bereft and vulnerable. It was good to have an old friend with whom to talk things over. And Russell Jennings was such an old friend; they had the same background, the same roots, the same early memories. Their relationship was something they could pick up and resume any time they wished, like an old piece of embroidery normally tucked away in a drawer, but taken out from time to time in order to add a few more stitches.

So now: 'Yes, it does get lonely,' she admitted. 'I get restless, too. I've brought up Pat from the age of ten, and Vivien from a little older. I feel I should like to do something with my life, but Rowe isn't keen on the idea of a working wife.'

'Do you still love him as much as ever?' The tone was impersonal; slightly curious.

'Yes. Strange, isn't it? From the very first moment I saw him, I was lost.'

'You don't need to tell me that,' Russell answered drily.

It was Christine's turn to be curious. 'Russ, I've asked you this before, but why on earth have you never married? And don't tell me again it's because of me. I simply won't believe it.'

He smiled, twisting his spaghetti expertly around his fork. 'All right,' he said. 'I shan't. I'm just not the marrying kind, I suppose. And I'm not bent, if that's what you're thinking.'

'Such a thought never crossed my mind!' She refuted the suggestion hotly.

'The fact is', he went on, as though she had not spoken, 'I've never met anyone else I wanted to marry, and over the years I've grown used to looking after myself. I'm very independent. I value my freedom. Mind, if you suddenly decided to divorce your husband – and, God knows, he's given you sufficient cause! – then I might just consider the notion.'

She replied quietly: 'Unless Rowe asked me for a divorce, that isn't likely to happen.'

'Well, then . . . But doesn't it ever strike you as odd that he hasn't, at some time, asked for his freedom? He hasn't exactly been faithful to you, and surely there must have been one, amongst those other women, he was in love with, at least enough to want to marry.'

Christine paused in the act of eating, to look at him. It was a small restaurant, rather dark, with high-backed bench seats and candles on the tables. Russell's face was partially in shadow, and it was difficult to see his expression very clearly.

'What do you mean, "odd"?'

Russell shrugged dismissively, as though sorry he had mentioned the subject. 'Oh, I don't know. I just thought there might be . . . well . . . a . . . a reason.'

'What reason?'

He laughed, a high affected laugh, and said uncomfortably: 'Look, forget it. I was just waffling. I'm sorry I spoke. I should have kept my mouth shut. If you've finished your spaghetti, let's get on to the serious business of choosing a pudding.' They both had a sweet tooth. 'They do the most marvellous praline and toffee ice-cream.'

Christine would have liked to pursue the subject, to probe further the question of what he had really meant by his remark, but she was Russell's guest, so, reluctantly but tactfully, she let the matter drop. But it niggled away at the back of her mind.

Later that night, alone in the double bed at Ingle-batch House, Russell's words kept her wakeful. He was right. It was odd that Rowland had never wanted a divorce; had always so adamantly set his face against it. He had never pretended he was in love with her. Fond, yes; friend, most certainly; and he had needed her for Patrick. And she had always suspected that neither Lisle Ingram nor Maxine Larson had meant that much to him. He had liked them, as he liked all women, and they had had something special to offer him at the time. But not enough to involve himself in the scandal of a double divorce. Faith Malyon, however, had been different. Not only had she been single, but also Rowland had so obviously had for her a deeper, a different kind of feeling. Christine had watched him change; had seen him fret, become jealous, grow thin and silent during her frequent absences on tour. And yet he still would not contemplate divorce; would not hear of it. She guessed that her husband's relationship with Faith had eventually foundered on that particular rock.

An owl hooted somewhere on the Heath. The new moon, a pale silver arc, hung low in the night sky, beyond her bedroom window. Was there a mystery, as Russell had implied? If so, she was incapable of solving it. She had never really understood Rowland, probably because, as he had once told her, he found it difficult to understand himself . . . her thoughts began to drift, becoming a jumble of nonsense; scraps of unrelated conversations; glimpses of scenes, like a camera shutter being raised and lowered; faces floating in a void . . . She was a child again, in Weston, running along the sands, the wind in her hair, the hot sun on her back as she raced towards the distant sea . . .

She woke with a start and switched on her bedside light, to discover that it was still only three in the morning. She turned off the light again and then lay wakeful, poignantly aware of Rowland's absence and the empty place in the bed beside her. She wondered where he was and what he was doing. Who he was with. Suddenly she found the tears were pouring down her face and she was aware of feeling more lonely than she had ever done in her life before. She thought of Russell. Was he really still in love with her? Was that the reason that he had never married?

Christine rolled on to her back and stared at the oblong of pearl between the drawn-back curtains. Did Russell still want her? Need her? Tonight, after their meal, he had suggested that she go back with him to his flat for a drink. Normally, she would have accepted without a second thought, but there had been something in his manner, something more lover-like than usual, which had made her refuse. Now she wished she had. She owed Rowland nothing, when it came to being faithful. If she could make Russell happy, even for a short time, what was to stop her? Only her wedding vows, and Rowland had demonstrated all too often what he thought of them. What was sauce for the gander must surely also be sauce for the goose . . .

The bed beside her felt empty and cold. She turned her face into the pillow to stifle her sobs.

It was the following day that she saw, quite by chance, the photograph in the arts pages of the *Guardian*. It showed Faith Malyon at some New York party with her husband; and there, in the background, but quite unmistakable, was Rowland. The caption underneath said that rumours of a split between the concert pianist and her jazz saxophonist husband were unfounded. The couple were determined to make a go of their marriage. Christine stared at the picture for a long time, while her early-morning coffee cooled and skimmed over. She was still sitting at the kitchen table, the newspaper spread in front of her, when Mrs Johnson, who had replaced Mrs Jones some years earlier as the daily cleaner at Inglebatch House, arrived for her morning duties.

'You all right?' she enquired, dumping an assortment of plastic bags on the draining-board and proceeding to take off her hat and coat. 'Proper white you're lookin'.'

'What?' Christine pulled herself together. 'Yes. Yes, I'm fine.' She folded up the newspaper and finished her coffee without being aware that it was cold.

'Mrs Saxelby senior not back yet, then?' Mrs Johnson shook out and put on a serviceable apron. 'Still over in France, is she, attending to the wedding?'

'Yes. But I think she's coming back for a day or two tomorrow.' Mrs Johnson sniffed, but was evidently not prepared to comment. Christine went on: 'There's no need to leave me any supper tonight, Mrs Johnson, thank you. I shall probably be out again.'

There was another sniff, of equal significance to the one before. Christine felt the colour begin to stain her cheeks and got resolutely to her feet before she was betrayed into a full-scale blush. She went upstairs to her bedroom and put through a call to Russell at his office.

When she was eventually connected, he sounded abrupt, as though he had someone with him.

'Russell Jennings.'

'Russ!' Christine was aware that she sounded breathless, more like a schoolgirl than a forty-one-year-old married woman. 'I wondered if . . . I mean, would it be all right if . . . if I came over and cooked a meal for you at your flat this evening?'

There was the briefest of pauses. Then he said, without any inflection in his voice whatsoever: 'Thank you. I should appreciate that.'

She felt deflated. 'Is it a bad moment? Aren't you alone?'

'No. But the arrangement is perfectly satisfactory. Does your offer mean what I think it means?'

It was her turn to hesitate, but only fractionally. 'Yes,' she said.

'That's very nice. I shall look forward to it. Goodbye.' He hung up, and she was left holding the silent receiver against her ear. Slowly she replaced it on its cradle. Crab, an old dog now and missing his master, came waddling into her bedroom and pressed his cold nose into her hand.

'I've nothing for you,' she told him with mock severity. 'And I wouldn't give it to you if I had. You're much too fat already.'

He waddled off, disconsolate, and made his way downstairs to the kitchen, to try his luck with Mrs Johnson. Christine sat where she was, on the edge of the bed, staring into space, her heart beating erratically. She had done it now. The die was cast.

CHAPTER THIRTY-TWO

'I'M SORRY,' she said, 'but I can't. I just can't do it.'

Christine slid out of bed, the light from the lamp on the bedside table bronzing her naked body, and crossed the room to the chair where she had left her pile of clothes. Hurriedly, and without looking round, she began to dress.

The evening had not gone well from the beginning. By the time she reached Russell's flat, at half-past six, with the necessary ingredients to cook dinner, she was already regretting the impulse which had made her telephone him that morning. She loved Rowland. She had no desire to go to bed with anyone else. If love, according to a popular film, never meant having to say you're sorry, it must surely also mean accepting the other person as he or she was, without having to get even.

Russell himself did nothing to salve her conscience. There was an air of suppressed triumph about him, a sense of smug self-satisfaction, which made her uneasy. She recalled suddenly that there was a ruthless domineering side to Russell, a manipulative core to many of his aims and actions. Had he been manipulating her these past few weeks? The thought remained and rankled. Throughout the meal – fillet steak, green salad, followed by ice-cream and coffee – Christine was aware of him watching her; much, she thought, as a spider watched its prey about to enmesh itself in the web. The analogy was an unpleasant one, and she wished it hadn't sprung to mind. She tried to make light conversation, but Russell was unusually silent and did not respond.

331

By the time they had finished eating, Christine was wishing herself anywhere but where she was, and bitterly regretting having landed herself in such a mess. But the evening had been her own suggestion. How could she now deny Russell's very obvious expectations? She tried delaying tactics, insisting on carrying all the dirty plates into the kitchen and stacking them on the draining-board. She even tried to start the washing-up, but was foiled by Russell coming up behind her and putting his arms around her waist. He turned her round to face him and pressed his mouth on hers.

She was unprepared for how much she disliked it. He must have kissed her in years gone by, but she could remember very little about that side of their relationship, so thoroughly had Rowland blotted out all memory of his rival. She disliked, too, the possessive way in which Russell said: 'Leave all that. Come on. Let's get to bed. That's what you're here for, isn't it?' A man's man, her father used to call him in approving tones; but what did it really mean? A man who, basically, did not like women? And it was that love of women, in its broadest sense, which was at the root of Rowland's attraction to, and for, her sex; to, and for, women of all ages.

She should have told Russell then how she felt and gone straight home. But guilt had made her walk with him to the bedroom, undress and get into the wide double bed, which seemed so incongruous in the small cell-like bachelor room. Did he entertain many women in it? she wondered. He also undressed, then paused at the dressing-table mirror to slick back his hair with a comb and pat on more aftershave. Christine found both actions faintly ridiculous. She watched him get in beside her, still gently patting his face, as though he found some sensuous pleasure in the feel of his own skin. Her heart sank, and she knew the urge to run. She gritted her teeth, however, remembering that she had brought this on herself. She had no option now but to endure the consequences.

But, the moment he touched her, her flesh shrank and all she could think of was Rowland. She knew then that, in whatever light she appeared to herself and to him, she could not let Russell make love to her. 'I can't. I just can't,' she heard herself saying; and, the next thing she knew, she was out of bed and scrambling into her clothes with shaking fingers. When she did at last pluck up the courage to turn and look at Russell, he was still lying in bed, propped on one elbow. His eyes were like flint.

'Well,' he said finally, in a voice as hard as his face, 'this is the second occasion in my life that you've rejected me in your own inimitably callous fashion. You'd have thought I would have learned my lesson the first time, wouldn't you? You must think me all kinds of a fool.'

'Russ, no!' she pleaded. 'It's not like that. I'm so terribly, terribly sorry. When I came here tonight, I intended . . . I fully intended . . .' She broke off, floundering, not quite sure what to say.

He supplied the answer. 'You fully intended going to bed with me in order to get your own back on that philandering husband of yours. Fair enough.' He lay back against the pillows, linking his hands behind his head. 'I was prepared to put up with that, because I also thought there might be some lingering spark of affection for me from all those years ago. A very small spark, but which might be fanned into a flame. However, you've made it quite plain that I can't compete, never shall be able to compete, with Rowland Saxelby.'

'Russ,' she said again, taking a step towards the bed, but he flung out one hand as though to ward her off; as though he could no longer bear her near him.

'Please go, Christine. There's nothing more to be said. Surely even you can see that. Just get out. Now.

And, if we ever run into one another again, don't expect me to be pleased to see you.'

She hesitated for a second or two, racked by guilt, searching for words with which to repair the irreparable. Then, realizing that it was hopeless, she picked up her coat and handbag from the chair and left the room. Quietly, she let herself out of the flat and walked to the parking-meter where she had left her car, sliding behind the steering-wheel and closing the door behind her. But when she tried to turn the key in the ignition and let in the clutch she discovered that she was shaking too much, and had to stay where she was for at least ten minutes. Finally, however, she felt in sufficient command of herself to try again, and this time the Renault moved smoothly out into the mainstream of traffic, the early darkness of the autumn night flickering past the windows.

The wedding was over, and the guests had returned to the Avenue Foch for a champagne breakfast. It had been Colette's decision to hold the breakfast at the Villa Dauphine, contrary to the wishes of both Solange and her mother, who had favoured somewhere grander with accommodation for far more guests. Neither Vivien nor Giles, however, had wanted a wedding on the grand scale, and had therefore backed Colette. Against this united and determined opposition, the two Mesdames de Bérenger found themselves powerless. Reluctantly, Solange had been prevailed upon to restrict her list to just over a hundred guests.

Christine had found the service, held in the English Roman Catholic church of St Joseph, in the Avenue Hoche, beautiful, but bewildering in its ritual. Unable to follow much of what was going on, she had contented herself with looking about her and contrasting this lush fashionable affair with her own register-office wedding at Caxton Hall, with only a handful of people present. She had been pleased to note that Vivien, entering the church on Julian's arm, looked extremely happy; although it was noticeable to discerning eyes, such as her own, that the bride never once looked or smiled at her father. Colette was right: Vivien still bore a grudge against Julian for his attitude at the time of her brief fling with Patrick.

Patrick himself was looking extremely handsome in his pale grey morning-suit and top-hat. Christine recalled the thin, shy, rather scared little boy she had met for the first time here, in this very city. But diffidence was no longer one of her stepson's characteristics. Money and education had laid a patina of self-confidence on him which was almost tangible; lent a kind of sheen to his skin, an arrogance to the tilt of his head and the way he carried himself. Rowland was unreservedly proud of him; but other people, including herself, were more inclined to have reservations.

The chief sensation of the day's events had undoubtedly been Sophie's arrival, ten minutes before that of the bride. She walked into the church, as cool as ice, in a tight-fitting red dress – very expensive and beautifully cut for all its lack of actual material – a huge black straw hat, black gloves and handbag, and black shoes with teetering four-inch heels. Tossed negligently across one arm was a honey-coloured mink coat.

'Typically Sophie,' Rowland had hissed with amusement in Christine's ear. 'Eye-catching and totally tasteless.'

She had agreed with a smile, taking the opportunity to study her husband's face. Since his return from America, she had watched him closely for any sign that he and Faith might have resumed their affair. But she was unable to find any. He had mentioned, quite casually, that he had met Faith and her husband at a party in New York; other than that, he gave no indication of any contact. He looked even leaner and paler than before he went away, but the business side of the trip appeared to have been successful. Both he and Julian seemed well satisfied, their only bone of contention at the moment being Patrick's inclusion in the firm and the large chunk of shares Rowland had made over to his son.

'He's a Saxelby,' he had replied succinctly, when Christine, too, had protested, asking him if he thought the action wise, and to that argument there had seemed to be no answer.

Sitting now in the Yellow Salon of the Villa Dauphine, listening to the babel of French and English all around her, Christine watched Patrick move smoothly through the crush, perfectly at home in either language. His early nomadic years with his mother had left him proficient in several foreign tongues, a fact which Rowland was quick to exploit when adducing Patrick's usefulness to the bank. Christine could not help noticing that he appeared to be very friendly, not only with Vivien and Giles, who were, after all, more or less his contemporaries, but also with Lucien. She remembered, with an inexplicable twinge of uneasiness, that he had returned from his summer holiday in Italy via Paris, and that his planned one-night stopover in the Avenue Foch had extended itself to more than ten days.

'Darling!' Sophie, brilliant as a macaw, grabbed another glass of champagne from a passing waiter, and settled into the chair beside Christine. 'I haven't seen you for an age. How are you keeping? Still doing your Patient Griselda act, I see, with darling Rowe.' Without waiting for an answer, she burbled on: 'They all thought they were going to keep me out of this, you know. All those damn Saxelbys, including my own dearest daughter. But they had to send me an invitation. Their consciences triumphed over their inclinations, but they were all hoping to God I wouldn't come.' She laughed. 'More fools them! They should have known me better. Julian should at any rate.' She glanced around her, wrinkling her nose. 'I don't think

336

much of all this foreign-looking furniture and gilded brass, do you? Worth a bit, though, I suppose.'

She rattled on in much the same style, pausing only to gulp greedily at her champagne. After a while, the raucous voice wore at Christine's nerves and she got up, excusing herself.

'I must go and speak to Solange.'

Sophie glanced up, smiling over the rim of her glass. 'Embarrassing you, am I? Think I'm getting tipsy? Well, what if I am? Nothing else to do. No one's speaking to me. And why? Because I got out while the going was good. I knew when my marriage had gone sour on me and I had the sense to cut my losses. Whereas you . . .' She tilted her head to one side and grinned. 'You're one of those women who excels herself in a lost cause.'

Christine turned away, forcing a path through the crowd of guests, out of the Yellow Salon, across the entrance-hall and into the Blue Salon, where the remains of the wedding breakfast were still on the long tables against one wall, and where Vivien and Giles were still holding court, the centre of a circle of well-wishers and friends. Christine touched Vivien's arm.

'I just wanted to tell you how wonderful you look,' she said, reaching forward to kiss her niece.

'And you!' Vivien flung her arms around Christine's neck, kissing her, Gallic fashion, on both cheeks. 'You should wear that shade of pink more often. It suits you. Gives you colour.' She added, suddenly serious: 'Chris, I haven't really thanked you properly before for all you've done for me over the years. You've been more like a mother to me than my own mother's ever been. I just want you to know that I appreciate it.'

Christine swallowed the lump in her throat and answered as composedly as she could: 'Thank you, darling. I just wish you'd be as generous to your father.'

Vivien's mouth shut tightly. 'He sent me away to France,' she said, 'just because he decided I'd disgraced him. He had me typecast as my mother all over again. I shan't forgive him for that in a hurry.'

Christine sighed. It was neither the time nor the place to start a discussion on the subject, with a dozen curious and interested pairs of eyes upon them. So she kissed Vivien again, embraced Giles and uttered all the banal things that one always does on such occasions, before going in search of Rowland. Soon it was time for the bride to go upstairs and change; then she and her husband were leaving on their honeymoon. Christine stood just inside the handsome wrought-iron gates of the villa with everyone else, waving them goodbye. She wished that it had been Julian, not Vivien's new father-in-law, Lucien, who had been the recipient of the bride's farewell kiss.

'I thought you'd prefer this place to some of the other night-spots,' Colette said, shepherding her party to one of the tables. 'I thought we needed to relax after the wedding.'

She had brought Rowland and Christine, Julian and half a dozen of the younger guests to Castel's in the sixth arrondissement – an area, according to Rowland, more akin to Chelsea than to Mayfair. None of them was a member, but Monsieur Castel had personally approved their admittance, having, it appeared, known Colette years before when he was the owner of a club in St-Tropez. It was a warm, friendly, almost cosy place, with a warren of dark bars and discos, and a great illuminated ivory galleon hanging from the ceiling. There was a restaurant upstairs. Everyone agreed, however, that they had already had far too much to eat. The younger members of the party immediately crowded on to one of the tiny dance-floors, gyrating in time to the incessant flow of music. Colette, her two sons and Christine preferred, for a while at least, to sip their drinks and merely be spectators.

'I think that all went off very well, don't you?'
Colette enquired. 'And Vivien looked splendid. That
deep ivory-coloured satin and the cream lace were my
inspiration.'

'And very self-satisfied you look about it, too,'
Rowland told her with gentle affection.

'And why shouldn't I?' She added a little petulantly:
'I wish Lucien and Solange had felt up to coming with
us tonight. If I'm not worn out, I don't see why Solange
should be. Maman I can understand; she's eighty-two.
But Solange is four years younger than I am, and she
hasn't carried half the responsibility that I have over
this wedding. I really think she might have made the
effort.'

Rowland grinned. 'What you mean is that you
wanted an even bigger audience than the one you
had to see Monsieur Castel bowing gallantly over your
hand and telling you that you don't look a day older.
Come on, Maman, admit it!'

Colette did not deign to reply, merely remarking:
'Patrick is an extremely good dancer.' She nodded
towards her grandson, on the tiny dance-floor. 'He has
obviously inherited my sense of rhythm.'

Julian winked at Rowland and sipped his Laphroaig
whisky. There was no stopping their mother tonight.
She was in high fettle and carried her sixty-five years
extremely well. Christine, looking at the three of them,
thought how alike, in some ways, they were. Julian, it
was true, was not so sensitive as the other two. He did
not seem to feel his daughter's disaffection as keenly
as the rest of his family did for him. In fact he hardly
seemed aware of it at all, dismissing Vivien's coolness
as 'just some silly female nonsense. She'll get over it in
time.'

Christine's eyes strayed to the dancers – Patrick,
wearing jeans and a striped silk shirt, attempting
to impress one of the young French female guests
– and then to a knot of people crowding round the

door, laughing and chatting, drinks in their hands. Most of them, as far as Christine could make out in the dim light, were in their early twenties, but there was one woman, standing a little apart, who looked older. Fortyish, perhaps; Christine could even discern a grey streak amongst the dark curling hair. After a few seconds, the woman turned, so that her face was illuminated by one of the shaded lights . . .

Christine set down her glass with a trembling hand, some of the vodka she was drinking slopping over on to the table. 'Rowe!' she said, in a voice which more nearly resembled a croak. 'It's Lucy! Over there, by the door!'

Rowland was on his feet at once, peering over the heads of the people nearest him. 'Where?' he demanded. 'Quickly! Show me!'

'Over there! Look! *Lucy!*' Christine raised her voice, regardless of people who were beginning to stare. She grabbed Rowland's arm and propelled him towards the door, pushing their way ruthlessly through the crowd.

But when they reached the place where Lucy – or, as Rowland pointed out, the woman Christine thought was Lucy – had been standing she had gone. A hurried search revealed no trace of her, nor did any of the bystanders recollect having seen her or know who she was. She seemed to have been attached to no particular party. At last Christine and Rowland returned to their seats.

'What was all that about?' Colette demanded.

Rowland shook his head. 'Nothing, Maman. Chris just thought she saw Lucy Brennan. But obviously she was mistaken.'

CHAPTER THIRTY-THREE

CHRISTINE'S CONVICTION that she had, indeed, seen Lucy Brennan began to waver.

'A trick of the light,' Colette said, when matters had been more fully explained to her.

'Impossible to see anything properly in these places,' was Julian's opinion. 'And, anyway, from what you and Rowe have always said about her, I shouldn't think this is quite her scene.'

Christine was unmoved by the force of this argument: Castel's seemed to her exactly the sort of place Lucy might choose. She was more convinced by Rowland's pointing out the unlikelihood of her recognizing Lucy Brennan after all these years, especially across a darkened room. By the time they all left the club, in the early hours of the following morning, she had persuaded herself that she had indeed been mistaken, and by tacit consent the incident was not mentioned to Patrick. Yet, deep down, a lingering doubt remained.

They flew back to London later that morning, Solange and Lucien coming to the airport to see them off. Once again, Christine noted how friendly Patrick seemed with his great-uncle. Just before boarding the plane, he and Lucien drew a little apart, deep in conversation. When she mentioned the fact to Rowland, however, he made nothing of it.

'Uncle Lucien's fond of Pat,' he said. 'I'm very grateful for the way everyone has accepted him.'

Much as she had enjoyed the wedding, Christine was still glad to be home. The narrow street lined with elegant Georgian houses, of which Inglebatch House was one, looked welcoming in the soft autumnal after-noon light. She realized that she felt tired, more tired perhaps than even the events of the past few days seemed to warrant. The abortive affair with Russell preyed on her mind. She felt she had treated him badly; made an enemy of him. Although what he could do to harm her she had no idea. Any sort of blackmail was out of the question. Rowland could hardly blame her if she had had any number of affairs, and Russell was intelligent enough to know that. Besides, what could he gain from it, except revenge?

She told herself that she was being ridiculous, blow-ing up the incident out of all proportion. And there was one sure way she could safeguard herself from any comebacks: tell Rowland the truth.

She told him that night, lying in the curve of his arm, in their own bed, listening to the quiet nocturnal sounds: the distant mewling of a cat, the swish of tyres as a late Sunday-night reveller drove home, the harsh-voiced call of a nightjar winging towards the Heath. When she had finished, his arm tightened about her shoulders.

'I don't deserve you,' he said, kissing the top of her head, her hair tickling his chin. 'I've told you that many times before, but repetition doesn't make it any the less true. Why do you put up with me? Why *aren't* you unfaithful?'

'Because I love you. I only want you. There isn't any particular virtue in the fact. Sophie referred to me as Patient Griselda, but I don't feel like that at all. I've always considered her as rather a saintly and insipid person. I look on loving you as a disease for which there is no known cure. But one can always live in hope.'

She could feel him laughing. She turned her face up to his, and he kissed her. They made love. Later, as she was falling asleep, she heard Rowland say: 'I've decided to give Pat a belated twenty-first-birthday present.'

She jerked awake. 'But you gave him that lovely set of golf-clubs, back in May!'

'I know. But it's time he was out on his own. I've been thinking for quite a while now that there should be just the two of us again, not three. You've been marvellous, all these years, but it's wrong to expect you to continue having him under the same roof. Besides, he needs space to be himself. So, before we left for Paris, I took a lease on a flat in a house in Half Moon Street. I haven't told him yet, but I shall tomorrow morning. He can be moved in by the end of the week. As I said, this will be my real twenty-first-birthday present to him.'

'Julian won't like it.'

'What I do with my money is none of my brother's business.' He kissed her again. 'Go to sleep now, and don't pretend you won't be pleased in many ways to see the back of Patrick.'

She was about to protest, but thought better of it. Rowland knew her too well. As she had told herself so often in the past, fond as she was of Pat, there was something about him which made her uneasy.

The following year, in the November of 1983, her mother died.

Gwen Chandos had been ill for some time. The discovery, just after Christmas, of a lump in her left breast, which had proved to be malignant, had resulted in a mastectomy from which she had never properly recovered. For the whole of those eleven months, Christine had divided her time between London, Hinton Malsherbes and Weston-super-Mare, the last eventually claiming the lion's share. From the end of September onwards, she moved permanently into the flat in Clarence Road North and waited, knowing there was nothing she could do except be there. She was thankful that when the end came it was peaceful. It was almost as if her mother had just drifted off to sleep.

Rowland came down for the service at the local Methodist church and at the crematorium, but afterwards he had to get straight back to London. The guests who returned to the flat were mostly friends and neighbours, and by four in the afternoon everyone, including the caterers hired by Christine to prepare a buffet lunch, had left. Only she and Lois Aylward remained.

'I must go soon, too,' Lois said. 'Barry and the girls seem congenitally incapable of getting a meal for themselves without making the most God-awful mess. You'd think, wouldn't you, that a grown man and two teenagers – eighteen and sixteen, mind you! – would be self-sufficient, but not a bit of it!' She added, looking concerned: 'Will you be all right?'

'On my own, do you mean? Yes, of course. I shall be going back to London, anyway, tomorrow.'

'What will you do with the flat? Sell it?'

'I suppose so. I just don't want to think about it at the moment.'

There was a companionable silence. They were such old friends that there was often no need for words. But eventually Lois remarked: 'I see from this morning's *Daily Telegraph* that Faith Malyon and her husband are finally divorced. There's some talk of her coming back to this country to live.'

Christine put up a hand and pushed a strand of hair away from her forehead. She looked extremely pale; but that, Lois decided, might be due to the black dress she was wearing or to grief for her mother. Nothing to do with Faith Malyon at all.

'Yes, I read that, too. But it's only conjecture at the moment. It's equally possible that she'll stay in New York.'

'It doesn't bother you?'

Christine shrugged. 'Maybe. Just a little. Look, let's not talk about something that may never happen. Thank you for coming. It's meant a lot having

344

you here. How about another cup of tea before you go?'

Lois shook her head and got to her feet. She was bulkier than ever, the picture of domestic contentment. Just for a moment, Christine knew a twinge of envy.

'No, thanks, love. I really must be off. I hate driving in the dark, and it will be pitch-black before I get home.' She enveloped her friend in a bear-hug. 'Take care of yourself. If things ever get really bad, you always have a second – or should I say third? – home with me.'

Christine laughed. 'I'm sure Barry would be delighted! And, anyway, it won't come to that. Give my love to the girls. I'll be down to see you all soon.'

When she had seen Lois off, waving as the old Ford Prefect rumbled down the road, she went back upstairs to the empty flat. Suddenly, in spite of the central heating, she was cold. She went into her parents' bedroom and found a cardigan of her mother's, which she wrapped around her shoulders. Somehow the softness of the wool against her neck, the faint lingering smell of Gwen's perfume comforted her. She made herself a pot of tea and thought about Rowland. He had seemed preoccupied throughout the funeral service, as though something were bothering him. He had looked ill, but when she questioned him he had insisted that he felt fine.

Christine drank her tea, sitting at the kitchen table. She was conscious of lassitude: she would have a bath and an early night. Tomorrow was time enough to come to terms with her grief for her mother and those other, nameless, inchoate worries lurking at the back of her mind. All she needed at the moment was sleep.

Seven months later, in June, Faith Malyon gave up her New York apartment and returned to London, with the well-publicized intention of making it her base. She needed, she said in an interview with one of the Sunday

345

supplements, to get back to her roots. As she originally came from Doncaster, the statement seemed suspect, to say the least. When she bought a house on the other side of Hampstead Heath, Colette was furious.

'I should like to cut her up in little pieces and fry her for breakfast,' she announced.

Christine could not help laughing at her mother-in-law's ferocity. Even Julian, who was present, said: 'Steady on, Maman! That's going a bit too far.'

'No, it's not! That woman means to get Rowland if she can. Christine! You are not to allow it. I refuse to have that *salope* as my daughter-in-law!'

Christine smiled. 'Don't worry. I don't mean to let her anywhere near Rowe, if I can prevent it.' But she was talking for the sake of talking, and the other two knew it. They knew that there was nothing she could do to stop Rowland seeing Faith Malyon again, if that was what he wanted.

Christine and Colette had been to Sadler's Wells to see a new revamped version of *HMS Pinafore*. Julian, who had been at his club for the evening, had joined them in the kitchen of Inglebatch House on his return. Rowland was at a meeting of the British Olympics Committee, the bank having been approached for some much-needed funding for the games in Los Angeles the following month. It occurred to Christine that she only had his word that he was there. Supposing – a cold hand gripped the pit of her stomach – he was really with Faith!

She wouldn't even think such a thing. Why should she? Rowland had given her no cause. His reaction to Faith's return had been muted, and his attitude to the news that she had bought Bowood Cottage had bordered on indifference. He was either acting, or he really did not care for Faith any more. Christine prayed fervently that it was the latter.

The kitchen door opened at that moment, and Rowland walked in. 'Ah, coffee,' he said. 'I thought

346

I could smell it.' He joined them at the kitchen table.

Christine got up and went to the stove. Colette enquired: 'How did the meeting go? You look exhausted, *mon cher*. When you have had your coffee, you must go straight to bed.'

'Don't worry, I shall.' Rowland sat down on one of the stools, hooking his heels over the rungs. Crab, who had not accompanied his master to his new home, got out of his basket and waddled across, sniffing affectionately around Rowland's knees. 'The meeting was OK,' Rowland continued. 'I've promised that Saxelby's will contribute a thousand pounds for every other thousand raised. As a matter of fact, it was over fairly early. For the past couple of hours, I've been in Half Moon Street with Patrick.'

Both Christine and Colette gave him a sharp suspicious look, but Julian seemed to have no difficulty in believing his brother.

'Discussing this bloody takeover bid, I imagine.'

'What takeover bid?' Christine and Colette spoke almost in unison.

Rowland darted his brother a reproachful glance. 'I wasn't going to worry either of you until I was more certain what was happening. Then I should have consulted with the board of directors and called a shareholders' extraordinary general meeting. As it is, I'm hopeful now that neither of those measures will prove necessary.'

'Patrick up to his tricks?' Julian asked bluntly, while Colette demanded irritably: 'Will you both please not talk in riddles. Christine and I want to know what exactly has been going on.'

Rowland sipped his coffee and seemed reluctant to say anything more. Julian, however, now that the subject was out in the open, displayed no such inhibitions.

'Bérengers have been buying up Saxelby shares for the past nine months and now have a forty-per-cent

347

holding in the company. Rowe didn't want to tell you, Maman. He thought you'd be upset.'

'Upset!' A torrent of invective, mostly in French, issued from Colette's lips. When she was finally mistress of herself again, he reiterated: 'Upset! Of course I am upset! My own brother to do such a thing to *my* family! It is *incroyable*! But I'm even more upset that you didn't tell me. If I had only known, I would have given Lucien a piece of my mind.'

Rowland set down his cup. His face, Christine noted, looked bloodless under the harsh strip-lighting. 'And that is precisely what I did not want you to do, Maman. This was strictly business. Your interference would have ripped the family apart, and that was something I wished to avoid at all costs.'

'If you think that I am ever going to speak to Lucien again, or to Giles—' Colette was beginning hotly, but Rowland interrupted her.

'I've told you, Maman, it's all right now. The remaining shares are all held by the Saxelby family. By you, Jules, Chris, myself – and Patrick.'

There was a sudden lull in their conversation. Julian, Colette and Christine exchanged speculative glances. Rowland stared at the surface of his coffee, tracing patterns in the layer of creamy bubbles with the back of his spoon. At last Julian broke the silence to ask: 'What did you promise him?'

'Wait a moment.' Christine leaned forward, clasping her hands together in front of her on the table. 'Are you telling us that Patrick was willing to sell his block of shares to Lucien? That he would have been prepared to give Bérengers control of the bank?'

'Of course he would!' Julian spoke scornfully, without giving his brother a chance to answer. 'Either that or – what in fact appears to have happened – use the threat to blackmail his father!'

'Is this true, Rowland?' Christine asked quietly.

He glanced up, but still avoided looking at anyone directly. There were very dark half-circles under his eyes. 'I think Julian is dramatizing things unnecessarily. Pat naturally felt that he had a . . . a bargaining-counter and that he would be . . . well, foolish not to use it. I can understand that.'

'Then, it's more than I can!' Colette snapped angrily. 'I should have expect a little more loyalty from a boy to whom I'd given as much as you have to Patrick.'

'I wasn't trying to buy my son's loyalty!' Rowland replied, equally angry. He had no difficulty now in looking at them all, and his gaze was unswerving. 'And, from Pat's point of view, I suppose I never have given him everything that he expected.' In answer to their questioning glances, his eyes dropped once more, again riveted on his coffee. 'Pat has always thought that I should adopt him legally. Make him my heir. He's . . . resented the fact that I wouldn't ditch Julian in his favour.'

'So what have you promised him now?' Julian asked. 'What have you bought him off with?'

Rowland shrugged, and it was a moment or two before he answered. 'A promotion. More money. A bigger office.'

'And will these be enough, do you think?' Christine demanded. 'Isn't it rather like being given a bag of toffees, when what you really wanted was the biggest, most expensive box of chocolates in the shop?'

Rowland gave a faint smile. 'Pat has promised me faithfully that he will not sell out to Lucien. I trust him.'

'It's more than I damn well do!' Julian exclaimed explosively, and for once Christine found herself totally in sympathy with her brother-in-law. She added her mite.

'I really don't see, Rowe, why you should do. No wonder he and Lucien were so thick last autumn after the wedding. They were probably hatching this up between them.'

Julian sneered. 'Well, poor old Lucien's in for a nasty surprise, isn't he? He's going to find out pretty soon what a two-timing little sod Patrick really is!'

Rowland looked at his brother and said quietly: 'I should like you to take that back.'

Julian's face set in familiar mulish lines. 'Why? Don't you relish hearing the truth for once about that little bastard of yours?'

Rowland got to his feet. 'Take it back!' he insisted.

Julian also rose. 'I'm buggered if I will. Who's going to make me? You?'

'Now, stop this, both of you!' Colette and Christine got up as well. The situation was turning unexpectedly ugly.

'Stay out of this, Maman!' Rowland commanded. 'This is between Julian and me. Now' – to his brother – 'are you withdrawing that statement?'

'Rowe!' Christine laid a hand on his arm. 'This has gone far enough. And Jules has a certain amount of justification on his side. Patrick has behaved abominably.'

Rowland shook her off. 'When I want your opinion, I'll ask for it,' he told her. He had never before spoken to her so roughly. She felt as though he had struck her. She walked round the table and stood between him and his brother. Her eyes were blazing.

'I'm going to bed,' she announced. 'And, for the time being at least, I shall be moving into Vivien's old room. I shall expect your apology in the morning. I don't think that either Julian or I deserve, in your estimation, to come second to Patrick. Good night.' She walked out of the kitchen, on legs that were shaking slightly, and quietly closed the door.

CHAPTER THIRTY-FOUR

ROWLAND APOLOGIZED TO HER over breakfast the following morning. But there was a formality about it, a lack of conviction, which riled Christine. She felt that loyalty to Patrick, probably engendered by a sense of guilt, had made him get his priorities wrong. She told him so, in no uncertain fashion.

'Pat's acted disgracefully, Rowe. He's blackmailed you into giving him undeserved promotion. And, understanding full well what he was up to, you let him. You can hardly be surprised if Julian's bitter.' Getting no reaction, she asked in exasperation: 'Why do you let Patrick behave so badly? If anyone else had attempted to pull a trick like that, you'd have frog-marched him out of the firm so fast his feet wouldn't have touched the ground.'

Rowland laid his knife and fork together on his empty plate. 'A prisoner's feet don't touch the ground when he's frog-marched,' he answered calmly. He got up. 'Look it up in the dictionary some time.' And he was gone.

After that, things seemed to go from bad to worse. The coolness which had developed between herself and Julian on one side and her husband on the other persisted. Rowland had erected a mental barrier which she found it impossible to penetrate. As Julian said, he was quite irrational on the subject of Patrick. But why?

'Rowe missed out on Pat's childhood,' was Colette's explanation. 'He's trying to make up to both of them for all the years he wasn't there.'

They went to Château Bérenger as usual in September, but the atmosphere was strained. Lucien and

Solange cut short their visit, intimidated by Colette's inimical silences and Julian's cold-shoulder treatment. Only Rowland behaved as normal, seeming to share his uncle's conviction that business was business and that nothing personal had been intended by the attempted takeover. Vivien and Giles did not appear at all. Giles was running the bank in his father's absence, and would in fact be taking full control when Lucien retired early in the following year. Patrick, too, for the first time, had declined to be part of the family holiday and had gone off to Corsica with his current girl-friend. Privately, Christine suspected that he did not want to spend a fortnight in the same house with Julian.

Old Madame de Bérenger demanded angrily of Colette what was going on. 'I will not have family quarrelling beneath my roof!' she said, thumping the floor with her ivory cane. 'Next time you go to Paris, you are to make up your differences with your brother.'

'Yes, Maman,' Colette agreed meekly, choking back all the things she felt she ought to have said, because she, too, disliked family quarrels. And, anyway, nothing had come of Lucien's machinations.

Christine had hoped that the peace of Château Bérenger would weave its own magic for herself and Rowland, and that there they might find again the relationship of mutual contentment and affection which had been theirs before the stupid dispute over Patrick. The silliest part of all was that Christine was still quite fond of her step-son. There was a charm about Patrick which not even his cupidity could undermine.

But things had not worked out between herself and Rowland. He continued to raise his defensive barriers, and even the charm of the château and the surrounding countryside failed to weave their usual potent spell. He was edgy, tense and, for him, strangely short-tempered. His mother and grandmother insisted that he could not be feeling well, and Christine herself was coming to believe it. But in answer to all their solicitous enquiries they received only a brief word of acknowledgement and the assurance that he was 'perfectly all right, thank you'.

And then, on the Thursday morning of their second week, Rowland announced that he would be leaving early; that morning, in fact. He was going to Paris for a few days before flying back to London on the Sunday.

'But why?' Colette wanted to know.

And Christine said: 'This is sudden. You haven't mentioned going to Paris before. Do you want me to come with you?'

Rowland shook his head, finishing his breakfast coffee. 'Not unless you'd like to hear Faith Malyon play. She's giving a recital in Paris tomorrow evening.'

After that, there did not seem much more to say, at least as far as Christine was concerned. Colette held forth at length; and even Madame de Bérenger, who always knew a great deal more about what was going on than most people imagined, said a few sharp words. Rowland, again with uncharacteristic rudeness, cut them both short by walking out of the room. An hour later, he was gone, driving his hired Peugeot northward.

By Christmas, Christine knew that the affair had been resumed. Several of her acquaintances on various charity committees, who thought, for her own good, that she really ought to know what was happening, reported that they had seen Rowland and Faith together.

It was one of the worst Christmases Christine could remember. They went, as always, to Hinton Malsherbes, but for once Mallerby House seemed cold and unwelcoming. Patrick and Julian spent the holiday ignoring one another, or, when forced to speak, doing so only in monosyllables. Colette was as subdued as it was possible for one of her temperament to be, and was complaining of twinges of pain in her left hip whenever she put her foot to the ground. Christine noted that when her mother-in-law walked she was beginning to do so with a slight limp. She mentioned the word 'arthritis' but was met with instant denial.

'Arthritis!' Colette exclaimed scathingly. 'That is for the old. I am still a comparatively young woman.'

And Christine supposed that at the age of nearly sixty-eight that was more or less true. With the advances in medical science, people of the mid-1980s were living longer than ever before.

As for Rowland, he seemed preoccupied, slipping away by himself, very often to the drawing-room, when Christine would hear the music of Rameau and Lully drifting out as she passed the door. A little while ago, they would have listened to it together. She had never been more miserable in her life.

She went to spend her usual day in Shaftesbury, taking her Christmas presents stacked in the back of the car. It was nice, she reflected, having so many people delighted to see her: Lois and the girls with extravagant displays of affection, Barry with more restrained but none the less genuine warmth.

While they were having lunch, Lois said: 'Barry had to go to a pharmaceutical convention in London, before Christmas, so I went with him. Now, don't jump down my throat! It was only for two nights, and there were so many social events crammed in for the wives that I didn't have time to let you know. But I did run into an old friend of ours. He enquired very particularly after you. Russ Jennings.'

Christine was startled. 'He enquired after me?'

'Of course. Why shouldn't he? I still think he's carrying a torch, you know. He's never married.'

Christine recollected that she had not told Lois of her abortive attempt at an affair with Russ, so she merely made the necessary polite enquiries and changed the subject as quickly as possible. Nevertheless, driving back to Hinton Malsherbes later in the day, she found herself thinking about him and the possibility that he might have forgiven her. If so, it was more than she deserved, and a wave of nostalgic affection swept over her. She had misjudged him when she thought that he would bear a grudge. But, then, she thought guiltily, she had been treating him badly all her life.

When she got back to Mallerby House, there was an atmosphere that could be cut with a knife. Colette informed her that there had been another disagreement between Rowland and his brother over something Patrick had said or done. Colette could not remember which.

'And to tell you the truth, *chérie*, I do not care. I shall be glad when we return to London.'

Christine agreed, and on New Year's Day thankfully packed her cases and loaded them into one of the cars. Even Hampstead, with Faith Malyon living on the other side of the Heath, seemed preferable to the claustrophobia and tensions of Mallerby.

She sat up in bed with a start, not knowing for a moment or two what had wakened her. Then she realized that the bed beside her was empty. Nor was Rowland anywhere in the room. After a few seconds, listening for sounds of him either on the landing or in the bathroom, she got out of bed, found her slippers and pulled on a dressing-gown. The April nights were still chilly.

During the past month, Rowland had changed. He was once more the humorous, tolerant, affectionate man she had always known. It was as though he had passed through a dark tunnel and come out at the other end. He seemed, for the first time in ages, more relaxed, and at pains to reconcile Julian and Patrick. He was going out of his way lately to be especially kind to his brother, as though wishing to make up for recent neglect. As far as the bank and Mallerby House were concerned, he made it plain that he regarded Julian as his rightful heir, and had nipped in the bud a scheme of Patrick's to change his name to Saxelby by deed poll. Yet there was no doubt that his affection for his son was as strong as ever; and this, too, he made perfectly clear.

What the present state of his affair was with Faith Malyon, Christine had no idea. Nor did she want to know. It was sufficient for her that she and Rowland were back on the old footing; that their friendship, their warmth and regard for one another, her deep abiding love for him, had come through unimpaired. But come through what? She was no nearer understanding what it was that had caused Rowland's bout of black depression.

She padded out on to the landing, but Rowland wasn't in the bathroom. The door stood wide, revealing the faint ghostly outlines of shower-cubicle and bath, frosted with moonlight streaming in through the uncurtained window. She stood still, straining her ears, but the house seemed silent. There was no sound from the floor above, where Julian had his self-contained flat, nor from Colette's suite of rooms on the floor below. Then, very faintly, from a long way down, Christine heard what could have been the rattle of a saucepan being placed on the stove. She descended the three flights of stairs to the basement.

Rowland was in the kitchen, crouched in front of the open refrigerator. There was a saucepan on the stove, but it was still empty and had obviously been abandoned. Glancing at the electric clock on the wall, Christine was surprised to find that it was only midnight. Somehow it felt much later.

Rowland looked over his shoulder and smiled. 'Sorry,' he said. 'I didn't mean to disturb you. I couldn't sleep, so I thought I'd come down for something to eat. A full stomach might make me sleepy.'

Christine went forward and firmly took the plate of cold leftovers he was holding out of his hands. 'You'll do much better with some hot milk,' she told him.

He grinned and stood upright, stretching his arms until she could hear the bones crack.

'I know that. Particularly if it's laced with rum. I was just too lazy to do it.'

'You don't look after yourself,' she scolded, and reached inside the refrigerator for a milk-bottle. There was one half-full, and she carried it over to the stove, then collected a couple of mugs from their hooks on the wall by the window. Rowland went to one of the cupboards and produced a flask of rum. He poured a generous measure into each of the blue-and-white-striped beakers.

When the milk had heated through, they sat at the kitchen table, sipping their drinks. The taste of the spirit was strong and, for a moment, Christine found herself almost choking. Rowland patted her energetically on the back.

'Anyone', he said, laughing, 'can see that you're not much of a toper.'

She smiled, but made no answer. It was warm and peaceful in the kitchen. The gentle hum of the refrigerator and the occasional bursts of energy from the gas-fired central heating were the only noises to disturb the quiet. The Formica-topped surfaces gleamed, spotless, under the light. The door to the laundry-room stood ajar, showing the flash of white tiles beyond.

'A penny for them,' Rowland said at last, and she glanced up to see him watching her, an odd expression on his face which she could not read. She shrugged.

'I was thinking of our first meeting, at Slapton. The caravan- and camping-site on the cliffs. What a beautiful morning it was.' To herself, she added: 'And I fell in love with you, and I've loved you ever since.'

He grinned. 'Outside the lavatories, if I remember rightly. Not what you'd call a romantic start.'

'That's right,' she said in mock indignation, 'burst the pretty bubble.'

They smiled at one another, then Rowland grew serious.

'Chris,' he said after a pause, but stopped, as though not quite sure how to go on.

'Yes?' she prompted.

He shook his head. 'Nothing . . . I can't remember now what I was going to say.'

'It's old age,' she teased. 'I get the same problem, if it's of any comfort.'

They had both finished their milk and now lapsed into friendly silence. Glancing again at the clock, Christine saw that an hour had passed. She got up, picking up the mugs.

'Time we went back to bed. You said you wanted to be in early in the morning.'

'Yes.' He rose, stretching and yawning, and made for the door.

She took the mugs over to the sink to wash them, running the hot tap and swilling them beneath the jet of water. Suddenly, she was aware that Rowland was standing beside her. He put an arm around her waist and kissed her cheek.

'There's a letter I want to write before I turn in,' he said. 'You go on up to bed. I'll be along later.'

Strangely moved by this spontaneous and unexpected gesture of affection, she struggled to keep the emotion out of her voice.

'Can't it wait until tomorrow? Surely you don't have to do it tonight.'

'I must. It's something I can't put off any longer.'

When he had gone, she dried and put away the mugs, then went back to bed, determined to stay awake until he came. But the rum had been too potent, and her eyelids were drooping almost before her head touched the pillow. She was unaware of anything else until the following morning, when the bed beside her was once again empty. Rousing herself, she looked at her bedside clock and saw that it was already eight-thirty.

As quickly as she could, she showered and dressed and went downstairs. In the kitchen, Rowland and Julian were just finishing their breakfast, while her mother-in-law, still in dressing-gown and slippers, was going through a pile of mail. The smell of bacon and eggs hung heavily on the air. Colette had obviously been cooking one of her favourite English meals.

As Christine entered, Rowland took a last gulp of his coffee, pushed away his dirty plate and stood up. As he passed her, he smiled and said: 'I'll see you this evening. I shan't be late. Expect me about six-thirty.'

Less than an hour later, he was dead.

PART SIX
1985 – 8

CHAPTER THIRTY-FIVE

THE MUSIC, Christine realized, had stopped a long time ago, and she had not even noticed, so absorbed had she been reliving past events. Slowly she got to her feet and crossed the room to remove the record and replace it in its sleeve, finally restoring it to its slot on the shelf. Outside, it was still raining, but less heavily now, and the clouds were beginning to lessen, allowing, here and there, a glimpse of the sun. She glanced at the clock on the mantelpiece and was startled to see that it was almost lunch-time. Colette and the two au pairs must have been back from the village some time ago. She went to the drawing-room door and opened it, just as Mrs James vigorously banged the gong. The housekeeper eyed her severely.

'I thought you'd gone to sleep,' she said, 'you've been so quiet. I've been waiting to clean the drawing-room all morning, but I didn't like to disturb you. I hope', she added, her rough tone concealing her unbounded sympathy, 'that it's done you good and that you'll be able to eat a bit of lunch. If there's one thing I hate more than another, it's seeing good food go to waste.'

Christine smiled gratefully at her. 'I'll try, Mrs James, I promise. My mother-in-law and the girls are back, I presume.'

Mrs James very nearly curled her lip. She had no time at all for the various au pair girls, who, from time to time, graced the Saxelby household, regarding them as lazy and, possibly, dirty; not because she had any proof of either of these failings, but because it was the attitude she adopted towards all foreigners, with the exception of Germans and Americans, who were 'more like us'.

'Mrs Saxelby senior's back,' she confirmed. 'But she's let those two flibbertigibbets go off shopping in Yeovil. I thought they were supposed to be here to work.'

Colette, however, merely shrugged when Christine repeated the housekeeper's strictures to her. 'I wish Mrs James would mind her own business. Just because she's worked at Mallerby most of her life, she thinks she owns us. I thought Marie and Françoise deserved a little treat; they were so disappointed at not going back to London. But it wasn't only that. I wanted to get them out of the way, so we could talk more freely. Sit down and tell me what happened this morning. Did you remember anything that might disprove this ridiculous story of Patrick's?'

Lunch – beginning with onion soup, made to a recipe of Colette's – had been laid in the breakfast-parlour, considered by Mrs James as cosier and friendlier than the dining-room when only the two Mrs Saxelbys were present. Christine took her place at the table just as Sharon Coombs came in with the soup. She waited until the girl had left the room again, and even then did not answer immediately, in spite of Colette's obvious impatience.

'Well?' her mother-in-law demanded.

Christine picked up her spoon. 'I suppose', she said, after a moment or two, 'that the answer is no, I haven't remembered anything which might prove Pat's story false. If I'm honest . . .' She hesitated, as though reluctant to continue, then went on: 'There were certain things which . . . which tend to confirm what he says.'

'What things?' Colette asked anxiously.

'Oh . . .' Christine drank some of the soup, noting vaguely that the rain had now ceased altogether and that it was turning into a fine afternoon. The pale blue wallpaper was patched with sunlight. 'Certain remarks that Patrick made when he was younger. The fact that . . . well, the fact that Rowland never wanted a divorce, even though he married me because he had to; even though I subsequently lost the baby and could have no more children; even though he was, at one time, I believe, very much in love with Faith.' She took another spoonful of the hot aromatic liquid and asked Colette: 'Hasn't that always struck you as peculiar?'

'Certainly not!' But her mother-in-law's emphatic denial seemed, to Christine, to lack conviction.

'Why not?' she demanded.

Colette waved her arms with a wealth of Gallic gesture. 'Because! And don't ask "Because what". I can't explain in so many words. Because he was Rowland, is the nearest I can get to it. You must know what I mean.'

Sharon Coombs reappeared to remove the soup-plates, followed by Mrs James herself carrying a laden tray. By the time she had arranged the bowl of salad, the platter of cold meats and fresh plates on the table, Christine had had an opportunity to mull over her mother-in-law's last remark. She did know what Colette was trying to say, and, at the back of her mind, in spite of surface worries, she agreed with her. But was that because she had to? Because she was unable to face the consequences if Patrick turned out to be right?

When they were once again alone, she said: 'I don't believe, any more than you do, that Rowe would have married me – gone through a ceremony of marriage with me – if he had already had a wife. Like you, I'm sure the man I knew would never have done something which was either illegal or, perhaps more important, likely to harm another person. But that only poses another question. How well does one person ever know another? I've no doubt that some bigamists are very nice men.'

Colette dropped her knife and fork with a clatter. 'I refuse to sit here and listen to you use that word in connection with my son!' she exclaimed fiercely. 'Why don't you just accept that Patrick's a liar and have done with it?'

Christine pushed her food around her plate, spearing pieces on her fork, without actually managing to eat anything. She answered quietly: 'Because I don't think Pat is lying. I don't know why I think he's not lying. I just do. I remember, years ago, when he'd had the measles that time, and I was reading to him in bed, we got on to the subject of secrets. He told me he knew a big one, and when I asked if it was something his father or I ought to know about he said "Maybe". At the time, I thought he was just talking for effect, to be interesting, so I didn't pursue the matter. Now I wish that I had.'

Colette helped herself to more salad. 'Children say these things. You were right. He was simply trying to make himself important. And in any case', she added, her practical French nature taking over, 'he has no possible way of proving this cock-and-bull story. I don't know why you and Julian don't just ignore it. Forget it. Get on with your lives. And if Patrick tells a few people what does it matter? With no proof to support his claim, they will soon dismiss it. What is the English expression? A nine days' wonder. And if we all treat it with the contempt it deserves it will soon be forgotten.'

Christine said nothing. She could see, and even appreciate, her mother-in-law's point of view, but Colette had nothing to lose by such an attitude. The truth, or otherwise, of the story made no difference to her status as Rowland's mother. But for herself and for Julian it was different. She knew that she could not go through the rest of her life wondering if she had been Rowland's wife or just another of his women. If they had married in different circumstances, if he had ever told her that he loved her, if he had remained with her because he was unable to do without her, then nothing else would have mattered. Whether she had been Rowland's wife or his mistress would not trouble her. But, as it was, all she had to hold on to was the fact that he had considered their marriage important enough not to want to leave her, even for Faith Malyon. The alternative was that he had stayed with her simply because to do otherwise was to compound the original offence and risk possible discovery. Somehow or other, she had to discover the truth.

The same, she imagined, went for Julian. He needed to know if Mallerby were truly his or not. He did not care for the thought that he might be masquerading as its owner, when all the time it rightfully belonged to his nephew, whom he cordially disliked. Christine could see that for a man such as her brother-in-law, a man of strong religious convictions, the antipathy he felt towards Patrick made it even more vital to find out the truth. Julian very much wanted to prove his nephew a liar, and Christine knew that the uncertainty and strain would be no good for him; that he could well go to pieces under it. Something must be done as quickly as possible.

'I'm going back to London tomorrow morning,' she said to Colette.

The older woman raised her eyes to the ceiling and threw up her hands in exasperation. 'But we have only just returned to Mallerby! I am too old, *chérie*, to keep running up and down like a yo-yo!'

Christine laughed. 'Then, of course, you must stay here for a few days. Mrs James will be only too happy to look after you. She enjoys having someone here, even if it does mean having Marie and Françoise as well. Come up to town again next week. But I want to talk to Pat again. I want to make absolutely sure that he's told me everything that he remembers.'

'He's spreading the story absolutely everywhere,' Julian said. 'The gossip columns are full of speculations and rumours. Everywhere I go, I can feel people are whispering about me behind my back.'

367

Christine was inclined to think this a wild exaggeration and said so, not mincing her words. 'Just ignore all the innuendoes, if there are any. Let people see that you treat the story with the contempt it deserves. Whatever little gossip there is will soon die a natural death.' In her anxiety to comfort him, she found that she was using Colette's arguments, and pulled herself up short. 'We must make every effort to find out the truth,' she amended. 'Anything you see fit to do, I'll support you.'

Julian smiled at her gratefully and, having finished the whisky in his glass, got up to pour himself another. He continued to occupy the top-floor flat of Inglebatch House, and in spite of a succession of women friends, of whom Trish Colmer had been the first, remained married to Sophie. His Roman Catholicism prevented him from divorcing her, while she had no wish even for a legal separation: she was perfectly happy so long as they went their different ways.

'I've already been in touch with Seamus Barrett,' he said. 'He has connections with private detective agencies all over Europe, and if anyone can find Lucy Brennan it'll be him. I've told him money's no object.'

Christine blinked a little at this, but she was too tired to contradict him just for the moment. She had had a long, hot, tiring drive up from Somerset, and was thinking now of an early supper, a cool shower and bed. She had been surprised, on her arrival in the late afternoon, to find Julian in. Usually, on a Sunday, he spent most of the day at his club, but it had transpired, when she questioned him, that socially he was becoming a bit of a recluse. It was then that he had told her about Pat and the stories he was spreading, and it was apparent to her that he needed to talk. She thought briefly of the unpacking she still had to do, then tried to forget it.

Julian returned to his chair. He had pulled the curtains against the early-evening sun, and the drawing-room was shadowed and quiet. Christine, sitting on the couch, curled her feet up under her, the burned-orange colour of her cotton dress swearing gently at the ruby-red velvet.

'Why have you come back so soon?' Julian suddenly enquired, as though her arrival had only that moment registered with him. 'I thought you'd gone down to Mallerby to think.'

She laughed. 'I've done so. In fact, for the past few days, I've done very little else. And I'm afraid that I still can't come up with any sort of answer. I've returned to London because I want to talk to Pat again. I want to see if I still believe him the second time around.'

Her brother-in-law snorted. 'The boy's a confirmed liar! There's not a word of truth in this story of his.'

Christine raised her eyebrows. 'In that case, why are you so keen to trace Lucy Brennan?'

'I should have thought that was obvious. To prove that he *is* a liar, of course!'

Christine finished her drink and put the empty tumbler on the floor. 'I wish I could be so confident.'

Julian frowned, and his tone was aggressive. 'You mean you'd rather take that little mongrel's word against Rowe's?'

She tried to keep her voice equable. 'Rowe isn't here, Julian, to argue his case. Nor did he ever assure me that he wasn't a bigamist.' She added ironically: 'The subject simply never arose.' She saw that his reaction to her forthright mode of speech was going to be the same as Colette's, and hurried on: 'The point is, I didn't feel that Pat was lying, much as I wanted to believe it. He described the coat of arms at the top of a British marriage certificate pretty accurately.'

'That's not proof!' Julian fetched himself another whisky, and Christine suspected that he had been drinking before she got home. He was growing more belligerent by the minute. 'Any fool could find out what a marriage certificate looked like.'

'I realize that.' She made an effort to keep her temper. 'It was just that . . . Oh, damn, I don't know! There was just something about the way he spoke that convinced me.'

'How can you say that?' he demanded, gesturing wildly and slopping some of his drink on to the carpet. 'How can you possibly think that Rowe would ever have done such a despicable thing? Good God! You lived with him for twenty years!'

'And I put up with his infidelities for twenty years!' Christine came abruptly to her feet, her anger now matching Julian's. 'Can't you see that I don't want to believe Patrick? That I loved Rowe with all my heart? That I shall continue to love him as long as I live? But he wasn't the "preux chevalier, sans peur et sans reproche" that you and Colette now want to make him out to be. He was a man with a great many failings, chief of which was that he couldn't resist women. To begin with, when I first heard this story, I thought like you; that it was preposterous, ridiculous, incredible. But I've had time since then to think; to sort through my memories; to stand back a little and take stock. For the first time in nearly twenty-five years, I've been able to look at Rowe dispassionately. And to be honest, Julian, I'm not certain any longer what he might or might not have been capable of doing.'

Her brother-in-law looked up at her, his eyes a little glazed, his speech a trifle slurred, but still sufficiently in command of his senses to observe: 'You've changed. I've never heard you talk like this before.'

Christine hunched her shoulders. 'I don't think I've changed. But it's as I said; I've never before taken stock of my life as a whole; never before realized how long I've drifted, in spite of frequent resolutions to do otherwise. Now, if it weren't for this story of Pat's, I should finally be free simply to love him without any fear of betrayal and, at the same time, to be myself. That's why I must, if possible, find out the truth.'

'And if we're unable to trace Lucy Brennan?' Julian asked.

'Then, I must reconcile myself to getting on with my life without ever knowing the truth.' She was glad that he did not ask her the follow-up question – 'What if Lucy confirms her son's story?' – because she was not yet sure of the answer to that. She sat down again, not in her former place on the couch, but drawing up another chair alongside her brother-in-law's and gently but firmly removing the glass of whisky from his hands. Ignoring his protests, she went on: 'Listen to me, please, Julian. What I'm about to say is very important to me. Now that Rowe's dead, there's a spare seat on Saxelby's board of directors. I want you to use your influence to make sure that I get it.'

He looked startled and asked ungallantly: 'You?'

'Yes, me.' She took a deep breath. 'Why not? I'm the bank's major shareholder, now that I own Rowe's shares as well as my own. I don't think any of the other directors would seriously object, do you?'

'But you know nothing about banking.' Julian reached for his glass again, where she had placed it on a side-table.

Christine laughed. 'If you think I've lived amongst the Saxelbys and the Bérengers for twenty years without absorbing some knowledge – a sort of process of osmosis – you must consider me very dull and stupid. Besides, I'm certainly not going to jump straight in with my advice. I shall be listening and learning for a long time to come. But I need something to fill my life, Julian. I've grieved enough. And this is what I want to do.'

'All right,' her brother-in-law agreed, with a far greater readiness than she had anticipated. 'I don't see why not. When the matter of a new director's raised at the next board meeting, I'll put your name forward. Maman's still a member of the Board, after all, even though these days she rarely attends. She'll probably vote for you, if you ask her.'

371

'I shall.' Christine got to her feet once more. 'But I fully intend, if I'm voted on, to take an active interest. And now I'm going to have a shower, after which I'll cook us both supper. Tomorrow, with your permission, I'll call in at the bank and speak to Patrick. You might like to be present at our discussion.'

Julian cleared his throat uneasily. 'No point,' he said. 'Calling in at the bank, I mean. He won't be there.'

'Why not?' She eyed him suspiciously. 'Is Pat unwell?'

Julian shook his head and, getting up, went across to the table where the drinks were set out, to fortify himself with yet another whisky.

'Well?' she demanded impatiently.

Julian refilled his tumbler and turned to face her. There was more than a hint of defiance in his attitude.

'Pat no longer works at the bank. I've sacked him.'

CHAPTER THIRTY-SIX

'HE'S DONE WHAT?' Colette demanded, her voice rising in disbelief. 'Surely even Julian can't be as stupid or as inept as that!'

Christine sighed, altering her position on the bed and nestling the telephone receiver closer to her ear. 'I'm afraid so,' she said. 'At least, that's what he told me, and I see no reason to doubt his word.'

She had unpacked, showered, changed, and cooked scrambled eggs for herself and her brother-in-law, which they had eaten together in the kitchen in almost total silence. Julian was aware of her unspoken disapproval and had taken refuge in a sulk. As soon as she had gone upstairs to bed, Christine had called Colette at Hinton Malsherbes. Her mother-in-law, too, was in bed, having had a day, she told Christine, when she had definitely felt her age. In other words, her hip had been giving her trouble. Rather reluctantly, Christine had imparted her news.

Colette's reaction was exactly what she had anticipated, and echoed her own. Colette said now: 'But what is Jules thinking of? Can't he see that sacking Patrick has made him a dangerous enemy and also fuelled all the rumours that are flying about? Oh! Why is he such a blundering fool? I shall return to London tomorrow to see if I can talk some sense into him and get him to reinstate Patrick.'

'It won't do any good,' Christine informed her mother-in-law regretfully. 'Before I telephoned you, I phoned Pat to make arrangements for our meeting tomorrow. He's very angry about his dismissal, but when I offered to talk to Julian on his behalf he said nothing would

373

induce him to return to Saxelby's. He's going to Paris. Apparently Giles has already offered him not only a position with Bérenger's, but also a substantial rise in salary.'

Colette swore fluently in French before reverting once more to English. 'Of course, he's bound to take it,' she said bitterly, without even the slightest inflection of doubt.

'Of course.' Christine put up a hand to her aching forehead. 'He'd be a fool not to. And, as you say, it will only give further ammunition to the gossipers and rumourmongers that he really is Rowe's legitimate son.'

When she spoke again, Colette sounded rattled. 'There has been no success in tracing Lucy Brennan, then?'

'It's early days yet,' Christine protested. 'She could be anywhere in the world. But I'm going to have another go at Pat tomorrow to see if there's anything more he can tell me, and to discover if my impression that he's telling the truth is still the same. So I'll let you know all about it as soon as you arrive. When do you think that will be?'

'About tea-time. Marie and Françoise will be coming with me. Ask Mrs Johnson please to make up their beds.'

'All right, if you insist on coming. But there's no need unless you want to. You won't be able to do any good.'

'I'll come just the same,' Colette answered grimly. 'Good night, *chérie*, and try not to worry.'

Christine laughed softly. 'I'll try not to worry any more than you,' she promised. 'Bonsoir, Colette. A demain.' And she replaced her receiver.

The first-floor flat in Half Moon Street was a little neater than the last time she had been in it, Christine thought, sipping coffee and looking about

374

her. Patrick had obviously made some attempt to tidy up. The magazines had been put away in a rack, and there were no dirty plates in evidence. Instead a tray of coffee things had been placed on a low glass-topped table between the two leather-upholstered armchairs. The coffee-pot, which was Royal Worcester, failed, it was true, to match the cups and saucers, which were Crown Derby, while the anonymous sugar-basin and milk-jug might have come from the bargain-basement of any department store. But the general effect was quite pleasing, and Christine conceded to herself that her step-son had, on this occasion, at least made an effort. When they were settled, she cut short the formalities and said: 'I want to go over your story again with you, Pat. I just want to be certain that I've got things straight.'

'OK.' He seemed perfectly agreeable. 'But I don't think there's much I can add to what I've already told you.'

'Well, let's see, shall we? You appear to remember pretty well the coat of arms at the head of the document. So what else can you recall? Do you remember anything that was written on it? The names of the parties concerned, for instance. Where they were married.'

Patrick shook his head. 'I've explained. I wasn't all that old and I wasn't all that interested. I was far more interested in the story my mother told me about the motto. You know, about Edward III and Joan of Kent. Purely apocryphal, I'm sure, but it makes a good yarn. Is that coffee to your liking?'

'Yes. Thank you. It's fine.' Christine frowned at him. 'Didn't you ever ask Lucy about it again?'

'No. Why should I? Until my mother abandoned me in Paris – and let me stress that that was as big a shock to me as to everyone else involved – and Rowland came into my life, I'd had absolutely no interest in my father. I wasn't old enough to begin wondering what my parentage was. That would have come later, as I grew up. But when I was ten my mother was all-sufficient. Even for the first couple of years after you and Rowe appeared, I was still coping with the fact that she could just go off and leave me like that. It wasn't until later, after I'd settled into my new life and begun to enjoy it, that I recollected that incident on the train. Mum giving me that satchel thing to play with, because I was tired and bored. Me scattering the contents on the floor, picking them up one by one, unfolding this paper and asking her what it was. Her reply. "That's the proof of my marriage to your father." Deciphering the motto at the top. *Honi soit qui mal y pense*. Her explaining what it meant, telling me the story. But I've told you all this before.'

Christine nodded, her eyes fixed on a Georges Seurat painting on the opposite wall, but in her mind seeing again the cliff-top in Devon, all those years ago, the contents of Lucy Brennan's satchel spilled on the grass; a couple of rings, a glittery brooch, the debris of old rail and bus tickets and various pieces of paper. And, as one of those pieces of paper had been caught by the breeze and started to blow away, Rowland had made a dive for it. 'You want to take care of that,' he had told Lucy, adding something offhand about it being the hire agreement for the car they had rented. Lucy had glanced at it, laughed and shoved it into the satchel with the rest of her belongings. She tried desperately to remember what the paper had looked like: an official document of some sort, or merely a piece of accumulated rubbish, part of the flotsam and jetsam of Lucy's nomadic life?

She became aware that Patrick was claiming her attention.

'More coffee?' he enquired politely, but she could see that he was intrigued by her obvious abstraction.

'No, thank you.' She returned her cup and saucer to the tray. 'You're sure', she asked after a moment, 'that there's nothing else you can tell me? Nothing at all that comes to mind?'

'I'm afraid not. You know how memories are, particularly childhood ones. It's like a shutter, opening and closing. While the shutter's open, you can see everything perfectly, but once it's down again there's nothing but a blank.'

Christine nodded. How could she contest a statement which was a common experience, particularly when she had just known one such moment herself? Instead she said: 'Your grandmother's returning from Mallerby today. If she and I can persuade Julian to change his mind and reinstate you, won't you give Saxelby's another chance? Surely it's in your own interests to remain in this country, at least until we know the truth.'

An angry flush stained Patrick's cheeks. 'I wouldn't work for Julian now', he replied scornfully, 'if he were to offer me a public apology and three times my previous salary! I've never liked him since that affair with Vivien, and I'm sure he's always resented me. He's incompetent and a fool. He's not fit to be running a major bank like Saxelby's. In many ways, he's done me a favour. I'll be better off with Giles.'

Christine thought of the controlling block of shares which her step-son owned and felt uneasy. It was on the tip of her tongue to say something to him, to ask him what his future intentions were, but in the end she decided against it. Perhaps it was better, for the moment, to let sleeping dogs lie.

'I must be going,' she said, getting to her feet. 'Thank you for the coffee and your time.' She moved towards the door of the room, then paused. 'You know that Julian has instigated proceedings to find your mother, don't you?'

'Of course.' Patrick also got to his feet. 'What I mean is I imagined he must have done. I wish him luck. Giles is going to do the same.'

377

'Giles?' Now she was really startled.

'Yes. Why not? With me going to work for him, naturally he's interested on my behalf. He knows it'll be a costly business, so he's offered to put up the cash. Decent of him, I thought. Don't you?'

'Very decent,' Christine said. 'And so disinterested.' But the irony was lost on Patrick, who had moved ahead of her into the flat's little hallway in order to open the front door. 'When', she added, 'do you go to Paris? Or hasn't that been settled yet?'

'Oh, it was all fixed last Friday,' he answered cheerfully, leaning forward to kiss her cheek. 'This flat is already in the hands of the agents. I leave at the end of the week.'

'Well?' Colette demanded impatiently. 'How did it go?' She had not even bothered to take off her cream silk jacket, but had come immediately, upon arrival at Inglebatch House, to find Christine. It was almost tea-time, and Christine was in the drawing-room, waiting for Mrs Johnson to bring in the tray. 'Your interview with Pat this morning!' Colette added, suddenly sitting down, as though caught by an unexpected pain. 'Tell me at once what he said!'

Christine grinned at her mother-in-law. 'Whatever happened to "Hello"?' she asked teasingly. 'And don't you want to go and freshen up before tea?'

'Don't be maddening!' Colette protested. 'My nerves won't stand it. Did you find out anything more from Pat?'

Christine sobered and shook her head. 'Nothing that he hadn't already told me. But I'm afraid *I* remembered something – something I'd half-remembered before, but with more clarity this time – which might or might not confirm Pat's story.' And she recounted the cliff-top incident.

Colette shrugged. 'I don't see that that proves anything. It probably *was* the hire-car agreement. I still think Patrick's lying.' But this last sentence was uttered with a certain amount of bravado.

Again, regretfully, Christine shook her head. 'I don't think so. As I told you on Saturday, he boasted to me of having an important secret when he was small. But the thing which convinces me most he's not lying is that he's allowing Giles to instigate his own search for Lucy. That, to me, is not the action of a man who has something to hide, or who has doubts about the validity of his story.'

'Giles is starting a search for Lucy?' Colette demanded incredulously. 'But why, in God's name? What has it got to do with him?'

Mrs Johnson came in at that moment with the tea-tray, and there was a pause while she arranged it on the table in front of Christine, at the same time enquiring in a long-suffering voice if she was supposed to be giving 'those two girls' their tea in the kitchen when she had her own. Upon receiving a reply in the affirmative, she sniffed loudly and withdrew.

Colette repeated angrily: 'What has it got to do with Giles?'

'Oh, come on, Colette!' Christine filled the two delicate china cups with the pale China tea and pushed one towards her mother-in-law. 'I should have thought that was obvious.'

The older woman bit defiantly into one of Mrs Johnson's freshly baked scones and said thickly: 'Not to me.' Then, when Christine made no comment, she cleared her mouth and asked belligerently: 'You really think my nephew wants to undermine my son?'

'I think he wants to make a friend of Pat,' Christine amended, 'and for a very good reason. He wants Pat to sell him his block of Saxelby shares. He tried once before, or his father did, to gain control of Saxelby's, and this time he means to succeed. Fate, in the shape of Julian, has played straight into his hands. An additional bonus is that, if Julian is thoroughly demoralized

379

first, Giles won't have any sort of fight to contend with. He's counting on Julian simply caving in.'

She waited for an outburst of condemnation from Colette against her nephew, but nothing came. Silently her mother-in-law helped herself to a second scone and nibbled at it thoughtfully. It was apparent that, once again, her maternal and practical instincts were at war. Giles was not only a Bérenger, Colette's own kith and kin; he was also doing what any astute business-man would do, given the circumstances. There was no room for sentiment, not even of the family kind, in business. That much, at least, Christine had learned. No, her mother-in-law's anger was directed against Patrick the traitor and possible liar, and Julian the blundering fool.

After a while, Colette gave a fatalistic shrug and said: 'Well, I suppose the more people looking for this Lucy Brennan, the better. The sooner we shall be able to settle this matter.' She sipped her tea, before adding: 'I don't know that it makes me believe Patrick any more than I do already. It's quite a good move to make, letting Giles search for her, if he's banking on the fact she won't be found.'

'I don't see how he can possibly bank on that,' Christine objected. 'The more people on her trail, the more chance there is of someone finding her eventually. But until that happens there's nothing to be done except for us to give Julian all our support and try to limit the damage that has already been done.' Christine took a deep breath, then added: 'Colette, I hope you won't think I'm being presumptuous, but I've asked Julian to use his influence to get me elected to Rowe's former seat on Saxelby's board of directors. I know you must think I've no experience—'

Her mother-in-law interrupted her imperiously. 'You do not know what I think! All sorts of people get elected to all sorts of boards of directors for all sorts of reasons. Sometimes it is just because someone has a title and it looks good on the letter heading. I can think of no one more suitable to take Rowe's place than his wife. Moreover', Colette added shrewdly, 'it will be good for you. It is as I said to you in the Feathers last week. You need a direction to your life, to make a fresh start, now that Rowland is dead. You need not worry about my vote. It's yours.'

Moved by a sudden impulse, Christine got up out of her chair and, kneeling beside Colette's, put her arms around her and kissed her cheek. 'Thank you,' she said huskily. 'It's always meant a lot to me, knowing that you were on my side.'

If this unexpected display of emotion took the older woman by surprise, she was careful not to show it. Colette had learned the hard way that the English were all too easily discouraged from exhibiting their feelings, so she merely returned the embrace with interest, kissing Christine resoundingly on both her cheeks.

'I'm so glad we're friends,' was all she said, knowing that anything more would embarrass her daughter-in-law. Indeed, Christine was already looking half-ashamed of her outburst and the fact that she was perilously close to tears. Changing the subject quickly and tactfully, Colette went on: 'You really ought to make a start on clearing out all Rowland's clothes. If you want me to help, or to make arrangements with Oxfam or some other organization, you have only to ask, you know that.'

Christine rummaged in her handbag for her handkerchief and blew her nose. 'Yes, I know, and thank you. But . . . well, I realize it's foolish, but I'll keep them for a bit longer. Seeing them hanging in the wardrobe, here and at Mallerby, makes him seem a little closer. Not so far away. Not so . . . so gone!' She smiled. 'Don't look so concerned. I accept Rowe's dead. Going back over our life together has helped me come to terms with his death. I'm able to see him more in perspective now. More in the round, if that's not a contradiction in terms. But I still need his presence now and then, and being able to touch his clothes gives me that. There's something very personal about the things which people have worn. After a while, they take on the personality of their wearer. So . . . I shall keep them a while longer. But as soon as I'm ready I'll turn them out.'

Her mother-in-law nodded. She understood, perhaps better than Christine imagined. She, too, had kept all Noel Saxelby's clothes for several years after he died, and for exactly similar reasons. Colette reflected, not for the first time, that she and Rowland's wife had a great deal in common; far more than she once had thought possible. She finished her tea and got up from the table, leaning over to kiss Christine yet again, but this time a light fleeting brush of the lips on her forehead.

'I must go and unpack,' she said. She added grimly: 'As soon as Julian comes home, tell him I want to see him, will you? In my sitting-room. Alone.'

'I'll tell him,' Christine promised. But when Colette had gone she grimaced at the tea-pot, from which she was pouring herself a second cup of tea. Fond as she was of her mother-in-law, she considered it unwise, to say the least, for Colette to continue treating Julian like an errant schoolboy. It was the way Rowland had always behaved towards his brother. It was one of the reasons, perhaps the chief one, why Julian was the sort of man he was today.

CHAPTER THIRTY-SEVEN

IN BED THAT NIGHT, Christine suddenly remembered something odd about her conversation with Colette. At no time had either of them mentioned the fact that Giles was Julian's son-in-law, or Vivien his daughter. Perturbed, Christine rolled on to her back and stared at the ceiling, where the glow from a street-lamp made patterns of light and shade. Had the omission been a subconscious acknowledgement that it was an irrelevance? That Vivien's animosity towards her father might even be a factor in her husband's determination to bring Julian down? No, no: that was too fanciful! Nevertheless, Christine had no hope that her niece would do anything to deter Giles.

The telephone beside her bed began to ring. Switching on the bedside lamp, she hastily snatched the receiver from its cradle before the ringing on the other extension, in Colette's sitting-room, should rouse her mother-in-law. A glance at her alarm-clock showed it to be well after midnight, and she wondered who could be calling so late, and for what reason.

'Hello?' she said cautiously into the mouthpiece.

'Hello. Christine!' It was Patrick's voice. He sounded excited.

'What's the matter?' she asked. 'Do you realize what time it is?'

'I know. I'm sorry. But I've just remembered something, and I thought you ought to know at once. About that marriage certificate. The date on it was some time in December 1961. I can't recollect the exact date, but I can recall the month and the year.'

She absorbed the information for a moment or two, before asking suspiciously: 'Why have you suddenly remembered this now?'

Her step-son's voice buzzed impatiently along the line. 'Because I've been thinking about it, of course, all day, ever since your visit this morning. I've been racking my brains to see if there was anything else I could recall. Trying to conjure up a mental picture. And quite suddenly, about ten minutes ago, while I was undressing for bed, I could see the date in my mind's eye.'

'Where was it?' she demanded.

'Where was what?' He sounded puzzled.

'The date. Whereabouts was it on the certificate?'

'Oh! Down at the bottom. There were printed bits in between, and I think the "19" of "1961" was printed. Doesn't that convince you that I really did see something?'

'Pat,' she said wearily, 'you could have looked at any British marriage certificate. You must have friends who have them. All right! All right!' she added, hearing the intake of breath as he prepared to voice his anger and indignation. 'Spare me the protests.' She wasn't able, at this stage, to confess to him that she considered he could be telling the truth. If she admitted that much, she admitted also that she might not have been Rowland's wife; and, whatever she had said to Julian on the subject, she was in no mood to make Patrick free of her thoughts. She softened her tone and added: 'Anyway, thank you for letting me know. But it doesn't really alter anything as far as I'm concerned. The only thing that's going to prove you right – or wrong – is for someone to find your mother. Good night. I hope you discover what you're looking for in France.' And on this somewhat enigmatic note she hung up.

She switched off the bedside lamp and once more settled down to try to sleep. But Patrick's words kept running around inside her head. December 1961. Why did that ring some sort of bell? Why did she feel that there was a connection she ought to make, if only she could capture the elusive fact which was spinning just beyond her reach? But it was no good. Her eyelids were growing heavy. Her thoughts were taking on a dream-like quality ... Within five minutes of replacing the receiver, she was sound asleep.

By late autumn, she had been made a director of Saxelby's and had attended her first board meeting. By Christmas, and the inevitable family migration to Mallerby House for the holiday period, she had cast her first vote and offered a single tentative opinion. It took until the following spring before she felt able to speak with any great authority. But she was learning all the time, and she found, to her secret surprise, that she picked up things fast. By the summer of 1986, when the world was still reeling from the Chernobyl disaster and a young German tennis-player called Boris Becker had powered his way on to the Wimbledon scene, she was able to speak with confidence at meetings, and discovered that fellow-directors were more inclined nowadays to look to her for a lead than to their chairman.

The reason for this, she supposed, was that she was the only member of the family on the board, apart from Julian and Colette. Her mother-in-law was rarely seen nowadays, unless her vote was needed; and after her hip-replacement operation Colette went to France for a long period of convalescence and recuperation. This was only what everyone had expected, and her frequent absences excited no comment. Julian, however, was a different story. Bodily present, he seemed increasingly absent in the spirit, and as the months passed it became apparent that he found his role as head of the bank and chairman of the board more and more difficult to sustain. Instead of going to Mallerby for Easter, he went into retreat at Downside Abbey, and had done so on two further occasions since then. At the end of June, he filed a suit in the papal courts for an annulment of his marriage.

'Why now, after all this time?' Sophie wailed to Christine over lunch at Le Gavroche. 'And on what possible grounds can he ask for an annulment?'

The years had not dealt kindly with Sophie. She had aged considerably since the last time Christine had seen her, at Vivien's wedding. The blonde mane of hair was now by courtesy of her hairdresser, and was done in far too youthful a style for a woman of forty-eight who was rapidly putting on weight, losing the contours of her once excellent figure. The skin-tight dresses, which she still insisted on wearing, made her appear vulgar rather than glamorous, and no longer gave her the slightly spurious allure which they had once done. The flesh around the eyes was puffy.

Christine shook her head, swallowing a mouthful of the grapefruit and vermouth water-ice which she had chosen to start her meal.

'I don't know. I'm not a Catholic, any more than you are. Perhaps,' she added, 'as you were married in a register office, that isn't regarded as valid by the Catholic church. Anyway, there isn't much you can do about it that I can see.'

'But what about my monthly allowance?' Sophie was getting indignant; beginning to think herself ill-used. 'I can't live on air, Chris, and so I hope you'll tell him.'

Christine refrained from remarking that her sister-in-law had made a very good living for years now, living off other men. But she could see that it might be more difficult for Sophie in the future.

'I'm sure Julian will do what's right by you,' she answered soothingly.

'What the hell's got into him?' Sophie asked viciously, breaking open a lobster claw with scarlet-tipped fingers.

Christine hesitated. 'Well,' she said after a moment or two, 'if you want my opinion – and I must stress that it is only my opinion: Julian has said nothing to me on the subject – I suspect that he may be thinking of applying for a novitiate.'

Sophie digested this, along with her lobster, a look of horror spreading slowly across her face. 'You mean he's thinking of becoming a monk?'

Christine was forced into a laugh by both the expression and the tone of voice, but she emphasized quickly: 'Don't say anything to anyone, for Heaven's sake! I've told you it's only my own idea.'

'But why?' Sophie was still incredulous. 'I know he got religion and turned RC, but he's got everything going for him now! He's head of Saxelby's, head of the family, owner of Mallerby . . . In God's name, why would he want to give it all up?'

'Because he can't cope!' The second course arrived, duck and wood-mushrooms in a red wine sauce, with apples. 'For goodness' sake, Sophie, surely you lived with him long enough to understand that Julian's a born second-in-command! He's an excellent lieutenant, but he hasn't the confidence to make decisions. It was the way he was brought up, to be dependent on his brother. And Colette's a very strong-minded woman. Between her and Rowland, Julian never stood a chance. And all this other business with Patrick has made him even more uncertain.'

Sophie speared a mushroom and enquired: 'What's happened about that? Of course, one's heard the rumours.'

'Yes, I dare say one has,' Christine responded drily. 'But at least they haven't been so prevalent since Patrick took himself off to Paris. People have at last begun to lose interest in the story, and as Lucy

Brennan's not yet been traced there's been no corroboration for his claim. Another six months, and most people will forget it entirely. But Julian won't and I shan't, because we're the two most nearly affected.'

'But it doesn't affect Julian's position at the bank!' Sophie's incipient double chin wobbled in exasperation.

'It affects his belief in himself as the owner of Mallerby and head of the family, and so affects his ability all round. Any undermining of his self-confidence is the last thing Julian needs at present.'

'So he's going to opt out. Cut and run!' Sophie's voice, through a generous portion of duck and mushrooms, was scathing. 'Just what one might expect of Julian. He never had any backbone. And, come to think of it, the celibate life will just about suit him. He was always bloody awful in bed.'

Christine sighed, wishing she had said nothing of her suspicions to Sophie, who had so clearly made up her mind that she was right. The best thing, sacrilegious though it might be, was to finish the meal as quickly as possible and leave.

As a result of this decision, the two women emerged into the sunshine of Lower Sloane Street shortly after two-fifteen, where they said their goodbyes and went their separate ways; Sophie to meet her current 'boy-friend', as she called him, an ageing member of an impecunious but aristocratic family, Christine in search of a cruising taxi to take her to Seamus Barrett's office in the Haymarket. She and Julian had arranged a meeting with the head of the detective agency for four o'clock. She could fill in the intervening time shopping. She had to buy a birthday present for her god-daughter.

As she settled into the back of the taxi, which she had eventually found in Buckingham Palace Road, Christine reflected that she had seen very little lately of Lois and her family. She had not gone to Hinton

Malsherbes at Easter. With Julian in retreat, it had seemed so pointless for her and Colette to go on their own. Now that Rowland was dead, Vivien and Patrick gone, the family was drastically depleted, and the memory of former, busier, happier days would have made too sharp a contrast.

Colette had suggested to Christine that she should accept Lois's invitation and spend the holiday in Shaftesbury with the Aylwards, but Christine had declined. She had known that her mother-in-law was nervous about the prospect of her forthcoming operation, and had therefore decided to stay with her in London and, as far as possible, take her mind off things. In some ways, now, she regretted the decision. She would have liked to see Cheryl, soon to be nineteen and already talking, according to Lois's most recent letter, of getting engaged.

'A nice enough boy,' Lois had written. 'A trainee pharmacist. This family can't seem to get away from the profession.'

Christine thought about Lois as the taxi rattled along Whitehall; about their long friendship which had survived two widely differing lifestyles, two widely divergent lives. And her mind was still on Lois as she glanced out of the taxi window and suddenly saw, coming towards her at a brisk pace, along the pavement, Russell Jennings. He was obviously in a hurry, dodging between the other commuters, intent on his destination, wherever that might be, and had no time to spare for glancing about him. He failed to see her, even though she rapped on the glass and futilely called his name. He had vanished almost before she opened her mouth, and she was left thinking once again how large and impersonal London was; a city where you could live for months, even years, on end without chance meetings or casual encounters . . .

Her thoughts were suddenly arrested. She had been thinking of Lois and had had a fleeting glimpse of

Russell Jennings. Now, why did those two facts grab at her attention? Why did she get a sense of *déjà vu*, and the feeling that it was somehow significant? The answer was there, somewhere, just out of reach, as it had been last summer, when Patrick had telephoned her in the middle of the night. She desperately cudgelled her brains, and for a split second almost had the answer. But just at that moment the taxi pulled into the kerb, and the driver slewed round in his seat to inform her that she had reached her destination. By the time she had alighted, paid the fare and tipped him, the elusive memory had gone. But as she turned to look in the nearest shop-window she found her head filled with the sound of tinkling piano music. It was an old tune from the late fifties, and she fancied that its title was 'Side Saddle'.

'So you've nothing to tell us?' Julian asked matter-of-factly, cutting across Seamus Barrett's flow of excuses and explanations as to why he had so little progress to report.

The head of the detective agency looked suitably embarrassed and muttered sadly: 'No.' He added hurriedly, getting into his stride again: 'But I do assure you both that it's not for want of trying. My contacts in Europe and America have been tireless in their efforts to trace Miss Brennan, but the lady in question is so far nowhere to be found. We have checked records of death and of marriage, working on the assumption that her son's story may not be true, and that, at some time or other, she has changed her name. But' – he shrugged expressively – 'nothing! We shall, however, go on trying for as long as you wish us to.'

'And as long as we're willing to pay you, eh?' Julian asked grimly. 'Yes, all right. Carry on.' He turned to Christine. 'You agree?'

She hesitated. 'It does seem rather a hopeless task,' she said after a moment or two, and with what she was quick to recognize as typically British understatement. 'But yes! We must persevere for a while yet. We can't let go that easily.'

Seamus Barrett raised his tufted eyebrows slightly, as though ready to cavil at her use of the word 'easily', but all he actually said was: 'I think I should tell you that I'm getting feedback from certain of my agents that other people – other agencies – are making enquiries about Miss Brennan's whereabouts as well.'

Julian nodded. 'We're aware of that. Mr Patrick Brennan and his present employer, Monsieur de Bérenger of Bérenger's bank in Paris, are also trying to trace Mr Brennan's mother.'

Christine noted that Julian had ceased to speak of 'my nephew' or 'my son-in-law' and sighed inwardly. Aloud, she asked: 'You are sure, I suppose, that Lucy Brennan's nowhere in Paris?'

Seamus Barrett regarded her solemnly, his round gooseberry eyes beneath the shaggy brows mournful with reproach. 'My dear Mrs Saxelby, after the information you gave us about a possible sighting there four years ago, naturally it is one of the places we have scoured the hardest. But, I regret to say' – he lifted his shoulders and spread soft podgy hands with dimpled knuckles – 'without success. That, of course, is not to say that Miss Brennan won't return there one day. We shall keep our ears to the ground and our eyes open for as long as you and Mr Saxelby wish.'

'Yes. Well, thank you, Mr Barrett.' She glanced at her brother-in-law. 'Julian. Is there anything more you want to ask?'

He shook his head. He seemed, Christine thought, almost indifferent, in direct contrast to his anxiety of a year ago; a fact which fuelled her speculation concerning his intentions. She picked up her handbag, which she had laid on Seamus Barrett's desk, and stood up. Julian rose with her, and they shook hands with the plump little detective, before making their way down the stairs and into the street. On the pavement, Christine paused, putting a hand on Julian's arm.

'Jules,' she said pleadingly. 'I'm flying to Paris tomorrow for a couple of days, to see Colette. She and Madame are staying with Giles and Vivien. Don't you think you ought to come with me? You haven't even seen little Lucien. Whatever you feel about Giles and his father, you can't go on ignoring your daughter and grandson.'

Julian's face set in predictably mulish lines. Today he was wearing, with his dark suit and white shirt, a particularly garish yellow tie. The colour of hostility.

'Vivien knows where to find me if she wants to bring the baby to see me,' he answered. 'I don't want to chance running into Pat.'

'Then, shall I give them your love?'

'If you wish,' her brother-in-law answered stiffly.

'Very well, then, I will. And you must admit that so far Pat hasn't succumbed to the temptation to sell Giles his block of Saxelby shares. Maybe we've both misjudged him.'

Julian snorted. 'No such thing. It would be impossible to misjudge that scheming little bastard. All it means is that the moment's not quite right. Cousin Giles hasn't come up with just the right offer.'

Christine, reluctantly, was forced to agree with him, so decided to say no more on the subject. 'Are you going back to the bank?' she asked.

'When I've been to confession. I'm going to cut through St James's Park and walk down to Ashley Place. The exercise will do me good. How about you?'

'I'll take a taxi home. I told Mrs Johnson I'd be in for tea. Julian, you don't recall a piece of music called "Side Saddle", or something like that, do you?'

He looked astonished at this abrupt change of subject, as well he might, but obediently puckered his brows. 'Piano,' he volunteered, after a moment's thought. 'Went to number one in 1959. I remember buying it. Played by that fellow Russ Conway.'

CHAPTER THIRTY-EIGHT

IT WAS NOT UNTIL that evening that it all came together, and even when it did Christine was not quite sure what to make of it.

Mrs Johnson had long since departed for Kilburn, and there were at present no au pairs to enliven the emptiness of Inglebatch House with their giggles and chatter: Marie and Françoise had both gone home to France the previous autumn. Julian had not as yet come in, and in any case would be poor company, retiring, as he did most nights, to his top-floor flat, erecting a barrier between himself and the world, withdrawing into increasing isolation.

Christine missed Colette more than she could say, and it was at times like this that her bitter sense of loss returned to haunt her. The loneliness and silence of the empty house weighed oppressively and sent her wandering edgily from room to room, switching on first the television, then the radio, pulling records at random from the shelves in the drawing-room, only to abandon them a few seconds later. She picked up a book, a magazine, the morning and evening papers, but never got past the first sentence. Her mind, her head, her whirling thoughts were full of Rowland. If she closed her eyes, she could feel his presence in the room, but when she reached out to touch him there was nothing there. She did not know which was the greater agony, her love for him or the knowledge that he had never loved her in return. Fondness, affection, these were not enough; nor, at such moments, did her own clearer perspective of him in any way help to lessen the pain. She remembered that he had spent his last night on earth writing a letter to Faith Malyon . . .

This had to stop. Lear's words came unbidden into her mind. 'Oh! that way madness lies. Let me shun that.' She got up resolutely from her seat on the sofa and searched the record-shelves for something cheerful. Not Rameau or Lully tonight; nothing to remind her of Rowland. She found the soundtrack of the film of *Kiss Me Kate*, and minutes later Ann Miller's powerful voice filled the room with the number 'Too Darn Hot'. Christine turned down the volume a fraction and put through a call to Shaftesbury, praying that Lois was in.

It was Judith Aylward who answered.

'Hello, Aunt Chris! Mum's in the kitchen, making strawberry jam. Hold on. I'll see if she can leave it.'

Making strawberry jam was just the sort of thing that Lois would be doing, and which Christine had never done in her life. She had a vivid mental picture of Lois, enveloped in the vinyl-coated Liberty-print apron which she wore on these occasions, weighing out fruit and sugar, good-naturedly yelling at the girls in the living-room that the television was too loud, ordering Barry to take off his shoes before he came in from digging the garden. Christine could identify with it immediately: normal, ordinary, sensible family life.

'Chris!' Lois's voice sounded cheerfully in her ear. 'Can't stop long, I'm afraid. The boiling's reached a critical stage. I've left Judy stirring, but she's fretting to get back to "EastEnders". How are you, my dear?'

They spent a few moments on the usual pleasanteries, then Christine said: 'I saw Russ Jennings this afternoon. He didn't see me. I was in a taxi. By coincidence, I was thinking about you at the time. Afterwards, I found I couldn't get that Russ Conway tune, "Side Saddle", out of my mind. Any idea why that could be?'

'Association of names, I should imagine. I can't think of any other reason, can you? Is this important or just an academic question?'

'I think it might be important. You remember I told you that Pat swears he can remember the date on the marriage certificate. December 1961. It ties up somehow in my mind with that.'

Lois was silent for a moment. Then she said: 'All I can suggest is that it has something to do with that Christmas shopping trip we had in London, that time we ran into Rowland in Regent Street. That must have been December 1961. And I seem to recollect that, a few moments before, I'd seen Russ Jennings crossing the road.'

'Yes,' Christine breathed. 'That's right. I remember now. I didn't notice, but you swore it was him. And Russ Conway came into the conversation somewhere.'

Lois laughed. 'You've a better memory than I have, but I'll take your word for it. It's all obviously an association of ideas. Oh hell! I can hear something boiling over. Oh my God! I'll have to go. Judy's shouting from the kitchen. 'Bye, love.' Her receiver slammed down, and Christine was left listening to the sudden silence. Slowly she replaced her own receiver and sat deep in thought, against a background of Howard Keel singing 'Were Thine That Special Face', trying to assess the importance, or otherwise, of this scrap of information, which had been buried for so long in her subconscious. What significance was it possible to attach to the fact that Russell had been in London that December day? Rowland, after all, had been there, too.

Other bits of information, gathered over the years and, at the time, not much regarded, began to rise to the surface of her mind: the fact that, according to Russell, he had met Lucy Brennan in the Lake District that autumn of 1961; the fact that he had subsequently remained in postal contact with her for a number of years; the fact that, in spite of being an

396

eligible, good-looking man, he had never married. She had never really believed his repeated assertions that love for her was the cause of his celibacy. Was it remotely possible that Russell was Lucy Brennan's husband? When he met her in Windermere that time, had she confided in him that she was expecting Rowland's baby? Could he, on the rebound from her own rejection of him, have offered her marriage? Was it likely that unconventional nomadic Lucy would have accepted him?

The first side of the record had finished playing, and Christine got up to turn it over. As she did so, the drawing-room door opened and Julian's head appeared round the corner.

'Hello,' he said. 'I'm just going up to the flat. Are you all right? What are you doing?'

She laughed and answered drily: 'Playing records and clutching at straws.'

He looked bewildered. 'Sorry?'

Christine shook her head. 'Nothing. If I don't see you tomorrow morning, do you still want me to give your love to Vivien and little Lucien?'

'If you must.' His facial muscles relaxed slightly into what might have passed muster as a smile. 'I suppose so. Tell Viv . . . tell her to bring the boy across to see me one of these days. But not to leave it too long.'

Christine regarded him straitly. 'Any particular reason?' she asked.

Julian looked uncomfortable and avoided her eyes. 'Not really. Well, I'm off upstairs. Have a good trip. How long are you going for?'

'Only three days. I think Colette's planning to come home with me at the weekend.'

'Good. She should have recovered from her operation by now, and there are things I want to discuss with her.'

Christine was suspicious. 'What sort of things? I mean . . . I don't want to sound nosy, but is there any way that I can help?'

397

Her brother-in-law shook his head. 'Thank you, but no. Tell Maman I shall be glad to see her again.'

The door closed gently, and he was gone. Christine decided against playing the other side of the record, and returned it to its place on the shelf. Her thoughts reverted to Russell and Lucy Brennan. They now seemed utterly fantastic. Russell was not the sort of person who indulged in Quixotic gestures like taking on the responsibility for another man's child. She had indeed, as she had told Julian, been clutching at straws. All the same . . . It wouldn't hurt, would it, to arrange a meeting with him? She would do it as soon as she got back from Paris, on Saturday morning.

'When I was young,' Vivien said, 'I used to think that Café des Deux Magots meant Café of the Two Maggots and, although I know better now, I can never get the original idea out of my mind.'

'Silly child,' Colette said fondly. 'But I know what you mean. Those early childish impressions are very hard to eradicate.'

She, Vivien and Christine, who had little Lucien on her lap, were seated in the mid-morning sunshine, outside the café which Jean-Paul Sartre and the other Existentialists had made famous after the Second World War. On the opposite corner of the *place*, the eleventh-century church of St-Germain-des-Près soared against an almost cloudless sky. As she sipped her coffee and kept her great-nephew amused with endless games of Peek-a-boo and Round and Round the Garden, Christine felt how absurd had been all her suspicions linking Russell and Lucy Brennan. She had allowed her imagination to run riot. For one thing, if Russ had read in the newspapers of Patrick's claim, he must surely have come forward to refute it, had he really been Lucy's husband. And, for another, her stepson's story had yet to be proved to have any foundation in fact. It had done her good to get away from London, if only for a few days, and to distance herself from the problem which continually occupied her mind.

Paris, however, was not without worries of a different sort. Vivien and Giles were the best of hosts and, as always, made Christine feel extremely welcome. There was, however, a certain restraint in all their conversations, as both Giles and Patrick, whenever he was present, assiduously avoided the subject of business. They must be only too well aware, Christine reflected, of the difficulties at present besetting Saxelby's; of the loss of custom, the downward trend in the price of shares; the lack of confidence in Julian in the city. But they made no mention of any of these things. They reminded Christine of two birds of prey, patiently waiting, with the scent of death in their nostrils.

Patrick had his own apartment now, in one of the turnings off the Avenue Kléber, but he spent a great deal of his spare time with Vivien and Giles in the house on the Avenue Foch, made over to them after the retirement of Lucien and Solange to the country. He was a frequent dinner-guest, as was Martine Didier, a distant cousin of Giles on his mother's side, who had recently arrived in the capital from her home in Champagne to study English and economics at the Sorbonne. Colette had confided to her daughter-in-law, almost as soon as Christine arrived on the Wednesday morning, that she considered Patrick to be *épris* in that direction . . .

Vivien's voice cut into Christine's wandering thoughts.

'You're very quiet, Aunt Chris. You were miles away. I don't believe you've heard a word we've been saying.'

'Yes, I have. You were saying something about . . .' About what? Of course. 'About thinking that Les Deux Magots meant the Two Maggots. Hardly an appetizing name for a restaurant.' And she smiled, jiggling little Lucien up and down on her knee. He gurgled with pleasure and flailed the air with his fists.

They all laughed, and Vivien leaned across to lift her son back into his push-chair, where he sat quite happily, kicking his heels against the foot-rest and watching the other occupants of the pavement chairs and tables. He was a sunny-natured child and indulged in very few tantrums.

Someone spoke to them, a little breathlessly, in French, and lifting her head Christine recognized Martine Didier. It was something of a shock to see her standing there, having been thinking of her so recently. She was a very pretty girl, tall and slender, with huge dark eyes, an abundance of curly brown hair, caught back in a bunch at the nape of her neck, and the high cheek-bones of a model. She lacked the sophistication of most Parisiennes, and there was a tentative quality about her which was extremely endearing. Christine could see why Patrick might be smitten.

Martine, who was carrying a pile of books, explained that she was between lectures, and had come with some friends in search of coffee. She indicated a couple of rather scruffy youths who were waiting patiently for her at a distance. She must go, but – with a special smile for Christine – it was lovely to have seen them all again.

'Don't forget you're having dinner with us tomorrow evening,' Vivien said. 'You and Pat. He told me he'd pick you up about seven.'

Christine said, holding out her hand: 'I'm afraid I shan't be there. Colette and I are returning to London in the morning.'

Later, she remarked to her mother-in-law: 'I think you're right about Pat and that girl. *She's* certainly very taken with *him*. You can see it by the way her eyes light up whenever anyone mentions his name. You do realize that if Pat marries her it will cement even further his bond with Vivien and Giles? The only thing which puzzles me is why he hasn't already sold out to Giles. I can't believe that Giles hasn't already made him a very attractive offer.'

She and Colette were on the plane the following morning, and it was at last possible to speak without restriction.

Colette wrinkled her nose thoughtfully, then said: 'I don't doubt Giles has. But Patrick's too canny to accept it out of hand. He'll wait for as long as he dares in the hope of pushing the offer up still further.'

'Or of proving his claim to be Rowe's legitimate son.'

Colette raised her eyebrows. 'You still think he might be able to do that, do you?' She sighed. 'I can't understand you. How you can have lived with Rowe for all those years and think him capable of . . . of such a thing is beyond me.' When Christine made no reply, she sighed and leaned back in her seat, momentarily closing her eyes as if in despair. After any protracted stay in France, she always became, for a while at least, more Gallic. 'All the same,' she added, opening her eyes again with a flick of her long dark lashes, 'Julian should try to do something about wooing Patrick back to the fold, and quickly. This Sword of Damocles hanging over the bank is no good for anyone's morale and certainly no good for Saxelby's image in the City.'

Christine glanced out of the cabin window at the grey waste of the Channel below them; at that narrow stretch of water which had separated Britain from the rest of the European continent for so long. Now there was talk of a Channel tunnel, with every prospect this time of it becoming a reality by the beginning of the next decade. Europe was growing smaller, whether Britain liked it or not. Takeovers of British businesses by Continental companies were becoming the norm. Even if Pat refused in the end to sell his shares to his cousin, Christine believed that Giles would find some other way of obtaining his goal. She wondered if she ought to voice her suspicions of Julian's intentions to Colette, but decided against it. If she were right, and her brother-in-law was seriously thinking of entering a monastery, then his mother would find out soon enough. For the time being, she would keep her own counsel.

Colette waved aside the stewardess's offer of another drink and demanded plaintively: 'What's this Seamus Barrett doing? Considering what we're paying him, he surely ought to have found out something by now.'

'The world's a big place to search in,' Christine reasoned. 'And Lucy never liked to stay in one place for long.'

'But she's growing older,' Colette objected. 'She must be at least your age. All right. I know forty-six isn't considered that old nowadays, but surely a woman feels the need to put down roots at some time. And what an unnatural mother she must be, never wanting to know what's happened to her son.'

'She knew he'd be all right with Rowe. And she wasn't like any other woman I've ever met. I think she was what is now called a "free spirit".'

Her mother-in-law snorted indignantly, but had no time to say more as the plane was coming in to land. People were fastening their seat-belts and gathering magazines and books together. Later, as they were waiting for their luggage to arrive, preparatory to checking through Customs, Christine suddenly became aware of a little ripple of interest among some of the other commuters. Turning her head, she saw Faith Malyon standing a few feet away from her, also waiting for her cases. The straight, fine-spun fair hair, the wide cornflower-blue eyes were immediately recognizable, as was the general air of fragility and vulnerability. Her pale-pink cotton dress was a wide-skirted affair, with puff sleeves and an old-fashioned sweetheart neckline. But it looked a little young on her these days, Christine thought nastily, now that Faith was almost certainly pushing thirty.

She must have been on the same flight from Paris. Strange that they had not noticed one another.

Colette's and Christine's cases came into view, and for the next few minutes Christine was fully occupied transferring them from conveyor-belt to trolley. By the time she had leisure to look around her again, Faith Malyon was already being ushered by one of the airport officials towards the VIP lounge. On a sudden impulse, Christine called out: 'Faith!'

She could tell at once by the reluctant way in which Faith Malyon paused, then slowly turned back to face her, that she was already aware of Christine's presence and had taken pains to avoid her.

Christine advanced towards her, hand outstretched. 'I'm Christine Saxelby.' She added ironically: 'You knew my husband.'

A faint blush stained the younger woman's cheeks, and she looked as though she might turn and run at any minute. Conscious, however, of the airport official's interested gaze, she stood her ground. 'Yes, of course,' she said in her high light treble.

'I just wanted to ask you', Christine said, surprising herself, 'if you received the letter Rowland wrote you the night before he died. I just wanted to know that it arrived safely.'

Faith Malyon blinked and, for the first time, looked Christine straight in the eyes. 'I never received any letter from Rowe,' she said. 'If he wrote one, he must certainly have forgotten to post it.'

CHAPTER THIRTY-NINE

THE IMPERSONAL VOICE of the answering machine said: 'This is Russell Jennings. I shall be abroad on holiday for the next three weeks, until the end of July. Please leave your name, telephone number and message, and I shall call you back as soon as possible.'

Christine hung up and glanced thoughtfully out of the window at the rain-washed deserted Sunday street. So that was that. There was no getting in touch with Russell for the present. She was almost relieved. Her theory now seemed so ludicrous as to be embarrassing. Only a tiny residue of suspicion had made her try to contact him this morning. Her mind was more exercised at the moment as to whether or not Faith Malyon had been telling the truth. And, if Rowland had not been writing to her, for whom had the letter been intended, and why had it been so urgent that it had to be written at one o'clock in the morning?

There was always a chance, of course, that it had been a business communication, and had been handed to Marcia Corby for posting when Rowland arrived at the bank. And yet it seemed highly improbable that he would have handwritten any sort of official letter, especially when he was tired and, as Christine now guessed, in some pain. And what about the brooch which Rowland had ordered, the true-lover's knot in sapphires and diamonds, which she had paid Garrard's for and then locked away in her safe-deposit box, along with most of her other jewellery? Of all the pieces Rowland had given her during their twenty-one years of marriage, she wore only the Chandos brooch with any regularity. Until recently, she had felt that it was the one item not tainted with 'conscience' money; the one item made especially for her, chosen with forethought and care. But since Patrick's revelation she had been forced to wonder even about that.

Christine's thoughts reverted to the letter. Had Faith Malyon really been telling her the truth? It had been an awkward moment for both of them: the words had been out before Christine even realized they were in her mind. It had been neither the time nor the place for a confrontation. She recalled, with a slight smile, the look of consternation on the airport official's face. Sensing the tension, he had feared a scene. His relief, when nothing further happened, had been palpable.

The drawing-room door opened, and Colette came in, still, although it was mid-morning, wearing her nightdress, over which she had wrapped a soft blue woollen dressing-gown. The previous day's flight had been bumpy, and she had looked pale and worn by the time they reached Inglebatch House. She had gone to bed early last night and had slept late this morning. Glancing in on her earlier, Christine had decided to let her lie: sleeping, Colette had suddenly appeared both old and vulnerable.

'You should have woken me sooner,' she accused Christine. 'You know how awful I feel when I oversleep. I'm going down to the kitchen to make some coffee. Do you want some?'

'Stay here,' Christine ordered. 'I'll get it. Then Julian's taking us both out to lunch.'

She was about to leave the room, when the telephone rang. She retraced her steps and picked up the receiver. Patrick's voice sounded excitedly in her ears almost before she had finished giving her name.

'Chris! I just wanted you and Grandmother to know that last night Martine and I became engaged.'

It seemed almost inevitable to Christine that, from the time of his engagement to Martine Didier, Patrick's future was bound up with the Bérengers. The question in her own mind was no longer whether or not her step-son would sell his block of Saxelby shares to Giles, but how soon. She gained the impression, when she and Colette flew to Paris early in September for the wedding – Julian had been pointedly excluded from the invitation – that her step-son's anxiety to prove himself Rowland's legitimate heir was waning. In marrying Giles's cousin, he had gained a security and an identity which he had previously lacked. Both Vivien and her husband were genuinely fond of him, and if Giles ever remembered the original reason for his wife's banishment to France it did not seem to worry him. It was only a matter of time, Christine felt certain, before Patrick succumbed to one of the many tempting offers which Giles regularly made him.

During that autumn of 1986, Saxelby's suffered several major financial reversals and the value of its shares plummeted drastically. Two companies in the high-risk area of hire purchase, in which the bank had invested heavily, went bankrupt. A military coup in one of the Third World countries which had borrowed extensively from Saxelby's shortly after Rowland's death only exacerbated matters. It was with very little surprise, therefore, shortly before Christmas, that Christine learned that Patrick had finally sold out to Giles, and that Bérengers were poised to take over their English rivals.

'I can't understand Jules,' Colette confided to her daughter-in-law, as they drove down to Hinton Malsherbes together a few days before Christmas Eve. 'He doesn't act as though it has anything to do with him. At that board meeting last week, when everyone else was in a panic, he seemed completely aloof and detached. We must try to talk some sense into him over the holiday. It's not too late, even now, to put up a fight, at least for his right to remain head of the firm.'

'I don't think you'll have any success,' Christine said gently. 'I believe Julian has his own plans, and now that Giles is at last in control of the bank they'll come to fruition.'

She refused to say any more, and Colette did not press her. Christine began to suspect that her mother-in-law had already divined her son's intentions. Instead, as she negotiated the new D-registration Renault clear of Andover's outskirts and on along the A303, Colette asked her abruptly: 'When are you and Julian going to call off this abortive search for Lucy Brennan? It's eighteen months since Barrett's started looking, and in all that time there's not been a single sighting.'

Christine kept her eyes steadily on the road ahead and said: 'Just for a little longer.'

Colette clicked her tongue impatiently. 'Does it still matter that much to you?'

'It will always matter to me. However, I agree with you, we can't go on for ever. And it seems to be of less importance than it once was both to Julian and to Patrick.' She hesitated, then went on: 'I did think, at one time, that I might have found a lead myself, but it came to nothing.'

'Oh?' Colette was curious. 'Tell me about it.'

Christine shook her head. 'There's nothing to tell. I decided I'd made a false assumption and didn't pursue it.'

Had she been remiss not to contact Russell Jennings again, when he returned to London at the end of July? But she had been so sure by that time that she would be making a fool of herself if she did that her pride had stopped her. She had never felt comfortable about Russell after leading him on and then rejecting him that evening. In fact, now she came to think of it, she had not felt comfortable about her treatment of him for the past twenty-five years.

The Christmas festivities were very muted. Julian arrived at Mallerby House on Christmas Eve, but had very little to contribute in the way of seasonal warmth or gaiety; although that, as Christine and Colette were the first to admit, was hardly surprising. But if he had been worried, preoccupied, they would have more easily understood. It was his detachment which made them so uneasy.

And then, late on Boxing Night, after the television had been switched off and the two women were making preparations for bed, he told them that he had something to say to them. Shortly before leaving London, he had received notification from Rome that his marriage to Sophie had finally been annulled, without in any way affecting Vivien's legitimacy. It was therefore his intention to be received as a postulant at Buckfast Abbey as soon as was practicably possible. He had always been attracted to the Benedictine Order.

When he had finished speaking, there was silence until Colette remarked quietly: 'Well, now we know. I've been wondering how long it would be before you told us.'

'You guessed?' Julian looked put out that his revelation had not had more impact.

'We both guessed,' Christine told him. She added, slipping her hand through Colette's arm and pressing it gently: 'If it's what you want, what you feel you must do, we both wish you every happiness.'

'I don't wish him happy,' Colette said fiercely, freeing her arm from Christine's grip and thumping the carpet with the walking-stick she still found it necessary to use. 'He's running away from his responsibilities. Rowland would never have done it, however bad things were. He was a fighter.' She turned and walked slowly, bent suddenly, like a much older woman, from the room.

'Of course,' Giles said, addressing his first meeting of the board of directors since becoming its new chairman, 'the name of Saxelby will be retained. There will naturally be one or two changes, but these, I'm afraid, cannot be avoided and will be kept to the minimum. Our first priority will be to turn the fortunes of the bank around and make it once again the force to be reckoned with that it was in the time of my uncle and cousin.'

He spoke very good English, Christine reflected; much better, she was sure, than anyone around the table could speak French. And when he was stuck for a word Colette would assist him. In spite of her feelings, in spite of being a Saxelby, she could not help being proud of her nephew; of being a de Bérenger and all that that entailed. Beyond the boardroom windows, Gresham Street was bathed in the warmth of the pale spring sun, the first really good day since the official end of winter four weeks before. There was a general mood of optimism in the air now that all the speculation was over and rumour had been resolved into fact. Since Julian's resignation at the end of January and the takeover by Bérenger's, Saxelby shares had once again started to climb. In the City, there was more confidence in the bank than at any time since Rowland's death and the newspaper gossip of Patrick's claim.

When the meeting was over, Giles asked Christine to stay behind. Alone, finally, in the big room with its dark oak-panelled walls, its long refectory table and leather-seated chairs, he poured them both a whisky and water from the concealed cupboard near the corner window.

'Santé,' he said.

She raised her glass in return. 'Cheers.'

'Chris,' he went on earnestly, 'I want you to have a permanent office here, like Tante Colette used to do. I want you to take a greater part in the everyday running of the bank.'

'But I'm a layman,' she protested. 'I've had no training in banking.'

'You have common sense and a cool head,' he answered. 'I can tell that the other directors respect your judgement. You do your – what is the expression? – your homework when there is an important decision to be made. I have been talking to people, finding out about you. I know that you have voted against Julian on several occasions, when others, unfortunately for the bank, were prepared to let him have his way. But, most important of all, you are a Saxelby, Rowland's' – there was only the tiniest hesitation – 'widow. That, for me, is essential, to have a member of the family here, in Gresham Street.'

She could not avoid asking: 'What, not Patrick?'

Giles shrugged. 'I need him in Paris. Besides, my cousin Martine does not wish to live in England, and Pat will not wish to come without her.' He smiled confidentially, his dark eyes crinkling at the corners. 'Since I was a child, I have always considered you a very intelligent woman. Now is your chance to prove that all these years I have not been wrong. Will you do it? There is no need for you to be here every day, all day. I am not asking you to give up too much of your time.'

'Very well. Who could resist such flattery?' She grinned. 'But you'll have to define the limits of my job. I want to earn my keep.'

Giles nodded. 'We'll discuss that and salary later. For now, I just wanted to sound you out. Is that the correct phrase?'

'Quite correct. Your English is extremely good.' They had finished their drinks, and she put her empty glass down on the table. 'We're expecting you at Inglebatch House for lunch, and we were rather hoping you might also stay the night. Do you really have to go back to Paris this afternoon?'

'Unfortunately, yes. Christine!' He paused for a second or two, then added: 'I want you to know that I have called off the search for Lucy Brennan, and I think, if you are wise, you will, too. We have done our best by Patrick. We have tried to do the right thing.

410

But without results, without proof, I would say that it is now time to forget his story. There is nothing more to be done.'

No, she thought, not now that you have got what you wanted; now that Patrick has served his purpose; now that you have driven Julian into embracing the religious life. But perhaps he had done his father-in-law a favour; perhaps it was what Julian had always secretly wanted. Certainly, he had put up a very poor fight. And Giles was right. It *was* time to call a halt to the search for Lucy Brennan. She and Julian had done what they could. They had nothing to reproach themselves with.

'Yes!' she said. 'I'll phone Seamus Barrett this afternoon and tell him that we no longer require his services.'

But, in the event, it was Seamus Barrett who telephoned her.

Christine, Colette and Giles were just finishing an excellent meal, cooked and served by Mrs Johnson, when the telephone bell sounded in the hall. A few moments later, the daily help poked her head around the dining-room door and said in her unceremonious way: 'Phone. For Mrs S junior.'

Christine excused herself and went out. She had barely identified herself to the caller, when Seamus Barrett's voice said excitedly: 'We've found her, Mrs Saxelby! We've found her!'

'Found her?' Christine repeated stupidly. 'You mean . . . Lucy Brennan?'

Seamus Barrett was jocular in his triumph. 'I don't think you've ever asked us to find anyone else! Yes, of course, Miss Brennan!'

Christine's head was spinning. 'Where . . .? Where is she?'

'Where you always thought we might find her in the end, Mrs Saxelby. Paris. The Arab quarter. She

411

has a room in the Rue Myrha. Our contact says she's only been there a few days, so we think she can't have been back long. One of my men left early this morning to keep a watch on the house, but if you still want to see her I would advise getting over there as quickly as possible, in case she moves on again. Miss Brennan is a very elusive lady.'

'Yes. Yes, thank you. I'll go this afternoon. Can you give me her full address?'

She returned to the dining-room, still in a daze, and when she had finished telling the other two the news said to Giles: 'I'll go and pack an overnight bag. I'm coming with you.'

'And I'm coming with *you*,' he answered grimly, 'when we reach Paris. The Goutte d'Or is no place for a woman to be on her own. It's a very rough district. It used to be full of Poles, Italians, Yugoslavs; now it's mostly Algerians, Tunisians, Moroccans. There are also a few Vietnamese and Filipinos.'

'Will you tell Patrick?' Colette asked.

Christine shook her head. 'Not yet. I want to know what Lucy has to say first.'

Her mother-in-law nodded. 'Very wise. You don't want him prompting her. Let her tell her own story.'

Once again, Christine excused herself and went upstairs. She put her nightdress, a change of underwear and her sponge-bag into the canvas and leather holdall which had been Rowland's, then sat for a moment or two on the edge of the bed, trying to calm her nerves. Her heart was beating with ragged suffocating strokes; her head felt as though an iron band were slowly being squeezed around it. In a few hours perhaps, certainly by this time tomorrow, she would know the truth; whether she had been Rowland's wife or just one of his women; whether Julian was the rightful owner of Mallerby, or Patrick. To think that only this morning she had decided to call off the search! Another twenty-four hours and no one would any longer have cared about the whereabouts of Lucy Brennan. Would she have been better off not knowing? Was it always wise to want the truth?

Well, it was too late to speculate now. She took a deep breath and, getting off the bed, went downstairs. Giles's taxi had been ordered for half-past one.

Colette and Giles were waiting in the hall. Colette came forward and kissed her, putting her arms around her in a gesture of comfort and encouragement. Christine returned her kiss and gave her mother-in-law a tremulous smile.

'You did warn me', she said, 'to leave well alone.'

'I know. I know. But I'm not sure that I meant it. Anyway, the damage is done. Chin up, *chérie*! Giles will look after you. He has been telling me how much he needs you at the bank.'

'Heaven knows why.' Christine gave a little laugh which broke in the middle. There was a ring at the doorbell. 'That's probably the taxi,' she said.

The taxi-driver took her bag and Giles's and put them in the back of the cab. Colette came out on to the pavement and once again hugged Christine.

'Promise to telephone me as soon as you have anything to tell. I shan't rest until I know what's happened.'

Looking at her mother-in-law's white tense face, Christine knew that she, too, was feeling the strain. Now that the moment of truth had almost arrived, she was not as certain of Rowland's innocence as she had always protested.

'Yes, of course I will.' Christine climbed into the back of the taxi, and Giles followed her. As it turned the corner of the street, she saw that Colette was still standing on the pavement, watching anxiously.

CHAPTER FORTY

GILES HAD TELEPHONED his office before leaving London, and a chauffeur-driven car was waiting for them at the airport. Christine eyed the bulky man behind the wheel with some misgiving.

'Wouldn't it be better if I went alone? I don't want to frighten Lucy to death.'

'Christophe and I will wait in the car,' Giles replied firmly. 'But we're both coming with you.'

Later, as the Citroën nosed its way along the Boulevard Rochechouart, and the crowding European and American holidaymakers gave place to gangs of Algerian youths, exotically garbed Berbers and a CRS coach parked by the side of the road, Christine conceded that Giles had been right: it would not have done for her to come here alone. Three of the soldiers from the coach, armed with FN rifles, were frisking a group of teenagers, while a fourth stood to one side, his eyes flicking nervously from side to side, alert for any sign of trouble. The paint on the shop-fronts was peeling, brickwork crumbling, and the whole district showed marks of the urban decay and social degradation so often associated, in the second half of the twentieth century, with the older quarters of populous cities which have become ghettos for the human flotsam and jetsam of disbanded empires.

The car turned left into the rue de Clignancourt, then right into the Rue Myrha, finally drawing up in front of a three-storey building which, at ground-level, was a shop, bearing the words *Boulangerie* and *Pâtisserie* one above the other in faded red lettering. As they came to a halt, a small man darted out from a neighbouring doorway and rapped on Christine's window.

'She's up there now,' he said a trifle breathlessly, as Christine opened the car door. The man stooped lower. 'I'm Stan Hitchins, by the way. I work for Seamus Barrett. The subject went out for a while this morning, around lunch-time, but she returned an hour ago and hasn't vacated the premises since.'

The semi-official jargon, and Mr Hitchins's earnest desire to please, made Christine want to laugh. She repressed the desire, however, and got out of the car, shaking her informant warmly by the hand.

'You've done a good job, Mr Hitchins. I shall tell Mr Barrett that I'm very impressed. Is it the first or second floor where Miss Brennan's living?'

'She has a room right at the top.' He beamed at her, plainly gratified by her praise. 'There's a door at the side of the bakery. There! D'you see? It's open. Just walk straight up, past the first landing and on until you reach the head of the stairs. The door facing you, that's Miss Brennan's.'

Christine did not ask him how he knew; she took his word for it and turned to speak to Giles who, by this time, had also got out of the car and was offering to accompany her if she needed him. Gently she refused.

'I think I'd rather see Lucy alone, if you don't mind.' She looked again at the little detective. 'Miss Brennan hasn't anyone with her, has she, as far as you know?'

Mr Hitchins pursed thin lips. 'A man, you mean? I may be wrong, but I don't think there's anyone else living with the subject. Certainly, I've seen no one since my arrival first thing this morning.'

Christine hesitated, feeling that this was no proof of Lucy's being on her own; but, if she did have a lover sharing her bed, there was nothing that she, Christine, could do about it. She took a deep breath and said: 'Well, here goes!'

415

The stairs were dark and dirty and smelt strongly of urine; whether human or animal it was difficult to say. The half-landing was lit by one small, very grimy window which showed a second flight of stairs even more rickety than the first. Christine, wishing she had worn a more sensible pair of shoes, made her way cautiously upwards. At the very top, as Mr Hitchins had said, was another landing and, immediately facing her, a door which had obviously once been painted yellow, but which now was stripped down almost to the wood. To her left, another small window let in fractionally more daylight than the one on the landing below.

Christine paused, her hand gripping the newel-post of the banisters, her heart pounding, but not from the climb. This was it then. It was no use standing here, hesitating. The sooner she got it over with, the better. She stepped forward, raised her hand and knocked.

The room was small and very close, with only a fanlight in the roof to give light and air. In one corner was a bed, unmade, the sheets and patchwork quilt thrown back in a heap, just as Lucy had left them when she got up that morning. The rest of the furniture comprised an armchair, out of whose seat the stuffing was protruding, a cheap deal table, an upright chair with several of the back rungs missing and a cupboard which presumably contained such necessities as food, crockery and cutlery. The cooking facilities were provided by a single gas-ring.

All this, Christine took in with a first comprehensive glance, but it was Lucy herself who occupied most of her attention. She looked extremely ill. Always thin, she was now emaciated. Her bones protruded through the sallow skin, and there were half-moons of discoloured flesh beneath her eyes. In spite of the fact that the April weather was still none too warm, and there was no heating in the attic, she was wearing only a thin cotton wrapper and leather-thonged sandals. Although no expert in the matter, Christine guessed that Lucy was on drugs, and had been for some considerable time. It was no doubt why she chose to stay in this particular quarter of Paris, where they were probably more readily obtainable.

Lucy had recovered from the initial shock of seeing her, and had slumped back on the bed after offering Christine the honour of the easy-chair.

'Be careful,' she warned with a laugh. 'One leg's broken.'

Christine lowered herself gingerly to the accompaniment of an ominous creaking. She placed her handbag on the floor beside her and gripped both the chair's arms. 'You must be surprised to see me,' she said.

Lucy made no answer, asking instead: 'How's Pat?'

'He's doing very well for himself. He's married now, a French girl, and living here in Paris.' If she had expected Lucy to show any excitement at this news, she was disappointed. There was no response, and she went on: 'He's working for Bérenger's bank. Giles de Bérenger, Rowe's cousin, is, of course, his cousin, too.'

Lucy gave a harsh laugh, which degenerated into a cough. When she could speak again, she said: 'That's a moot point.'

Christine frowned. 'What do you mean?'

'I mean I don't really know whether Pat is Rowland's son or Russell's.'

There was silence. Then Christine asked: 'How could he possibly be Russell's? You never had a chance to . . . to sleep with him.'

Lucy laughed and coughed yet again. 'What a delightfully old-fashioned turn of phrase. If you mean Russell never had a chance to fuck me, why not say so? But, in any case, you'd be wrong. You went for a walk with Rowland one morning during that holiday, do you remember? It happened then.'

The walk to Slapton village to look at Sir Guy de Brian's chantry, and then on to Torcross . . . And, when she and Rowland got back, Russell had been looking smug and pleased with himself, not sulky and resentful as she had expected. Lucy wasn't there; she had gone into Plymouth, but there had been plenty of time for love-making before she left. Christine recalled, with a sudden jolt of memory, that she and Rowland had been gone for nearly three hours. Why had it never occurred to her that that was what might have happened?

She said slowly: 'When you met Russ again, later that year – in the Lake District, wasn't it? – you told him you were expecting a baby and that the baby was his. Quite how you convinced him of the fact, I don't know, but you obviously did. He offered to marry you and, for some reason which only you understand, you accepted. You were married in London just before Christmas.'

'You seem to know an awful lot about my affairs,' Lucy said resentfully. Then she smiled faintly, leaning back against the wall, pushing the jumble of bedclothes out of her way, so that most of them fell on the floor. 'But you're quite right. Russ did offer to marry me. As to why I accepted him . . .' She shrugged impatiently. 'I suppose I was bored. I thought marriage might be amusing. A new experience. I never intended it to last.'

'Poor Russell,' Christine said. 'How long did you stay with him? And why did no one else ever know about you? His parents and friends, for instance. Why did you pose as a single man?'

'It was one of my conditions for marrying him that he wouldn't say anything until I gave him leave. He wasn't very difficult to persuade. I think he knew, deep down, that he was making a terrible mistake – in answer to your question, it lasted exactly four weeks – and he was afraid of making a fool of himself a second time. It was only a month or two, if you remember, since you had refused him, after everyone believed that you were as good as engaged. Which, of course, was why he offered to marry me. He was mad to prove to himself that someone found him attractive enough to want him, and the baby was a splendid self-justifying excuse. But, as I said just now, in his hearts of hearts he knew what I was like, that he was making another big mistake; but his precious male ego had taken such a battering, he just wasn't thinking straight.' Lucy shifted her position on the bed, as though she were in pain. 'Anyway,' she asked, 'what's all this about?'

Christine told her. When she had finished speaking, Lucy said: 'Well, I'm sorry. I can't even remember showing Pat the marriage certificate, or anything about the incident. But it apparently made a great impression on him.' For a moment, something like maternal pride glowed in the sunken eyes. 'Fancy him remembering it for all those years. He must have hugged that secret to him, working out how best to turn it to his advantage. The scheming little bastard! But he always had a streak of cunning in him. I used to try to work out whether he got it from Rowland or from Russell.'

'And what did you finally decide?' Christine asked quietly.

'Oh, Russell, wouldn't you say?' Lucy gave a high-pitched laugh, and her hands twitched nervously.

Christine did not answer, but asked instead: 'So what happened after you and Russ were married?'

Lucy shrugged, and her voice sounded peevish. 'He wanted to take me home to Weston to tell his parents. He'd married this wealthy woman and he was going to be a father. Clever old Russ! Only, of course, it wasn't really his parents he wanted to impress, but you. He wanted to show you that he could succeed where Rowland had failed. Except that Rowe never asked me to marry him!'

'And then?'

'Oh, I fobbed him off with some excuse or other. I was living in a rented flat in Paddington at the time. I'd only taken it for a couple of months, but Russ didn't know that. He came up to see me every weekend for the next four weeks; he even managed to come and visit me over Christmas. He kept on making plans for our future together. He'd actually been house-hunting in Weston, he told me. Inevitably, his patience was wearing thin, and he said he was going to tell his parents and the people at the office. I persuaded him to give me one more week's grace, but I knew by then that I just couldn't stick to my original intention.'

'Which was?' Christine prompted, as Lucy lapsed into introspective silence.

'What? Oh, well . . . I told you I was bored. I thought marriage might be fun for a year or two, until the baby was old enough to leave with Russell. I didn't really want a child dragging behind me. I thought it would cramp my style, and I was right. Men aren't interested in a woman with a baby. But at the end of only four weeks I knew I should go mad if I had to settle down and play the devoted wife, even for a couple of months, so I just took off. Later on, after Pat was born, I wrote to Russell and told him the truth, that I didn't really know who was the father. I told him to divorce me, but he wouldn't. Said everyone still thought he was a single man, and as far as he was concerned it could stay that way. He'd finished with women. I suppose, between us, we had given his ego a bit of a battering.'

'I see.' Christine made no further comment for a while, trying to sort out her thoughts. Eventually she went on: 'So, when the time came for you to offload Patrick, there wasn't much choice but to tell Rowland that the child was his.'

'And he might be.' Lucy's voice was suddenly faint, as though she had had enough. Her eyelids drooped, and she was sweating slightly from weakness. 'But, as you say, Rowe was the obvious choice. He was able to give Pat far more than poor Russell ever could. And then there was you, a frustrated mother.' The eyelids lifted a little to reveal a gleam of mockery. 'I'd kept in touch, you see, over the years, with what had been happening to you and Rowland.' She slumped even further down the wall, now plainly exhausted. When she spoke again, her words were almost inaudible. 'But I didn't know about the trouble Pat has been causing. I've been travelling in India and Pakistan for some years now. I was in Tibet for a while. I got arrested there and locked up . . .' Her voice was now a mere thread of sound, but she rallied sufficiently to say: 'You can see the marriage certificate for yourself, if you want. In fact you can have it. No good to me. It's in that canvas bag in the corner.'

She was dropping off to sleep, so Christine picked up her handbag and got softly to her feet. Looking around, she saw a battered canvas holdall, as battered as the old leather satchel had once been, in a corner of the room. When opened, it revealed a jumble of papers, some unwashed clothes, a few cheap trinkets, the pathetic detritus of Lucy's nomadic life. The marriage certificate was almost at the bottom, dog-eared and dirty. But the writing was still plain, the ink faded but legible, and attested to the marriage, in December 1961, of Lucy Maeve Bridget Brennan to Russell Bertram Jennings. Christine glanced at it, then folded it up again and put it in her handbag. She crossed the room to Lucy, gently shaking her by the shoulder.

'Lucy. I'll let you have the certificate back as soon as I can. But there are a few people who ought to see it, so I'll have it photocopied. You did say I could take it.'

'Keep it,' Lucy mumbled. 'Told you . . . Don't want it.'

'I'll let you have it back just the same.' Christine hesitated, then asked: 'Is there anything I can do for you? Anything I can get you? Don't you think that . . . well, that you should see a doctor?'

A faint spark of animation kindled Lucy's eyes as they once more fluttered open. 'Piss off!' she whispered. 'Leave me alone.'

Christine straightened her back. 'OK,' she said. 'If that's what you want.' She paused, looking over her shoulder. 'Goodbye, Lucy.'

There was no reply. She went out, closing the door thankfully behind her.

'What a strange woman she must be,' Vivien said.

Dinner was over at the Villa Dauphine, and she, Giles and Christine were gathered round the fire in the Blue Salon, the marriage certificate spread out on the coffee-table in front of them. Over the years, the folds had become splits, and Giles was gumming the edges together with sticky tape.

He said: 'I'll get a photostat of it made first thing tomorrow morning at the bank.'

'What do we do about Patrick?' his wife asked, after a pause. 'Do we tell him the truth? The whole truth, I mean. That he might not be Uncle Rowland's son.'

Christine sipped her coffee and stretched her feet to the blaze. She felt desperately tired, but pleasantly so; more genuinely relaxed than she had felt in years.

'I don't think we'll say anything about that.' She glanced at the other two. 'Or to anyone else. I don't want Colette thinking all the time that he might not be her grandson. Because he might be. We don't know, and never shall know. If Lucy herself isn't certain . . .'

Vivien nodded decisively. 'I quite agree. That part of the truth is just between us three. But what about Lucy's assurance to Pat that the certificate was proof of her marriage to his father? That's always been the linchpin of his story.'

Both women looked towards Giles for inspiration. He nipped off the surplus end of the last piece of sticky tape between a set of excellent teeth, and shrugged.

'She lied to him. A woman like that, why should that be so surprising?'

Christine nodded slowly. 'She did lie to him,' she said. 'Lucy told him as a fact what could only be a surmise. I don't think we have anything to reproach ourselves with if we tell him that. And I'm sure Pat would much rather believe he was Rowe's bastard than Russell Jennings's legitimate son.'

'You're quite right.' Vivien poured herself a second cup of coffee. 'And he does look like Rowland after all.'

'He looks like Russell Jennings, too,' Christine responded drily. 'He and Rowe were always similar in appearance – only, of course, I was always convinced that Pat was Rowland's son and that his resemblance to Russ was coincidental. Now I can see he could belong to either of them.'

'Oh well!' Vivien shrugged, adding comfortably: 'We'll invite him and Martine to dinner tomorrow and tell him all about it then. I don't think he'll be too disappointed, as long as we stick to what we've agreed.' A thought struck her. 'Do you think he'll want to visit his mother?'

'If he does, or feels he ought to, try to dissuade him,' Christine advised. 'Seeing her like that could upset him; and, frankly, I don't think Lucy wants to know.' She smiled wearily. 'And now, if you'll both forgive me, I'm going to bed after what seems to have been the longest day of my life. It feels like light-years since that board meeting in London this morning. And I still have to phone Colette.'

She got up as she spoke, and Giles escorted her to the door, where he gallantly stooped and kissed her hand.

'Bonne nuit,' he said. 'Sleep well.'

'Oh, I shall,' Christine answered. 'I shall sleep the sleep of the just, now that I know who I am at last. Now that I know I'm really Christine Saxelby.'

CHAPTER FORTY-ONE

IT WAS HIGH SUMMER AGAIN, mid-June, but the warm sunny days of 1988 were few and far between. Everyone agreed that it was one of the most miserable summers anyone could remember – although, as Colette pointed out, the English said the same thing practically every year – so a sudden brief good spell of weather had sent Christine and her mother-in-law hurrying down to Hinton Malsherbes for a long weekend. The faithful Claud Laing had been chivvied into accompanying them, but he did not enjoy the country, and on this bright Saturday afternoon, while the two women dragged sun-beds on to the terrace, he took himself off to Yeovil to browse around the bookshops.

'Bring me back something nice,' Colette had scolded him, and he had made her an old-fashioned little bow.

'Of course. Sweets to the sweet,' he had answered.

'I wonder he puts up with you,' Christine told her mother-in-law, as they settled themselves comfortably, side by side. 'You pick him up and cast him aside like some old glove. You don't see him for months, then he's commanded to drop everything at a moment's notice and come with you down here. Are you ever going to marry him?'

'Certainly not,' Colette replied indignantly, adding with a giggle: 'The very idea would frighten him to death. He's a confirmed bachelor. You wouldn't catch Claud giving up his cosy chambers in Albany for all the fuss of running a house in London as well as a big estate.' She was silent for a moment, then went on: '*You* shouldn't be having all the fuss of it, either. It's Julian's responsibility. If only he hadn't run away . . .!'

'He's happy,' Christine said, linking her hands behind her head and staring up into an almost cloudless sky. 'That's what matters. And I don't mind in the least running things for him. In fact I positively like it. What with that and my job at the bank, I've enjoyed this past year more than I can say. I've found out that I'm capable of doing all sorts of things that I'd never dreamed I could do. I feel . . . I feel fulfilled.'

Colette glanced sideways at her. 'Completely fulfilled? You have a great capacity for love, Christine. You proved that with Rowland. What about fulfilment as a woman?'

There was another silence. A flight of rooks rose suddenly from the trees in the park, cawing and screeching their way across the heavens. Christine watched them until they were nearly out of sight, a scatter of black dots on the horizon.

'I don't want to get hurt again,' she said after a while. 'And I still love Rowland.'

They that love beyond the world cannot be separated by it. Death is but crossing the world, as friends do the seas; they live in one another still. William Penn's words came back to her, as they had done so often in the past, and they were as true for her as they had ever been. But she knew, too, that Rowland's failure to feel the same way about her had left an emotional scar which might never heal; might prevent her from ever falling in love again. She was not a whole person and probably never would be, but she had become reconciled to the fact. In every other way, as she had told Colette, she was enjoying living.

Sharon Coombs appeared, carrying a tray. 'Mrs Renshaw thought you might like a cold drink,' she said, setting her burden down on top of the broad stone balustrade. 'Iced lemonade,' she added, handing each woman a tall frosted glass.

Christine wriggled into a more upright position. 'That's very kind of her. Thank her for us, will you, please?' She noticed the ring on the third finger of the girl's left hand and said: 'Is that the engagement-ring? May I see?' She turned to Colette. 'Sharon and Phil Pollard, Geoff Pollard's son, are being married next spring. They told me when I was down here last month, seeing about the matter of that new fencing.'

Colette offered her congratulations and, when Sharon had gone, said slyly: 'You make an excellent chatelaine, *ma chère*. You're much better at it than Julian would ever have been. Perhaps, after all, things have happened for the best. One must always trust in *le bon Dieu*.'

Christine laughed and sipped her lemonade. After a while, she volunteered: 'I went to see Russell Jennings after I came back from Paris last year. I don't think I told you.'

'No,' Colette said, 'you didn't.' She might have asked, 'Why are you telling me now?' but she forbore. At seventy-one, she was old enough to realize that there were right times and wrong times for confidences. 'What did he have to say for himself?' she enquired.

Christine finished her lemonade and put the empty glass on the ground beside her. 'I wanted to know why he hadn't told me the truth about his marriage to Lucy Brennan. I said he couldn't have been unaware of Patrick's claim. There was enough about it, at the time, in the newspapers. He admitted to having seen something.'

'So? What was his excuse?' Colette prompted, as Christine fell silent.

'He didn't offer one. What he did offer me was pure unadulterated hatred.' Christine drew in her breath sharply. 'I never realized how much he had grown to dislike me. And he hated Rowland. He'd never forgiven him for what he called "ensnaring my affections". God! All those years, that loathing was festering away inside him. If he could have got me back, he wouldn't have minded. Honours would have been even. A few years ago, I almost let myself have an affair with him, but at the last minute I couldn't go through with it. I was still too much in love with Rowland. I actually went to his flat, and then left before anything happened. I treated him badly, I have to confess it. I suppose he had every right to be furious, to want to get his own back. And I suppose Pat's claim seemed like the answer to prayer. So he didn't say anything.'

Colette also put her empty glass down on the ground and once again leaned back in her chair. 'It is never nice', she observed, 'to discover that other people dislike us, but it is an unfortunate fact of life. Take consolation from the fact that only complete nonentities have no enemies. You must try now to put it all behind you. Go on building a new life, as you have been doing this past year.' She put out a thin arm on which the veins were knotted, an old woman's arm, and took hold of one of Christine's hands. 'Keep your heart open,' she said. 'Don't close it against love for ever because you're afraid of being hurt again.'

Christine returned the pressure of her mother-in-law's fingers, but made no answer. After a protracted silence, she said: 'You and Claud will be able to have a day on your own tomorrow. I've arranged to go to Shaftesbury to see Lois. I phoned her before we left town.'

'Ah, yes,' Colette murmured sleepily. 'Making plans for your godchild's wedding.'

'That's one reason for my visit, yes. But, also, Lois is now heavily involved with her local branch of the Red Cross. Amongst other things, as you know, they collect unwanted clothing for sending to disaster areas, and apparently they're always particularly short of men's. So, you will be pleased to hear, I've at long last decided I'm strong enough to get rid of Rowe's things. I brought two big suitcases of his stuff down with me from Inglebatch House, and I'll pack up what's left here tonight. I'll get Mrs Renshaw to help me.'

Colette nodded. 'I *am* glad to hear it,' she confirmed. 'And I'll give you a hand as well. We must remember to turn out all the pockets.'

Christine smiled at her affectionately. 'Thank goodness for French common sense. That would never have occurred to me.'

Which was how she came to find the letter.

When, with Mrs Renshaw's assistance, they had finished emptying the wardrobe in Christine's bedroom, carefully searching and packing each garment, Colette insisted on the two cases which had been brought from London being opened.

'Now, make sure there's nothing in these pockets, either,' she instructed.

It was a boring job, and one which promised to yield little beyond the odd pound coin, a theatre-ticket stub, screwed up and forgotten, a fountain-pen and two biros. But almost at the bottom of the second case was the dressing-gown Rowland had worn that last night, in the kitchen; dark blue silk with two deep patch pockets. After his death, Christine could not bear to look at it and had pushed it to the very back of his wardrobe. It brought a rush of memories crowding into her mind; and, even now, three years on, she found it difficult to touch it without wanting to cry.

As she put her hand into the left-hand pocket, she heard the crackle of paper and, a moment later, her fingers felt the stiff smooth edge of an envelope. She knew at once what it was. The letter to Faith Malyon, still unposted . . .

The room was suddenly very quiet. As though aware that something momentous was about to happen, Colette and the housekeeper had stopped talking and were both watching her, hands quiescent, making no attempt to pick up another garment.

'Christine?' Colette queried gently. '*Chérie*, are you all right? You're looking very pale. What is it?'

'It's a letter,' she answered dazedly, twisting the heavy cream envelope between her hands. 'It's from Rowe, and it's addressed to me.' She continued to stare, not at Faith Malyon's name and address, but at the single word 'Christine' scrawled in Rowland's large impatient hand. 'That night, he wasn't writing to her after all. He was writing to me.'

Colette came to sit beside her on the edge of the bed, putting a comforting arm around her shoulders, her eyes full of tears. Mrs Renshaw tactfully slipped out of the room.

'Take it somewhere quiet and read it,' Colette said softly. 'Go down to the drawing-room. There's no one there this evening. Claud's in the library, smoking his pipe, and after I've finished here we're going for a stroll in the garden. He likes looking at the roses. And I'll tell Mrs Renshaw to see you're not disturbed. Go on,' she urged, giving Christine a little push. 'Don't sit here, hesitating, wondering what's in the letter. It might be very important.'

Christine's fingers tightened on the envelope. She looked at her mother-in-law as though she had not heard her, but after a while she said: 'Yes, you're right. There's no point in putting it off. I'll go now.' She stood up, then leaned down to kiss Colette's cheek. 'Whatever it says, I have to know.'

The drawing-room was very quiet in the evening sunlight. Tomorrow, according to the forecasters, more rain was on its way, but for now summer still offered peace and warmth and contentment. The French doors stood open on to the terrace, and somewhere a bird was singing, a shower of golden notes pouring into the silence. Christine put on one of Rowland's favourite records: Rameau, *La Princesse de Navarre*. Then she sat down and opened the letter.

My love, I have been meaning to tell you for a very long time just how much you have come, over the years, to mean to me. And tonight, sitting there in the kitchen, I finally admitted to myself what, deep in my heart, I must have always known: that I love you. You are my past, my present, my hope for the future. I have ordered from Garrard's a true-lovers' knot in sapphires and diamonds. When it is ready, you will receive it, together with this letter.

Why am I not saying all this to your face, instead of taking refuge in a letter? The truth is I haven't the courage. I want you to know the facts before you speak; before I see that little half-smile of disbelief which is so characteristic of you. And why not? You have every reason to be cynical. I have treated you abominably. I would not let myself be tied to any one woman. I was afraid of becoming too like my father, whose overwhelming passion for my mother weakened him in all other ways.

I realize now how unforgivably foolish I've been. You are not my mother; you, of all women, are capable of giving love without demanding anything in return. No other woman has really meant anything to me, although, for a while, I deluded myself that Faith Malyon was necessary to my life. She wasn't. She never has been. I know that now. I shall spend the rest of my life trying to make amends.

You see that I am confident of your forgiveness. Am I making too great an assumption? Knowing you, your love, your generosity, I don't think so. And I pray to God I'm right. When you have read this letter, come and tell me that I am.

It's very late, and I'm tired, and there's a nagging pain in my chest and all down one of my arms. I've been overdoing it, I suppose, and it's

430

got to stop. I want to spend much more time with you. We'll go away to our beloved France, just you and me and nobody else. I'll tell Gran'mère that we need the Château to ourselves. She'll understand.

I'm going to bed now for what's left of the night. By this time tomorrow you'll have read this letter. Good night, my darling. I love you.

ROWE

Slowly, very slowly, Christine let the letter drop into her lap and leaned back in her chair, closing her eyes, listening to the music which flooded the room. The blackbird in the tree outside was singing frantically in competition. The tears were pouring down her face, but they were tears of healing. Of peace. Life stretched before her, full of hope and promise. She was a whole woman at last.

A SELECTION OF FINE TITLES
AVAILABLE FROM CORGI BOOKS

THE PRICES SHOWN BELOW WERE CORRECT AT THE TIME OF
GOING TO PRESS. HOWEVER TRANSWORLD PUBLISHERS
RESERVE THE RIGHT TO SHOW NEW RETAIL PRICES ON
COVERS WHICH MAY DIFFER FROM THOSE PREVIOUSLY
ADVERTISED IN THE TEXT OR ELSEWHERE.

All Corgi/Bantam Books are available at your bookshop or newsagent, or can
be ordered from the following address:
Corgi/Bantam Books,
Cash Sales Department,
P.O. Box 11, Falmouth, Cornwall TR10 9EN

UK and B.F.P.O. customers please send a cheque or postal order (no
currency) and allow £1.00 for postage and packing for the first book plus 50p
for the second book and 30p for each additional book to a maximum charge of
£3.00 (7 books plus).

Overseas customers, including Eire, please allow £2.00 for postage and
packing for the first book plus £1.00 for the second book and 50p for each
subsequent title ordered.

NAME (Block Letters) ....

ADDRESS ....

....